So Well Remembered

JAMES HILTON

So Well Remembered

AN ATLANTIC MONTHLY PRESS BOOK

LITTLE, BROWN AND COMPANY

BOSTON

1945

ATLANTIC—LITTLE, BROWN BOOKS
ARE PUBLISHED BY
LITTLE, BROWN AND COMPANY
IN ASSOCIATION WITH
THE ATLANTIC MONTHLY PRESS

PRINTED IN THE UNITED STATES OF AMERICA

So Well Remembered

Part One

THAT DAY so well remembered—a day, indeed, impossible to forget—was the first of September, 1921; on the morning of which George Boswell—then only Councillor Boswell, then sandy-brown-haired with not a trace of gray—woke before dawn, looked at his watch, and promptly slept again till Annie brought in the morning paper, a cup of tea, and some letters that had just arrived. Amongst them was a note from Lord Winslow's secretary, saying that His Lordship would arrive at Browdley station by the noon train, in good time for the foundation-stone laying; and this made George very happy and proud, because Lord Winslow was not an ordinary kind of lord (a type which George, never having met any, imagined for himself and then proceeded to scorn on principle), but a special kind who had not only devoted a lifetime to public service but had also written several distinguished books.

At half past seven George got up, put out his blue serge suit (the one reserved for big events), and shaved with especial care, scanning meanwhile the cheerful headlines of the paper propped against the mirror, and noting with approval, whenever he looked beyond it, the misty promise of a fine summer day. By eight he was at the breakfast table, eating ham and eggs and exchanging good-humored chatter with Annie, the elderly "help" who looked after the house and did her best to overfeed him during his wife's absence; by nine he was at his desk, composing an article for the *Browdley and District Guardian,* which he owned and edited. He did not write easily as a rule, but this time the phrases came on a wave of exhilaration,

7

for though he had a few private doubts that the Treaty of Versailles was not all it should be, he was prepared to give the future the benefit of them, the more so as it was natural for him to give the future the benefit of anything. Anyhow by ten George had composed a suitably optimistic editorial; noon saw him at the railway station to welcome Lord Winslow; by one o'clock he had made a short speech at the Town Hall luncheon; and by a quarter to two he was in his seat on the improvised dais at the corner of Mill Street, blinking in the sunshine and beaming his satisfaction to the four winds, one of which, then prevalent, wafted back the concentrated smell of Browdley's industries. But George did not mind that—indeed, it was the remembered perfume of his childhood, of days spent on the banks of the canal that threaded its way between factory walls, taking waste water hot from each one, so that a fog of steam drifted over the surface and spread a low-hanging reek of oil, chemicals, and machinery. Waiting on the platform for the ceremony to begin, George sniffed and was happy.

A great day for Councillor Boswell and for Browdley, and also (one gathered) for England and for the world. History, George reflected, could not have done a better job of dramatization—August Thirty-first, the Official End of the Great War—September First, the Foundation-Stone-Laying of Unit One of the Mill Street Housing Scheme that was to replace some of Browdley's worst slums. A great day, indeed. George, as his glance roved around, was proud to have the dedicator (a Bishop) on his left, the guest of the occasion (Lord Winslow) on his right, and various local bigwigs beyond and behind; but he was proudest of all to see the crowd, and only wished it as large as it would have been if Browdley folk weren't such notorious slackers about civic affairs. He said so later, when he got up to speak, and was applauded for his downrightness. George, in fact, was invariably downright; it was natural for him, and a quality which, sometimes disconcerting but always good-humored, did as well in Browdley as the smooth tongue of the diplomat, and perhaps better. There was a legend that when he had wanted a rich local manufacturer to donate a mansion for use as a municipal museum, he had said: "See here, Bob, I'm not *asking* this—I'm *demanding* it. You and your folks have exploited this town for the best part of a century—if there was any justice you'd have been hanged long ago. But as there isn't—let's have that house." And he had got it.

Furthermore, George thought, it was a shame that only a few hundreds, instead of thousands, had turned out to welcome a man like Lord Winslow—or was it possible they didn't know how distinguished Lord Winslow really was? But George's personal enjoyment of the proceedings was not to be lessened—not even when the town brass band began to play Sousa rather badly in the shadow of a large Union Jack hung upside down—a detail that remained unnoticed save by a solitary busybody who afterwards wrote a letter about it which the *Guardian* did not print. Altogether the scene was typical of many a quietly happy English occasion during those distant years when Englishmen could be quietly happy.

George's face was also typically English (which means, perhaps, nothing more than that he might have passed, in their respective countries, for a Dane, a Norwegian, a Swede, a German, or a Norman-Frenchman, but not so easily for an Italian, a Greek, or a Spaniard); at any rate, he was blue-eyed and ruddy-cheeked, the mouth expanding into smiles of shy benevolence as greetings came from the crowd, the chin steady and square, with none of the false dynamism of the acute angle. George, at thirty-five, was a good-looking man, if one cared to call him that, but he seemed to merit some solider adjective than could be applied equally to youthful film actors and tennis champions; there was a touch of earthiness in him that matched well with his wide shoulders and strong hands and genial provincial burr. It was a quiet, almost a humorous touch, behind which, in a sort of ambush, there lurked ambitions and determinations that had already left their mark on Browdley.

This housing development was one of them—a modest triumph (George called it) of practical idealism over the 90 per cent of apathy and 10 per cent of pure selfishness that comprise idealism's biggest enemy. George could justifiably smile as he stared about him that September afternoon, for this was the first fruit of his Councillorship and the first postwar improvement in Browdley to get beyond the talking stage. Only George knew the struggle it had been through almost incredible thickets of vested interests and government red tape; but here it was at last, something actually begun after all the argument, and his friends and fellow citizens might well give him a cheer. Even the Mayor, who was among his strongest political opponents, could not restrain a reluctantly cordial smile.

George was telling the Bishop that he had been born in one of the slum houses just demolished—Number 24, Mill Street, to be precise—and the Bishop was chaffing him about not having had it preserved as a place of historic interest with a mural tablet to commemorate the great event. George laughed and said he would have taken such an idea far more seriously twenty-odd years ago, and then he confessed that as a small boy he had once read how the desks at Harrow School were carved with the names of famous men; and that in order not to disappoint posterity he had carved his own name on the inside of the privy door at the end of the backyard of Number 24—not a very romantic substitute for a desk at Harrow, but the handiest available in his own limited world.

"Ah, dear me," exclaimed the Bishop, who was a Harrovian and a little shocked at first, but then when he looked at George's face, so clearly that of a man telling a simple story of something that had very simply happened, he was won over, as people nearly always were by George; so he added with a smile: "Ah well—a harmless occupation, I daresay."

George went on without realizing the extent of his conquest: "Aye, it was the only place I was ever left alone in those days, because we were a large family, and a four-roomed house doesn't allow for much privacy. Fortunately my father started work at five in the morning and didn't come home till six at night—I hardly saw him except on Sundays when he marched us all off to chapel."

"Ah, grand folks, those old Nonconformists," murmured the Bishop, turning on the magnanimity.

"He was a local preacher too," George continued, pointing suddenly up Mill Street. "There's the chapel, and there—" swinging his arm in the opposite direction—"there's Channing's Mill, where he worked—"

"*Channing's?* Not—er—Channing and Felsby?"

"Aye, that's what it used to be. You knew of it?"

"I'm afraid so." The Bishop smiled ruefully. "I—er—I once had a few shares in it."

"You were better off than my father, then, because he had a

lifetime in it. From the age of ten to the day he died—fifty years, and for half of every year, except on Sundays, he only saw daylight through the mill windows."

"Ah, terrible—terrible—" murmured the Bishop.

George chuckled. "Maybe, but he didn't feel that way. I don't believe it ever occurred to him. He was quite content all week looking forward to Sunday."

"When he enjoyed his preaching, no doubt."

"You bet he did, and he was a dab hand at it too. I've heard him last a couple of hours, without a note, and fluent all the time."

The Bishop sighed. "Ah, that's a wonderful thing—to possess the gift of tongues, so that one never has to think for a word—"

"Maybe that's it," said George. "It's the thinking that spoils it." His eyes twinkled and his voice, as nearly as a voice can, nudged the Bishop in the ribs. "Once I remember my father started off a prayer with 'Oh God, if there be a God—' but he said it in such a grand booming voice that nobody noticed it any more than he had."

"Except you," interjected Lord Winslow, who had been overhearing the conversation from the other side. George turned, a little startled at first, and then, seeing a smile on His Lordship's face, smiled back and replied thoughtfully: "Aye, that's so. I suppose I was always a bit of a one for noticing things."

By then the band had finished playing and it was time for George to open the proceedings. He did so in a speech that lasted a few minutes only; one of his virtues, innocently acquired because he regarded it as a drawback, was that ceremonial oratory did not come easily to him. But he had a pleasant voice and a knack of using simple words as a first-class workman uses tools; his newspaper editorials were not so good, because he "polished" them too much. There was also a hint of the child in him that appeared now in his unconcealed and quite unconcealable pleasure; he could not help letting Browdley know how pleased he was, not only with the town for having elected him one of its councillors, but doubtless also with himself for having so well merited the honor. A certain inward modesty made tolerable, and even attractive, an outward quality that might have been termed conceit. And when, having briefly introduced Lord Winslow, he sat down amidst another gust of applause, the life of the gathering seemed to center on his still beaming countenance rather than on the tall, thin, pallid stranger who rose to pay him conventional compliments.

Winslow, of course, was a much better speaker by any erudite standards. To the acceptable accent of English aristocracy and officialdom he added an air of slightly bored accomplishment that often goes with it, and the chiefly working-class audience gave him respectful attention throughout an address that was considerably above their heads. Had he been of their own class they might have shouted a few ribald interruptions, but they would not do this to a stranger so clearly of rank; indeed their patient silence implied a half-affectionate tolerance for "one of the nobs" who eccentrically chose to interest himself in Browdley affairs instead of in the far more glamorous ones they imagined must be his own—the sort of tolerance that had evoked an audible exclamation of "Poor little bugger!" from some unknown citizen when, a few years back, a royal prince had passed through the town on an official tour. To Browdley folk, as they looked and listened now, it seemed that Lord Winslow was all the time thinking of something else (as indeed he was), but they did not blame him for it; on the contrary, the cheers when he finished were a friendly concession that he had doubtless done his best and that it was pretty decent of him to have bothered to do anything at all.

Then the Bishop prayed, the foundation stone was well and truly laid, sundry votes of thanks were passed, the band played "God Save the King," and the ceremony petered out. But Councillor Boswell seemed loth to leave the scene of so much concentrated personal victory. He gripped Winslow's arm with proprietary zeal, talking about his plans for further slum clearances while from time to time he introduced various local people who hung around; and finally, when most had disappeared to their homes and the Bishop had waved a benign good-bye, George escorted his principal guest to the car that was to take him back to Browdley station. It was not only that he knew Winslow was important and might at some future date do the town a service; nor merely that he already liked him, for he found it easy to like people; the fact was, Winslow was the type that stirred in George a note of genuine hero worship— and in spite, rather than because, of the title. After all, a man

couldn't help what he inherited, and if he were also a high government personage with a string of degrees and academic distinctions
after his name, why hold mere blue blood against him? It was the
truer aristocracy of intellect that George admired—hence the spell
cast over him by Winslow's scholarly speech, his domelike forehead,
and the absent-minded professorial manner that George took to be
preoccupation with some abstruse problem. He had already looked
him up in *Who's Who*, and during the drive in the car through
Browdley streets humility transformed itself into naïve delight that
an Oxford Doctor of Philosophy had actually accepted an invitation to have tea at his house.

George was also delighted at the success of his own ruse to sidetrack the Mayor and the other councillors and get Winslow on his
own, and most delighted of all, as well as astonished, when Winslow said: "Good idea, Boswell—I had been on the point of suggesting such a thing myself. My train is not for an hour or so, I
understand."

"That's right, no need to hurry," George replied. "And there's
later trains for that matter."

Winslow smiled. "Well, we have time for a cup of tea, anyhow."
And after a pause, as if the personality of George really interested
him: "So you come of an old Browdley family?"

"As old as we have 'em here, sir, but that's not so old. My great-
great-grandfather was a farm laborer in Kent, and our branch of
the family moved north when the cotton mills wanted cheap labor.
I haven't got any famous ancestors, except one who's supposed to
have been transported to Australia for poaching." He added re-
gretfully: "But I could never get any proof of it."

Winslow smiled. "At any rate, your father lived it down. He
seems to have been a much respected man in Browdley."

George nodded, pleased by the tribute, but then went on, with
that disconcerting frankness that was (if he had only known it, but
then of course if he had known it, it wouldn't have been) one of
his principal charms: "Aye, he was much respected, and for
twenty years after he died I went about thinking how much I'd
respected him myself, but then one day when I was afraid of
something, it suddenly occurred to me it was the same feeling I'd
had for my father."

"You mean you *didn't* respect him?"

"Oh, I did that as well, but where there's fear it doesn't much matter what goes with it. There was a lot of fear in our house—there always is when folks are poor. Either they're afraid of the landlord or the policeman or employers or unemployment or having another mouth to feed or a son getting wed and taking his wage with him—birth, marriage, and death—it's all summat to worry about. Even *after* death, in my father's case, because he was what he called God-fearing."

Winslow smiled again. "So you didn't have a very happy childhood?"

"I suppose it wasn't, though at the time I took it as natural. There was nothing cruel, mind you—only hardships and stern faces." George then confessed that during the first six years of his life he was rarely if ever told to do anything without being threatened with what would happen if he didn't or couldn't; and the fact that these threats were mostly empty did not prevent the main effect—which was to give him a first impression of the world as a piece of adult property in which children were trespassers. "Only they weren't prosecuted," he added, with a laugh. "They were mostly just yelled at. . . . D'you know, one of the biggest shocks of my life was after my parents died and I was sent to live with an uncle I'd never met before—to find out then that grown-ups could actually talk to me in a cheerful, casual sort of way, even though I *was* only a boy!"

"Yes, there must have been a big difference."

"Aye, and I'll tell you what I've often thought the difference was," George went on, growing bolder and smiling his wide smile. "Just a matter of a few quid a week. You see, my father never earned more than two pound ten at the mill, but my uncle had a little business that brought in about twice that. Not a fortune—but enough to keep away some of the fears."

"There's one fear, anyhow, that nobody had in those days," Winslow commented. "Wars before 1914 were so far off and so far removed from his personal life that the average Englishman had only to read about them in the papers and cheer for his side."

"Not even that if he didn't want to," George replied. "Take my father and the Boers, for instance. Thoroughly approved of them, he did, especially old Kruger, whom he used to pray for as 'that great President and the victor of Majuba Hill, which, as Thou knowest, Lord, is situated near the border of Natal and the Transvaal Republic. . . .' He always liked to make sure the Lord had all the facts."

Despite Winslow's laugh, George checked his flow of reminiscence, for he had begun to feel he had been led into talking too much about himself. Taking advantage, therefore, of a curve in the street that afforded the view of a large derelict weaving shed, he launched into more appropriate chatter about Browdley, its history, geography, trade conditions, and so on, and how, as Councillor, he was seeking to alleviate local unemployment. Winslow began to look preoccupied during all this, so George eventually stopped talking altogether as he neared his house—smiling a little to himself, though. He suspected that Winslow was already on guard against a possible solicitation of favors. "Or else he thinks I'm running after him because he's a lord," George thought, scornfully amused at such a plausible error.

The factor George counted on to reveal the error was the room in which they were both to have tea. It was not a very large room (in the small mid-Victorian house adjoining the printing office in Market Street), but its four walls, even over the door and under the windows, were totally covered with books. One of George's numerous prides was in having the finest personal library in Browdley, and probably he had; it was a genuine collection, anyhow, not an accumulation of sets for the sake of their binding, as could be seen in the mansions of rich local manufacturers. Moreover, George really *read* his books—thoroughly and studiously, often with pencil in hand for note-taking. Like many men who have suffered deficiencies in early education, he had more than made up for them since; except that he had failed to acquire the really unique thing a good early education can bequeath—the ability to grow up and forget about it. George could never forget—neither on nor off the Education Committee of which he made the best and most energetic chairman Browdley had ever had.

What he chiefly hoped was that during the interval before

Winslow must catch his train back to London, they might have a serious intellectual talk—or perhaps the latter would talk, Gamaliel-wise, while George sat metaphorically at his feet.

Unfortunately the great man failed to pick up the desired cue from a first sight of the books; indeed, he seemed hardly to notice them, even when George with an expansive wave of the hand bade him make himself at home; though there was consolation in reflecting that Winslow's own library was probably so huge that this one must appear commonplace.

"Make yourself thoroughly at home, sir," George repeated, with extra heartiness on account of his disappointment.

"Thank you," answered the other, striding across the room. He stood for a few seconds, staring through the back window, then murmured meditatively: "H'm—very nice. Quite a show. Wonderful what one can do even in the middle of a town."

George then realized that Winslow must be referring to the small oblong garden between the house and the wall of the neighboring bus garage. So he replied quickly: "Aye, but it's gone a bit to pieces lately. Not much in my line, gardening."

"Must compliment you on your roses, anyhow."

"My wife, not me—she's the one for all that if she was here."

"She's away?"

"Aye—on the Continent. Likes to travel too—all over the place. But books are more in my line."

"It's certainly been a good season for them."

George wasn't sure what this referred to until Winslow added, still staring out of the window: "My wife's another enthusiast—she's won prizes at our local show."

George still did not think this a promising beginning to an intellectual conversation, but as Annie was just then bringing in the tea he said no more about books. Winslow, however, could not tear himself away from the spectacle of the roses—which were, indeed, especially beautiful that year. "Too bad," he murmured, "for anyone who loves a garden to miss England just now. . . . So you're not keen on foreign holidays, is that it, Boswell?"

"Oh, I wouldn't say no if I had the chance, but I don't suppose I'd ever be as keen as Livia is. Anyhow, I've got too much to do in Browdley to leave the place for months on end."

"*Months?* Quite a holiday."

"Aye, but it's not all holiday for her. She has a job with one of those travel tours—'Ten Days in Lovely Lucerne'—that kind of thing. Pays her expenses and a bit over."

"Convenient."

"For anyone who likes seeing the same sights with different folks over and over again. I wouldn't."

"Sort of guide, is she?"

"I reckon so. She runs the show for 'em, I'll bet. She's got a real knack for managing folks when she feels like it."

"I wouldn't say you were entirely without it yourself."

"Ah, but with her it's an art." George was too genuinely modest to realize that his own sterling naïveté was just as good a knack, art, or whatever else it was. "Maybe you won't believe me, but when I was a young fellow I was so scared of meeting folks I could hardly get a word out. And even now I'm not as happy on a platform as I am sitting alone in this room with a good book." He jerked his head towards the surrounding shelves in another attempt to steer the conversation, and when Winslow did not immediately reply, he added more pointedly: "I expect you're a great reader yourself?"

"Oh fairly—when I can find the time."

"Aye, that's the worst of being in public life." At least they had *that* bond in common. "You know, sir, there's only one reason I'd ever wish to be young again—*really* young, I mean," he added, as he saw Winslow smile—"and that's to have summat I missed years ago—a right-down good education. . . . I'll never forget when I visited Oxford and saw all those lucky lads in the colleges . . ." A sincere emotion entered his voice. "And the professors in their libraries—I tell you frankly, I . . ." He saw that Winslow was still smiling. "Well, I'll put it this way—there's only one thing I'd rather be than in politics, and that's one of those university dons, as they call themselves."

"Yet I doubt if many of them are doing any better work than you are here—judging by what I've seen today."

George was pleased again, but also slightly shocked by the comparison; he could not believe that Winslow really meant it, and he was surprised that such a distinguished man should stoop to mere flattery. "Oh come now, sir, I'll never swallow that. After all, think of the books they write—I've got shelves of 'em here—heavy stuff I admit, but grand training for the mind."

"Yes, books are all right." Winslow gave a little sigh. "Though it's remarkable how little help they offer in some of the more curious problems of life." George was thinking this a rather strange remark when an even stranger one followed it. "Look here, Boswell, I'm going to do something I wasn't sure about before I met you—partly because I wasn't sure you were the right man, and partly because even if you were, I couldn't be positive how you'd take it."

George looked up with a puzzled expression. There flashed through his mind the intoxicating possibility that Winslow might be going to ask his advice about some matter of departmental policy —low-rent housing, say, or an extension of the school-leaving age.

But Winslow continued: "Quite a coincidence meeting you like this. Several months ago when I promised to speak at your ceremony today I hadn't even heard of you—when quite recently I did, I decided it might be a good chance to—to approach you—if—if you seemed the sort of man who might be approachable. You see, it's a somewhat unusual and delicate matter, and there aren't any rules of etiquette to proceed by."

And then there flashed through George's already puzzled mind another though less welcome possibility—that Winslow was an emissary of the Government deputed to find out in advance whether George would accept a title in recognition of his "public services" to the town of Browdley. It was highly unlikely, of course, since he was a mere town Councillor and did not belong to the Government party, but still, anything could happen when parties and politics were fluid and Lloyd George was reputed to cast a discerning eye upon foes as well as friends. Anyhow, George's reply would be a straight "no," because he very simply though a trifle truculently did not believe in titles.

He saw that Winslow was waiting for a remark, so he called his thoughts to order and said guardedly: "I'm afraid I don't quite catch on so far, but whatever it is, if there's any way I can help—"

"Thanks, that's very kind of you. I hope there is. So if you'll just let me go ahead and explain . . ."

George nodded, now more puzzled than ever; he could not help thinking that Winslow was terribly slow in getting to the point, whatever it was. Meanwhile the great man had opened up into an account of a semiofficial tour he had lately undertaken to inspect housing projects, mostly on paper, in some of the Continental countries. At this George nodded with enthusiastic comprehension, and to show that, even without foreign travel, he kept himself well abreast of such matters, he reached for a book that happened to be to hand. "You'll have seen it, I daresay," he interrupted eagerly. "I got the architect of our local scheme to adopt several of this fellow's ideas—I've always said we should all pool our postwar experience—allies and ex-enemies alike. Take Vienna, for instance, where the Socialists are very strong—"

"Yes, yes indeed," Winslow agreed, though with a note in his voice to check all chatter. However, he seemed willing enough to take Vienna, for he continued: "That was one of the cities I visited recently. Apart from business, I had a special reason because my son Jeff happens to be there too. He has a job—er—connected with the Embassy." He paused and pulled out a small pocketbook; in it he found a snapshot which he passed to George. It showed a smiling young man in ski costume in company with several pretty girls against a background panorama of snow-covered mountains. "Taken at Kitzbühel," he added.

George had not heard of Kitzbühel, but he knew a fine-looking fellow when he saw one, and now quite sincerely expressed his admiration. To reciprocate the intimacy he pointed to one of a number of photographs on top of a revolving bookcase of encyclopedias. "Reminds me a bit of the lad just behind you."

Winslow turned to look and confirmed after a scrutiny: "Yes, quite a resemblance. Your *son?* I wouldn't have thought you were old enough—"

"I'm not. . . . That's one of my brothers—killed on the Somme on July first, 1916. Fifty thousand killed with him the same day— according to the records. Something for folks to remember when they attack disarmament."

"And *this?*" said Winslow, still seemingly preoccupied with the photographs.

"That's my wife."

"Ah, yes."

George then felt it was time to relieve his guest of any further

obligation to appear interested in his family, so he returned the
snapshot with the comment: "Aye, he's a bonny lad—and brainy
too, by the look of him."

"They seemed to think so at Oxford."

"He did well there?"

"Pretty well."

"What did he get?"

"Get? Oh, a Rowing Blue and he was also President of the
Union—"

"And a good degree? A First, I suppose?"

"Er . . . yes, I think so."

"Double First?"

Winslow smiled. "I believe he took several Firsts in various subjects, but they don't seem to use the term 'Double First' any more."

"Gladstone got it."

"Did he? You seem to know a good deal about these matters,
Boswell. . . ."

"Aye, as an outsider. Though it was my father who told me
about Gladstone. I think he was the only man except Bible characters whom my father really admired. . . . But go on about your
boy."

"Well, as I said, Jeff did pretty well at Oxford till the war cut
into his career. Then he served in Egypt and got a D.S.O., and soon
after the Armistice he went to France and Germany for languages,
because he was entering the Diplomatic Service and the usual thing
is to get attached for a few years to one of the embassies or legations.
He's only twenty-five."

"Sounds like a future in front of him."

"That—er—is what I have hoped. We've always got on excellently together—good friends, I mean, as well as father and son.
When I arrived in Vienna recently the first thing he did was to take
me off to some restaurant where we could talk—because I hadn't
seen him for six months, and that's a long time for family gossip to
accumulate." Winslow began to smile again. "I thought from the
outset he didn't seem exactly himself—he was preoccupied, somehow, in the way he behaved and talked—and later I asked if there'd
been any trouble at the Embassy, but he said no, nothing like that.
At last I got out of him what *had* caused the change." The smile

became suddenly forced and wan. "Perfectly natural, you may think."

"Been worrying about conditions in Austria? I understand things are pretty bad, what with the famine and inflation—"

"No—not even all that. . . . He'd fallen in love."

George chuckled. "Well, sir, that quite often happens to good-looking chaps of twenty-five. The only surprising thing is that it hadn't happened before."

"Oh, but it had. That's one of the—er—complications. He was engaged to a very charming girl, a neighbor of ours in Berkshire, but he said he'd already written to her to break it off—on account of the—er—new attraction."

"I see." And at this George frowned slightly. A whiff of truculence was generated in him as, momentarily, he saw in Winslow no longer an unworldly scholar but a hidebound aristocrat conforming to type; for already the probable outlines of the story seemed clear—a father anxious for his son to make a socially correct marriage, the son's romance with some pretty but penniless Austrian girl . . . and George, of course, was all on the side of the son and the girl, though he would wait to say so till Winslow had finished. All he commented now was a blunt: "Everyone has a right to change his mind."

"Of course. It wasn't my place to interfere—provided the supplanter was all right."

"Not even if you thought she wasn't. A chap of twenty-five must choose for himself."

"Yes, in theory, though when—"

"In theory *and* in practice, sir. I don't say a father can't give advice in these matters, but that's about all he *can* give. And if a young fellow makes a mistake, well, it's his mistake, and he can't blame anyone else. Haven't we all made mistakes? And besides, even if she is a foreigner and recently an enemy—"

"Oh, that wouldn't worry me, and anyhow, she isn't—she's English."

"Then what does worry you?"

"Perhaps I'd better go on with what happened. Jeff naturally described her to me in glowing colors and suggested an early meeting, so we all three dined together the next day, and I must admit my first impression was favorable—at any rate, she struck me as both charming and intelligent. . . ."

George was about to pour his guest another cup of tea, but Winslow made a declining gesture. "Very kind of you, Boswell, but—but I really feel in need of something a little stronger—I wonder—if you—if it isn't too much trouble—if I could have a whisky-and-soda?"

At which George could only in his own turn look embarrassed. "To tell you the truth I don't have such a thing in the house—you see, I'm teetotal. But if you're not feeling well I could send Annie out for a drop of brandy—"

"Oh, please no, I'm perfectly well—just tiredness, that's all. I really shouldn't have mentioned it. Of no consequence at all, I assure you." What had really been demonstrated was a social distinction far more revealing than any question of blood or accent—the fact that Winslow, though he drank sparingly, nevertheless belonged to the class for whom whisky is as much a household commonplace as salt or soap; whereas George, though by no means a bigot, had inherited enough of his father's puritanism to think of liquor in terms of drunkenness and social problems.

After the gulf had been bridged by renewed apologies on both sides, Winslow continued: "To come to the point—" (*at last,* thought George)—"I told Jeff afterwards that if they'd both made up their minds there was nothing much for me to say. I was just a bit worried, though, because I gathered it had been a very sudden affair, and I didn't think he could really know enough about her."

"You mean her family and so on?"

"Partly. You may think me a snob, but I had to ask myself whether, as a diplomat's wife, she would have the right background."

"Aye, I suppose that's what counts." George's voice was severe.

"Yes—though not as much as it used to."

"I'm glad to hear it. I don't know much about the Diplomatic Service, but I'm all for democracy in these things. And since you have to admit the girl was all right herself—"

"Oh yes, she seemed so. I could imagine her a good hostess, and she certainly had intelligence enough to pull wires."

"Do diplomats' wives have to do that?"

"They don't have to, but it can help. Don't the wives
cal councillors sometimes do it?"

George grinned. "Not mine, anyhow. I could never get her to
take an interest in local affairs at all. . . . But about your son and
this girl . . . So I suppose you consented to the match?"

"I should have done, but for finding out something about her
that was—as I think even you will agree—rather insuperable.
Simply that she was already married. The fact came out quite acci-
dentally—someone I happened to meet in Switzerland on my way
home was able to tell me about her. She had, it appeared—at least
there was no other conclusion to be drawn—deliberately misled
Jeff. And a rather pointless deception too—unless of course she was
prepared to commit bigamy."

George pondered a moment. "Well, you found out in time, that's
the main thing."

"Perhaps not in time, though, to stop him from making an utter
fool of himself."

Winslow paused and seemed suddenly aware of the extent of
George's library, though his ranging glance was hardly one of interest in it. At the same moment Annie entered with some letters
and was about to hand them to George, but the latter shook his
head and gestured her to put them on his desk. Winslow intervened: "Don't mind me if there's anything important you ought to
attend to."

"They can wait, whatever they are."

"It's good of you to let me take up your time like this."

George was amazed at the humility of such a remark from a man
of Winslow's age and importance. He could only reply: "Not at
all, sir. Besides, you say I can help—though I wouldn't pretend to
be much good at advice about—er—family matters and so on."

"Perhaps because your own family affairs have been happy?"

"Oh, I've had my troubles, same as most folks, I reckon."

"But you've settled them all?"

"I've never had any to settle about a grown-up lad." And George
added, wryly: "Worse luck."

"Perhaps that itself makes a sort of trouble? I mean if—if—of
course I don't know what your—"

"Aye . . . aye . . . but let's get back to *your* lad. What's the
mistake he made? Surely when you told him—"

Winslow leaned forward with his hands pressed down on his knees; he seemed to be seeking mastery of some strong emotion. "Forgive me for not keeping to the point. . . . Yes, I told him. We had long conversations, but only by telephone, unfortunately, because I was compelled to return to England for an important government conference. That was a further complication—not being in personal touch with him. It was very hard to telephone. Of course if he'd been his normal self the mere facts would have been enough —he's always been quick to do the right thing. But—you see—he's *not* his normal self any more. This emotion—love or whatever you call it—perhaps madness or infatuation's a better word—"

"Doesn't seem to matter much what you call it if it's there."

"I agree—provided one doesn't fall into the error of idealizing. I'd say, for instance, that I love my own wife, but I can easily think of things I wouldn't do to please her—things which, even if she asked me to do them, would destroy the bond between us—like betraying my friends or my country. . . . But infatuation's different —it seems to glory in doing things *in spite of,* rather than *because of* . . . if you know what I mean."

George made no comment.

"Well, anyhow, the point is, he hasn't dropped her, even though he knows the truth and she's been forced to admit it. He's behaving, in fact, as if he *can't* drop her. The last time I talked to him, which was from Paris, I gathered he'd not only forgiven her for the deception, but she's made him believe a long story about an unhappy past and a husband she ran away from because she couldn't stand him . . . and the upshot of it all is, Jeff's now urging her to get a divorce so that he can marry her himself."

"What's *her* attitude?"

"I only know through him—and of course he's so completely prejudiced in her favor that it's not much to go by. But remember he's quite a catch, even if it does ruin his career."

"And it would? Because of the scandal?"

"Possibly. . . . But worst of all, as I see it, is the thing itself— to put himself at the mercy of someone who has such evident power to distort and overthrow his judgment . . . *judgment* . . . the most valuable attribute a man of his profession can have . . . because if he still had any of it left, he'd drop her. After all, how could he *expect* a marriage of that sort to turn out a success? . . . It's a sad thing, Boswell, to see a first-class intelligence functioning like a baby's."

"Why don't you go out and talk to him personally as soon as you have the time?"

"Yes, I shall do that—I wired him today about it. But somehow I'm not sure that I can do much on my own—that last telephone talk was simply shattering—the most I could get was a promise that he'd think it over, but he *can't* think, that's the trouble—he's in a world utterly beyond logic and argument—you can't prove anything to him—he just believes this woman's a sort of martyr heroine and her husband's an impossible brute and—"

"How do you know he isn't?"

Winslow got up suddenly, walked to the window, then came back and touched George on the shoulder with a queerly intimate gesture. "I didn't know—definitely—until today. But I'm a bit positive at this moment. . . ." And after a second pause, standing in front of George, he stammered unsurely: "I hope I haven't been so damned tactful that you're going to ask me what all this has got to do with you. . . ."

. . .

Then George looked up and saw in a flash what it *had* got to do with him.

He felt himself growing cold and sick, as if a fist were grasping him by his insides. Try as one might, he reflected with queer and instant detachment, the actual blow of such a revelation must be sudden; there was no way of leading up that could disperse the shock over a period; one second one did not know, the next second one did know; that was all there was to it, so that all Winslow's delicacy had been in a sense wasted. He might just as well have blurted out the truth right at the beginning.

George knew he must say something to acknowledge that Oxford had managed to convey with subtlety in an hour what Browdley could have tackled vulgarly in five minutes. After a long pause, he therefore spoke the slow Browdley affirmative that, by its tone, could imply resignation as well as affirmation.

"You mean you *do* understand, Boswell?"

"Aye," George repeated.

"I'm terribly sorry—I could think of no other way than to put it to you—"

"Of course, man, of course."

Winslow gripped George's arm speechlessly, and for several minutes the two seemed not to know what to say to each other. Presently George mumbled: "Is that—all—you can tell me—about it? No more details of any kind? Not that they'd help much, but still—"

"Honestly, Boswell, I've told you just about everything I know myself."

"I understand. . . . But how about the people on the tour whom she was supposed to be looking after?"

"Maybe she just left them stranded. . . . It would be crazy and irresponsible—but no more so than—than—"

"Than anything else. That's so."

"I admit the whole thing sounds—must sound to you, in fact—well, if you were to tell me you simply didn't believe a word of it, I'd—"

"Aye, it's a bit of a facer."

"But you *do* believe it?"

"Reckon I have to, don't I? After all, you took a good look at that photograph. . . ."

"Yes, it's the same. I knew that at once. . . ." Winslow's voice grew almost pathetically eager. "And you *will* help me, won't you—now that you know how it is? What I had in mind was this—if you agreed—that we go out there together—quite soon—immediately, in fact—before there can be any open scandal involving him—you see what I mean?"

"Aye, I see what you mean."

"And you agree?"

To which George retorted with sudden sharpness: "Why not, for God's sake? He may be your son, but she's my wife too. Don't you think *I'm* interested?"

"Of course. I'm sorry. I'm afraid I—I—"

"Now, now, don't apologize. Come to that, we've neither of us much to apologize for."

"I thought we might leave tomorrow—"

"Aye, if we're going, might as well—"

"Boswell, I can't tell you how much I—"

"None o' that, either, man. Let's get down to some details. I'll need a passport—"

And somehow from then on, in spite of what might have been held more humiliating for George than for Winslow in the situation, it was nevertheless George who took the leadership, a certain staunch four-squareness in his make-up easily dominating the other. They both belonged to a world in which the accomplishment of any suddenly urgent task requires the canceling or postponement of other less urgent ones; and now, as they eased themselves back into chairs, there was nothing left but such routine adjustments. Winslow pulled out a little black notebook and began crossing off this and that; George reached for a sheet of paper on his desk and jotted down a few memoranda. Into the momentary silence there came the distant chiming of the hour on Browdley church clock, and a newsboy shouting familiarly but incoherently along Market Street. *Good* news, perhaps, about the international situation . . . but it did not seem to matter so much now, so quickly can world affairs be overshadowed by personal ones in the life of even the most public man.

Winslow looked up. "You're optimistic, Boswell? From your own knowledge of her—do you feel that—that somehow or other you'll be able to persuade her to—to—"

George's face was haggard as he replied: "I wouldn't call my own knowledge so very reliable—not after this."

"Then perhaps you could talk to my son—try to influence him—"

"Aren't you the one for that?"

"But a new angle, Boswell—*your* point of view in the matter— he may not have realized—"

"All right, all right—no good badgering me." The first shock had been succeeded by anger—helpless anger, which Winslow's concern for his own son merely exacerbated. "I'm damned if I know what I'll do—*yet.*"

"I'm sorry again." And the two faced each other, both driven out of character and somehow aware of it, for it was not like George to be angry, nor was Winslow accustomed to pleading and apologizing. Presently an odd smile came over his face. "Badger . . .

badger . . . " he repeated. "It's a long time since I heard that word, and you'll never guess why it makes me smile."

"Why?"

"My nickname at school—Badger."

Then George smiled too, glad of the momentary side issue. "Because you looked like one or because you did badger people?"

"Both—possibly."

"They once called me Apple-Pie George in Browdley, but it sort of died out."

"Apple-Pie George?"

"Aye . . . because somebody threw some apple pie in my face during an election. The pie stuck but the name didn't." He laughed and Winslow laughed, and it was as if one of several barriers between them were from then on let down. "Too bad I haven't that drop of whisky for you," George continued. "But how about changing your mind about another cup of tea?"

"Thanks, I will."

George went to the door and shouted down the corridor to Annie, then came back and began to search a timetable on his desk. "If we're both going to start in the morning, maybe you'd like to spend the night here?"

"That's very kind, but I think I'd better go back to London as I planned and join you there tomorrow."

"Just as you like. There's a good train at five-eighteen—that still gives you an hour, so take it easy."

Winslow seemed now better able to do this, and until the time of leaving they both relaxed, arranged further details of their meeting the next day, and talked quite casually on a variety of subjects— some even verging on the intellectual, though George was not in the best mood for appreciation.

Then he took Winslow to the train, and only in the final minutes before its departure did they refer to the personal matter again. Winslow muttered, leaning out of a first-class compartment: "I—I must say it, Boswell—I—I really don't know how to thank you for —for taking all this in the way you have . . ."

"What other way was there to take it?"

"I know, I know . . . but it's such an extraordinary situation for you to have been able to come to terms with."

"Who says I've come to terms with it?"

"Yes, but I mean—when I try to imagine myself in your place—"

"*Don't.*" And there was just the ghost of a smile on George's face to soften the harsh finality of the word.

"All right . . . but I can't help feeling more hopeful already—thanks to you. Of course the affair's still incomprehensible to me in many ways—for instance, to fathom the kind of person who could do such a thing . . . of course you know her, but then I know Jeff, and he's not a fool—that's what makes *his* side of it so hard to understand."

"Oh, maybe not so hard," George replied. "It's probably what you said that you couldn't find a name for."

"Infatuation?"

"If you like." And then, abruptly and without caring for the awkwardness of time and place, George began to tell something about Livia that he had never mentioned to anyone before. Perhaps it was the atmosphere of a railway station that reminded him, for it had happened (he said) at the end of their honeymoon when they were to catch a night train from a seaside place back to London. They had spent the last day pottering about the promenade between showers, and during one of these, while sheltering, they had got into conversation with a well-dressed and rather distinguished-looking man of sixty or so. It was one of those chance acquaintanceships that flourish amazingly without either background or future prospects; almost immediately the stranger offered to conduct them through an adjacent art gallery which, though full of very bad canvases, gave him the chance to talk so fascinatingly about paintings that they thought he must belong to that world himself until later he talked with equal fascination about literature, music, and politics. Within an hour they were all chattering together like old friends, and as evening approached it seemed perfectly natural to accept the stranger's invitation to dine. (He had given them his name and told them he was French, which had further amazed George because of his completely accentless English.) The two newlyweds were presently entertained in a manner to which they were wholly unaccustomed and which they could certainly not have afforded—George smilingly declined to break his temperance pledge, but ate two dozen oysters with gusto while Livia drank champagne and laughed a great deal. After dinner it seemed equally natural that the stranger should drive them back to their hotel in his car and later take them on to the railway station. The train was already drawn up at the platform, so the three of them sat together in an otherwise unoccupied compartment with half an hour to wait. Suddenly George discovered the hotel-room key in his pocket and, excusing himself, walked down the platform to the station office to arrange for its return. He wasn't away more than ten minutes, and when he got back the three resumed their conversation until the train's departure.

About a year later (George went on), Livia exclaimed suddenly, during a rather trivial quarrel: "That Frenchman sized you up all right—*he* said I oughtn't ever to have married you!" More startled than angry, George then asked for an explanation. She wouldn't give any at first, but on being pressed said that during the few minutes he had left her alone in the train with the stranger, the latter had made her an ardent profession of love and had actually implored her to run off with him.

When George reached this point in the story he commented rather naïvely: "I suppose that *could* happen, with a Frenchman, even though he'd only set eyes on her a few hours before."

"Perhaps in that particular way he was unbalanced."

"No—or at least there wasn't much other evidence of it. You see, having once got interested in the man, I'd found out a few things about him and followed his career. He'd been married and raised a family long before his meeting with us, and recently he's become fairly well known as one of the financial experts to the Peace Conference. You'd recognize the name if I told you, but I don't think that would be quite fair because a few months ago he and his wife came to London on some official mission, and there were photographs of them in the papers looking as if they'd both had a lifetime of happiness."

"Maybe they had."

A sudden commotion of door banging and engine whistling drowned George's reply and caused him to repeat, more loudly: "I shouldn't wonder."

"There's one other thing that occurs to me, Boswell, if you'll forgive my mentioning it—"

"Of course—"

"How do you know the incident really happened?"

The train began to move and George walked with it for a few seconds, hastily pondering before he answered: "Aye . . . I can see what you mean. . . . Funny—I hadn't ever thought of *that*. And yet I should have, I know." His walk accelerated to a scamper; there was now only time to wave and call out: "Good-bye . . . see you tomorrow. . . . Good-bye. . . ."

When the train had left he stood for a moment as if watching it out of sight, but actually watching nothing, seeing nothing. A porter wheeling a truck along the platform halted and half-turned. " 'Night, George."

"Good night," responded George mechanically, then pulled himself together and walked down the ramp to the station yard.

. . . . .

He felt he must at all costs avoid the main streets where people would stop him with congratulations on the success of the day's events. There was a footpath skirting the edge of the town that meant an extra half-mile but led unobtrusively towards the far end of Market Street. Nobody went this way at night except lovers seeking darkness, and darkness alone obscured the ugliness of the scene —a cindery wasteland between town and countryside and possessing the amenities of neither; it had long been a dream of his to beautify the whole area with shrubs and lawns, to provide the youth of Browdley with a more fitting background for its romance. But Browdley youth seemed not to care, while those in Browdley who were no longer youthful objected to the cost. Perhaps for the first time in his adult life George now traversed the wasteland without reflecting ruefully upon its continued existence; he had far more exacting thoughts to assemble, and in truth he hardly knew where he was. The day that had begun so well was ending in trouble whose magnitude he had only just begun to explore, and with every further step came the deepening of a pain that touched him physically as well as in every other way, so that he felt sick and ill as he stumbled along. He was appalled by the realization that Livia still had such power to hurt him.

Somberly he reached his house and, as he entered it, suddenly felt *alone*. Which made him think; for he had been just as alone ever since Livia had left six months before; and if he had not felt it so much, that proved how hopefully, in his heart, he had looked upon the separation. She would come back, he must all along have secretly believed; or at least the bare possibility had been enough to encourage his ever-ready optimism about the future. Night after night he had entered his empty house, made himself a cup of tea, spent a last hour with a book or the evening paper, and gone to bed with the comforting feeling that anything could be endured provided it might not last forever. There was even a half-ascetic sense in which he had found tolerable his enforced return to bachelorhood, and there was certainly a peace of mind that he knew her return would disturb—yet how welcome that disturbance would be! And how insidiously, behind the logic of his thoughts, he had counted on it! . . . He was aware of that now, as he entered his house and felt the aloneness all-enveloping. Heavily he climbed the stairs to his bedroom and began to throw a few necessary articles into a suitcase. Even that he did with an extra pang, for it reminded him of times when Livia had packed for him to attend meetings or conferences in other parts of the country; she was an expert packer as well as very particular about his clothes. And the first thing she did when he returned was to unpack and repair the ravages of his own carelessness about such things. There was that odd streak of practicality in her, running parallel to other streaks; so that she not only loved classical music but could repair the phonograph when something went wrong with it. And the garden that Winslow had admired was further evidence; it had been a dumping ground for wastepaper and old tin cans before she started work on it. Recent months without her attention had given the weeds a chance, but still her hand was in everything, and the roses seemed to have come into special bloom that week as if expecting her return. In a sort of way she had done for that patch of wasteland what George himself had tried to do for Browdley as a whole (yet would never have bothered to do for his own back garden); but of course she had done it without any civic sense, and for the simple reason that the place belonged to her. George sighed as he thought of that, recognizing motives that were so strong in her and so absent in him; but with the sigh came a wave of tolerance, as for someone who does simple natural things that are the world's curse, doubtless, but since they cannot be changed, how pointless it is to try. Yet the world *must* be changed . . . and so George's mind ran on, facing an old dilemma as he snapped the locks on his suitcase. All at once the house, without Livia in it, became unbearable to him; he knew he would not sleep that night, and as his train left early in the morning he might as well not even go to bed; he would take a walk, a long walk that would tire him physically as well as clarify some of the problems in his mind. He went downstairs and put on a hat, then passed through the partition doorway that separated the house from the printing office. It was the middle of the week, the slack time between issues; copy for the next one lay littered on his desk—mostly local affairs— council meetings, church activities, births, marriages, and funerals. Occasionally he wrote an editorial about some national or international event, and the one he had composed that morning faced him from the copy desk as unfathomably as if someone else had written it in another language. It read:—

These are times when the clouds of war roll back and THE SUN OF HUMAN BETTERMENT shines out to be a lamp of memory for the future. Let us hope, therefore, that AUGUST 31st, NINETEEN HUNDRED AND TWENTY–ONE, the date selected as that of the official end of the Great War, will have more than a merely legal significance, that it will symbolize the actual dying out of hatreds and bitterness both at home and abroad. In this connection it is good news that the Washington Conference is soon to convene, and that the problem of world-wide DISARMAMENT will then be tackled in real earnest. We of this town, who have just dedicated our first postwar plan for a BETTER BROWDLEY, can feel especially proud, for our own achievement makes us part of a mighty movement in which men of goodwill all over the world are straining to participate.

(A pretty fair example, incidentally, of George's editorial writing —typical, at any rate, in its use of capitals, in its opening metaphor that almost gets out of hand, and in its tendency to glib phrases. Typical also of George's fondness for linking local and world affairs into a pleasing dish of optimism.)

But now, reading it over, he had difficulty in gathering what it was all about. Disarmament? *Disarmament?* . . . The word echoed meaninglessly in his mind as he sought, even for a moment, to concentrate on something non-personal. What did he know about disarmament? And at the form of that question he smiled, because of the oddest recollection that came to him there and then, as he crossed the printing office to the door leading into Market Street.

It was of something that had happened several years before, when he had just acquired the almost bankrupt *Guardian* and was full of visions of the kind of influence a small-town paper could wield, perhaps even nationally, if its editor were the right sort, and surely the right sort must be well-educated, which surely in its turn could mean nothing less than a university degree. So that had become one of his numerous ambitions, and since Oxford and Cambridge were out of the question for a man who had a job to do, he had concentrated on a near-by provincial foundation of decent repute that offered degrees by examination only. It had been a hard struggle, even so, for he had originally left school at the age of thirteen, and though the following decade and a half had contained a good deal of self-education there were many deplorable gaps. He could write and speak forcefully, for instance, but before beginning to study he had scarcely heard of the technicalities of grammar, he had small knowledge of history, and none at all of any foreign language. At the first of the two necessary examinations he was baffled by the academic atmosphere, by the courtesy bordering on indifference of the pedagogue in charge (so unlike the nagging, shouting schoolmasters of his boyhood days), and he was rather dashed by an English paper which, though offering the most generous choice of questions, could not avoid the discovery of so much that he did not know. To one question, couched in that very phrase—"What do you know of the Pathetic Fallacy?"—he had replied, pathetically enough: "Nothing"; and there were other matters nearly as hopeless. Leaving the examination hall after that three-hour battle he had been fairly certain of failure.

But a few weeks later he received a note asking him to appear at the same place for oral questioning—which, he was cautioned, did not necessarily imply that he had passed the written tests. The coolness of the warning reinforced his pessimism, so that he was in a thoroughly black mood by the time he faced the ordeal. A tall, thin, spectacled man with a domelike forehead and very precise clipped speech presided at the interview. (Ever afterwards he was the personification of an ideal in George's mind—the pure scholar, un-worldly, incomparable, serenely aloof; so that on meeting Lord Winslow, for instance, he felt he already knew the type.)

The prototype had talked pleasantly and informally with George's examination papers before him, and also (though George had not known this) notes of reminder that the examinee was thirty-two years old, had had nothing but an elementary-school education, but was already owner and editor of a local newspaper as well as a town Councillor with reputedly advanced views—altogether a rather remarkable specimen. Clearly George both puzzled and at-tracted him, though he gave no sign of it; he merely steered the conversation from one subject to another—which was not difficult, for George loved to talk. After half an hour or so the older man nodded, picked up the examination papers, cleared his throat, and began rather uncomfortably: "A pity, Mr. Boswell, that you have done so badly in one paper—English—that your total marks do not reach the required minimum."

George's conviction of failure, which had somehow become sus-pended during the conversation, now returned with a hard hit to the pit of the stomach. "Aye," he said heavily. "I guessed as much."

"Do you think you will try again, Mr. Boswell?"

"I dunno, sir. I dunno if I'll have the time to."

"Why not?"

"You see I'm on the local Council and I run a newspaper—there's a heap of work in all that—work that I can't cut down on. If it was just a question of giving up fun or a hobby I wouldn't mind, but when it means important things . . ."

"Such as?"

"Well, sir, I doubt if you'd be interested in all the details, but I'm trying to get a postwar slum-clearance scheme adopted by the Council, and that's a job, I can tell you—if you knew the sort of place Browdley is."

"H'm, yes . . . I understand. And I do not dispute the im-portance of such work, or the priority you feel you must give to it. What does puzzle me—a little—is your motive in entering for this examination at all. Did you feel that a university degree would help you politically—or professionally?"

"No sir, it isn't that. But I thought it might help me—sometimes—inside myself—to feel I was properly educated."

"And what do you mean by 'properly educated'?"

George pondered a moment, then replied: "I'll put it this way, sir—sometimes I read a book that seems to me just plain stupid, but because I'm not properly educated I can't be sure whether *it's* stupid or whether *I'm* stupid."

A smile creased over the older man's face as he burrowed afresh among the papers, finally discovering one and holding it up before his spectacles. "H'm . . . h'm. . . . Such a pity, Mr. Boswell— such a pity. . . . Mind you, I didn't mark these English papers myself, so of course I don't know whether . . ." And then a long pause, punctuated by more throat clearings and spectacle fidgetings. "Take this question, for instance—'What do you know of the Pathetic Fallacy?' I see, Mr. Boswell, that your answer is 'Nothing,' for which you have been given no marks at all."

George felt it was rather unfair to rub it in; if he had failed, he had failed; and when (since the examination) he had found out what the Pathetic Fallacy really was, it had turned out to be so different from anything he could possibly have guessed that he thought he had at least done well not to try. So with this vague self-justification in mind he now blurted out: "Well, sir, it was the truth, anyway. I did know nothing and I said so."

"Precisely, Mr. Boswell. I have no reason to suppose that your answer was not a perfectly correct one to the question as asked, and if the questioner had wished to judge your answer on any other merits it seems to me he should have used the formula *'State* what you know'—not *'What* do you know?' I shall therefore revise your rating and give you full marks for that particular question— which, I think, will just enable you to reach the minimum standard for the examination. . . . My congratulations. . . . I hope you will find time to work for the final examination next year. . . ."

"Oh yes, sir—yes, *indeed,* sir!"

But George hadn't found time, after all, because the year ahead was the one during which he had met and married Livia.

And what did he know of Livia, for that matter?

.   .   .

Browdley streets were deserted as he closed the door of the newspaper office behind him. From Market Street he turned into Shawgate, which is Browdley's chief business thoroughfare; he walked on past all the shops, then through the suburban fringe of the town —"the best part of Browdley," people sometimes called it. But the best part of Browdley isn't, and never was, so good. The town consists mainly of four-roomed bathroomless houses built in long parallel rows, dormitories of miners and cotton operatives who (in George's words to Lord Winslow) had piled up money like muck for a few local families. George had not added that his wife belonged to one of those families, even when the mention of Channing and Felsby's Mill would have given him a cue. For Livia was a Channing—one of the Channings of Stoneclough . . . and suddenly he decided that, since he was trying to kill time by walking, he would walk to Stoneclough. It was even appropriate that he should take there his problem, his distress, and that brooding subcurrent of anger.

Presently his walk quickened and his head lifted as if to meet a challenge; and in this new mood he reached the top of a small rise from which Browdley could be seen more magically at night than ever in the daytime; for at night, especially under a moon, the observer might be unaware that those glinting windows were factories and not palaces, and that the shimmer beneath them was no fabled stream, but a stagnant, stinking canal. Yet to George, who had known all this since childhood, there were still fables and palaces in Browdley, palaces he would build and fables he would never surrender; and as he walked to Stoneclough that night and looked back on the roofs of the town, he had a renewal of faith that certain things were on his side.

The trouble with Livia, he told himself for the fiftieth time, was that there was no *reason* in so many things she did; or *was* there a reason this time—the reason he had been reluctant to face?

He climbed steadily along the upland road; it was past one in the morning when he came within sight of Stoneclough. The foothills of the Pennines begin there; there is a river also, the same one that flows dirty and sluggish through Browdley, but clean and swift in its fall from the moorland, where it cuts a steep fissure called a "clough," and in so doing gives the place a name and provides Browdley citizens with a near-by excursion and picnic ground. The first cotton mills, driven from a water wheel, were set up in such places towards the end of the eighteenth century, and one of them belonged to a certain John Channing of whom little is known save that he died rich in the year of Waterloo. The shell of the old gray-stone mill that made his fortune still stands astride the tumbling stream; but the rows of hovels in which the workpeople lived have long since disappeared, though there are traces of them on neighboring slopes, where sheep huddle in rain against weed-grown fireplaces.

Gone too is the first Channing house that adjoined the mill; it was demolished about the time of Queen Victoria's accession, when the Channing family, by then not only rich but numerous, built a new and much more pretentious house on higher ground where the clough meets the moorland. About this time also it became clear that steam would oust water power in the cotton industry, and with this in their shrewd minds the Channings took another plunge; five miles away, on meadows near what was then the small village of Browdley, and in partnership with another millowner named Felsby, they built one of the first large steam-driven mills in Lancashire. Other speculators obligingly built Mill Street for the new workers to live in, and the same process, repeated during succeeding decades with other mills and other streets, made Browdley what it is and what it shouldn't be—as George said (and then waited for the cheer) in his popular lecture "Browdley Past and Present," delivered fairly frequently to local literary, antiquarian, and similar societies. Yes, there was one question at any rate to which he could return a convincing answer—"What do you know of Browdley?" —and that answer might well be: "More than anyone else in the world."

Suddenly George saw the house—the house which, like the locality, was called Stoneclough. It showed wanly in the moonlight against the background of moorland and foreground of treetops. The moon was flattering to it, softening its heavy Victorian stolidity, concealing the grim undershadow that Browdley's smoke had contributed in the course of half a century of west winds. This was the house the Channings had lived in, the Channings of Stoneclough. A succession of Channings had traveled the five miles between Stoneclough and the Browdley mill on foot, on horseback, by pony carriage and landau, by bicycle and motorcycle and car, according to taste and period; and the same succession had added to the house a hodgepodge of excrescences and outbuildings that had nothing in common save evidence of the prevalent Channing trait throughout several generations; one of them might construct a billiard room, another remodel the stables, yet another add terraces to the garden or a bow window to the drawing room—but whatever was done at all was done conscientiously, always with the best materials, and with a rooted assumption of permanence in the scheme of things.

George saw Stoneclough as a symbol of that assumption, and—because the house was now empty and derelict—as a hint that such permanence would have received its virtual deathblow in 1914, even apart from the special fate of the Channings. Only the gardens had any surviving life, the shrubs growing together till they made an almost unbroken thicket around the house, the fences down so that any straggler from the clough could enter the once-sacred precincts out of curiosity or to gather fuel for a picnic fire. All the windows were broken or boarded up; everything lootable from the interior had long ago been looted. Yet the fabric of the house still stood, too massive to have suffered, and in moonlight and from a distance almost beautiful. George wondered, not for the first time, what could be done with such a property. No one would buy it; no one who could afford repairs and taxes would want to live there or anywhere near Browdley, for that matter. Once or twice he had thought of suggesting that the Council take it over for conversion into a municipal rest home, sanatorium, or something of the kind—but then he had cautioned himself not to give his opponents the chance for another jibe—that he had made Browdley buy his wife's birthplace.

He did not walk up to the house, but turned back where the road began its last steep ascent; here, for a space of a few acres, were the older relics—the original Channing Mill, the broken walls of cottages that had not been lived in for a hundred years. George never saw them without reflecting on the iniquity of that early industrial age—eight-year-old children slaving at machines for fourteen hours out of the twenty-four, sunlight falling on the treetops in the clough as later on rubber forests of the Congo and the Amazon. Thus had the first Channings flourished; and it might be nemesis, of a kind, that had given their grand house to the bats and the rats. But its quality showed even in ruin; it was a substantial ruin.

By four o'clock George was back in Browdley, tired and a little footsore. As he turned into Market Street and fished in his pocket for the door key there came a voice from the pavement near his house. " 'Ow do, George. Nice night—but I'd rather be in bed all the same."

"Aye," answered George mechanically. Then, recognizing the policeman on his beat, a friendly fellow always ready with a joke and (at election times) with a vote, George pulled himself together and made the necessary response. "How do, Tom."

"Fine, thanks—bar a touch of rheumatics. . . . I was at the stone layin'. It's bin a grand day for ye, and I wouldn't say ye don't deserve it."

"Thanks, Tom."

"Ye've worked for it hard enough. I can remember when ye used to swear ye'd have those Mill Street houses pulled down, and folks'd laugh at ye then, but I'll bet they can see it's no joke now. Aye, ye've made a grand start. How long d'you reckon the whole job'll take?"

"Years," George answered (but he would have been shocked if he could have been told how many). His voice was rather grim, and he did not amplify as he usually did when anyone encouraged him to discuss his plans. Tom noticed this and muttered sympathetically: "Well, I'll be gettin' along—mustn't keep you talkin' this hour. . . . 'Night, George—or rather, good mornin'."

George fumbled the key in the lock and re-entered his house. He felt, as he had hoped, exhausted, but not, as he had also hoped, insensitive to the aloneness. It flew at him now like a wild thing as he strode along the lobby and heard, in imagination, Livia's call from upstairs that had so often greeted him when he came home late from meetings—"That you, George?" Who else did she expect it to be, he would ask her waggishly, and feel sorry that she was such a light sleeper, since his meetings were so often late and the late meetings so frequent. . . .

He went to the kitchen and made himself a cup of tea, sitting there at the small scrubbed table till dawn showed gray through the windows; then he went to the room with the books in it which he called his "study." The timetable lay open on the desk, reminding him of the impending journey for which his tiredness now gave him even physical distaste; and next to the timetable was the small pile of letters that Annie had brought in during the interview with Winslow. George glanced through them idly, and with equal distaste. Suddenly then his glance changed to a gaze and his gaze to a stare, for the writing on one of the envelopes was Livia's and the postmark was Vienna.

He read it through, and through again, stumbling to his armchair with the aloneness all around him as he faced the issue. Time passed in a curious vacuum of sensation; he did not realize it was so long until he saw the sunlight brightly shining, glinting already on the gilt titles of his books. Then he crossed the room to his desk and reached for pen and paper.

He wrote out a wire first of all: REGRET MUST CANCEL VIENNA TRIP FOR REASONS WILL EXPLAIN FULLY IN LETTER.

Then he wrote the letter without pause as follows:

DEAR LORD WINSLOW—By now you will have got my wire, and are probably surprised by my change of mind. The reason for it is simply that I have just read a letter from my wife. It came yesterday—actually while you and I were discussing things. I put it aside with other letters and only noticed it an hour ago. Though short, it is a very frank letter, and in view of what it says there seems little that I can do now—except what Livia asks. I do not pretend to understand how these things happen, and why, but I have to take into account her age, which was not much more than half mine when I married her, so that if it was a mistake, I'd blame myself more than her. Anyhow, it would be unjust and stupid to expect her to cling to it for the rest of her life. Maybe she is old enough now to know what she really does want, and if your son is also, I won't stand in their way—no, I *can't*—neither on moral grounds nor for social and professional reasons such as you might have. So there's nothing I could do in Vienna except make the whole thing more troublesome for all concerned. Please excuse what may strike you as a hasty reconsideration and perhaps even the breaking of a promise, but I've already thought it all over as much as a thing like this can be thought over. As for what I feel, that matters to no one except myself, but I would like to say how deeply I appreciate the way you approached me yesterday. No one could have been kinder and I shall never forget it.

> Yours sincerely,
> GEO. BOSWELL

George always signed himself "Geo." in important or official letters because that was how Will Spivey set up his business letterheads —"Geo. Boswell, Printer and Bookbinder." And under that, in smaller type: "Proprietor of the Guardian Press, Market Street, Browdley." And under that, in even smaller type: "Estimates Free. Good Work Guaranteed."

About seven o'clock he went to the corner, posted the letter, and re-entered his house to find that Annie had returned from spending a night with her mother across the town and had already noticed his bag half-packed on the bed upstairs. *"Another* conference?" she exclaimed. "Why, it's only last week end you was away at the last one. . . ."

"It's canceled," George answered. "I'm not going after all."

"Then I'll unpack your things and have breakfast ready in a jiffy."

George was suddenly aware that he had none of his usual healthy early morning appetite, but she was in the kitchen before he could say so, and by the time he followed her there he had decided he might as well say everything else that had to be said and get it over.

He stood in the kitchen doorway wondering how to make it sound not too dramatic, yet not so commonplace that she would miss the full significance. He began: "By the way, I've had news of Livia." (He always called her "Livia" to Annie.)

"You have? . . . Well, that's nice. Did she say when she was coming home?"

That was a good opening. "I'm—er—afraid she's—she's *not* coming home."

"What?" Annie swung round in consternation as she interpreted the remark in the only way that occurred to her. "Oh, my goodness, she's not—she's not—you don't mean—" And then a flood of tears.

It was quite a minute before George realized what was in Annie's mind. Then he had to comfort her and meanwhile explain matters more specifically. "Good heavens, no—she's all right—she's quite well—nothing at all's happened to her. She's just not coming home. . . . She's decided to—to leave me. It does happen, sometimes— that people don't hit it off together. . . . I just wanted you to know, so that you can get her clothes in order—I expect she'll be sending for them soon. No need to talk about it in the town yet, though of course people will have to know sooner or later." (And no need, yet, to tell even Annie the other details.)

Annie, having been heartbroken, now became furious. She belonged to a world in which women do not leave their husbands, but regard themselves as lucky to get and keep any man who does not drink, gamble, or beat them. And George not only possessed these negative virtues, but others to which Annie had for years accorded increasing admiration. She really believed him to be a great man, and for a wife to be dissatisfied with such a paragon seemed to her incomprehensible as well as shocking. She had never liked Livia as much as George, and that made her now feel that she had never liked Livia at all. "She's a bad lot," she whimpered scornfully. "And it's all you could expect from where she comes from."

"Nay . . . nay . . ." said George pacifyingly. "She's all right, in her own way. And maybe I'm all right in mine."

"I never really took to her," Annie continued. "And I'm not the only one. . . . There was something queer about her, or folks wouldn't have talked the way they did about her father's death and what she had to do with it—because there's never no smoke without fire—"

"Oh yes, there is, often enough," George interrupted sharply.

"Well, anyhow, there was something queer about Stoneclough altogether—what with ghosts and drownings and everything—and I'm sorry if I've let out something I wasn't supposed to. . . ."

She was on the point of weeping again, so George made haste to reassure her. "Oh, that's all right, Annie. I don't think you could tell me much that I didn't hear at the time. But it was all gossip—not worth repeating now or even remembering—that's the way I look at it. I doubt if we'll ever know the whole truth about what really happened." He found something he could force a smile at. "And as for the ghosts—why, that's only an old yarn—a sort of local legend. . . . I heard it long before Livia was born. . . ."

Part Two

Livia had first heard it from Sarah (combined cook, nurse, and housekeeper to the Channing family for half a century); it was the story of three girls who had lived about a hundred years ago in the cottages in the clough. They had been little girls, not more than nine or ten, and in those days children of that age went to work at the Channing Mill (the original one that straddles the stream where the water wheel used to be); and what was more, they had to get up in the dark of early morning to be at their machines by half-past five. Because they were always so sleepy at that hour the three had an arrangement among themselves that while they hurried from their homes they should link arms together, so that only the middle girl need keep awake; the two others could then run with eyes closed, half sleeping for those few extra minutes. They took it in turns, of course, to be the unlucky one. But one winter's morning the middle girl was so sleepy herself that she couldn't help closing her eyes too, with the result that all ran over the edge of the path into the river and were drowned. And so (according to legend—the story itself might well have been true) the ghosts of the three are sometimes to be seen after dark in the clough, scampering with linked arms along the path towards the old mill.

Sarah told this to Livia by way of warning to the child never to stray out of the garden into the clough, for it was always dark there under the trees, and also, added Sarah, improving the legend to suit the occasion, the ghosts were really liable to be seen at any time of the day or night. But that made Livia all the more eager to stray. She was an only child, without playmates, and it would surely be

45

breathlessly exciting to meet three possible playmates all at once, even if they were only ghosts. She was not afraid of ghosts. In fact she was not then, or ever, afraid of anything, but she had a precocious aversion to being bored, and it *was* boring to sit in the Stoneclough drawing room with her nose pressed to the windowpane, staring beyond the shrubs of the garden to that downward distance whence she believed her father, in some mysterious way, would return, since that was the way Sarah said he had gone.

One gray October afternoon she managed to elude Sarah and escape from the house. There was a wet mist over the moorland; the shrubs of the garden dripped noisily as she ran among them and through the gate into the forbidden clough. She ran on, under the drenched trees, keeping watch for the ghosts, and presently the moisture that had been mist higher up turned to heavy rain; then she grew tired and cold, and—though still not in the least afraid—considerably disheartened by not meeting anyone. At last she came to the road to Browdley, though she did not recognize it, never having been walked so far by Sarah or her mother; but as she stared round, a horse and carriage came along which she did recognize. The horse was William, and Watson was driving, and inside the carriage, calling to her from the window, was her mother.

So she was promptly rescued and made to sit on the familiar black cushions through which the ends of hairs stuck out and pricked her legs. It was an unfortunate encounter, for it doubtless meant that her mother would tell Sarah and Sarah would be cross (which Livia did not fear, but it was tiresome to anticipate), and worst of all, she would be watched henceforward more carefully than ever. So she made a quick and, for a child, a rather remarkable decision; she would say she had met the three little girls—the ghostly ones—in the clough, and had run after them because they beckoned her. That could serve, at worst, as an excuse; at best, it might completely divert attention from her own misdeed. Yet as she began, a moment later, she was curiously aware that her mother was showing little interest in the story; nor did she seem angry, or startled, or impressed, or any of the other things that Livia, aged four, had ideas but no words for. Her mother merely said: "Livia, you're wet through—you must have a bath and change all your clothes as soon as you get home."

Nor later on was there any crossness even from Sarah, but in-stead a strange unhappy vagueness, as if she were thinking of some-thing else all the time. When Livia retold her yarn, Sarah answered disappointingly: "It's only a story, Livia, you mustn't really believe it. There aren't any such things as ghosts."

"Isn't there the Holy Ghost?" Livia asked, remembering religious instruction imparted by Miss Fortescue, who came to the house every weekday morning, and seemed already to Livia the repository of everything knowable that one did not particularly want to know.

"That's different. . . . Go to sleep now."

Not till the following morning was Livia told that her father was dead; and this was not true.

. . .

She had been a baby at the time of her father's trial and sentence, so that the problem of how much to tell her, and how to explain his absence or her mother's distress, had not immediately arisen. The year had been the last one of the nineteenth century or the first of the twentieth (according to taste and argument); events in South Africa had gone badly, and men were being recruited for the least romantic, though by its supporters and contemporaries the most romanticized, of all England's wars. Emily Channing, who was a romanticist about that and everything else, had concocted a dream in which her husband obtained his release to enlist, and eventually, on *kop* or veldt, "made good" by some extraordinary act of gallantry which would earn him the King's pardon and possibly a V.C. as well. It was an absurd idea, for British justice is unsentimental to the point of irony, preferring to keep the criminal fed, clothed, and housed in perfect safety at the country's expense, while the noncriminals risk and lose their lives on foreign fields. Channing knew this, and was not in the least surprised when the appeal his wife had persuaded him to make was turned down. But Emily was heartbroken, the more so as she had already told Livia that her father was "at the war." It was a simple explanation in tune with the spirit of the times; Emily had found no difficulty in giving it, but Livia was really too young to know what or where "the war" was, and only gradually absorbed her father's absence into a private imagery of her own.

A couple of years later, however, the South African War was history, and there came that gray October day in 1903 when even a prison interview between husband and wife could not avoid discussion of the matter. For John Channing, after several years to think things over, was in a somewhat changed mood. Till then Emily and he had always comforted each other with talk of her waiting for him and the ultimate joys of reunion; but now, during the half hour that was all they were allowed once a month, he suddenly told her they must both face facts. And the facts, he pointed out, were that with the utmost remission of sentence for good conduct he would not be released until 1913, by which time he would be fifty, she would be thirty-eight, and Livia fourteen.

But Emily (as before remarked) was a romanticist, and the interview was distressing in a way that no earlier one had been. Sincerely loving her husband, she could accept only two attitudes as proof of his continued love for her; that he should, as heretofore, expect her to wait for him, or that he should melodramatically beg her to "try to forget" him. And now, in this changed mood, he was doing neither. He was merely advising her that she should live her life realistically, feel free to make any association elsewhere that might at any time promise happiness, and forget him without feeling guilty if that should seem the easiest thing to do. If, on the other hand, this did not happen, and at the end of the long interval they both felt they could resume their lives together, then that would clearly be an experiment to be attempted. As for Livia, the suggestion he made was equally realistic—that the child should be told the plain truth as soon as she was old enough to understand it. "Why not? You certainly won't be able to carry on with the war story now that there isn't a war."

"I could tell her you were abroad," Emily suggested, "doing some important work. Or I could say you were an explorer. . . . And perhaps there *will* be another war somewhere soon."

John Channing smiled—and his smile, Emily felt, was also different from usual. It was a slanting, uncomfortable smile, and it lasted a long time before he answered: "No, Emily—just tell her the truth. Of course you'll have to be judge of the right moment, but there's really no way out of telling her, once she begins to have school friends. And it would be far better for her to learn the facts from you than to pick them up in garbled scraps from other children."

"I shall tell her you're innocent, of course."

The smile recurred. "Oh no, *no*, Emily—don't ever do that. First, because I'm not, and second, because it would give her a grudge to go through life with—the worst possible thing for a youngster. Say that I'm guilty of what I'm here for, but you can add, if you like, that I'm not personally a vile character. . . . That is, if you agree that I'm not."

"Wouldn't that be very hard for her to understand at her age?"

"At any age, Emily. Sometimes even *I* find it hard to grasp. But I'd rather have her puzzled about me than indignant on my behalf."

But Emily, distressed as she was, nevertheless declined to accept that alternative herself. To be puzzled was the one thing she abhorred, and to avoid it she could almost always discover a romantic formula. That accounted for her mood when, towards twilight as she returned home after the interview, she saw Livia wandering in the road below the clough; it was why she failed to scold her, or to listen to her prattle about ghosts; and it was why, next morning, after long consultations with Sarah and Miss Fortescue, she told Livia the only possible romantic lie about her father except that he was innocent—and that was, that he was dead. He had been killed, she said, in South Africa, and the war for which he had given his life had ended in victory. Emily found it possible to say all this convincingly, with genuine tears, and without going into awkward details. Doubtless in a few years (she reckoned) the truth would have to come out, but when it did it might even seem relatively *good* news to a child of maturer intelligence; while for the time being it surely could not upset Livia too much to think that a father whom she did not remember had died a hero. Pride more than grief seemed the likely emotion.

Livia felt neither, however, so much as a queer kind of relief. She wept easily when her mother wept, for much the same reason that she made imitative noises when the dog barked or the cat mewed; but she had stared out of the drawing-room window with such protracted hopes of her father's return that it was almost pleasanter not to have to expect him any more. Instead, she promptly added a new legend to that of the three little girls whose ghosts were supposed to haunt the neighborhood. She persisted in telling people (the people at Stoneclough, for she never met anyone else) that she often saw her father's ghost in the clough, smoking and walking slowly and looking at the trees. She was so circumstantial in describing all this that Miss Fortescue grew nervous about driving to Browdley after dark, though there were several flaws in Livia's story when Miss Fortescue analyzed it. For instance, how could Livia, who did not remember her father, even pretend to recognize his ghost? And then, too, the detail about the smoking. Not only had John Channing been a non-smoker, but Miss Fortescue was also sure that ghosts could not smoke. Livia, however, replied stoutly: "My daddy's ghost *does.*"

Which presented a problem that Emily, Miss Fortescue, Sarah, Dr. Whiteside (the family physician), and a few others were wholly unable to evaluate, much less to solve. Could it be that the child, in addition to *believing* a lie (which was only right and proper, in the circumstances), was also capable of *telling* one? Miss Fortescue thought not, again adducing the "smoking" detail. If Livia had uttered a falsehood with deliberate intent to deceive, surely she would not have invented such an incongruity; therefore, did it not prove that she was speaking what at least she regarded as the truth?

In fact, it was neither a lie nor the truth, but some halfway vision in a child's-eye view of the world, a vision that could start as easily from a lie deliberately told, and as easily end by sincerely believing it. Those three children, for instance; Livia had undoubtedly lied in claiming to have seen them, but later her fancy convinced her that she *did* see them, more than once; and this made her forget that she had lied in the first place. Nor was it ever a conscious lie that she saw her father, for by that time the clough was a place where she could see anything and anybody. The high trees arching over the stream as it tumbled from the moorland, the ruins of the old cottages where grass grew through the cracks of the hearthstones, the winding path leading down from the Stoneclough garden to the road—these were the limits of a world that did not exist elsewhere save in Grimm and Hans Andersen and the *Tanglewood Tales*—a world as young as the children who lived in it and the belief that alone made it real.

And in the other world, meanwhile, she continued to learn mathematics, spelling, geography, history, and "Scripture" from Miss Fortescue, who was everlastingly thrilled by the secret that could not yet be told and by her own forbearance in not telling it; she also understood children just enough to feel quite certain that she understood Livia completely, which she never did. Old Sarah, who professed no subtleties, came much closer when she remarked, leaning over the child's first attempts at arithmetic—"Queer stuff they put into your head, Livia—no wonder you see ghosts after it." And it was Sarah who saw nothing queer at all in Livia's question, when Miss Fortescue had informed her that Ben Nevis was the highest in the United Kingdom: "Please, Miss Fortescue, what's the *lowest?*"

.   .   .

Another war did begin, as Emily had envisaged (but it was between Russia and Japan, and so not one in which an English household had to take sides); meanwhile Livia passed her sixth birthday; meanwhile also the cotton trade boomed and then slumped. This would have mattered more at Stoneclough had not Emily possessed a little money of her own; indeed, it was a subject of bitter comment throughout Browdley, where hundreds had been ruined as a result of the Channing crash, that the family responsible for it seemed to be flourishing just as formerly. But this was not quite accurate. Browdley did not realize how much had been abandoned —the town house in London, the holidays at Marienbad, the platoon of servants; and while to Browdley life at Stoneclough was itself a luxury, to Emily it was an economy enforced by the fact that the house was of a size and style that made it practically unsalable, and thus cheaper to stay in than to give up. So they stayed—she and Livia and Miss Fortescue and Watson the gardener-coachman-handyman (a truly skeleton staff for such an establishment); and the blacker the looks of Browdley people, as trade worsened and times became harder, the more advantageous it seemed that Stoneclough was so remote although so close—a moorland fastness that no one from the town need approach save in the mood and on the occasions of holidays. All of which, in its own way, conditioned Livia's childhood. Sundays in summertime were the days when she must, above all things, remain within the half-mile of garden fence; weekdays in wintertime permitted her the greatest amount of freedom. It was easy, by this means, to keep her ignorant of everything except Miss Fortescue's teachings and a general impression that all nature was kind and all humanity to be avoided.

And Emily, who liked to put things off anyway, kept putting off the time for correcting all this. "Next year perhaps," she would say, whenever Dr. Whiteside mentioned the matter. He was an old man who had brought both Livia and Livia's father into the world; he did not greatly care for Emily and doubted the wisdom of most things that she did. "It's time the child went to school and mixed with people," he kept urging. "Why don't you tell her the truth and get it over? You'll have her self-centered and neurotic if she stays here seeing nobody but you and Sarah and Miss Fortescue. . What does John think about it?"

"He left it to me to tell her when I think the moment is right," replied Emily, with strained accuracy. "She's only eight, remember."

But it was just the same when Emily was able to say "She's only nine" and "She's only ten." And by that time also another thing had happened. John had been transferred to a prison in the South of England, and Emily no longer saw him every month. After all, it was a long journey just for the sake of one short interview, and it was possible also to wonder what good it did, either to him or to her; letters were much easier.

Not that Emily was a hardhearted woman—far from it. She had no bitterness against her husband for either the crash or the crime, or even against the country for having jailed him; she had no conviction that he deserved his punishment—nor, on the other hand, that he had been monstrously overpunished. The whole situation was one she could no longer come to terms with at all, since it had passed the stage of romantic interpretation. She was still able to weep whenever she thought of him, but equally able to do without thinking of him for long periods, and the idea of raking the whole thing up by telling Livia was not only distasteful, but something she was a little scared of. Already she was aware of something in Livia —character or personality or whatever one called it—that outclassed her own. For one thing, Livia had no fear—of ghosts, or being alone, or anything else. And also she would sometimes make scenes—curious, nerve-racking scenes that made Emily feel peculiarly helpless. Perhaps Dr. Whiteside was right and the child *was* neurotic—but would the knowledge that her father was in prison make her any less so? It was easy to think not.

Nor was it clear that Livia would be made happier by school, for in addition to hating the idea of it, the child also seemed perfectly happy at Stoneclough. She had far more freedom than children have in many homes; she could play with dogs, cats, chickens, tame rabbits, and William the horse; she liked and was permitted to make cooking experiments in the kitchen and planting experiments in the garden; she could walk endlessly over near-by moorland and through the clough on weekdays; she could read library books sent up from Mudie's in London, and there was that new invention, the phonograph, to amuse her. And on Sundays, to brighten the one day of restriction, old Mr. Felsby usually called. But it did not brighten things so much for Livia, who early formed the opinion that Mr. Felsby was a bore.

Richard Felsby was seventy-eight, oaken in physique, the last of a generation destined to glower (within gilt frames) from above thousands of mantelpieces upon dwindling families. Both the Channings and the Felsbys were, in this matter, typical; once so prolific, they seemed now in danger of reaching a complete full stop, for only the surviving Richard, the absent John, and the infant Livia could claim direct descent from the original Channing and Felsby who had built up the firm. The last of the Felsbys could not forgive the last of the John Channings—not so much on personal grounds (for Richard, disliking John's newfangled business ideas long before the crash came, had dissolved partnership and retired a rich man), but because of the disgrace to the Channing name in a world that still associated a Channing with a Felsby. It was said that the trial and the scandal connected with it had aged Richard considerably, and if so, there were many in Browdley who wished it had done more, for the old man was generally disliked. When younger he had been against drinking, smoking, gambling, dancing, and theatergoing (anything, indeed, that might lessen the weekday efficiency of his employees); but of later years he had mellowed to the extent that he only scowled wordlessly if he came across Livia sewing or reading a novel during one of his Sunday visits. He did not much care for Emily, though he felt he ought to keep an eye on her; he was disappointed in Livia, because she was not a boy to carry on and rehabilitate the Channing name; and, as before remarked, he could not forgive John. But he was old enough both to remember and to revere the memory of John's father, who had died some years before the turn of the century. Friend, partner, and contemporary, this earlier John had been, in Richard's opinion, the last of the "good" Channings; and it was for his sake, chiefly, that the old man now visited Stoneclough.

Besides being thus a tribute to the dead, the weekly visits were an undoubted trial to the living, for Richard honestly believed he conferred great benefits by patting Livia on the head and by discussing the state of the cotton trade in a loud voice with Emily. He discussed this because, with Livia hovering about, and in his usual mood by the time he arrived at the house, it was practically the only thing he dared discuss; for Dr. Whiteside had warned him against undue excitement, however caused. If he had anything to say about John he would therefore take Emily into a corner for a session of mysterious sibilant whispering, and sometimes in the middle of this Livia would burst into the room, whereupon Richard would boom out again about the state of the cotton trade. After this sort of thing had happened a few times Livia grew convinced that there was a "mystery" about her mother and old Mr. Felsby, and once the idea got into her head she was quick to notice other evidences of mystery —certain occasions, for instance, just before and just after her mother went away for a few days, when a curious air of tension filled the entire house, when even Sarah and Miss Fortescue seemed to rush from room to room with secrets as well as pins filling their mouths. Livia noted too the almost guilty look they had if she interrupted them at such times; it made her determined to discover what everything was all about, like the detectives in some of her favorite stories. Actually "the Mystery of Stoneclough" (as she privately decided to call it) gave her an added interest in life, since it was clearly more exciting to *live* in a detective story than merely to read one, especially when the detective was herself. For that matter, she sometimes imagined she was the criminal also, or the suspected person who was really innocent, or the stupid policeman

who made all the mistakes, or any other of the familiar characters
. . . it was so easy, and so fascinating, to climb on the moors and
lie down and imagine things.

On the afternoon of Christmas Day, 1910, Livia entered the
drawing room just in time to catch Mr. Felsby inveighing against
"any man who makes a proposal of that kind." In truth, there was
nothing particularly mysterious about the words, since they referred
to the wickedness of the Chancellor of the Exchequer (Mr. Lloyd
George, who was still bent on increasing taxes), but from force of
habit Emily shot the old man a warning look, whereat Richard
assumed his glassiest Christmas smile and reached out his less
arthritic hand. Livia then allowed herself to be patted on the head
as usual; but later, while Mr. Felsby enjoyed his usual nap, she
pondered alone in the downstairs room which was her own whenever Miss Fortescue was away, since it was there that she received
lessons, played quiet games, and felt entrenched in extra-special
privacy. She was still pondering, with a book on her knee, when she
overheard something else—her mother telephoning from the hall
outside. Without any intention to eavesdrop at first, she gathered it
was a long-distance call from London, and after that she listened
deliberately. The talk continued, with long pauses and a lowering
of her mother's voice in short staccato replies; at last she heard her
end up—"I can't hear you—yes—no—I still can't hear you—I'll
write . . . yes, I'll think about it . . . yes, dear, happy Christmas
to you too. . . . Good-bye. . . ." Livia then put aside her book
and abandoned herself to wondering who "dear" was and what
"it" was that her mother had promised to think about; and suddenly, as she speculated, an idea came that she instantly labeled as
absurd, yet instantly allowed to take possession of her; supposing
"it" had been a proposal of marriage? Doubtless the remark of Mr.
Felsby's she had overheard was really responsible; anyhow, during
the next few minutes the idea became a perfectly tenable theory,
and by the time her mother called her to tea the theory had developed into a near-certainty, strengthened by the absence of any
comment about the telephone call. It would have been natural,
Livia thought, for her mother to say, "Guess who rang up just
now?"—and because this did not happen Livia stifled her own
natural impulse, which was to ask.

Presently, however, the near-certainty slipped back into a mere theory again, and then into its proper place as an absurd idea; a few guests began to arrive for the Christmas dinner, and the whole thing passed out of mind till it was revived hours later by a remark of Mr. Felsby's about something else altogether—he was discussing the state of the cotton trade and trying to be seasonably cheerful about it. "There's only one thing I can say, Whiteside—booms come after slumps just as slumps come after booms."

Dr. Whiteside, who wasn't particularly interested in the cotton trade, though indirectly, like any other Browdley professional man, he depended on it for the quality of his living, responded absently: "That's about it, Richard. It's always been the same."

"How do you know it always *will* be the same?" Livia asked, with an air of casualness. "How do you know that this time it isn't different?"

Every eye was turned on a girl of eleven who could put such a question; Dr. Whiteside blinked quizzically, and after a rather awkward pause Mr. Felsby cleared his throat and snorted: "Never you mind. You'll know what we mean when you grow up."

All at once Livia became really interested, but with a faraway rapt look that drew even more curious stares around the table. "But I know what you mean *now*," she said quietly. "And I don't think it's right."

Richard Felsby snorted again, then gave a cross look to Emily, as if this were all her fault for not bringing up the child to have better manners; while Emily, with her own typical gesture of helplessness, began to expostulate: "Now, Livia dear, how *can* you contradict Mr. Felsby?"

"Nothing's ever just the same," Livia repeated, cryptically and with the utmost adult solemnity. She had an odd feeling of being actually adult at that moment, of being carried along by an emotion that grew with its own momentum—as if she were dramatizing something in a rather marvelous extempore way. The drama she had constructed that afternoon was now an even bigger one in which she heard herself speaking lines as if they were being dictated by some inner yet half-random compulsion.

"Livia dear—what on earth do you mean?"

"Nothing can be just the same, even if it does happen again. It can't, Mother." Gradually, inexorably, the words moved to the vital point of attack, and her eyes flashed as she challenged the other eyes across the table—no, across the footlights that she had read about and imagined, but so far never seen. She knew she was acting, yet she could have vowed that her emotion was not wholly counterfeit.

"But—Livia—whatever's the matter? Has anything upset you?"

"Nothing, Mother, except that . . . Oh, how could you even *think* of such a thing? . . . After being married to Father . . ."

And at that moment she really meant it; the man whom she did not remember was now more than a ghost, he was at last a holy ghost, in his daughter's imagination.

A short time afterwards Livia, weeping and exhausted in her bedroom, gave way to equally sincere remorse. She knew that the strange scene had spoilt the evening, that it had distressed her mother, embarrassed Dr. Whiteside, infuriated Mr. Felsby, and caused the party to break up early; she knew she had in some way been rather wicked. "Oh Mother, I'm so *terribly* sorry. I don't know *what* could have possessed me. I'll never, *never* say such things again. . . . It all sprang out of nothing—I just heard you talking on the telephone to someone, and the idea got hold of me that it was a man proposing to you. . . ."

Livia felt her mother's hand tighten over her own. "But—darling . . ."

"Yes, I know, Mother. I know it's silly."

But Emily didn't think it was silly so much as uncanny. There was, of course, no question of her marrying; that was impossible under the existing conditions of British law. But she had fallen in love, and it was that man who had telephoned, begging her to come to London again as early as possible in the New Year. His name was Standon, and he had met Emily by chance in a London restaurant on her return north from one of those no longer monthly visits. He was several years her junior, and lived in a studio in Baron's Court, painting portraits when he could get commissions, and idling when he could not. He liked Emily because she was easy going and had money; she loved him because he was attractive and also (though she did not realize this) because she was starved for

the kind of attention he was always most happy to provide. It
was not a bad bargain, in the circumstances.

． 　　　　． 　　　　．

After the scene at the Stoneclough Christmas dinner table of
which Dr. Whiteside had been a witness, he pressed his argument
that Livia should be told the truth and then allowed to mix with
children of her own age; and even Emily (thinking of Mr. Standon)
realized that something had to be done. However, a solution occurred to her of a kind that she delighted in—one that really solved
nothing, but merely delayed the issue. Why not send Livia to a
good boarding school in another part of the country? In such surroundings could she not mix with children of her own age *as well as*
remain in happy ignorance about her father? If the headmistress
were let into the secret beforehand, surely there was no reason why
the plan should not work out perfectly?

So Livia went to Cheldean, in Sussex, where for the first time in
her life she was thoroughly unhappy. She had tried to look forward
to meeting other girls, imagining that they would all be eager to
know her; but the facts of school life, and even more the fictions,
brought quick disillusionment. She could not fit herself easily into
the patterns of school-girl right and wrong, of not doing things that
were "not done," of avoiding taboos. And questions that Miss
Fortescue would have tried to answer even though they were unan-
swerable were thought merely exhibitionist or absurd at Cheldean;
so after a few unwelcome experiences Livia ceased to ask them.
That helped to lessen her initial unpopularity, the more so as she
was growing up rather personally; she was a girl one would look
at twice, even if one did not agree that she was beautiful.

Meanwhile the cotton trade in and around Browdley slumped
further, giving Mr. Felsby more to shout about during family din-
ners that took place at least once during every school vacation. And
also during one of these vacations Livia was introduced to this man
called Standon, who spent a week end at Stoneclough for the os-
tensible purpose of advising Emily about a color scheme for the
drawing room. The visit was not an entire success, for Sarah thought
it nonsense that a man should travel all the way from London to
tell anyone how to paint a house, while Miss Fortescue could not

believe that a youth with such exquisite manners was not somehow a deceiver. Livia simply did not like him. All this was a rather poor reward for Mr. Standon's efforts to be agreeable to everybody, as well as for Emily's carefully planned scheme to introduce him to the family without causing too much comment. But it was impossible for Mr. Standon not to cause comment, and though Mr. Felsby did not meet him, rumors of his visit got through to the old man and gave him material for unlimited banter afterwards. "And how's your painter friend?" he would ask, nudging Emily in the ribs. "Still sleeping with nothing on?" (This was according to a horrified report made by Sarah after taking a cup of tea up to Mr. Standon's bedroom early one morning.) Of course Mr. Felsby did not for a moment suspect that Emily was privileged to know how Mr. Standon slept.

Standon, on his side, also realized that the visit had not worked out as well as had been hoped, but he was less disappointed than Emily because he had found the entire week end rather a bore—awful house, undistinguished food, uncouth servants, wet days, bleak scenery, and a precocious brat of a girl on holiday from a boarding school who (he could see) continually got on her mother's nerves. Altogether he thought Emily much more fun in Baron's Court, and hoped that all their subsequent meetings would be on his own ground. He really *did* like her, and forbore to sponge more than a poor artist must on a better-off woman. (For instance, she was going to buy him a motorcar, but in return he had promised to teach her to drive.) Knowing all about her past, having investigated it from newspaper files long before she told him, he could feel with some justification that he was being as good to her as to himself.

As for Livia, she immediately connected Mr. Standon in her mind with the secret, or the mystery, or whatever it was; the more so as he was always whispering privately to her mother—*more* secrets, *more* mystery. And Emily, who had romantically set store on Livia liking him, was chagrined that the girl didn't, and told her (truthfully but far too outspokenly on one occasion) that *of course* she wasn't going to marry Mr. Standon. Whereupon Livia, surprised at the denial of something that had not been suggested, could feel only extra certainty that there *was* something between them—*something*, at any rate. A few terms of Cheldean had even given her a vague idea of what, and because she did not like Mr. Standon, she did not like the idea of that either. Whereupon a rift opened between mother and daughter, more insidious because neither would tackle it frankly; it was as if they understood each other too well, but also not enough. Anyhow, Livia went back to Cheldean with thoughts that cast a shadow over a term that happened to be her last. The shadow made it hard for her to write home, and once, when she had composed a letter in which she tried to be affectionate, a feeling of guilt, almost of shame, made her tear it up.

It was Livia's last term at Cheldean because of another unpleasant thing that happened.

For some time there had been an epidemic of minor thieving on the school premises—money and small articles missing from dormitories, coats left in the locker room, and so on; the sort of thing that, if it for long goes undetected, can poison the relationships of all concerned—pupils, teaching staff, and school servants. Miss Williams, the Cheldean headmistress, had done all she could to probe and investigate, yet the thefts continued, culminating in the disappearance of a wrist watch belonging to Livia's best friend. When news of this reached Miss Williams she summoned the whole school into the main hall—an event which, from its rarity, evoked an atmosphere of heightened tension.

Miss Williams began by saying that, being convinced the thefts had been perpetrated by one of the girls, she had decided to call in a detective who would doubtless discover the culprit, whoever she was, without delay. She (Miss Williams) therefore appealed to this culprit (again *whoever she was*) to come forward and confess, thus avoiding the need for distasteful outside publicity, and also— here Miss Williams began to glare round the room—earning perhaps some remission of penalty.

This appeal was followed by a long and, to Livia, terribly dramatic silence during which the word "detective," as spoken by Miss Williams, turned somersaults in her mind.

Then: "Well, girls? How long is one of you going to keep me waiting?"

Still silence.

Miss Williams glared round again before raising her voice a notch higher. "Girls . . . *girls* . . . I simply cannot believe this.

Surely I am to get an answer? . . . Remember—I am particularly addressing myself to *one* of you—to one of you who is a *Thief*—*here*—*now*—in this hall! Some of you must be so close that you could *touch* her. . . ."

Suddenly Livia felt herself melting into a warmth that seemed to run liquid in her limbs; she could not check it, and in excitement let go a book she was carrying; everyone near her turned to stare, and she knew that her face was already brick-red.

"Come now, girls . . . I will wait for sixty seconds and no longer. . . ." Miss Williams then pulled an old-fashioned gold watch on a long chain from some pocket of her mannish attire and held it conspicuously in the palm of her hand. *"Ten* seconds already . . . *twenty* . . . *thirty* . . ." And then, in a quite different voice: "Dear me . . . will somebody go after Olivia?"

Somebody did, and presently Livia was sitting, limp and still, on the couch in Miss Williams's study, while Miss Williams, stiff and fidgety, drummed her bony fingers on the desk top.

"But, Olivia . . . why do you keep on saying you didn't do it?"

"I didn't, Miss Williams. You can punish me if you like—I'm not afraid. But I really didn't do it."

"But nobody's even accusing you—nobody ever *has* accused you!"

"They thought it was me—they all saw how I looked—and then when I dropped the book—"

"My dear child, if they did think you behaved suspiciously, whom have you to blame but yourself? What made you run out of the hall like that? Surely, if you knew you weren't guilty—"

"I knew, Miss Williams, but I couldn't help it. I wasn't guilty, and yet—and yet—"

"Yes, Olivia?"

"I *felt* guilty."

Miss Williams's eyes and voice, till then sympathetic, now chilled over. "I cannot understand how you could *feel* guilty unless you *were* guilty," she said after a pause.

"But I did, Miss Williams. I feel guilty—often—like that. Punish me if you like, though. I don't care."

After another pause Miss Williams replied: "Suppose we say no more about it for the time being."

And there the matter had to remain, for the plain fact was that Miss Williams did not know whether Livia was guilty or not. She rather liked the girl, who had never been in any serious trouble before; yet there was something odd about her, something unpredictable; yet also something stoic—which was another thing Miss Williams rather liked. She could not avoid thinking of the secret that Livia did not know, and perhaps ought to know, at her age . . . or *did* she know already . . . partly . . . in the half-guessing way that was the worst way to get to know anything? That feeling of guilt, for instance (assuming there had been no grounds for it at Cheldean)—could it be that Livia suspected something in her own family to which guilt attached, and (by a curious psychological twist) was becoming herself infected by it? Miss Williams had not received a very good impression of Mrs. Channing from the correspondence they had had; she seemed a weak, dilatory person, incapable of facing her own or her daughter's problems with any kind of fortitude. Whereas fortitude, and problems, were Miss Williams's specialties—whether, for instance, a headmistress should tell one of her girls something she had promised not to tell, if she believed it was in the girl's best interest? For several weeks Miss Williams debated this problem with herself, while she continued to find things likable in Livia; she even admired the girl for the way she faced up to the deepening mistrust with which the school as a whole regarded her; she admired the girl's proud yet stricken eyes as she continued to take part in games and lessons; but she had had enough experience as a schoolmistress to know that nothing but absolute proof of someone else's guilt could ever put things right, and if this did not soon appear, then there would arise a final problem—could Livia remain at Cheldean without harm to herself and to the morale of the school?

One day towards the end of term Miss Williams reached a decision. She called the girl into her room and very simply told her the plain truth about her father. There was no scene, but after a long pause Livia said: "Can I go home now, Miss Williams?"

"*Home?* You mean—to your mother?"

"Yes."

"Why do you want to go home?"

"I—I *must* go. Everything's different. I said it would be. Nothing can ever be the same again."

Miss Williams did not ask when Livia had made this cryptic prophecy; she merely remarked: "I hope you're not angry with your mother—she did what she thought was for the best."

"I'm not angry with anybody. Not even with Mr. Standon any more."

"And who's Mr. Standon?"

"The man my mother goes with."

"Oh come now . . ." And Miss Williams, coloring a little, felt the ice getting thin even under her own experienced feet. (But not, perhaps, so experienced in certain directions.) She added hastily: "Livia . . . I think we had better not discuss this any further for the present. And I'm not sure whether you ought to go home now or wait till the end of term. I'll think it over and let you know in a few days."

Miss Williams planned to write Mrs. Channing a long letter of explanation which would arrive ahead of Livia; but this intention was frustrated by a much simpler act by the girl herself. She ran away from the school that same evening, taking nobody into her confidence, but leaving for Miss Williams a note in which there was, perhaps, just a whiff of histrionics:—

DEAR MISS WILLIAMS—I am going home, and since you think I am a thief, I have stolen money for the fare from Joan Martin's locker. I took a pound. Please give it back to her out of my bank money.

OLIVIA

The note was not discovered till the next morning, by which time Livia would have reached home. All Miss Williams could do, and with great luck, was to replace the pound before the loss of that was discovered also. She knew that Joan was Livia's best friend and would willingly have lent the money had she been asked. . . . A strange girl, Livia—perhaps not a bad girl; but still, it was just as well not to have her back at Cheldean.

.   .   .

Livia reached Browdley before six o'clock on a windy March morning. Throughout the night-long train journey she had thought out the things she would immediately ask her mother; she wanted to know *all* the secrets, all the details that Miss Williams had not told because she probably had not known them herself. The list of these was mountainous by the time the cab came within sight of Stoneclough, gray and ghostly in the first light of dawn. In the yard beside the stables she was startled to see a new motorcar, with her mother in the driver's seat and Mr. Standon hastily stowing bags into the back.

"Livia! *Livia!* What on earth are you doing here?"

As her mother spoke Livia noted the exchange of glances between her and Mr. Standon. The latter dropped the bags and came over with a smile of rather weary astonishment. He was a very elegant young man, but he did not look his best at six in the morning; and he had, indeed, received so many astonishments during the past twelve hours that he felt incapable of responding to any more. "Hello, Livia," he remarked; it was all he could think of to say.

Livia ignored him. "Mother—I've left Cheldean—I've run away—I'm never going back there—and I want to talk to you— I've got things to ask you—"

"But Livia . . . not now. . . . Oh, not now. . . ." And a look of panic came over Emily's face as she turned again to Mr. Standon. "Lawrence, *do* make haste . . . we can't stop because of—because of *anything*. . . ." Then: "We've—that is, dear— your mother's in a hurry—"

Livia knew from experience that Emily always called herself "your mother" to put distance between herself and the facing of any issue; it was like a shield behind which she could retire from a battlefield before the battle had begun.

"Mother, you *can't* go away yet. I've got most important things to talk to you about . . . *alone.*"

"No, no, dear. . . . Lawrence, put those bags in and let's be off. . . . If you've got into any trouble at Cheldean, don't worry. . . . Mother will write to Miss Williams and have it all put right."

"It isn't that, Mother. . . . Mother, *please*—please will you come into the house and let me talk to you for a while."

"Darling, I can't—I just *can't*—"

But this was too much even for Mr. Standon. "Perhaps you'd better, Emily," he advised. "You can't let her go in without— without—" And the look between them was exchanged again.

Emily slowly climbed out of the car, her face pale and distraught. She walked with Livia a few paces towards the side door leading through the kitchen into the house. They did not speak, but from the doorstep Emily gave one despairing look over her shoulder towards Mr. Standon, as if scared of going out of his sight. Then suddenly and hysterically she cried out: "Lawrence, I can't tell her —I can't, I *can't*. . . . *You'll* have to." Whereupon she ran back to the car and with almost absurd alacrity jumped in and drove off, leaving him to shout after her in vain and to turn to Livia with the faintest possible shrug.

"Your mother's upset," he remarked mildly; and then, detaining her as she stepped towards the house: "I wouldn't go in yet if I were you. Let's have a little chat first."

Livia shook her head. "It's cold here. And it's my mother I wanted to talk to, not you."

"I know . . . but there's something *I* can tell you, perhaps."

"You don't have to. I know. And I don't think it's any of my business."

Mr. Standon looked nonplused for a moment, then shifted uncomfortably. "That isn't what I . . . er . . . well, what I *do* mean *is* your business. It's about your father."

He draped his hand over her shoulder at that word, as if to lessen the shock, but the fact that there was none made him so uncomfortable that he took away his hand before Livia could reply: "I know about that too. Miss Williams told me. He's not dead as my mother always said. He's in a prison."

Mr. Standon gulped hard. "No . . . Not any more."

This time there *was* a shock, perceptible but well-controlled; the girl looked up at him inquiringly. "You mean he *is* dead now? He's died?"

"No, Livia. He's—he's been released. And—he's here—now—in the house. He got here a few days ago."

"But . . . but . . . my mother . . . why . . ."

"I can't explain all that."

She stared at him, incredulously, and while she did, the sound of a motor horn echoed from the road down below.

He said hastily: "I'm sorry, Livia, but you see . . . well, that's how it is."

The horn sounded again, peremptorily. Mr. Standon fidgeted as he went on: "Perhaps you'd like to come along . . ."

"Come along? Where? With you?"

"Not with me, exactly—with your mother. I'm sure that would be all right—"

"But with *you?*"

"Well . . . only in case . . . in case you wanted to be with *her.*"

"But where's she going? When is she coming back? Why must she go away at all?"

"Livia, it's no use asking me these questions. If you want to walk down the road and talk to her about it, come with me now."

"With *you?*"

And the horn sounded a third time, causing Standon to exclaim, under his breath: "Damnation, she shouldn't have run off like this . . ."

Livia added quietly: "I don't want to go anywhere with you."

"Well, then . . . I'm afraid that settles it." He walked a few steps away, then turned again for a last appeal. "But what are you going to *do?*"

"Stay here."

"But—but your *father's* here."

"That's all right."

"You mean you don't mind?"

"I mind my mother going away, but if she goes away I don't mind anything else."

"Livia . . . I wish there were something I could . . ."

She was moving towards the door. He continued, for he was not an entirely insensitive young man: "Livia, you *want* to see him? You're *sure* of that?"

"Where is he? Is he in bed?"

"No . . . he's been up all night. That's why, if you'd like to think things over first . . ."

"What is there to think over? Anything *else?*"

The question was so direct, yet so free from irony, that he could only reply: "Maybe I'd better come in with you and—and—er—" It sounded idiotic to say "introduce you," but for the life of him he could not think of another way to finish the sentence.

"No, I'll know where to go."

"In the drawing room, I think. That's where he was."

Livia then went in without another word, while Mr. Standon, after staring at her retreating figure for a moment, slowly lit a cigarette and began to walk down the driveway towards the road, quickening his pace when he heard the horn a fourth time. He still felt extremely uncomfortable.

. . .

The lights throughout the house were unlit, but a flickering glow, as of firelight, showed beneath the drawing-room door where the carpet had worn; everything else was dark, except the high window at the end of the corridor, which showed the dawn in a gray oblong. Livia turned the door handle and entered. Her eyes were dazzled at first by the firelight, but she was somehow aware of a person in the room.

"I can't *see* you," she said—the first words she ever spoke to him.

She saw then a tall shape striding across the floor to the light switch; next she saw his shoulders, a little stooping; then, when he turned, all such details as his gray thinning hair, wide forehead, and odd smile merged into a general first impression that he was *tired*.

"Livia, isn't it?"

"Hello," she answered; and they shook hands.

When one is young, everything has a stereoscopic clarity, even if it is not properly understood; no hoard of experience both makes and compensates for a blurred background. To Livia as she shook hands with the stranger who was her father, it seemed that her life hinged in a new direction, terrifyingly new, puzzling, even shattering, yet somehow not to be feared. But for the moment she thought her mind would break with such a mixture of emotions as she began to feel: angry love for her mother, cold dislike for Mr. Standon, and a growing shock over the entire situation, as if her physical existence were coming out of numbness. I shall never be the same again, because *nothing* can ever be the same again, and I am not *nothing*—she reflected suddenly, remembering the first lesson in logic that had been almost the last thing she learned at Cheldean. But the frantic syllogism comforted her, all the more because it had not occurred to her till just that moment; and as she stared from the firelight to the tired face of the man standing before her, she repeated it to herself: Whatever happens, whatever they do to me, however much I am torn apart, *I am not nothing.*

She saw that he was still smiling, waiting perhaps for her to speak. She wondered how long she had been silent—minutes or only seconds? But the words could come now; she began abruptly: "Are you hungry? *I* am."

He answered: "Not very. But don't let me stop you—"

"Wouldn't you even like a cup of tea?"

"Well . . . er . . . hadn't we better wait till Sarah—"

"Oh, I'll make it. Let's go into the kitchen."

"All right."

She made not only a cup of tea, but a substantial meal of eggs and bacon, which they both ate, talking of nothing in particular meanwhile—just the weather, and the sharp frost that morning, and how they liked their eggs done. It was beginning to be easier now—like the first morning of term when you go into a new class with a new teacher and you do not exactly expect to get on with her at first—in fact you pine for the old one all the time, though you would not, if the choice were given, stay down in the lower class just to escape the trials of newness.

When he lit a pipe she commented: "They said you never used to smoke."

He did not ask who "they" were, or why the matter should ever have been mentioned. He answered lightly: "Oh yes, I have most bad habits."

"You mean you drink too?"

"Well . . . I *have* been known to touch a drop."

She laughed, because the phrase "touch a drop" had amused her when she was a child; it was so funny to touch a drop, if you ever went to the trouble of doing it, and she had often in those days puzzled over why old Mr. Felsby should boast so much about never having done it in his life.

"I don't suppose there's anything here," she went on. "I think Watson takes whisky, though—on the sly. Perhaps he keeps a bottle somewhere—I can ask him—"

He smiled again. "Don't worry—I never did drink at breakfast."

For that matter, I never drank much at any time. Not to excess, that is."

"Then it's not a bad habit."

"All right—so long as you don't think too well of me."

They talked on, as unimportantly as that. She did not ask him any direct questions, nor he her, but by the time the first rays of sunshine poured in through the kitchen window they knew a few things about each other—such as, for instance, that they had both arrived at Stoneclough before their time; she from school, having run away, he from prison, having been released a few months earlier than he had counted on, due to a technicality in the reckoning. She gathered also that his arrival had led to other events in which her mother and Mr. Standon were involved. He did not tell her much about that, but he said it was an odd coincidence that she should have come that morning, an odd and perhaps an awkward one, but not so awkward as if she had come a few hours sooner.

"I don't know why she didn't tell me everything before," he added, as if thinking aloud. "It would have been all right. I wouldn't have blamed her. . . . I don't blame her now, for that matter. She just couldn't face facts—never could. . . . Oh well, give me another cup of tea."

While Livia did so he puffed at his pipe and went on: "Things never turn out quite how you expect, do they?"

She knew that he was addressing her as an adult, either deliberately or absent-mindedly, and in order not to break the spell she said nothing in reply. But he relapsed into silence, and presently, still under the spell herself, she said brightly: "Don't I make good tea?"

He seemed to wake himself up. "You certainly do." Then he yawned. "*Very* good."

"I expect you're tired."

"Yes. Dead tired. I was up all night."

"So was I—in the train."

"Perhaps we'd both better get some sleep."

She nodded. "Sarah knows you're here, of course?"

"Oh yes. *And* Miss Fortescue *and* Watson. We'll meet at dinner, then."

He walked out of the kitchen and a few seconds later she heard him climbing the stairs. It was odd to reflect that he knew his way about the house.

She slept soundly most of the day and was wakened during the afternoon by the sound of commotion in the yard. When she ran to the window, with almost every possibility in mind, she saw it was only Miss Fortescue driving off in a cab. Somehow it did not seem to matter what Miss Fortescue did, but it gave her something to begin the conversation with when she went down to the dinner table that evening.

"She left," he said, "because the whole situation was revolting to her sensibilities."

Again he was talking to her as to an adult; and she knew what he meant, if not all the individual words. Throughout the rest of the meal he veered between more trivial gossip and silence, but when Sarah had left the room for good he said: "I don't know what your plans are, Livia. . . ."

"Plans? I haven't any."

"I mean—what are you going to do?"

"I'm not going to go back to Cheldean."

"Well . . ." And he began to light his pipe. "Some other school, perhaps?"

"You mean you don't *want* me here?"

"Livia . . . it isn't that. It hasn't much to do with what I want. Let's not discuss it yet, though. All kinds of things can happen."

Which was the kind of world that Livia dreamed of—one in which all kinds of things could happen.

She said cheerfully: "The school holidays begin next week, so I'd have been here soon anyway."

He smiled. "Naturally . . . and—er—while you *are* here, there's another thing . . . you mustn't feel you have to entertain me. I don't want to interrupt any of your habits. . . . What do you usually do after dinner?"

"Sometimes I take a walk in the garden, but I think it's already begun to rain. Sometimes I read, or play records."

"Then please do just what you like—as usual."

Without another word she went to the phonograph and put on

Mozart; after it finished she closed the instrument and called from the doorway: "Good night." When he gave no answer she went back to his chair and saw that he was asleep, so she took the warm pipe out of his hand in case it set fire to something; then she laid another cob of coal on the reddened embers in the grate.

It was all very easy the next morning, so far as Livia was concerned. But as the day proceeded it became clear that other people were bent on making difficulties. First there arrived Richard Felsby, and a somewhat stormy scene took place from which Livia was excluded, though she tried to listen at the door and gathered that the old man was just as shocked as Miss Fortescue. She was also vaguely aware that matters of importance were being arranged over her head, and decided there and then to insert her own personal clause into whatever plans were being concocted. And that was simply that she would not, in any circumstances, go back to Cheldean. As soon as the chance came she reiterated this. "And if you send me," she added, "I'll run away again." Neither she nor her father knew that Miss Williams would not have had her back in any event; it would have saved them an argument. "Very well," he said at length, "I'll see about somewhere else." But it was already too late for the girl to begin the new term at any other school.

And the sensation of John Channing's return, combined with the scandal of Emily Channing's departure, raged like a hurricane through Browdley and neighborhood for several weeks, then slowly sank to the dimensions of a zephyr.

.   .   .

They became good friends. It was not that Livia liked him instantly, still less was she aware of any submerged filial emotions, nor was there any conscious effort to like him; but a moment came, quite a casual one, when she realized that she had already been liking him a good deal for some time.

She did not call him "Father." It was hard to begin, and since she did not begin soon enough, it became impossible to begin. Eventually, since she had to call him something, she asked if he would mind "Martin."

"*Martin?* Why Martin?"

"I like the name. I used to have a friend at school called Martin . . . Joan Martin."

"Used to have? It's not so long ago." He was rather relieved to find she had had a friend, after what Dr. Whiteside had said when they met a few days before. "Don't you keep in touch with her?"

"No."

"Why not?"

"Because she thinks I stole her watch."

The answer was devastating, and out of it came the story of the Cheldean incident. After she had given him the somewhat curious details he said quizzically: "And did you?"

"Good heavens, no—what do you think I am?"

"Well, what do you think *I* am?"

She pondered gravely for a moment, whereupon he laughed, not because there was anything to laugh at, but because he had at last found a way of introducing a matter which he wanted to clear up once and for all. "You see, Livia, I don't wish you to get any false ideas. Don't think up excuses for me. Don't dramatize me innocent, for instance, as you dramatized yourself guilty. . . . On the other hand—don't believe everything you read about me in the papers. . . . Know what I mean?"

She nodded and he knew she did.

She added hastily: "I must tell you something else though . . . I didn't steal her watch, but I did steal her money afterwards."

"*What?*"

Then more explanations. He finally laughed again and said: "That's all right. Perhaps we're neither of us quite as bad as we're painted—or as good as we ought to be. And I still think you ought to keep in touch with Joan. Mustn't center yourself on Stoneclough altogether. . . . Get out more. Meet people. What did you think of doing this afternoon, for instance?"

"Nothing in particular."

"There's a farm sale I'm going to. Watson said he wanted more tools for the garden and I thought I might pick up a few bargains. . . . Come with me if you like."

"Oh yes, Martin. . . . I *can* call you that? You don't mind?"

"Not a bit. . . . On the contrary, you've settled what name I'll give if I bid for anything."

It wasn't only his name, however, so far as Browdley itself was concerned. He was recognized by many in the town, despite the long interval, and one day, after he had called on Dr. Whiteside at his house in Shawgate, a stranger accosted him in the street and made offensive remarks. After that he never visited Browdley again, but in the other direction, at a somewhat greater distance, lay country towns and villages where no one knew him by sight; and here he liked to take Livia with him on casual expeditions—to that farm sale, for instance (at which he bought some spades and hoes, and quietly said "Martin" to the auctioneer); or on other occasions to an agricultural show, or a cricket match, or a local fair. He liked outdoor scenes and functions—the smell of moist, well-trodden earth, the hum of rural voices blown full and then faint on a veering wind, the pageantry of flags and bunting against low-scudding clouds. Frankly he did not much care whether Livia enjoyed every moment of these occasions or not; she took the chance when she agreed to accompany him, and if she were bored, that was her lookout. Sometimes she admitted afterwards that she had been. "But I don't *mind* being bored with you, Martin." To which she added quickly: "I mean I don't mind being bored when I'm with you . . . no, no, not even *that* exactly—what I *really* mean is, I don't mind being bored *provided* I'm with you."

Of the schools to which he wrote, all declared they had no vacancies. Whether they had received unsatisfactory reports from Miss Williams, or whether the newspaper scandal had scared them off, was hard to determine; they gave no such reasons, of course, but after the same kind of letter had arrived from half a dozen headmistresses he felt there was not much use continuing. Perhaps there were schools in France or Switzerland; he would have to look the matter up. He did not tell Livia of his lack of success so far, preferring her to think he had merely dropped the matter; which she did, without much delay and with great satisfaction.

For it was very pleasant to be at Stoneclough as the seasons rounded and another spring brought new green to the trees. After the battles and scandals of the previous year, peace seemed to have descended on the house and its occupants; even Sarah, shrill-voiced as she shared the domestic work with Livia, nagged less if only for the prosaic reason that she was getting deaf and could hear less.

She too had made her truce, whether of God or of the Devil; without giving up one jot of her religious scruples, which were of the strictest kind, she nevertheless contrived to mate them with an old conviction that a Channing could do no wrong. He could, and had done, obviously; and yet, in another sense, it was not so. Surely that was no harder to believe than some of the things she heard, and with relish, from her favorite pulpit every Sunday? She was a devout attender at one of the Browdley Methodist chapels, where, as deafness slowly gained on unobtrusiveness over a period of years, she had worked her way up to the front pew immediately beneath the preacher's oratory. She liked the preacher in a grim, prim way —the same way that she liked Mr. Felsby. She had never liked Emily, or Miss Fortescue, or Watson, or anyone at Stoneclough who was not a Channing. And she only half-liked Livia, who was only half a Channing. Livia wrangled with her, tolerated her, and thought her at time insufferable—which she was. She was also stupid, hard-working, not very clean, and intensely loyal.

Whereas Watson was not so loyal, rather lazy, and occasionally drunk. But he had a knack with plants and machines, and an affection for the place he worked at rather than for the people he worked for. He liked his employer well enough, did not much care for Livia, whom he thought arrogant, and hated Sarah, who had once floored him with a saucepan when he came into her kitchen tipsy.

And yet, out of these strains and stresses, a queer equilibrium emerged—a tideless sea in which all the storms were in teacups. It was Browdley, that almost foreign land five miles away, where rancors increased as trade worsened and mill after mill closed down. Even Mr. Felsby was rumored to be losing a small part of his fortune; one could not be sure, however, since he forbore to come up the hill and grumble about it. And Dr. Whiteside, his closest friend, gradually absented himself also, though he was cordial enough with Livia when they met, as they sometimes did, in the streets of the town.

Livia shopped, kept house, and helped with the cooking; while Martin (since he may as well be called that) spent hours in the garden, turning wasteland into vegetable patches, thinning trees, repairing terraces and fences. There was much to be done after so many years of Watson's neglect and Emily's indifference.

One day he told her she was to go to a school in Switzerland, and that she would like it very much because Geneva was a very beautiful city. Livia was surprised and disappointed; she had hoped that the whole idea of school might be dropped, but of course it was quite exciting to be going abroad for the first time, and doubtless a Swiss school would be nothing like Cheldean. So there followed a great scurry of preparation—travel tickets had to be obtained, clothes to be bought, and the old Cheldean trunk taken down from the attic over the stables. Martin, who had visited Geneva in his youth, told her what she would see and what she must on no account miss, and that part of the value of being at a foreign school was merely to be living in a foreign country.

Livia was to leave by a night train on the Wednesday after Easter week. During the afternoon she had some last-minute shopping in Browdley, and returned towards dusk in the rather shabby old car that Martin had picked up at a bargain price and that only Watson's constant attention kept in going order. The trunk was in the hall, roped and labeled; it was understood that there would be early dinner while Watson loaded up the car for the drive to the station. Livia, excited in a way she could not exactly diagnose, walked into the drawing room where she found Martin standing in front of the fireplace reading the paper. There was nothing odd in that, but when he put the paper aside to talk to her, Livia was transfixed by the sight of tears in his eyes.

The conclusion she reached was inescapable.

"Oh Martin, Martin—what's the matter? If you don't want me to go, I won't. I don't really care about Geneva or Switzerland or any place except here! I'd *rather* stay with you, Martin—"

"Come here—" he interrupted. And then he stepped towards the girl and took her arm with a curious nervous pressure. "It isn't that. . . ."

"Martin—what's happened?"

He picked up the paper, folded it to a certain place, and handed it to her. But she did not look at it; she kept staring at him till he had to say: "I'm afraid it's bad news. . . . Or would you rather have me tell you?"

She looked at the paper then. It was a small paragraph on an inside page, reporting that Mrs. John Channing had been killed instantly when the car she was driving overturned on the road between Chartres and Orléans, and that a Mr. Standon, who was a passenger, had been severely injured. The reading public was further reminded that Mrs. John Channing was the wife of the same John Channing who, etc., etc.

Livia did not speak. She read the paragraph over and over, trying to grasp not only what it meant, but what it signified in her own life; and then, because of the tears in Martin's eyes, she began to weep herself. "Oh Mother . . . *Mother* . . ." she sobbed. But even while she did so a thought came to her in such a guise that she felt dreadful for having the kind of mind in which it could even exist—the thought that in his distress, which was also hers, Martin might now want her to stay at Stoneclough for company's sake. Yet how could one help one's thoughts, whatever they were? And she *was* distressed; her tears, imitative at first, were perfectly genuine as they proceeded. But she knew now, for certain, how much she wanted not to leave Stoneclough, and that all the excitement of packing to go abroad would be nothing to the quiet relief, even the sad relief, of unpacking.

But it was not to be. As soon as she hinted at it, he said no; if the news had upset her very much she could postpone departure for a day or two, but that was all; and really, he thought it best for her to go; the change of scene and new companions would prove a great help, he assured her.

"And it wouldn't help *you*, Martin, if I stayed?"

He half-smiled. "That's very kind of you, my dear, but I really don't think it would."

After that she was proud enough to leave that night, as had been planned, and not accept the short delay that was so pitiable a substitute for what she had hoped.

But she was not long away from Stoneclough. The time was April 1914; she had one term at the Geneva school, then returned to England for the summer holidays just before the war broke out. And when the next term began, in September, the Germans were on the Marne and it was thought inadvisable to send English girls across France, even to the best Swiss finishing schools.

One day, to escape a heavy shower, Livia entered the Browdley Public Library, and by sheer chance as she wandered in and out of the alcoves came upon a section dealing with law cases and jurisprudence; one of the books, conspicuous by its worn condition, proved to be a verbatim report of the Channing case. The name was a shock that set her heart beating, but a greater one came when she opened the book and found, against the title page, a photograph of her father as he had been at the time of the trial all those years before. So young, so handsome, so dashing; she could hardly believe it was the same man . . . and against the photograph, scrawled in pencil, was a word unknown to her, but which she guessed to be foul. It brought a flush to her face that she thought everyone in the library must notice, but no one did, and with a curious hypnotized fascination she took the book to a secluded table and began to read carefully. Later, when she had to leave, she hid it behind some other books, so that nobody should borrow it before she continued reading the next day. Not being a library member she could not borrow it herself, nor did she want to order a copy from a bookseller. But every afternoon for a week she spent an hour or two in the library alcove, trying to understand the crime that her father had committed. And for the most part she was mystified. It was all to do with another world—a world of complicated details and strange jargon—false estimates of reserves, duplicated stock certificates, and so on. What puzzled her was the intention behind it all, and to this she found no positive clue until she came to the defending counsel's speech, in which her father was portrayed as a brilliant visionary who had wished to amalgamate a large group of cotton mills with a view to preventing their eventual bankruptcies as separate competitors. But then, when she came to the judge's summing-up, the whole picture was different—that of an ambitious, unscrupulous adventurer, greedy for power, employing deliberate deceit to tempt unwary investors. . . . The two pictures made the problem harder than ever, the more so as neither bore the slightest resemblance to the man she herself knew. She then reread the examinations and cross-examinations, seeking to disentangle some corroboration of one or other viewpoint out of the mass of opposite and bewildering evidence. The main thing she gathered was that her father had once been in a position to deal with vast sums of money, whereas now he could hardly afford the extra hundred pounds by which the taxes on Stoneclough had lately been increased.

Some day, she thought, he would tell her all about it; and then he would be surprised to find out how much she knew already. But what *did* she know? The chief clue was missing . . . *why* had he done whatever it was that he had done? Not only why had he defrauded people, for that question had already been given two conflicting answers, but why had he been either the adventurer greedy for power, or the visionary with dreams of reorganizing an industry? Why? For it had been stated over and over again during the trial, as if it were against him, that the Channing Mill itself was sound until his own course of action ruined it; everything would have been all right, therefore, if he had let things alone. Only he hadn't let things alone.

And then, too, she realized with a sense of discovery, though it was obvious by simple arithmetic, that he had spent many years in the industrial and financial world before the crash. His career was referred to at the trial as having been an "honorable" one; distinguished connections were cited with a number of companies besides his own. Why, then, had he suddenly broken whatever were the rules of the game?

There was yet a third character reading, scattered throughout the book in sundry penciled remarks. "Liar," "Thief," "Swindler," were among the mildest of them; but on the last page was a clue, if not to her father's motives, at any rate to his anonymous accuser's. For in the margin alongside the judge's pronouncement of sentence was the scribbled comment: "And not half of what the —— deserved for ruining me and hundreds more."

Long after she had finished the book and had learned all she could learn from it she found that even passing the library gave her an itch of curiosity—was it still being read, was some other unknown borrower adding new penciled insults to the printed lines? She would sometimes dash into the building just to see, and one day she reflected how simple it would be to put the book under her coat and take it away as she walked out. But she could not make up her mind to do this. It was no question of the morals of stealing, or of risk in being discovered, but rather of her personal attitude

towards Browdley: to remove the book would somehow be accepting defeat, whereas to leave it was—if not victory—at least a challenge and a defiance. So she left it, and the library took on a curious significance in her mind: the place where the book was, and
where people went who hated Martin.

.   .   .

He never spoke to her about the past, or gave her any opening
to ask him direct questions about it; but sometimes, apropos of
other things, he made remarks that connected themselves with it in
her mind—remarks that did not so much reveal the light as illumine
the darkness. Once he said: "The hardest thing in the world is to
understand how you were once interested in something that no
longer interests you at all." And another time, standing with her in
the garden on one of those rare clear days when all Browdley could
be seen in the distance, he said: "The factories look big, don't they?
They dominate the town like the cathedrals at Cologne or Amiens
. . . perhaps they *are* cathedrals, in a way, if enough people believe
in them." And then he mentioned a lecture by a young fellow
named Boswell who was trying to get on the Browdley Council—a
lecture Richard Felsby had told him about in great indignation because it had blamed the Channing and Felsby families for much
that was wrong about the state of Browdley. "There's some truth in
it, though. Whenever I think of those rows and rows of drab streets
huddling under the cathedrals I have the feeling that if somebody
were to send me to jail for *that,* I'd consider it a just sentence. . . .
We're all guilty, Livia, of everything that happens. Read the papers
and see how." (It was the autumn of 1917, the blackest time of the
war.) "And if guilt had to be paid for by punishment, then the
earth would be one vast prison. Perhaps that's what it is."

"The animals would have a good time if everybody was in
prison," Livia commented cheerfully. *"They* aren't guilty, anyhow.
In fact they don't know anything about our wars and peaces—how
can they? What does it matter to a worm whether he gets cut in half
by a garden spade or by a shell bursting?"

He smiled. "It would certainly be hard to convince him of the
difference. Probably about as hard as to explain to Man the mind
of God." He turned with her into the clough. "By the way, I'm go-

ing to London for a few days. Anything you'd like me to get for you there?"

"Can't I come with you?"

"Wouldn't be much fun for you. It's—it's mostly a business trip."

"You mean—you're going to—to start doing financial things again?" That was the nearest she ever came to a direct question.

"Good God, no. Don't you think I had enough?"

That was the nearest he ever came to a direct answer.

. . .

While he was gone she realized she was enjoying even the loneliness, because of the image of his return. That image hovered over the edge of every page of every book she turned to, was called to life by every loved phonograph record. Her eighteenth birthday came during his absence, and somehow she was not even disappointed that he had chosen to be away at such a time; maybe he had had no choice; there were still many things in his life of which she knew nothing. The long interval of the prison years, for instance. He never even hinted at them, yet—she argued—what else could have caused the disconnection between the kind of person he had been and the kind he now was? Some day, perhaps, he would tell her about that also. Some day, when she was old enough, he would think of her as a complete adult, within range of every possible adult confidence. She already felt she was, however little it might have occurred to him so far. She was also beginning to appraise herself physically, though without vanity, for she considered her body too small and her mouth too big; but in being thus ruthless she was merely, of course, denying herself what she did not want. She knew no boys or young men, and when sometimes in Browdley they would stare at her as if she attracted them, she herself was aware only of disinterest. She did not want—was sure she would never want— to attract anyone that way. There were other ways for which she felt herself far better equipped; she liked to think there was something rare and talismanic about her that could appeal to an older man.

Yet she must not dramatize; he had once cautioned her about that, and ever afterwards she had known she had better not act before him; and this, by a subtle transition, meant that she need not act before him, thus (if she chose to look at it that way) relieving her of a burden rather than imposing on her a restriction. It was pleasant, anyhow, to think of the future that stretched ahead; she and Martin at Stoneclough, pottering about the garden, taking walks in the clough and on the moorland, visiting places together—the eventless days, the long firelit evenings. And, of course, to complete such felicity, the war would end sometime.

Sarah, growing deafer and more asthmatic in her old age, seized the chance of Martin's absence to urge her to "get out" oftener, to make friends with young people, to enjoy herself more. And this, from Sarah, who had always connected "enjoyment" with the Devil, was an amazing suggestion if Livia had been interested enough to think about it.

But she merely replied, offhandedly as she always did to Sarah: "I *do* enjoy myself. I'm perfectly happy."

"It's a pity you gave up school," said Sarah.

"Well, I never enjoyed myself much there, anyhow. And besides, I didn't give it up—the school gave me up. Didn't you know that? I was practically expelled, and then other schools wouldn't have me —Martin didn't tell me that, but I once saw some letters on his desk saying they couldn't take me. . . . *I* knew why even if *he* didn't. . . . You see, I'm a bad lot—like father, like daughter— isn't that rather natural?"

She knew, of course, that she was acting then; she was always ready to do so in order to shock old Sarah.

.   .   .

When Martin came back she had been waiting for him for hours, but without urgency. Snow had fallen during the day, and this presumably had made his train late. It had also covered the drive as far as the road so thickly that Watson could not clear it in time to take the car to the station; so Martin would doubtless arrive by taxi. Earlier in the evening she had put on galoshes to enjoy the garden, where the snow lay piled in knee-high drifts—a rare enough sight to be novel, and so were the white slopes of the clough, through which the path ran untraceably except to one as familiar with it as she. The sky was blue-black and full of stars; they and the snow made a paleness bright enough to read by. And all around, especially when she listened for any car noise, there was a great blanket of silence that seemed to follow her into the house when she re-entered.

He arrived about ten o'clock, having walked the last mile along the road because the taxi couldn't get any further.

"And with those thin shoes, Martin? You must be soaking wet. . . . And carrying that bag all the way . . ."

"It's not heavy. I'll go up and change immediately."

"Let me carry it for you."

"No, no . . . I'm all right. If I want anything I'll ring for Sarah."

"She's got a bad cough and went to bed hours ago."

"All right. . . . I won't want anything."

By the time he came down she had the drawing-room fire roaring high, and a tray of refreshments by the side of his favorite armchair —hot soup, sandwiches, whisky and soda.

"Nice of you, Livia, but really and truly I don't want anything —except the fire."

"But I'm sure you didn't have any dinner—"

"I managed all right. Don't worry about me. *Please* don't worry about me."

The way he said that made her instantly begin to do so. She noticed how more than usually tired he looked, his whole face drawn a little, hands trembling as he held them to the fire.

"When you were so late I wondered if perhaps you weren't coming back till tomorrow."

"No . . . it was just the weather."

"I thought perhaps your business had taken longer than you expected."

"No . . . there wasn't much business." His face lightened as he added: "I didn't forget your birthday, but—I have an awful confession—I left what I bought you in the train. They were some special records—of Mozart. I knew you'd like them. I don't know how I could have been so stupid, but it's quite possible they'll be turned in by the finder. Unless he's so disappointed when he unwraps the parcel that he smashes them in disgust."

"Oh no—*nobody* could deliberately smash Mozart records!"

He smiled. "Maybe not. Anyhow, I left word about it—and if we don't get them back I'll buy you some more."

"Martin . . . I'm so sorry . . . don't worry about it."

"Who said I was worrying about it?"

"Well, you're worrying about something—I can see from your face."

"I told *you* not to worry."

Suddenly, leaning forward to warm his hands, he slipped and fell to his knees. Only her nearness and quickness saved him; another few inches, another second, and he would have been burned. As it was, she managed to pull him back and saw then that it had been more than a slip, more than just tiredness. She was calm, yet uncertain what to do—call Sarah?—call a doctor?—but first, anyhow, there was the whisky. She forced a stiff drink between his lips, then began loosening his collar. While she was doing this his eyes refocused themselves.

"I think you fainted, Martin."

He nodded, gulping over the taste of the whisky.

"Seems so . . . and by the way, I shouldn't have had that."

"Why not? It pulled you round."

"Maybe . . . only I'm not supposed to have it—now."

"Why *now?*"

"Well, any time for that matter."

"You said *now!* Martin, what's wrong? What's happened? Are you ill? . . . Shall I call a doctor?"

He shook his head. "No, I've had a doctor. That's really what I went to London for. It's nothing you need worry about. . . . But perhaps I'd better go to bed now—and rest. I *assure* you it's nothing you need worry about. . . . It's—er—to do with my eyes. I've known for some time they weren't quite as they should be. Old Whiteside diagnosed it wrong, of course. . . . Well, anyhow, let's hope those records turn up. At least I can *hear* properly."

He got up and walked to the door, while she ran past him to open it.

"Martin . . ."

"I'm really all right, Livia—I didn't even intend to tell you but for—"

"Martin, *I'll* look after you. You know that?"

"Why, yes, but—"

"Even if you were to go blind—"

"Oh come now, there's no question of that. . . ." And then a laugh. "You *do* like to dramatize, don't you? . . . But you're very kind. I sometimes wonder why. I never did anything for you—except bring you into the world, and God knows whether you'll thank me for that, in the end. . . . Yes, it puzzles me sometimes—why you are so kind to me."

"Because I love you," she answered simply, and then she laughed too, as if to join him in any joke there was. "Good night, Martin."

"Good night."

Back in the drawing room she listened to his footsteps creaking on the floor above. Then she ate a sandwich and walked to the window, opened it, and breathed the cold air. The blanket of silence was still covering the world.

.   .   .

The next morning he asked her not to tell Sarah anything about his fainting, or the trouble he had mentioned, because Sarah would fuss, and fussing was just as bad as worrying. And it was useless to tell Sarah not to fuss, because she would do so anyway; whereas if he told Livia not to worry, then he was sure of her compliance. Livia said she was far too happy to worry about anything, which was the truth, and it puzzled her. Perhaps it was because he looked so much better after his night's sleep. Or perhaps it was just that he was home again. Or perhaps it was her own penchant for having the oddest emotions at the oddest times.

Anyhow, she was so happy she decided to put the old work horse between the shafts of the garden cart and drive over the hill to fetch eggs and butter from one of the farms; Watson usually did this in the car, but he was afraid the snow might be too deep in places, though the horse would manage all right. So she sat on the plank seat, surrounded by the rich smells of the empty cart, and jogged down the road as far as the side turning that climbed again steeply to the moorland. The sky over the snow was an incredible deep blue, and when she had gone a little way and looked back, there was Stoneclough, a huddle of white roofs against the black-and-white trees. And above her now, the mountain lifted up. In that strange snow-blue light it seemed to her that she had never been so near it before, though actually she had climbed to the summit many times; she felt a sudden wild ecstasy that made her lie down on the floor of the cart amidst the smells of hay and manure, to exult in the whole matchless beauty of that moment. The horse jogged on, presently stopping before a closed gate. She jumped down to open it, laughing aloud. Then the lane narrowed to a stony track, and there were other gates. At last she reached a farmhouse and saw a fat woman standing at the doorway wiping her arms on an apron and smiling. "Laws amussy," she cried, as Livia approached, "I didn't expect anybody'd come up this morning. Are you from Stoneclough?"

Livia said she was, and had the impression she was being taken for a servant girl; and that, somehow, added to the pleasantness of the occasion. Smiling also, she handed over the note on which Sarah had written out so much butter, so many eggs, and so on; but then another strange and pleasant thing happened. The fat woman pushed back the note with a loud chuckle. "Nay, that's no use to me, girl—ye'll have to tell me what it says. I never was a scholar."

"You mean you can't *read?*" queried Livia.

"That's so—and I don't know as I'll ever bother to learn, now I've let it go so long."

Livia then told her what she wanted, whereupon the woman disappeared into the farmhouse, returning after a few minutes with the various items, a handful of carrots for the horse, and a jug containing a pale frothing liquid. "Nettle drink," she cried, triumphantly, "and it'll be the best ye've ever tasted."

That could be easy, thought Livia, who had never tasted any before. But it *was* delicious, whether because of the woman's special brew, or for some curious extra congeniality of time and place . . . but the truth was, everything that morning was to Livia miraculously right—the drive, the sky, the sunshine, the mountain, the nettle drink, and the fact that the woman could not read. Never again, as long as she lived, was she quite so happy.

.   .   .

She would hold his arm firmly (for he was apt to stumble a little), and walk with him up and down the level paths along the terraces, sometimes as far as the fence, but not much beyond, because there might be strangers in the clough, and he did not want to be seen. All at once a secret between them was removed, so far as this was concerned; he made no more effort to conceal from her certain things that he still wished to conceal from others. She was a co-conspirator in a small but necessary deception. For some reason he did not want outsiders to know that his eyes were bad; he seemed not to realize that few would care, or even think that a man walking slowly along with a girl holding his arm was behaving in any abnormal way for father with daughter. But she did not mind the pretense, if it satisfied him. And inside the garden, with no one to see or hear, with the empty moorland above and the dark clough below, she learned the special trick of sharing whatever mood he was in, even to extremes; if he wanted to laugh, she would laugh too, and if he had wanted to cry she believed she could have done that also. Sometimes she would tell him the only funny stories she knew, which were about Cheldean or the Geneva school; they were mostly rather silly yarns, even if they were funny at all, and it was odd to feel their schoolgirl importance dwindling in retrospect while she narrated them, so that she could tick them off afterwards as things never to be told again. He seemed interested, however, and often asked about her school friend, Joan Martin, suggesting again that she should write and try to re-establish the friendship. But Livia said it was no use now; she was sure they wouldn't have a thing in common, even apart from the doubtful incident of the watch.

"But you ought to have friends, Livia—*young* friends. I know it would be hard for you to make them in Browdley—for various reasons . . . but you ought to have them—there ought to be people of your own age whom you could spend holidays with at their homes."

"Or they could come here to spend holidays with me—how would you like that?"

The point was taken. He replied: "I wouldn't mind it so much. I wouldn't have to see a great deal of them, and if they were *your* friends, I'd do my best to make them feel at home."

She smiled. "But they wouldn't be, they couldn't be, and I'd mind them here, anyway. Martin, don't you worry about me, either." And then sharply: "Who's been talking to you? Sarah? She had no business to . . . Why should she interfere?"

He did not deny that Sarah had talked to him.

"All right," he said temporizingly, "but don't go and nag Sarah about it. She means well."

"That's not always a good defense," she said, thinking of it suddenly, "when people do the wrong thing."

She often gave him cues like that, as they occurred to her on the spur of the moment, hoping they might lead him into talk of the past. But they never did, and she wondered if he ever guessed that they were deliberately put out, and if he just as deliberately ignored them. One evening, however, without any cue at all, he began to talk of his years in prison. They were walking in the garden, with the stars especially bright in the frosty air, and that drew him to remark that the books he had read in prison were mostly about astronomy and philosophy. "You see, in prison after the first period of getting used to it, which is rather dreadful, you slip into a mood of timelessness that isn't either happy or unhappy, and in that mood—for me, at any rate—the things to think about were the timeless ones—the mysteries of life and existence that have sent many men into cells not very different from mine . . . the cells of monasteries, or the other kind where mad people are put. Not that I invented any special philosophy or had any special vision to match those I read about. I don't have the right quality of mind."

"Neither do I," she answered. "You liked that kind of book because you were in prison, but I'd feel in prison if I had to read that kind of book."

"I know," he smiled. "But a very kind and gentle prison. A prison within the other prison. It wasn't so bad—although, as I said, my mind wasn't exactly equal to it—because, after all, I'd only been a smart businessman most of my life."

"And not even so smart," she said softly, taking his arm.

"That's so. Well, let's say just a businessman. Perhaps that's why I think now of the end of a man's life as a sort of taking over by a junior partner—some cheeky young fellow whom at first you thought of no account, but he grows and grows inside your affairs till he begins to touch them all—you'd like to get rid of him but you can't, he's the fellow you try to forget when you go to sleep, but he wakes you in the morning with his nagging and needling . . . the first step you take you know he's still there, at your elbow, jogging and shoving and hurting like the devil . . . you're at his mercy—his strength grows all the time at the expense of yours—he knows he's going to have his own way in the end—it's only a matter of time, and a horrible time at that . . . and from his point of view, of course, everything's going exactly as it should—he is healthy, striving, spreading —you are just an old decaying out-of-date thing he feeds on." He checked himself. "Am I talking too much?"

"No," she answered, transfixed.

"Do you know what I'm talking about?"

"Not altogether." She added quickly: "But I don't mind not knowing altogether. You remember once I said I didn't mind being bored. When you don't mind being bored, it isn't boredom, really. And it's like that when you don't mind not understanding—perhaps it means that you *do* understand—a little."

"I hope so," he said, holding closely to her as they reached an up-hill part of the path. "Now tell me some more about Cheldean."

She racked her brains to think of a story because she knew that in some obscure way those yarns about school life took his mind in a pleasant direction, even if he did not always listen carefully; but she had already told him most that had happened, and now she could only think of something that had not happened. It was an incident she had once invented during a rather dull service in the Cheldean School chapel. The preacher was a local divine who came regularly and always devoted a large part of his extempore prayer to the weather; he was never satisfied with it and always wanted God to change it to something else, so that the slightest sign of floods, drought, a cold wave or a heat wave, gave him an excuse. One sunny Sunday after a week of consecutive fine days, he prayed most eloquently for rain—which the girls definitely did not want, since there was a school holiday the next day; and Livia, sharing this resentment, suddenly noticed a sort of trap door in the roof of the chapel just over the pulpit.

What fun, she thought, if one had climbed up there with a bucket of water and, at the moment of the appeal, had poured it down over the preacher's head! The thought was so beguiling that she had giggled quietly in the pew; but now, telling the story to Martin as a true one, she had him laughing aloud.

"What really made you do it?" he asked. "Just for a lark?"

"I wanted to see his face when he looked up," she said, still using her imagination. "I thought he might think I was God."

She had to invent the sequel of her own discovery and punishment, at which he kept on laughing. In doing so he half stumbled to his knees; and while she was helping him up Watson entered the garden from the yard. He gave them both a rather long and curious stare, and a few hours afterwards, catching Livia alone, asked how her father was. She answered "All right," as she always did to that question.

Watson grinned. "Just a little drop too much sometimes, eh?"

"What do you mean?" Then Livia realized what he did mean and was immensely relieved. She had been afraid for a moment that he might have deduced some real illness, and his mistake seemed the happiest and simplest alibi, not only for past but possibly future events also.

She therefore smiled and retorted: "You ought to know the symptoms, Watson, if anyone does."

From then on, Livia cared less about what was seen and heard, even though Watson's knowing impertinences increased.

.   .   .

One evening Martin called her attention to a white dog walking along the path towards them, but she saw it was not a dog, but a piece of newspaper blown in the wind; but he still insisted it was a dog and stopped to touch it, then said it had run away. That made her realize how bad his sight was becoming, and she begged him to see some other eye doctor; perhaps a special kind of glasses or treatment would help; even if Dr. Whiteside were no use, surely there must be someone in Mulcaster or London . . . But he said no; it had all been diagnosed and prescribed for before; there was really nothing anyone could do about it—perhaps it would not get any worse. And he could still see many things perfectly well—colors, for instance. The red geraniums, the blue lobelias, the yellow sunflowers; he welcomed them all each day. That gave her the idea to put on a scarlet dress the next time she walked with him, and he was delighted. From which she promptly derived another idea, and that evening, though she was poor at sewing, she worked hard after he had gone to bed, cutting up an old patchwork quilt and making it into a multicolored dress to wear the following day. And he was delighted again.

She then thought he might like a real white dog, and asked Watson to get one; but when the dog appeared and was duly presented to his master in the garden, he wriggled loose and scampered into the clough. "There you are," Martin laughed, when she fetched the animal back. "That's what happened before. The white dog will have nothing to do with me."

"Then I must be a white cat," she answered, breathlessly. She had noticed before that the silliest repartee of this kind seemed to lift his mood; it was strange, indeed, how much of their talk had recently been either silly or abstruse, seeming to skip the ordinary world in between. And as usual, the silliness worked; he was lifted. "Come along, little white cat," he laughed again.

"Yes—and the white cat won't run away," she answered.

She could see that he was recalling something. "But a holiday, though . . . that would be all right. Why don't you take one?"

"A holiday?"

"Yes, why not?"

"Away . . . from *you?*"

"Well, only for a time. . . ."

Suspicion filled her mind. "One of Sarah's ideas?"

"Now, now, don't get cross with Sarah. She's not the only one who thinks you need a holiday."

"Who else, then?"

"Oh . . . several people. . . ."

"Who? *Who?*"

He wouldn't tell her, but it was easy to worm the truth out of Sarah, and the full truth proved even darker than her suspicion. For it seemed that old Richard Felsby (he of all people) had visited Stoneclough recently and talked to Martin not merely about her taking a holiday, but about her leaving Stoneclough altogether. Some friends of Richard's who lived on the coast of North Wales had been approached and had agreed to have her stay with them indefinitely; Richard had offered to pay all expenses, and Martin had actually approved the idea. This was the biggest blow of all; yet after a wild scene with Sarah she could only reproach him somberly. How could he have even considered such a thing? And that awful old man, Richard Felsby—how dared *he* interfere with her and her affairs? "Oh, Martin, I thought he never visited you any more. I thought you'd quarreled. I hoped you were enemies forever."

"Livia, he just called on business the other day—while you were out. Something about a new mortgage on the house."

"But he talked about *me*—you both did—planning to have me sent away—and Sarah already getting my clothes ready—all of you —behind my back—against me—plotting—and then pretending it was just a holiday—"

"Livia, please—it wasn't like that at all—"

"Do you know what I'll do? I'll hate them both as long as I live —I'll *never* forgive them—either of them—"

"They were only thinking of what might be your own best interests—"

"To send me away from you? Is that what *you* think too? You don't want me here?"

"Livia, please. . . . You know how much I like you—"

"I like you too. I love you. I've told you that before. And I wouldn't go, even for a holiday. I'll never leave you. They'd have to drag me out of the house and if they took me anywhere else I'd run away and I'd fight them all the time. I'd kill anybody who tried to send me away from you."

"Now, Livia, Livia . . . why should you talk like that?"

"Because I'm so happy here. What on earth would I do alone in a strange place?"

"You wouldn't be alone—"

"I'd be alone if I left you alone. I won't go anywhere unless you go with me. Then I'll go—wherever it is. Even if you went out of your mind I'd go out of mine too. That's a bargain. . . . So don't try to get rid of me." She put her hands up to his face and clawed him gently with her fingernails, suddenly and rather hysterically laughing. "The little white cat will scratch you to death if you even think of it."

· · ·

Dr. Whiteside happened to meet Livia in Browdley one afternoon. She did not mention her father, until asked, and then she said he was "all right." The doctor was an old man now, long retired from practice, and for that reason even readier to think out the problems of the families he had once attended. He well remembered advising Emily to tell Livia the truth and send her to school lest the life at Stoneclough, without playmates of her own age, should make her grow up neurotic and self-centered; he had not seen the girl often since then, but now, even to his dimmed perceptions, she looked as if everything had happened just as he had feared. There was the peculiar rapt expression, the angular tension of her whole body as she stopped to speak to him in the street. And he made up his mind there and then to visit Stoneclough unasked; he did not care how John received him, it was the girl he was thinking about. She ought to be sent away, and he would tell John this and be damned to the fellow.

So a few days later, amidst pouring rain that had already flooded the low-lying districts of Browdley, Dr. Whiteside had his old coachman-chauffeur drive him up to Stoneclough. Admitted by Watson, he was glad to find Livia out, and made his own way across the hall to the drawing room. He walked in without ceremony, being both in the mood and at an age when such things were possible. John Channing sat alone by the fireside, with a white wire-haired terrier on his lap. It was one of the almost lucid intervals, less frequent now and more fragmentary; the younger man shook hands, invited the doctor to sit down, remarked on the weather, and in all ways but one seemed perfectly normal. The exception lay in the fact that though he clearly did not recognize Dr. Whiteside, he showed no surprise that a stranger should walk in unannounced.

It would have puzzled a man less subject to freaks of behavior than Dr. Whiteside himself. "Good God, man, don't you *remember* me?" was all he exclaimed. "Whiteside . . . *Doctor* Whiteside. I've been meaning to look you up for a long while. . . . How are you getting on?"

"Oh not so badly, thanks. Yes, of course I remember you now. It's—it's just that I don't *see* very well."

"Still the same trouble?"

"No. It never was what you diagnosed."

"You don't say?" Dr. Whiteside was somewhat discomfited. "Well, of course, I'm not a specialist. I hope you consulted one."

"I did."

"And what did he say?"

"That's my business, if you don't mind."

"Why . . . certainly. I beg your pardon." But by this time Dr. Whiteside's interest, both private and professional, was thoroughly aroused. He was not really a stupid doctor, only a rather perfunctory one when people came to him with vague complaints, such as "a little trouble with my eyes." On the occasion of that visit several years before, he had discovered a few symptoms of strain and had recommended a local oculist who would make a more detailed examination. As he never heard that Channing visited the oculist, he had concluded that whatever was wrong had got right of its own accord, as so many ailments do; but now, staring closely, he detected other symptoms—much more serious ones. Of course he couldn't be sure, but if what he instantly thought of were possible, then it was rather appalling. . . .

He continued, automatically turning on the jaunty air that he always adopted at such moments, yet at the same time reflecting that the real object of his visit was now more necessary than ever: "Matter of fact, I didn't come to talk about you at all."

"Good—because it's the one subject I try not to be interested in. What *did* you come to talk about?"

Dr. Whiteside answered bluntly: "Livia."

"Livia? Fine—go ahead. Too bad she's out shopping now, or you could talk to her yourself. . . . What about her, though?" Then with sudden darkening urgency: "She's not ill, is she? There's nothing happened to her?"

Dr. Whiteside saw a loophole into the argument which he knew had to come. "If she *were* ill, John, or if anything *were* to happen to her . . . and I'm telling you this frankly, mind . . . it would be nobody's fault but yours."

"But she's not ill . . . tell me . . . tell me . . ."

"No, she's not exactly ill. She's just in a rather nervous state. . . ."

"I know—she ought to go away. Matter of fact it was all arranged—"

"Yes. Richard told me, but he didn't tell me she hadn't gone."

"He doesn't know that yet. . . . But she's not *ill?* . . . You're not keeping something from me?"

"I've said she's in a rather nervous state. That describes it pretty well. A *very* nervous state . . . as apparently you are yourself."

"Oh never mind me. Leave me out of it."

"But I can't entirely—in what I have to say."

"Then for God's sake get on with saying it!"

After a pause Dr. Whiteside resumed: "She's very fond of you, isn't she?"

The question seemed to bring instant calm to the discussion.

"I daresay. I am of her too. She's kind to me. You'd never believe how kind to me she is. I often wonder why, because—as I've told her —I never did anything for her except bring her into the world, and that's a doubtful privilege . . . but she's so kind—so *wonderfully* kind."

Dr. Whiteside cleared his throat; he would soon be on delicate ground. "Has it ever occurred to you . . ." He hesitated, then leaned forward to pat the head of the terrier and was disconcerted when the animal growled at him. "A faithful dog, I can see."

"Livia gave him to me. Becky, his name is. She gave me this pipe too—though I can't smoke any more—it hurts my head to have a pipe in my mouth. She doesn't know that—please don't tell her. She's always giving me things. I give her things too, but I can afford so little nowadays . . . and those records were never returned. The railway people never found them. They were Mozart records—she loves Mozart."

Dr. Whiteside nodded grimly. Presently he said, beginning afresh: "Has it ever occurred to you that she never remembered you as a child . . . so that when she saw you a few years ago it was like meeting a stranger for the first time?"

"Why, of course. That's what makes it so remarkable. Two strangers. And very much at odds with the world—both of us. We've managed to get along pretty well. But I agree with you—that is, if the point you're making is about her health . . . a long holiday . . . Richard's right . . . she needs it. Sarah says so too. . . ." Then suddenly, in a changed voice: "Dr. Whiteside, I'm not well— I have to admit that. In fact, there are times when I'm very far from well. Will you please tell me—quickly, please—because there's not a great deal of time . . . exactly what are you driving at?"

Half an hour later Dr. Whiteside left the house, having discovered a great deal more than he had allowed the other to realize, and having said perhaps more than he himself had intended.

．　＞　．

Livia's shopping was considerably delayed that afternoon. She was not temperamentally a very good driver of a car, and after such rain as had fallen during several consecutive days there were extra hazards in traveling to and from Stoneclough. It was quite a phenomenal rain; all the streets near the river were under water, with basements engulfed and families living in upper floors; the *Advertiser* and the *Guardian* both reported it as the worst flood within living memory. This would have been enough for Browdley to gossip about, yet when Livia entered shops to make her purchases she could feel she was changing the subject of scores of conversations. For the town was already full of rumors about Stoneclough. A few words from Watson had been sufficient; their very fewness gave larger scope to theory, interpretation, pure invention. The whole history of the Channing family, their crimes, scandals, and downfall, was revived under a new spotlight. It was impossible not to wonder what secrets lay behind the eyes of a girl who looked and talked as if she were half a child and half an adult, but nothing at all of an eighteen-year-old.

She shopped at the butcher's, the grocer's, the pastry cook's. It was remembered afterwards (by individuals) that she had bought some pipe tobacco at the tobacconist's, and some lengths of colored ribbon in the drapery department of the Co-operative shop. She was quick-spoken, as always; knew exactly what she wanted, what it should cost, and if it were of good quality. A true Channing in that respect, at least.

After dusk she set out on the return journey. The old Citroën spluttered slowly uphill with water leaking under the hood; it was a car that did not take the hill too easily at the best of times, but now both wind and rain were beating against its progress, and every cross street sent rivers of muddy flood waters swirling against the wheels. It was all she could do to hold the road, and no more easily as she climbed, because the stream through the clough had become a torrent breaking bounds in places. She hoped Martin would be asleep by the time she reached the house, because if not, he might be worrying about her safe arrival. He usually dozed off about dusk and would often wake again past midnight, when it was her habit to cook a small meal which they would eat in the kitchen; after which they would talk until he felt like dozing again, or sometimes, in fine weather, they would pace up and down the garden in the darkness.

The strain of the drive had tired her, and when she finally slewed the car into the garage she saw with relief that there was no chink of light at the drawing-room window. That meant he had already gone to bed and might well be asleep. Suddenly as she closed the garage door she noticed tire marks in the yard that were not from the car, or from Watson's motorcycle; and a moment later, seeing Watson wheeling his machine out of the shed where he kept it, she asked if anyone had called during the day.

"Only Dr. Whiteside."

"*He* called? Why?"

"Oh, for a chat, I suppose. He didn't stay long."

She remembered then that when she had recently met the doctor in Browdley he had said something about calling round to see her father; though she hadn't expected him to do so with such promptness, especially during the rain. "You'd better be careful," she warned Watson. "The road's nearly washed out down the hill."

"Oh, I'll be all right, miss."

He jumped on his machine and was off. She idly wondered where he could think of going on such a night; she was as far as ever from guessing that Stoneclough's inhabitants were beginning to get on his nerves.

She entered the house through the kitchen. As she passed Sarah's room, near by, she heard a voice and listened; but it was only Sarah herself, praying aloud in a curious wheezy whine. The whine was based on jumbled recollections of Methodist local preachers whom Sarah, in the past, had admired; the wheeze was merely asthmatic. Sarah had always prayed aloud before going to bed, and it brought back to Livia memories of a thousand childhood nights when she herself (at Sarah's command) had done the same, kneeling and shivering in a nightdress, and how the nightdress popping over her head just before she began had become a symbol of prayer, so that the words "Night is drawing nigh" in the hymn had meant "Nighties drawing nigh" to her until long after she began to read.

She went upstairs to her own bedroom and was asleep within minutes. She did not pray; somehow the act of prayer seemed more fitting before a whole night's sleep, not just a few hours until midnight. And besides, she was apt to pray harder during the day, while she was doing other things as well.

But that night, had she known, she might have said an extra prayer, for when she awoke it was almost dawn; from utter exhaustion she had slept eight hours. Immediately—and perhaps it had wakened her—she heard the bark of a dog in the distance, the little white dog whom Martin had called Becky, because (they had both noticed) it never seemed to follow them when they walked, but liked to run on ahead and then turn round, as if beckoning.

The bark continued, giving her a sudden premonition of tragedy. She hurried through the dark house and across the garden, following the sound, and Becky came running forward to meet her at the top of the clough.

Martin's body was wedged between rocks where the river poured in spate; she made the discovery quickly because Becky jumped into the torrent near the exact spot. She tried to drag the body out of the water, but lacked the strength. She noticed later that where the path came nearest to the rocks there had been a small landslide.

.   .   .

It was full dawn as she returned to Stoneclough. Sarah was still asleep, Watson had been out all night; the house was cold and gray and silent. Entering it she knew she could not tell anyone yet; she felt herself spinning into unconsciousness as she flung herself on a couch in the drawing room. Just a little while to gain control, and then hold it for a lifetime—just half an hour, maybe, until the sun was up, until Sarah, taking tea to his room, would herself discover the absence. Presently she noticed that Becky was wet and shivering, and the dog's simple need roused her to equally simple action. But a moment later, while she was in the kitchen rubbing him with a towel, some men appeared in the yard outside. They were Browdley Council workmen, in charge of an engineer; they had walked up the clough to see if the flood water was abating; and in so doing they had found Martin's body.

One of the workmen claimed afterwards that when Livia was given the news she said in a low voice "Yes, I know—" but she denied this later in the morning to Dr. Whiteside, and under his tactful handling the matter was not raised at the inquest, though it was freely gossiped about in the town. She was so distracted, anyhow, that (as all the men agreed) she might not have known what she was saying even if she *had* said it. But it was still a little odd, as were a great many other things.

Part Three

CHRISTMAS and the Christmas number of the *Guardian* came a few weeks later, and George Boswell, summarizing the local events of the year in a special article, then wrote as follows:

. . . In November Browdley suffered its worst floods within living memory, while in the same month the death, under suspicious circumstances, of Mr. John Channing, of Stoneclough, recalled the Channing Mill crash of a generation ago—an event notable in the history of our town both on account of the number of its victims and the sensational criminal trial that followed it. . . .

When George handed this to Will Spivey, his subeditor, printer, proofreader, ad salesman, and general all-purposes assistant, the latter scrutinized it, grunted, then carefully blue-penciled the word "suspicious."

"You can't say that, George."

"Why not? Isn't it true?"

"Have ye never heard 'the greater the truth the greater the libel'?"

"Libel? Who's libeling who?"

"The verdict at the inquest was 'accidental death.' "

"Aye, and everybody knows why—because old Whiteside was coroner and made 'em believe what the girl said. . . . As if anyone sober or in his right mind would be taking walks in the clough at night during the worst storm for years—"

"I know, George. And there's some say he wasn't sober and there's others say he wasn't in his right mind and I've even heard it whispered that—"

"Nay—I'm not saying or whispering anything, because I simply don't know and I refuse to believe gossip. I'm just content with the word 'suspicious.' "

"No good, George. The jury found it was accidental—you can't contradict 'em. Change to 'tragic' and you'll be safe."

George reluctantly made the substitution. It was his first year as editor and he did not want trouble. Already he had discovered that the written word had more pitfalls than the spoken, and that the *Guardian* was a rather sickly infant whose survival could only be contrived from week to week by the most delicate nursing.

"There you are then," he muttered, handing back the corrected copy. "And if I'm safe, that's more than Channing's ever was. . . ."

.   .   .

Ever since he could remember, the Channing name had been part of his life. He had known that his father worked at "Channing's" before he had any idea what Channing's was, and when he was old enough to associate the word with the humming three-storied soot-blackened cotton mill at the end of the street, it had taken shape in his mind as something fixed, universal, and eternal. As a child the rows of windows had seemed endless to him as he walked under their sills, and it became an exciting dream to think that as he grew up he would presently be tall enough to see through them. When that time did come he found there was nothing to see—just the faint suggestion of moving wheels behind the wired and murky glass, with the humming louder when he put his ears to it. He had grown up to feel that work at Channing's was in the natural order of events, like play along the canal bank and chapel on Sundays. Indeed, it was the shrill Channing's "buzzer" that marked Time, and the Channing's brick wall that marked Space, in his own small boy's world.

Even after the death of his parents, when he had gone to live with his uncle in another part of the town, Channing's merely acquired an extra attribute, for Uncle Joe called it "safe." George soon learned that it paid his uncle, who did not work there, just as regularly as it had paid his father, who *had* worked; though why this should be, he could not imagine. It was, however, of importance because his uncle had promised to send him to Browdley Grammar School and pay the fees out of "the Channing's money." Then suddenly disaster struck.

Even to an intelligent schoolboy it was all rather incomprehensible, for the mill still stood, not a brick disturbed, not a cadence lost from the call of its early morning and late afternoon siren; and yet, in a way that undoubtedly hurried Uncle Joe to his grave, Channing's proved no longer "safe."

So George, because of this, had left an elementary school when he was thirteen, and had taken various jobs that gave him nothing but a series of pointless and not always pleasant experiences, and then had come the war, with more pointless and not always pleasant experiences—in France and elsewhere. During this time, however, his dissatisfactions had acquired a pattern, and the pattern had acquired a trend; so that on seeing Browdley again, war-injured but recovering, at the age of thirty, he had known what he wanted to do and had begun right away to do it. At a Council by-election he won a victory that surprised even himself, while about the same time he took over the almost bankrupt *Guardian*.

And after seven months the *Guardian* was still almost bankrupt. For one reason, it had no monopoly (the *Browdley Advertiser,* one of a chain of local papers, enjoyed a far bigger circulation), and Browdley folk remained obstinately fixed in their reading habits even when an increasing number of them favored George's political opinions. He would have been badly off indeed but for the small printing establishment (two hand-presses with three employees), which not only put out the regular weekly edition but also received official printing jobs from the Browdley municipality. And here, of course, lay an obvious opening for George's political opponents, some of whom whispered "graft" whenever the Council (George scrupulously absenting himself from the vote) decided to hand him another contract. That they did so at all, however, testified to his rising popularity as well as to the fact that the enmities he made were rarely bitter or lasting. The truth was, as an enemy once remarked, it was damned hard to hate George, and whispers of graft did not stick very well because, graft or no graft, it really was quite obvious that he was not lining his pockets with any considerable success. He lived modestly in the oldish, inconvenient house which, adjoining the printing works, he had acquired when nobody else wanted either; and he often found it as hard to pay his newsprint bills as to collect from some of his customers. He dressed rather shabbily and rode a bicycle except when official business entitled him to the use of a municipal car. The local bank manager and income-tax assessor knew all these and other pertinent details, but as they belonged to the opposition party they were constrained to attack him in reverse: if, they argued, George succeeded so meagerly with his own small business, how could Browdley feel confidence in his capacity to run the town? But humbler citizens were not much influenced by this. Most of them knew George personally and felt that his total lack of prosperity made him all the more human, municipal contracts or not. They *liked* him, in fact, and a great many fought his battle, and if a few of them fought it bitterly, he would sometimes reward them with a speech that made them think he was secretly as bitter as they were. But in that they were wrong, for George was just fiery, effervescent, genuinely indignant over much that he saw around him, but incurably romantic about what he saw in his own mind. He was also naïve in the way he tackled his opponents—first of all overwhelming them with a sort of Galahad impetuosity, then wondering if perhaps he had been a little unfair, and later—as often as not—making some quixotic gesture of retraction or conciliation.

There was that Council meeting, for instance, in the spring of 1918, at which he first spoke Livia's name—and with a ring of challenge as he pitched his voice to the public gallery. "I've always held," he began, "that no accident of birth should ever stand in the way of merit (*cheers*)—in fact it's one of the few things I'm prepared to be thoroughly consistent about. (*Laughter.*) Councillor Whaley has just referred to the great injustice done to our fellow citizens many years ago by one whose name has a certain prominence in the history of this town. I think Councillor Whaley put the matter far too mildly in using the word 'injustice.' I'd prefer myself to call it the most damnable piece of financial knavery ever perpetrated by a self-acknowledged crook at the expense of thousands of honest hard-working folks. (*Loud cheers.*) Oh yes, I know the saying *De mortuis nil nisi bonum*—if I've got the pronunciation wrong perhaps some of the gentlemen on the other side who have had the advantage of a better education than mine will correct me (*laughter*)—at any rate, they'll agree with me that the Latin words mean that you should speak no evil of the dead. . . . But may I ask *this* question of Councillor Whaley—suppose the dead reach out from their graves

to continue the harm they did during their lives—are we *still* to keep
silent about them? (*Loud and prolonged cheers.*) Gentlemen . . .
I wouldn't have referred to such a matter unless the other side had
thought fit to mention it first. But since they did, I'll say this much—
that in my opinion our town is *still* suffering from the effects of the
Channing Mill crash and the iniquitous swindle that caused it! Its
victims are to be found in every street—nay, almost in every house.
Certainly in *one* of our houses—the workhouse. (*Cheers.*) What
shall we say of any man, living or dead, who can be accounted personally responsible for such a thing? To inherit control of an industrial concern and then behave with such callous dishonesty that
working people lose jobs and life savings together, so that hundreds
of homes are sacrificed and broken up, so that health is imperiled and
countless lives are embittered, so that children have their educations
interrupted and old folks are hastened to their graves—if one man
causes all this havoc, then in God's name what shall we call him, or
the system that gave him such power and opportunity?"

Here the cheers and shouts of the gallery were interrupted by a
shabby little man in the back row who yelled out with piercing
distinctness: "Don't matter what you call 'im now, George. The
bugger's dead." Whereupon cheers dissolved into laughter and
George, sensing the moment for a change of mood, dropped his
voice to a much more prosaic level and continued:—

"Aye . . . let's cut the cackle and get down to the business in
hand. There's a war still on, and we must save a bit of our bad
language for the Germans. (*Laughter.*) I was just then tempted—
as we all are sometimes—to speak my mind. (*Laughter.*) I couldn't
help it, and I think those who elected me to this Council didn't really
expect me ever to do anything else. (*Cheers and laughter.*) And
that's why I'm urging you now, as a man still speaking his mind, not
to pay off an old score on an innocent person. To begin with, the
score's too big. And then also, though we're often told that the sins
of the fathers get visited on the children, there isn't one of us who
thinks that's really a fair thing, or ought to be encouraged. . . .
Well, now let me really come to the facts of the matter. We have
tonight a subordinate municipal post to fill for which we invited public applications. As I see it—and not as some folks here seem to see
it—there's only one thing we ought to do, and that's what we always

have done—choose the best person for the job and let no other consideration matter. It's a simple method, and I'm all against changing it." And then, dropping his voice to a monotone as he consulted a sheet of paper: "I have here the list of applicants for the position of junior library assistant, together with their qualifications. On the basis of these facts, and these alone, I move that the application of Miss Olivia Channing be accepted." (*Cheers and some cries of dissent.*)

The foregoing has been worth quoting verbatim, not only because it was one of the events that shaped George's destiny, but as a sample of his speechmaking in those days. He always said he was no orator, and sincerely believed it, but his opponents, though reluctant to use the complimentary term, were not so sure; at any rate they could call him a rabble-rouser. The speech is typical in its astute and somewhat excessive preliminary agreement with the other side (in this case his own side), putting them in a good humor by stating their case better than they could themselves, so that afterwards George's real point came as an intended anticlimax. He had often by this means won victories almost by default. The jibe about his fellow members' superior education was also typical; it was true that many of them had been to better schools, but extremely unlikely that any could remember as much Latin as George had recently learned.

But most typical of all was his quixotic impulse to be fair; it was as if, having called the father a crook, he felt in duty bound to find the daughter a job.

On this occasion victory was anything but by default. His speech failed to silence objectors, and there was further argument, some of it rancorous. But the motion was eventually passed by a narrow margin, with much cross voting; so that in due course Miss Olivia Channing did indeed become junior assistant in the Browdley Public Library at a commencing salary of forty-five shillings a week.

"And a nice problem you've handed me," Dick Jordan remarked, meeting George a few days later in Shawgate. The librarian was one of George's closest friends and political supporters.

"Why, Dick, isn't she any good?"

"She does the work all right, but—well, when you remember her father there's a lot of things you can't feel sure of."

"Aye, and one of them's heredity," declared George, advancing stoutly to a favorite topic. "Thank goodness it's not as important as environment, because environment's something you can change."

"Not when you've already had it. What d'you think *her* environment was like at Stoneclough—up there with a man who'd done a stretch in prison and drank heavily and was so impossible to live with that . . . oh well, you've heard some of the rumors, I daresay."

"I've heard 'em, but I don't see why they should make us condemn the girl. Seems to me it's more a case for sympathy."

"She'll not find much of that in Browdley, George. It's one thing to swing the Council by a speech, but when it comes to changing the minds of ordinary folks who've lost their hard cash—"

"But *she* didn't steal it—"

"No, but she lived at Stoneclough, and for years that's been the symbol in this town of being luckier than you deserve. And it's still the symbol, George, in spite of all the mortgages on the place and no matter what the girl herself had to put up with there. . . ."

.   .   .

George did not meet her till some weeks after she had begun work. He was then studying hard for the final examination that might earn him a university degree, and it was this that occupied his mind when he entered the Reference Department of the library on a sunny April afternoon. But when he left, a couple of hours later, he could only think of the girl who had brought him Volume Four of the *Cambridge Modern History*.

He always remembered her first words to him as she took his slip of paper, scanned it, then him, then stepped back a pace. *"Councillor Boswell?"*

And his own first words as he stared at her for the first time: "Aye, that's me."

"Then I want to thank you for—for—"

"Oh . . . so you're Olivia Channing?"

"Yes, that's why I want to thank you. It was kind of you to put in a word for me."

"I didn't mean it as kindness—just fairness, that's all. But I'm glad it turned out the way it did. How are you managing?"

"You mean the work? Oh, it's easy."

"Like it?"

"Pretty well."

"Only that?"

She smiled—a curious smile, for which George, who saw it often afterwards, long sought an adjective, and in the end could only use Jordan's description of the girl—he had said she looked "haunted."

She said now, with this smile: "People don't like *me,* that's the trouble."

He smiled back, robustly, cheerfully. "Can't expect them to, yet awhile. You'll just have to live things down a bit."

"Live things down?"

"Aye . . . If you know what I mean."

He wondered if, or how much she did, especially as that ended their conversation rather abruptly. She fetched him his book and did not resume it.

. . .

After that first meeting he began to feel emotionally the full force of the argument he had stated in abstract terms at the Council meeting—that the child should not suffer for the sins of the father. In this case the sins of the father had been so considerable that the sufferings of the daughter might well be on the same scale unless someone intervened on her behalf; and George, having intervened once, could not help the growth of a feeling of personal responsibility to match his awakening interest. He knew that John Channing had died practically without means, despite the fact that he had lived at Stoneclough from the time of his release from prison until his death; and though the daughter's need to go out and earn her own living did not stir George to any particular pity (for, after all, that was what most Browdley girls had to do), he was nevertheless concerned that she should be happy in her job, the more so as he had obtained it for her. Not till he met her for the second time did it occur to him to wonder why on earth she had applied for any job at all in a place where there was so much local feeling against her family.

He spoke this thought aloud when (on a bus top where he found himself next to her) she admitted having encountered a good deal of coldness and even a few personal insults at the library.

"Then how about giving it up?" he asked, suddenly seeing things from her angle and becoming indignant about them. "Would you be happier?"

"I need the money," she said simply.

"Aye, but there'd be other jobs in other places—why not try London, for instance?"

"I'd rather stay here."

"You mean you *like* Browdley?"

She shook her head.

"Then why?"

"It's my home—Stoneclough."

"Stoneclough? You mean the actual house? It means so much to you? You still live there?"

"Yes, it's my home."

"I should have thought you'd have been glad to leave a place that had such—er—unhappy associations."

She shook her head again.

After an awkward pause George continued: "Well, don't worry. Most people have short memories."

"I haven't."

"Oh, I didn't mean *that* . . . I meant other people—they'll change their minds about you if you stick it out."

(And yet as he said this he was aware of another phenomenon that became familiar to him later—the ease with which, to her or in her presence, he said things he did not really mean, or that his own judgment did not support. For instance, it simply was not true that Browdley people had short memories—on the contrary, though the Channing crash had taken place a generation before, it was still remembered with bitterness, and the fact that the girl had had unpleasant experiences at the library proved it.)

She said: "Please don't think I'm complaining about the job. It was you who asked me what it was like, otherwise I shouldn't have said anything."

"Well, I'm glad it doesn't bother you much. If it does, let me know."

(But that also was absurd. What could he do, even if she did let him know? Any other job in Browdley would have the same drawbacks, and outside Browdley he had no influence to find her a job at all.)

She said, smiling: "Thanks. It's very kind of you. . . . I'm afraid this is my stop. . . . Good night."

It was at the corner where the lane to Stoneclough left the main road. He suddenly realized that and detained her for a few seconds with an astonished: "But—but—are you going home *now?* How do you get from here?"

"I walk."

"But it's three miles."

"I don't mind. I love walking. . . . Good night."

After she had gone and the bus had restarted he began to think it over. Six miles a day on foot oughtn't to have shocked him (he was a good walker himself and had often, when he was her age, walked to and from jobs to save bus fares), but it was strange to realize that till then he had never wondered how or where the girl did live, travel to her work, and so on. So she was still at Stoneclough? . . . Too bad there were no other houses in that direction, or he might have asked the Transport Committee, of which he was a member, to start a new bus route.

He met her several times again on that same trip and each time he found himself more interested. Up to a point they seemed to get along excellently; she was quick-minded and charmingly friendly, and when she spoke it was with a sort of grave ardor that made even chatter sound significant; yet beyond that a shadow seemed to fall between them. After thinking it over with some deliberation he decided what the shadow was; it must be the fact (doubtless known to her) that he had publicly attacked her father and family. He was prepared for some inevitable mention of this sooner or later, and planned to be completely frank and outspoken. "Now please," he would say, "let's not waste time over that. I said what I meant and I still mean it. But I don't expect *you* to see things my way—after all, he was your father, whatever else he was."

But she never gave him the cue. One day, however, he met Dick Jordan in the street again and heard the story of a rather odd incident that had taken place at the library.

"I was in my office, George, when I heard a bit of a row going on at the counter, so I went out to see what it was, and there was old Horncastle calling the girl names and shouting about her father having ruined him. You know Bob Horncastle?"

Yes, George knew him. He was a gnarled industrial veteran who had lost both job and money in the Channing crash and had lived ever since on the verge of penury, his embitterment becoming a shade nearer lunacy each year. Browdley knew all about him. His was a hard case, but no harder than some others.

"The girl was standing there, George, pale and not saying a word and with that haunted look I told you about, while the old chap poured out a stream of abuse. When he saw me approaching he stopped, and then the girl said very quietly—'I'm sorry, Mr. Horncastle.' She had to get his name from the library card she was holding, and the way she did that—the way she looked down, I mean, and then looked up again and spoke his name . . . well, it was just like a play, especially when she went on—'But why don't you scribble it in the margins of the book, as all the other people do?' Then she just walked off and left him to me to calm down. Of course there wasn't much I could say—he's too old, for one thing, and the way he was carrying on I was afraid he was going to have a heart attack. Finally I got him to go, and then I went back to my office and nearly had a heart attack myself. That kind of thing upsets me."

George was troubled. "I must admit I didn't think folks would take it out of the girl so much. And from what you say, Dick, it wasn't her fault—she gave no provocation."

"The bare fact of her being there was provocation enough to Horncastle. . . . But there's a sequel. After he'd gone I was curious about the girl's remark about people scribbling in the margins of the book. . . . *What* book? There's only one it could have been, and that's the detailed report of Channing's trial, so I thought I'd look to see if it was on the shelves. It was, and sure enough, the margins were messed up with penciled comments—including just about the foulest language I ever heard of—and in different handwritings too. Looked as if a good many Browdley readers had had a go at expressing their opinions. . . . Of course it was our own negligence not to have spotted it earlier—we're supposed to go through all the books at the annual stocktaking and rub out anything of that sort, but apparently this book had been overlooked. So I put it aside and thought I'd do the job myself as soon as I had the time. But then another queer thing happened. Later in the afternoon the girl came to my office and asked where the book was. Seems rather as if she kept an eye on it and had already noticed it was gone—for of course she could check to see it hadn't been lent out. I told her I'd taken it and that I intended to have the objectionable remarks removed, and then she said—and again I thought of somebody in a play—she said: 'Oh please don't on my account.' I gave her a bit of a sharp answer—I said—'It's not on your account at all, young lady, it's simply a library rule.' And that ended the matter. . . . But I must say, she's a queer customer. You'd have thought she'd be glad I was going to do it. Frankly, I can't make her out."

George nodded thoughtfully. "Aye, she's a problem, I can see that. Maybe I made a mistake in getting her the job, but it's done now and can't be undone. If I were you, though, I'd try to find her some kind of work where she doesn't have to meet folks so much. . . . Isn't there something?"

"She might tackle the indexing. Yes, that's not a bad idea, George. I daresay she's smart enough."

"Attractive-looking too, don't you think?"

Jordan gave George a shrewd glance. "Can't say. Maybe I'm no judge, or maybe she's just not my style. She attracts *attention,* if that's what you mean, but whether it's by her looks or a sort of personality, or something else, I can't be sure. I know I wouldn't want her in my office."

"She'd give you more heart attacks, is that it?" said George, laughing.

The librarian joined in the joke, as boisterously as a man may who actually does have a weak heart as well as a nagging wife.

. . .

So it was arranged that the girl should tackle the indexing, and George wondered how it had worked out when next he met her, for she certainly seemed happier and greeted him with a smile whose warmth he felt, for the first time, was somehow intimate and personal. They chatted—on the bus top as usual—without mentioning anything important till she said, apropos of nothing in particular: "Aren't you soon taking a university degree?"

"Aye, if I can pass the exam, and that's a pretty big 'if.' Who told you?"

"I heard someone saying something about it at the library. You see, you ask for so many books." She added: "Such *difficult* books too . . . and yet . . ." And then she hesitated.

"And yet what?"

"Those 'ayes' of yours."

"My *eyes?*"

"I mean the 'ayes' you say instead of 'yes.' "

He flushed, and for a moment fought down a humorless impulse to be offended. Then he laughed. "Aye," he answered, with slow deliberation. "I daresay I could drop them if I disliked them enough. But I don't. And if anybody else does . . . well, let 'em." And then he suddenly gave himself the cue that he had waited for in vain from her. "Maybe you feel about your dad like that. You just don't care what other people *think*—because it's what you yourself *feel* that matters. I don't blame you. I've done my share in attacking your family in this town—you probably know about that—and I'm not going to make any apologies or take back a single word. But I can't see why that should come between you and me, and for my part it doesn't have to."

He paused to give her a chance to say something, but she said nothing, so he went on: "Well, thank goodness that's off my chest. I've been looking for the chance to say it, because if you and I are going to get to know each other well there has to be some sort of understanding about how we both feel about ancient history. Aye, ancient history, that's what it is." He was relieved to have found the phrase until he saw her face, turned to him with a look so uninterpretable that it might have been slight amusement or slight horror, but mixed, in either case, with a preponderance of simple curiosity. She seemed to be waiting to hear what he would say next, and that, of course, put him off so that he stopped talking altogether. Just then the bus reached the corner of the Stoneclough lane, surprising them both, and as she sprang down the steps with a quick smile and a good-night he had an overmastering urge to follow her, if only not to leave the conversation poised for days, perhaps, at such an impossible angle. So he ran after her and overtook her a little way along the lane. "I don't need to study tonight," he said breathlessly (she knew that he spent most of his evenings with the difficult library books). "I can walk part of the way with you—that is, if you don't mind. . . ."

"Why, of course not. I don't mind at all. But on one condition."

"Yes?"

"Let's not mention my father again . . . *please.*"

"All right."

"*Ever* again? You promise?"

"Why, certainly—if that's what you wish, but I assure you I *do* understand how you feel—"

"No, no, you don't—you *can't* . . . but you've promised, remember that. From now on. From this minute on." And over the strained emphasis of her words there came, like a veil slowly drawn, that curious "haunted" smile.

So he walked with her, puzzled and somewhat discomfited at first, as he changed the subject to Browdley and its affairs. He did so because, after his promise, that seemed the easiest way to keep it; and sure enough, he was soon at ease amidst the torrent of his own plans and ambitions, both personal and for the town. She made few comments and when they said good-bye at the gates of Stoneclough he could not forbear the somewhat chastened afterthought: "I hope that didn't bore you. Or weren't you listening?"

She answered, smiling again, but this time differently: "Well, not *all* the time. But I don't have to, do I? Can't I like you without liking the new gas works?"

"Aye," he said, smiling back as he gave her arm a farewell squeeze. "But I can like you and *still* like the new gas works. Why not?"

.   .   .   .   .

But *could* he? That was to some extent, both then and afterwards, the question.

He soon realized that he loved her—probably on the way home after that first walk to Stoneclough. And immediately, of course, she became the object of a crusade, for in those days that was the pattern of all George's emotions—his passion for education, his eagerness to tear down the slums of Browdley (already he had a scheme), his secret ambition to become the town's Member of Parliament—all were for the ultimate benefit of others as well as to satisfy personal desire. And soon, eclipsing everything else in intensity, came his desire to marry Livia—that is to say, to *rescue* her. To rescue her from Stoneclough, from the thraldom of ancient history; and now, additionally, to rescue her from a situation he had himself got her into, where she was at the mercy of casual insults from strangers as well as of her own morbid preoccupation with a book about her father's trial. All this, as George had to admit, totaled up to a rather substantial piece of rescue work, but he had the urge to do it, and his Galahad mood rose as always to put desire into action. It did not take more than a few weeks to bring that desire to fever point, especially when the chance of prompt action was denied. For she refused his first proposal of marriage. She seemed genuinely bewildered, as if it were the last thing she had ever expected. She *liked* him, she admitted—oh yes, she liked him a great deal; but as for marrying—well, she thought she was far too young, and anyhow, she didn't think she would ever want to marry anybody. And she was quite happy where and how she was—at Stoneclough. In fact, to bring the matter to its apparently crucial issue, she couldn't and wouldn't leave Stoneclough.

George took his "no" for an answer exactly as he had begun to do on the Council whenever he brought up his housing scheme—that is to say, he seemed to accept it good-humoredly and as final while all the time he was planning how he could best bring the matter up again. Besides which, in this case, he was in love. He had supposed he had been in love before, on several occasions, but the difference in what he felt for Livia convinced him that *this* was love; because why else should he begin to neglect his Council work—not much, not even in a way that could be noticed by anyone else, but enough to give him qualms of conscience only to be stifled by reflecting that as soon as he had won her he would make up for lost time. He gave himself the same consolation over similar neglect of his examination studies. After all, even in battles, the first must come first. He had confidence that he would win her eventually, not only because he had confidence about most things in those days, but because—as he saw it—there was no considerable rival in the field—only Stoneclough, and he felt himself more than a match for bricks and mortar, however darkly consecrated. How could she long hesitate between the past and the future, especially as there were moments when he felt so sure of her—physical moments when she seemed to withdraw into a world of her own sensations that offered neither criticism nor restraint, in contrast from her usual behavior, which was to make of most contacts a struggle for mastery? He was a clumsy lover, and ruefully aware of it; as he said once, when she emerged from her private world to laugh at him: "Aye, I'm a bit better on committees. . . ."

The fact that she would never say, in words, that she loved him mattered less after she had said, both doubtfully and hopefully, in reply to his fifth or sixth proposal: "I *might* marry you, George, someday. If I ever marry anyone at all. . . ."

He never passed beyond the gates of Stoneclough; she never invited him, and he never suggested it. She told him little about herself, and the promise he had given not to mention her father set limits to his personal questions about other matters, though not to his curiosity. He wondered, for instance, why old Richard Felsby, her father's former partner, had not helped her financially, for Richard had dissolved partnership and sold out his interest in the firm before the crash, so that he was still rich and could well have afforded some gesture of generosity. But when once George spoke Richard Felsby's name he knew he had in some way trespassed on forbidden territory. "I don't see him," was all she said, "and I don't want to. I *never* want to see him."

She said little, either, about her life at Stoneclough, except to reiterate, whenever he brought up the matter, that she would rather live there than anywhere else, despite the inconvenience of the three-mile walk. He gathered that there was some old woman, a kind of housekeeper, living there also, and that the two of them shared cooking and other domestic jobs; but she gave him few details and he did not care to probe. Most of his time with her was spent along the Stoneclough road, walking evening after evening during that long fine summer; but as the days shortened and the bad weather came, they sometimes met in the library at midday, when she had an hour off and they could talk in one of the book-lined alcoves of the Reference Department. They spoke then in whispers, because of the "Silence" notice on the wall; and there was piquancy in that, because as Chairman of the Municipal Library Subcommittee he had a sort of responsibility for seeing that library rules were enforced.

One lunch hour she greeted him in such a distraught way that he knew immediately something was wrong. Soon she told him, and even in face of her distress his heart leapt with every word of the revelation. By the time she had finished he knew that fate had played into his hands, so he proposed again, with all his quiet triumph hidden behind a veil of sympathy. For George could not avoid a technique of persuasion that made his last thrust in battle—the winning one—always the kindest. And by sheer coincidence, in that odd way in which at important moments of life the eye is apt to be caught by incongruous things, he noticed while he was talking that just above her hair, and glinting in the same shaft of sunshine, lay an imposing edition of Creasy's *Fifteen Decisive Battles of the World*. He couldn't help smiling and thinking it a good omen.

The news that had so distressed her was that the bank had foreclosed the mortgage on Stoneclough, so that she would have had to leave the house in any event. George tried to feel that this did not detract from his triumph, but merely contributed to it. He assured her that she would find it more fun living in a small house than in a great barracks of a place like Stoneclough. "I'd like to know what the bank thinks it can do with it. . . ."

She made no comment, but asked after a pause: "Do you like dogs?"

"Aye, I like 'em all right. Used to have one when I lived with my Uncle Joe—a big black retriever."

"My dog's small—and white. His name's Becky."

He suddenly realized what she was driving at. "You mean you want to bring your dog to live with us? Why, of course. . . . And I like any dog, for that matter."

They were married a few weeks later at Browdley Registry Office, with only a few friends of George's in attendance. She was nineteen, and the fact that he was getting on for twice that age was only one of the reasons why the affair caused a local sensation.

Councillor Whaley, a seventy-year-old confirmed bachelor and one of those political opponents whom George had converted into a staunch personal friend, took him aside after the ceremony to say: "Well, George, she's smart enough, and ye've got her, so God bless ye both. . . . I doubt if it'll help ye, though, when ye come up for re-election."

"And d'you think that worries me?" George retorted, with jovial indignation. "Would you have me marry for votes?"

Tom Whaley chuckled. "I'll ask ye ten years hence if ye'd vote for marriage—that's the real question." George then laughed back as he clapped the old man on the shoulder and reflected privately that Tom Whaley mightn't be alive ten years hence, and how lucky he himself was, by contrast, to have so much time ahead, and to have it all with Livia. For he was still young enough to think of what he wanted to do as a lifework, the more so as the world looked as if it would give him a chance to do it.

George, ever ready to be optimistic, was particularly so on that day of his marriage.

So were millions of others all over the earth—for it was the month of November, 1918.

.   .   .

The honeymoon, at Bournemouth, was a happy one, and by the time it was over George knew a great many things—a few of them disconcerting—about Livia, but one thing about himself that seemed to matter and was simple enough, after all—he loved her. He loved her more, even, than he had thought he would, or could, love any woman. When he woke in the mornings and saw her still sleeping at his side he had a feeling of tenderness that partly disappeared as soon as she wakened, but somehow left a fragrance that lasted through the day, making him tolerant where he might have been unyielding, amused where he might have been antagonized. For she was, he soon discovered, a person with a very definite will of her own. He thought she was in some ways more like an animal than any human being he had ever met; but she was like a *real* animal, he qualified, not just a human animal. There was intense physicality about her, but it was unaware of itself and never gross; on the other hand, she had a quality of fastidiousness that human beings rarely have, but animals often. He could only modestly wonder how he had ever been so confident of winning her, because now that he had done so she seemed to him so much more desirable that it was almost as if he had to keep on winning, or else, in some incomprehensible way, to risk losing. And when he returned to Browdley that was still the case. He had hoped, after marriage, to concentrate more than ever on his Council work and on study for the university examination—to make up for such splendidly lost time with a vengeance; yet to his slight dismay there came no relief at all from a nagging preoccupation that he could not grapple with, much less analyze. He found it actually harder to concentrate on the *Cambridge Modern History,* harder to generate that mixture of indignation and practical energy that had just barcly begun to move the mountains of opposition to everything he wanted to do as town Councillor. It was as if the fire with which she consumed him were now seeking to consume other fires.

For instance, her sudden change of attitude in regard to Browdley, and her naïve question, within a few weeks of their return: "George, I've been thinking—couldn't you do your sort of work somewhere else?"

"Somewhere else? You mean move into a better part of the town?"

"No, I mean move altogether. Out of Browdley."

He was too astonished to say much at first. "Well, I don't know . . ." And then he smiled. "That's just what I suggested to you once, and you said you'd rather stay here."

"I said I'd rather stay at Stoneclough. But I haven't got Stoneclough now."

"Well, I've still got the *Guardian* and my Council position. Wouldn't be so easy for me to give all that up."

"You think it would be hard to find a newspaper or a council job in some other town?"

"Aye, that's true too. But what I said is just what I meant. It wouldn't be easy for me to give up Browdley."

She was not the sort of woman to say "Not even to please *me?*"— and although he did not think it was in her mind, he knew it was rather uncomfortably in his own.

"It's probably silly of me, George, even to ask you."

"No, I wouldn't call it silly—it's just not practical. Of course I can understand how you feel about the place, but surely it's easier to put up with now than it used to be when you worked at the library?"

"Oh, it isn't a question of that. I can put up with anything. I did, didn't I? It's just that—somehow—I don't think Browdley will bring us any luck."

"Oh, come now—superstitions—"

"I know—I can't argue it out. It's just a feeling I have."

He laughed with relief, for the unreasonable in those days did not seem to him much of an adversary. "All right, maybe you won't have to have it long, because I've a bit of news to tell you. . . ."

He told her then what he had known for several days—that the Parliamentary Member for Browdley was expected to retire on account of age within a few months. When this happened there would be a by-election and George would be a possible candidate; if he won, he would be obliged to live in London during Parliamentary sessions, so Livia would enjoy frequent escapes from Browdley that way.

She was much happier at the thought of this, and soon also for another reason—she was going to have a baby.

.   .   .

The Member for Browdley duly applied for the Chiltern Hundreds; the writ for the by-election was issued; George was selected as his party's candidate, and the campaign opened in the summer of the following year. George's opponent was a rich local manufacturer who had made a fortune during the war and declined to entertain the notion that this was in any way less than his deserts. His party's majority at the coupon election just after the Armistice had been large, but already there were signs of a change in the national mood, especially in the industrial areas, and it was generally agreed that George had a chance if he would put up a fight for it. And there certainly seemed no one likelier or better able to do so.

When George looked back on his life from later years, it was this period—those few weeks and months—that shone conspicuously, because upon Livia, always unpredictable, pregnancy seemed to confer such deep contentment. George then realized the power she had over him, for immediately he felt freed for effort just when effort was most needed. Never did he work harder than during that election campaign; every morning, after a few necessary jobs in the newspaper office, he would leave for a whole day of canvassing, meetings at street corners and factory gates, culminating in some "monster rally" in the evening that would send him home tired but still exhilarated, long after midnight. Usually Livia would then have a meal awaiting him, which he would gulp down avidly while he told her of the manifold triumphs of the day. In her own way she seemed to share his enthusiasm, if only on account of what could happen after his victory, for it was already planned that they would rent a house in some inner London suburb—Chelsea, perhaps—

where she could live with her baby while George made a name for himself in Parliament. Who could set limits to such a future? Well, the electorate of Browdley could; and that, of course, sent him out in the morning to work harder than ever, with Livia still in bed and himself strangely refreshed after no more than a few hours of snatched sleep. He had never been so happy, had never felt so physically enriched, or so alert mentally. Things that had seemed a little wrong between him and Livia just after their marriage had worked themselves right—or something had happened, anyway; perhaps it was just that they had needed time to get properly used to each other.

One thing, naturally, had to be postponed for a while—his studies for the university degree. But of course he could pursue them just as easily—nay, more so—in London later on. And it would be an added pride to put B.A. after his name when he could already put M.P.

Gradually during those busy weeks Browdley's long rows of drab four-roomed houses took on splashes of color from election cards in most of the windows—George's colors were yellow, his opponent's blue. The latter's slogan was "Put Wetherall In and Keep Higher Taxes Out." George, however, struck a less mercenary note. "A Vote for Boswell Is a Vote for Your Children's Future," proclaimed his cards, banners, and posters.

(George would remember that one day.)

But he really meant it. He told the voters of Browdley exactly what he intended to do if they should choose him to represent them; he mixed the dream and the business in a way that was something rather new to the town, and could be both praised and attacked as such. He had plans, not merely promises, for slum clearance, education, medical insurance, and relief of unemployment; and (to redress the balance, as it were) he had visions, not merely opinions, about international trade, India, the League of Nations, currency, and world peace. He was eager, cheerful, spontaneous, sincere, and a little naïve. He battled his opponent trenchantly, yet with rough-spun humor that took away most of the sting; it was another of George's special techniques, and he had already become rather expert at it. "I don't like to hear Mr. Wetherall attacked because he made a lot of money during the war," he would say. "Let's be fair to the man—he couldn't help it. (*Laughter.*) It wasn't his brains that did it. (*Laughter.*) He didn't even have to try to do it. (*More laughter.*) The money just came rolling in, because we hadn't got the laws or the taxes to stop it. So don't blame poor Mr. Wetherall. Blame the laws and the tax system of this country that enabled one man to become half a millionaire while others had to fight in the trenches for a shilling a day. And let's get things changed so that it can't happen again. (*Cheers.*) But of course you mustn't expect Mr. Wetherall to vote for any such change. After all, why should he? (*Laughter.*) . . ." And so on. Political prophets tipped George as the winner, but whether or not, Browdley had certainly never enjoyed a more bracing political contest.

Election day dawned unseasonably windy and wet, which was his first item of bad luck, for the other side had more cars to take voters to and from the polling stations. He left his house for the central committee rooms at an early hour and was kept busy all day with routine matters; meanwhile, as the rain increased, his spirit sank a little. His agent, Jim Saunders, was already giving him revised last-minute opinions that it would be "a damned near thing."

Polling closed at eight o'clock, and an hour later the count began in the Town Hall. George paced up and down amongst the green-baize-covered trestle tables, keeping his eyes on the mounting piles of ballot papers; his opponent was absent, preferring to spend the anxious hours more convivially in a hotel room across the street. The atmosphere in the Town Hall became tenser as it also grew thicker with tobacco smoke and the smell of wet mackintoshes.

Towards midnight most of the ballot boxes had been brought in from outlying districts and half the count was over, with George leading by a narrow margin. Watching the proceedings, he found it hard to realize that his fate lay in those slips of paper—his own fate and Livia's. And then, whimsically, he thought of his election slogan—"A Vote for Boswell Is a Vote for Your Children's Future." It was a vote for *his* children's future, anyhow, he reflected.

By midnight he knew what his fate was, for the last few ballot boxes, drawn from the suburban fringe where mostly professional and retired people lived, had contained a heavy preponderance of votes for Wetherall. The final figures were not even close enough to justify a recount; George had lost the election by a hundred and forty-eight.

As in a trance he received the impact of the news and went through the ritual prescribed for defeated candidates on such occasions. He stepped out on the balcony to make a short speech to his supporters, congratulated and shook hands with the victor, seconded a vote of thanks to the returning officer; it was all over by one o'clock in the morning, and the rain had not stopped.

As he was leaving the Town Hall Jim Saunders handed him a throw-away leaflet printed in the opposition colors that had been given eleventh-hour circulation throughout the town.

George scanned it over and shrugged more indifferently than he felt. "Poor stuff, Jim. And not even true. I'll bet it's not libelous, though."

"I wasn't thinking of that. But there's a good many voters it may have influenced."

It was an artfully worded suggestion that George had secured a municipal appointment for his wife—concealing the all-important fact that he had not even met her till after she took the job.

"It's the sort of thing that swings votes," Saunders went on. "Shouldn't wonder if you'd have been in but for this."

"I doubt it, Jim. . . ." And all the way home George kept telling himself that he doubted it.

Not till he turned the corner of Market Street and saw the familiar printing office (now plastered, and how ironically, with adjurations to "Vote for Boswell") did he contemplate the really worst penalty of failure, and that was having to tell Livia. He wondered if she would already have heard.

When he entered the house he waited to hear her voice, but only Becky came up to him rather forlornly; and then he saw a note on the table. It told him she had had to call the doctor early that evening and had been sent to the hospital.

.   .   .

An hour later he sat at her bedside, realizing that for a new and far happier reason this was one of the memorable days of his life. His child was born—prematurely, but thrivingly—a boy. And as he looked first at his son, and then at Livia, a great tenderness enveloped him, so that he took her hand and could not find words for anything in his heart or mind.

"I didn't want you to come earlier," she said weakly. "I wouldn't let them tell you because I knew you'd be busy. . . . Is it over yet?"

"Why . . . don't you know?" He realized afterwards that he had doubtless been left the job of breaking the bad news gently, but it seemed so trivial then that he answered outright and almost casually. "Aye, it's all over. I lost. By a hundred and forty-eight. . . ."

"You *lost?*" He was still so happy that the look of disappointment on her face startled him, especially when she added: "No luck, George. I said so, didn't I?"

"*Luck?* Why, isn't *this* luck?" And he pointed to the child.

.   .   .

Of course his own personal disappointment returned, though he knew he would not have felt it so keenly but for hers. She had, and always had, that curious capacity to weight or lift his mood with her own, to give him peace or no-peace at will. In his own mind the loss of the election need not have been tragic; after all, he was still young, and there would be other chances—possibly within a short time. But she made it seem tragic by the way she regarded it, and he, as if in defense of Browdley against this attitude, plunged anew into work for the town.

Foremost was his plan to stir some civic spirit among the richer citizens. There were no millionaires, but a few who were well off, and one was Richard Felsby, partner of Livia's father and grand-father in the days when the firm had been Channing and Felsby. George had never been able to understand what exactly the trouble was between Livia and the old man, perhaps a family feud of some kind, certainly no concern of his own; and since Richard was over eighty, ailing, a bachelor, and the owner of some land on Browd-ley's outskirts that would make a fine municipal park if given to the town, George called on him one evening—quite prepared to be kicked out unceremoniously, but unwilling to neglect even a hun-dred-to-one chance.

Richard Felsby, dressing-gowned, nightcapped, and from a bed-room armchair, astonished him by saying, during their first minute of conversation: "Let's not waste time, Boswell. . . . When ye

married Livia, ye married a problem, and it's not a bit of use com-
in' to me about it."

"But—" George protested, and then let the old man have his say,
since the saying might be of interest.

"And neither of ye need think ye're going to get a penny o' *my*
money, because I'm leavin' it all to Sarah."

George did not even know who Sarah was, and perhaps his look
showed it, for Richard went on: "Sarah looked after Livia and her
mother and father and grandmother and grandfather for the best
part of sixty years . . . and where'd ye think she'd be now but
for me? . . . Why, in the workhouse. That's all Livia cared. I know
the woman's stone-deaf and cranky and no beauty either, but she
deserved better than to be left stranded when Livia ran off to marry
you."

"I never knew that," George gasped.

"Aye, and I don't suppose ye know a good many other things.
But it's the truth, and ye can tell her so. Sarah gets my money, and
if ye've come to talk me into anything else it's not a bit of use."

George then felt that his simplest disclaimer was to tell the old
man frankly what he *had* come for, and now it was the latter's turn
to be astonished. It had clearly never occurred to him that he owed
anything to the town, and George's suggestion that he did so aroused
a host of vaguely associated antagonisms—to mollycoddling and
spoon-feeding and high taxes and socialist agitators and what not.
But the odd thing was that as the interview proceeded, Richard
Felsby found himself rather liking George personally. (He was not
the first to fall under that spell, or the last either.) And when
George rose to go, he grunted: "It's all a pack of nonsense, Boswell. This boom that's on now isn't going to last, and when it's over
Browdley'll need jobs, not parks."

"So you won't let go any of that land, Mr. Felsby?"

"Not a yard, except at a fair price. . . . But ye can stay and
have a drink, if ye like."

"Thanks, but I don't drink."

"Just as well, because the drink ye'd have got here is tea. . . .
I've often caught chaps that way. To my mind it's a misuse of the
word that it should only apply to alcohol. . . . So ye're a teetotaler,
eh?"

George nodded.

"Teetotal family?"

"Not all of 'em. My Uncle Joe drank plenty."

"The black sheep?"

"Maybe, but I liked him better than some of the white ones."

"Ye did? . . . Sit down, lad, and what about a cup?"

George accepted, and then had a chance to verify that Sarah was indeed as had been described. Meanwhile Richard Felsby, who had enjoyed no such congenial human contact since the death of his best friend, Dr. Whiteside, made the most of the occasion and became almost garrulous. He admitted that he wasn't a big "giver" (George had known this already), but when he did give, he said he liked to suit his own ideas—as when, for instance, he had offered an annual prize to the Browdley Grammar School for the boy who achieved "the best all-round lack of distinction." "It was the prize I'd have won myself when I was there," he chuckled asthmatically, "but they wouldn't even let me offer it." It appeared, too, that sometimes he amused himself by sending checks for small sums to people momentarily headlined in the news—the farmer who refused to let a fashionable Hunt cross his fields, the postman's wife with her second set of triplets, and so on. "I reckon ye think I'm a queer sort of chap," he added, after these confessions.

"Aye," answered George, unconsciously giving his voice a riper Browdley burr to match the other's. "Ye're queer enough. And I suppose ye think *I'm* queer for wanting Browdley to have a park?"

"Oh, to blazes with the park—are we on that again? . . . I hear ye've got a baby."

George nodded. "A boy."

"Let's hope it takes after you, then. Because I'll tell ye this, Boswell, the Channings are queerer than you and me combined. . . . Must ye go?"

"Getting late," said George, with a smile.

"Drop in again some time."

"Aye . . . but I won't promise not to mention that park."

.   .   .

George did not tell Livia about his visit, because he felt it would not please her, however well he could justify it. And a few weeks

later he visited Richard again, partly in case there was any change
of mind about the park, but chiefly because he was passing the house
and was touched by a sudden vision of the old man's loneliness in
that upstairs room with no one to talk to but a deaf servant. A moment later, having acted on impulse, he was touched again by the
evident warmth of Richard's welcome.

"Sit down, lad, and make yeself at home. . . . See this?" And
he waved, of all things, a check he had been busy writing. "I'm giv-
in' it away for charity. . . . Doesn't it make your mouth water?"

George laughed, while Richard went on to explain that he was
sending it to a man he did not know, but whose name and address
had appeared in that morning's paper—some fellow who had grown
a hollyhock taller than his house. "Mebbe ye'll drop it in the post
for me when ye go, Boswell. He'll get a nice surprise when he opens
my letter tomorrow. . . . Well, what are ye starin' at me for?
D'ye think I'm daft? Or don't ye like hollyhocks taller than houses?"

"I like 'em all right," answered George, "and houses too. I'll
count it as one of your *better* benefactions. Why didn't ye make it a
bit more, though? What's a pound from you?"

Whereat Richard enjoyed the best laugh he had had in years,
for despite his reputation for being tight with money, no one had
dared to hint it to his face until George, in sheer naïveté, stumbled
into doing so. But it made such an instant hit that George was never
quite sure afterwards whether he kept it up out of candor or to give
the old man more fun.

For he formed quite a habit of dropping in to see Felsby, whose
house was not far from the Town Hall. The visits did not have to
be long ones, and George enjoyed their brevity as much as the out-
spokenness of what was said on both sides.

"The trouble with you, George, is that ye think too much of yourself. I always thought ye did, ever since ye got on the Council. I've
sacked hundreds of better men than you for a tenth of the things
ye've said to me tonight."

"Aye," retorted George. "And ye'd sack me too, if I was an em-
ployee of yours. But I'm not. My father was, though, for the best
part of a lifetime. Or the worse part, whichever way ye look at it."

That sort of thing. . . .

(George reflected afterwards that the old man must like it, or he would get offended; but then it occurred to him that he would have got offended already if he had thought that George really meant what he said, but he doubtless supposed he didn't. Yet George *did*, in a way, and knowing this found himself up against a familiar dilemma: that to say what you mean without ever offending people is usually to say what you mean without making them believe you mean what you say—and what was the use of that? Well, maybe *some* use, sometimes. For, as a victim expressed *his* side of it once: "George tells you what a bastard you are, and you laugh, and then after he's gone you suddenly say to yourself—'Of course, George was only joking—it's a good job he doesn't really know I *am* a bit of a bastard!' ")

Richard was frank enough also. He once said: "George, I'm sorry for ye, married to a Channing. Her father was no good, and her mother wasn't much better, and the life she lived up at Stoneclough that last year before he died—well, it was no Sunday School picnic, believe me."

It was impossible to resent this, in its context, yet George felt impelled to answer defensively: "Oh, Livia's all right"—before curiosity made him add: "She had a bad time, you mean?"

Richard Felsby said impressively, "There's only one man who could have told you—and that's Dr. Whiteside, and he's dead. He never told me, for that matter—but I knew how he felt, because I remember what he said when he got news of her father's death —'Thank God,' he said, 'for everybody's sake.' . . . Well, well— maybe that's more than I should have passed on. But I'll tell ye this, George—the Channing blood's had a streak of moonshine in it lately. That's what made me leave the firm. I found I was getting too sensible for it."

"You're not as sensible as you think," retorted George, allowing the conversation to become bantering again. He guessed it would be good policy not to press his inquiries at this stage, especially as the old man would doubtless return to the subject at a later meeting and tell all he knew. George had had enough experience of wheedling information to know that an air of not too much concern is the best wheedler. And besides, he must keep in mind the other object of his wheedling. So he added, still banteringly: "If ye *were* sensible ye'd give me that land for a park. Think of the taxes ye'd save."

At which the old man shook and spluttered with merriment to a degree that quite possibly imposed a strain on his heart.

.   .   .

Suddenly it all came to an end.

Livia found out about the more or less regular visits and flew into the kind of tantrum that George had certainly not anticipated; if he had, he would doubtless not have called on Felsby in the first place. He had been prepared for her coolness over the association, but he was amazed to discover how profoundly the whole thing must matter to her. "Oh George," she cried as if she had discovered him in some mortal sin, "how *could* you do it? I *hate* him—I don't want to have anything to do with him. You knew that. And to think that secretly—all the time—so that I only got to hear of it by accident—"

Perhaps because he did feel a little guilty in that one respect, he was more than usually ready to defend himself. "Nay, let's keep a sense of proportion, Livia. No harm's been done to anyone just because I've had a few chats with an old man—even if you do count him an enemy for some reason I've never been told about. Besides, I went to him chiefly on business—I wanted him to give the town a park."

"Oh George, what does a park matter?"

"Just what *he* said."

"The main thing is, you must never, *never* go there again."

George stared at her, for the first time in his life, with a look of disenchantment.

"I couldn't promise that, Livia."

"*What?*" And she was facing him, the issue suddenly alive between them.

"I'm sorry, Livia. I don't like to upset you, but I've got to think of the town's interests. If you know what I mean."

"Oh yes, I know. I didn't know—but that's unimportant. It makes no difference."

(She knew what? What was it she hadn't known? What was

unimportant? What made no difference? He was by now accustomed to the mental gymnastics that her talk often demanded; she spoke in a sort of verbal shorthand, so that one had to grab at the meaning as it flashed by, and even then not be sure of getting it. Basically, he felt it to be a species of natural arrogance; she used the dotted line of her own immediate thoughts and expected others to follow her without that advantage.)

He said again: "I'm sorry." But in his look there was still the absence of any surrender.

She returned that look for an instant, then quietly went out of the room.

Yet left alone, he had no sense of victory—only a feeling of emptiness that made him wonder if the issue had been worth facing at all.

Would he, despite the stand he had taken, visit Richard Felsby again?

The next morning, after a troubled night of thinking the matter over, he was still unsure, and to the end of his life he did not know what he would have done eventually; for on the evening of that next day Richard Felsby died peacefully in his sleep.

A few weeks later George happened to meet Ferguson, the lawyer who was settling the estate. "Too bad, George," he commented. "You nearly pulled it off."

"Pulled what off?"

"You nearly got that park." Then Ferguson explained in confidence that a few days before he died Felsby had talked about leaving some land as a gift to the town, but on one condition—"and this'll make you sit up, George—on condition that it's called The Channing Memorial Park! You'd have had a fine job persuading Browdley to *that*—some of them have enough to remember the name Channing by, without a park. . . . Perhaps it's just as well he didn't have time to give me definite instructions."

"Aye," said George, "it'd have put me in a tight corner." But then he began to laugh. "And that's just where he wanted me, the old devil. . . ."

Ferguson went on: "As matters stand, his housekeeper gets the lot, and *she's* made a will leaving everything to a training college for Methodist ministers. . . . So there goes the last of the Channing

and Felsby fortunes, George—and you can add that to your lecture
on 'Browdley Past and Present'!"

.   .   .

The child was called Martin (Livia's choice) and took after
George, in appearance at least, enough to have given the old man
a measure of sardonic satisfaction. During the first year of his life
Martin grinned far oftener than he cried, almost as if he knew he
had been born on the day his father only narrowly missed becoming
a Member of Parliament; and when George grinned back, it was as
if to say: Don't worry, I'll manage it next time. But political affairs
are incalculable, and as events developed, it began to seem highly
unlikely that any next time would come soon.

This revived Livia's plea that George should pack up and leave
Browdley. He tried to avoid serious argument on the issue, yet it
was clear his attitude had not changed, and there grew a hard core
of deadlock between them, always liable to jar nerves and send off
sparks if any subordinate differences occurred. They did occur, as
in all married lives; nevertheless, by and large, Councillor and Mrs.
Boswell could have been called a fairly happy couple—except on
those few occasions when they could have been called Councillor
and Mrs. Boswell. For Livia's dislike of the town made her scorn
the slightest official recognition of her existence. After a few experiments, she declined to attend civic functions so persistently that
George ceased to ask her, and in the end she was not even invited.
This must have helped rather than hindered him, for Livia was still
unpopular in Browdley, especially when the world-wide postwar de-
pression brought sudden distress to the town. It was easy to choose a
local name as a scapegoat—easier than to figure what the whole
thing was about. And who *could* figure what the whole thing was
about, anyway?

George evidently thought he could, for on a certain day in July,
1920, he wrote the following in one of his *Guardian* editorials:

The signing by Germany of the protocol containing the disarmament
terms of the Allies marks another landmark on the long road towards
world recovery. There are some who profess to be concerned about the
future of thousands of workers in the arms industry if production is cut
down to a minimum; but to that naïve misgiving every economist and

social worker has a ready answer. For the real wealth of the world consists, not merely in things created by hand or brain, but in things so created THAT ARE WORTH CREATING. For this reason we may regard yesterday's event as a step not only towards PEACE, but *because* of that, towards PROSPERITY.

George himself needed a step towards prosperity as much as anyone, for his paper was losing both circulation and advertising revenue, and he found himself suddenly on the edge of a precipice which a financially shrewder man would have foreseen. Everything then happened at once, as it usually does: people to whom he owed money (the bank, the newsprint company, the income-tax authorities) demanded payment; those who owed George money, and there were hundreds of them, made excuses for further delay. In this crisis Livia stepped into the breach and proved herself, to George's utter astonishment, a thoroughly capable business woman. The first thing she did was to produce some sort of order in the printing office, where Will Spivey's slackness had held sway for years. By making Will's life a misery she pared expenses to a minimum and increased the margin of profit on whatever small printing orders came in. Then she began a campaign to secure at least part payment of what was owing, while at the same time she made contact with creditors and persuaded most of them to have patience. Altogether it was an excellent job of reorganization, carried out so expeditiously that George made the mistake of supposing that she enjoyed doing it.

"The fact is, I'm not cut out for business," he admitted, after ,congratulating her on having saved the *Guardian* from bankruptcy.

"And do you think *I* am? Do you think I *like* asking Browdley people for favors? Do you really think I'm doing this for your sake or my sake or for your old *Guardian?*"

There was another thing that she did. It so happened that Councillor Whaley carried influence at the bank where the *Guardian* had an overdraft, and with this in mind Livia readily agreed to something she had long balked at, and that was simply to have Councillor Whaley to tea. She had always said she knew Whaley disliked her and she had no desire to meet him, and George had always urged that Whaley was his friend and that she ought at least to give him the chance to change his mind about her. Her sudden surrender on the matter brought joy to George that was unmarred by the slightest suspicion of an ulterior motive, and when the day came and Tom Whaley arrived (for a "high tea," according to Browdley fashion), George was sheerly delighted by the result. It was almost ludicrous to see a cynical old chap like Tom falling so obviously under her spell, yet no wonder, for George thought he had never seen her in such a fascinating humor—warm, gay, sympathetic. Tom—it was his weakness as well as George's—liked to talk, and Livia not only listened, but gave him continual openings, making his chatter seem at times even brilliant (which it never was); and as George looked on, quietly satisfied that all was going so well, he could not help adoring her with such intensity that he wondered what exactly caused the feeling in him. Would it have been the same had there been some fractional mathematical difference in the angle of her nose and forehead? His experience of women before Livia had been limited, but enough to know or think he knew what sex attraction was; yet now, honestly though he tried, he could neither confirm nor deny that what he felt for Livia had anything to do with sex. It puzzled him enormously and quite happily as he sat there, staring at her face across the crumpets and cold ham.

When, having stayed much longer than they had expected, Whaley put on his overcoat to go, he seized a chance to whisper to George at the street door: "George—she's a winner—whether she wins elections for ye or not!" He was in a mellow, sentimental, patriarchal mood—so utterly had Livia bewitched him.

A moment later George, still beaming from the effect of his friend's remark, found Livia on her knees on the hearthrug, warming her hands at the fire. Her face was turned away from him as he approached; he began cheerfully: "Ah, that's been a grand time! You should have heard what Tom thinks about you—he just told me—"

All at once he stopped, because she had turned round, and the look on her face was as startling as her first words. "Oh George, what a *bore!* Such a *silly* old man! How can you possibly endure him? That awful, high-pitched voice, and the way he talks, talks, *talks*—"

George gasped incredulously: "You mean you don't *like* him? You don't like Tom Whaley?"

"What is there to like?"

"But—but—he's a good fellow—he's against me on the Council, I know that—but he's really all right, Tom is—"

"George, he's dull and he's pompous and he loves the sound of his own voice. And he *will* go on explaining the same thing over and over again. I thought I should have screamed while he was telling me the difference between the Local Government Board and the Ministry of Health—"

"He's one of my best friends, anyhow."

"Oh, George, I'm sorry . . . maybe I was in the wrong mood."

"You didn't seem to be."

"Couldn't you see I was pretending?"

No; he hadn't seen it. He said, anxious to ease matters: "Well, if you were, I appreciate that much. It was nice of you to give such a good impression."

Not till long afterwards did he guess why she had done so, but Whaley's visit undoubtedly led to a second social occasion, far less pleasant, that showed how much further she was prepared to go. It began by her asking George if he would meet some friends of hers, Mr. and Mrs. Wallington by name, for dinner one evening in Mulcaster. It seemed she had picked up a chance acquaintance with Mrs. Wallington in a Mulcaster dress shop, and George, who thought it odd that he should be dragged into it, demurred at first, but on being reminded of how hospitably she had behaved towards Tom Whaley consented on one condition—that he himself should be the host. "Then if I don't like 'em I don't have to invite 'em back," he explained, with sturdy if not too flattering independence.

So in due course Livia took him to a Mulcaster restaurant where the appointment had been arranged. There he was presented, not only to the couple, but to an extra man, and also to the revelation that all of them seemed to know Livia far better than he had anticipated. Although he was usually able to get on well with strangers from the outset, he felt curiously ill-at-ease that evening, and as it progressed he became less and less happy for a variety of reasons, one of which was quite humiliating—he didn't think he would have enough money to pay the bill, especially as they were all ordering expensive drinks. But apart from that, he found none of his previous pleasure in witnessing Livia's social success; it was one thing to introduce her to a friend of his own and watch the magic begin to operate, but to see the *fait accompli* in the shape of already established friendships with strangers was another matter. He did not think it was jealousy that he felt, but rather a sense of annoyance that, after sneering at Whaley, she should show her preference for men like those two. For they were both of the blustery, aggressive type, especially the one who was not the husband and had not been invited. His name was Mangin, and from certain boastful references George gathered that he had lately made a good deal of money in the advertising business. There was a cold swagger about him that met more than its match in Livia's repartee, but George himself could not come to terms with it, and was made even less comfortable by his wife's peculiar ability to do so.

As the dinner went on and more drinks fed the bluster, he fell into a glum silence that became equally a torture to maintain or to try to break. He was relieved when Mangin made a move to leave, mentioning a train he must catch; but then came the problem of the bill; why on earth had Livia chosen such a swank establishment, and would such a place be satisfied with his personal check? He was trying rather clumsily to signal the waiter and learn the worst when Mangin shouted: "What the deuce are you bothering about, Boswell? Everything's taken care of at source—don't you know me yet? Anyhow, your wife does—that's the main thing. . . ." Whereupon, with a lordly gesture amidst ensuing laughter, he intercepted the waiter whom George had summoned and ostentatiously tipped him a pound note, then adding to George: "By the way, Boswell, I'd like a word with you if you can spare a moment."

George could say nothing; to argue without enough in his pocket to pay the bill would have been even more humiliating. In his confusion he somehow found himself leaving the table and being piloted by Mangin into the restaurant lobby.

"So you're a newspaper man, Boswell?"

George nodded, still inclined to be speechless.

"Know much about advertising?"

"Advertising? . . . Er . . . Well, I take in advertising, naturally."

"Ever *written* ads?"

"Oh yes, my customers often ask me to help them—"

"I mean big stuff—campaign advertising—things like patent medicines—"

"No, I can't say I—"

Mangin threw a half-crown into the plate on the cloakroom counter and began putting on his overcoat.

"Well, I'll tell you what . . . You don't seem to have had any experience, but I'll give you a chance . . . start at six pounds a week for the first three months and we'll see what happens. . . . But you'll have to *learn*, Boswell, and learn plenty if you want to stay in the game."

"But—but—" George was slowly recovering his voice. "But I don't understand—I don't know what you're talking about."

"I'm offering you a job, that's all. In my London office."

"But I don't want a job. I've got a job already—"

"You mean that newspaper—in—what's the name of the place —in—"

"Aye, in Browdley. I'm owner and editor of the *Browdley Guardian.*"

"But I thought you wanted to give it up! Wasn't that the idea . . . to try somewhere else?"

George suddenly flushed. "There must have been a mistake."

"*Mistake,* eh? Looks like it. . . ." Mangin smirked as he signaled the doorman for a taxi. "Better have that out with Livia. . . . I've got to rush for my train. . . . G'bye."

George did not go back to the table immediately; he calmed himself first, then discovered (as he had hoped) that the rest of the party was breaking up. He murmured his good-byes, and could not find words to address Livia during the first few hundred yards of their walk together along the pavement from the restaurant. Eventually she broke the silence herself. "Don't be so angry, George, just because Mr. Mangin paid for the dinner. You know you only asked the other two—and then all those drinks . . . they wouldn't have felt free to have what they wanted if they'd thought you were paying for everything."

"Why not? How do they know what I earn? I'm not poor just because I can't afford to buy champagne cocktails."

"That's it, George, you can't afford them and Mr. Mangin can —and besides that, you don't drink yourself—that's another thing."

He said, half to himself: "Seems to me there's a more important matter than the one we're discussing."

She answered eagerly: "I hope so. I don't know what Mr. Mangin said to you outside. I was afraid you hadn't given him much of an impression of how clever you are—because you *are* clever, George—I know you are—in your own way."

"Thanks," he retorted. "And perhaps you'll tell me why in God's name you should care *what* impression I make on a man like that?"

"Only because he might find you some work. I thought it was a stroke of luck when I met somebody who knew him—he's very influential in the newspaper world, so Mrs. Wallington told me. And it would get us out of Browdley—that is, if he *did* say he could find you something."

George gritted his teeth and replied: "Aye, he said he could. He offered me six pounds a week in his London office—provided I learned enough."

"Oh, but George, that's—that's *wonderful!* You don't make nearly so much out of the *Guardian*—not lately, anyhow."

"Livia . . ." He stopped suddenly in the street and faced her. "Do you really mean you'd have me give up my own paper and all the work I do on the Council—just to have a job under a man like that? And *what* a job—writing patent-medicine ads. . . . Livia, would you *really* have me do that?"

He knew what her answer would have been but for the look on his face, which made her temporize: "Maybe it isn't exactly the life you'd choose. But *I* don't choose the life I have, either. . . . And why keep on saying 'a man like that'? They can't all be men like you."

He began walking again. "Livia, let's not quarrel. You did a silly thing, but I daresay you meant well. You asked this man to find me a job—you made yourself agreeable to him—you were pretending just as you were with Tom Whaley, weren't you?" His eagerness to think so fanned a warmth between them. "I believe you really thought you were doing the best for me."

"No. . . . I was thinking about Martin more than you. That was the real reason."

Then she told him the bare economic facts of his own household (which he had hardly guessed, so preoccupied had he been with the bare economic facts of the whole town)—the fact, for instance, that sometimes lately she hadn't been able to afford the kind of food and clothing the child most needed, and had had to make do with the second-best. Though this was a condition common all over Browdley, and formed the subject matter of countless speeches he made, he was nevertheless shocked to find it so close to his own personal affairs—not because he thought he ought to have been exempt from what afflicted others, but simply because it had never occurred to him. And once it did, of course, why, *of course,* something must be done about it. But what *could* be done? persisted Livia, coolly stemming his indignation. It was no use her asking for more money because she knew, and none better, that the *Guardian* didn't make it; she knew also there were no more business economies possible. Nor were there domestic ones; she herself did all the housework, and some of the office work too, now that she knew how careless Will Spivey was. As she very calmly explained: it had become her honest opinion after George's electoral defeat that it would be a wise thing to leave Browdley, even apart from her own desire to do so.

"But—my Council work, Livia—"

"Where's it getting you?"

"I don't know, but I've not been defeated in *that* . . . *yet.* I don't have all my own way—after all, who does?—but I am *on* the Council, pretty safely on too, judging by my last majority. And the job's worth doing. I know you're not interested in it—I don't ask you to be, but do believe me when I say this—*it's worth doing.* . . . Livia, don't hinder me in it—even if you can't help me. . . . And as for the extra things you need for Martin, you shall have them. Of course you shall—I had no idea you were doing without. . . . I'd rather go without everything myself—"

"But you can't, George. You don't drink or smoke—there's nothing you could give up . . . except Browdley. *That's* your hobby, or your luxury—whatever you'd rather call it. And I don't say you're not entitled to it—you personally, that is—everyone has his own tastes. But what sort of a place is it for a child to grow up in?"

But that only gave him his own private cue for optimism, as she would have known if she had attended more of his meetings. For he answered, beginning quietly but with rising confidence as he proceeded: "Not such a bad place as it used to be . . . and I'll make it better. You wait. You don't know all the plans I have. And they're not just dreams—they're practical. I don't tell you much— because I know you don't want to hear about it—I *wish* you did . . . but never mind that. Mark my words, though, I'll *do* things with this town. I'll get the slums off the map. I'll build schools . . . and a new hospital. . . . I'll . . . well, laugh at me if you like—I don't care."

She did not laugh, but she smiled as she took his arm. "I wouldn't care either, but for Martin. You'd do anything for Browdley—I'd do anything for him."

"So would I too—I just don't see any conflict between them. Don't you think I'm as devoted to the kid as you are?"

He was; but nevertheless in his heart he looked forward to the time when Martin would be a little older—old enough for the friendly father-and-son relationship to develop, old enough also to start the kind of education on which George set so much store. Whereas for Livia every tomorrow seemed a future far enough ahead and complete in itself; it was almost as if she hoarded the days of babyhood, unwilling to lose the separate richness of each one.

. . . .

She was wrong, though, in saying there was nothing he could give up. There was, and he gave it up. She never knew, because she had never known anything about it at all. The fact was, after his electoral defeat George had gone back to his earlier ambition, the university degree. The long interval he had let pass meant digging over a good deal of old as well as new ground, but he tackled the job, as he did all his chosen jobs, with enthusiasm. Most of the necessary time he put in late at nights, in the room which he had now begun to call his "study"; and without actually telling Livia a direct lie, he allowed her to think he was busy preparing material for the *Guardian*. As she was generally asleep when he came up to bed she did not know how long he worked; sometimes it was half the night. He had a curious unwillingness to let her know what he still hankered after, partly because he was not sure he would ever succeed in winning it, but chiefly out of a sort of embarrassment; he was sure she would smile as at a grown man caught playing with a toy, for book learning to her was something you had forced on you during youth and then were mercifully released from ever afterwards. She might also (a more valid attitude) feel that if he had such time to spare it would be better spent in trying to sustain his own precarious livelihood. Anyhow, he did not tell her, and having not done so, it was easy to give the whole thing up without a word to anyone in the world. There were the examination fees he would now avoid, and he could also sell some of the expensive textbooks he had had to purchase. He did this and gave her everything thus saved, spreading it over a period so that she needed no explanation.

But the habit of reading in his study at night continued—in fact, the whole habit of study continued, for it was something bigger than a mere competitive examination that had inspired George. The fringe of scholarship he had touched had left him with an admiration for learned men all the more passionate because he almost never met them either in business or in politics; and there came to him, a constant vision, the memory of the dome-headed spectacled examining professor who had been so indulgent to him about the Pathetic Fallacy.

Perhaps Martin would grow up into a learned man—which was another reason for not discussing the matter with Livia.

One thing, however, became both an immediate and a practical ambition—that the boy should have a vastly different childhood from his own. Not that his own had been cruel or vicious; merely that, in recollecting it, he was aware of how far it had been from the ideal. Perhaps equally far from the worst that it might have been, in Browdley, for George's father had always had regular employment in a job that set him among the aristocracy of cotton-mill labor—a spinner's wage being at that time more than twice that of the lowest-paid. And though Mill Street became a byword later, it was no worse during George's childhood than nine tenths of Browdley; for the Boswells, like many other families, had lived in a four-roomed bathroomless house more because there were no others available than because they could not have afforded better. Anyhow, Number 24, in which George was born, had been clean and decently furnished, and its occupants, though overcrowded, were never without enough plain food and strong soap and good winter fuel; they were "respectable chapel folk," moreover, which meant that their children were nagged at without the use of technical bad language; and if the young Boswells feared their father too much, and their father feared his Heavenly Father, it was doubtless on general principles rather than for any more definite reason.

Even George's early education, which was poor enough, had had a few passable things in it; indeed, at the old-fashioned prisonlike elementary school he was taught reading, writing, spelling, and arithmetic far more thoroughly than were the youngsters in the luxurious modern school that George persuaded the Council to build years later. But there was a drawback to the thoroughness, for the teacher, a Mr. Rimington, was dull-witted enough to think history and geography "easy" subjects, and therefore somewhat to be despised. All George learned of the former was that somebody was a "good" king and somebody else a "bad" one, plus a few scraps of information such as that Henry the Second never smiled again and that Oliver Cromwell had a wart on his nose; while geography consisted largely of memorizing "what belongs to England," and of copying maps—an occupation which Mr. Rimington approved of because it took so long and kept the class quiet. He was also dull-witted enough to think that a boy who turned over a page during a reading lesson without waiting for the order to do so was guilty of a serious breach of discipline. George had been punished for this once or twice, after which he hated and feared Mr. Rimington and formed a self-protective habit of concentrating his attention and disengaging his intelligence whenever he crossed the school threshold. Not till years afterwards when, as Chairman of the Browdley Education Committee, he had the task of choosing applicants for teaching posts, did he realize that Mr. Rimington had made himself thus terrifying because when he first became a teacher the rougher products of Browdley homes had terrified *him*.

And now, as the father of the product of another Browdley home, George turned over in his mind his own childhood memories, not without a certain nostalgia, but with a resolute determination that Martin's early life should contain happier ones. He remembered the crowded house in Mill Street, his mother's continual nagging (behind which he had failed to diagnose the harassed affection that was really there), his father's doomful voice at home and from the pulpit; the canal bank where he sneaked off to play when his father was at work and his mother was ill (the only time of real freedom he enjoyed); the elementary school round the corner and Mr. Rimington's classroom, with its torn maps and dirty walls, the smell of wet clothes and steaming waterpipes in winter, and of sweat in summer; the slabs of dust-laden sunlight into which he so often stared after finishing tasks adjusted to the speed of the stupidest pupil; terrifying Mr. Rimington himself, and the not-quite-so-terrifying headmaster, old "Daddy" Simmons, whose habit, fascinating to all, was to stick his little finger into his ear and waggle furiously; and the paragraph in the tattered reading book that said: "Harrow is one of the great schools of England. Many famous Englishmen went there when they were boys. Some of them carved their names on the school desks, and these names can still be read. You must not carve your name on your school desk, but you can make up your mind to become a famous Englishman when you grow up. . . ."

George's own ambitions, even if he should ever become both a Member of Parliament and a Bachelor of Arts, had never permitted themselves to soar as far as being "a famous Englishman." But for Martin . . . why not? What obstacles were there? Surely not boyhood in Browdley, since winning scholarships was no harder from there than from anywhere else. Perhaps Martin might win such scholarships—not to Harrow (for George, though he could admire some of their products as individuals, was of the opinion that public schools encourage snobbery), but to Oxford—or Cambridge, at least. That faint preference in favor of Oxford was nothing but a recollection of Gladstone's Double-First.

There came a day when Martin seemed old enough to be taken by his father to the Browdley Town Hall, there to imbibe some vague first impression which George could hardly seek to clarify at such an early age, but which would later, he hoped, inspire the lad to an interest in civics, local government, the history of his country, the parliament of man, and the federation of the world. (After all, there was no limit to the effects of a child's first impression.) So George held the boy lovingly in his arms in front of the rather bad stained-glass window in the main lobby of the Town Hall—stained glass depicting a woman carrying some sheaves of wheat in one hand and what looked like a coffee grinder in the other ("mechanical power," it was supposed to represent) ; he hoped Martin would at least notice the bright colors. And in due course the child's eyes rounded with all the excitement, nay more than the excitement that George had hoped for, but unfortunately those eyes were not on the stained glass at all.

George looked down and saw a large rat scampering across the Town Hall floor.

He was horrified, not only that the child should have seen such a thing, but that such a thing should exist; it argued bad drains or something—he would certainly bring the matter up at the next meeting of the Building Committee.

But Martin was by no means horrified. He knew nothing about rats, but perhaps he thought that what he had seen was some extremely swift and fascinating kind of pussycat (for pussycats *were* known to him), and with this to wonder about the visit to the Town Hall did indeed enshrine an experience.

Martin loved his father less than his mother and perhaps even than Becky, but George did not mind this, reflecting magnanimously that the balance would be evened up later on. After all, it was a result of the physical contacts of mother and child, the domestic routine, the humble, seriocomic intimacies; and Livia made a perfect mother—unexpectedly so, indeed. It was as if all the nonsense that cropped up so often in her behavior with adults were resolved into complete naturalness between herself and Martin; she never raised her voice to him, or was angry, or even irritated. In an odd way she gave the appearance of being with the boy in his own world, rather than of looking into it from hers; perhaps there was a sense in which she had never grown up herself, or perhaps it was just the animal quality in her that George had noticed before, that extraordinary paradoxical knack of being shameless and fastidious at the same time. When George came upon his wife and child romping together, he sometimes felt that to make them even aware of him was an intrusion, the breaking of a lovely spell, and he would tiptoe away rather than do this; for again he was able to fortify himself by thinking that his own time would come later.

One night, as he sat with a book in his study, the impulse came to write something that might, if anything untimely should happen, be a help to the boy or at least a reminder that a man had once existed who had dreamed things about him and hoped things for him; and in this mood, rare because of its slightly melancholy flavor, George wrote:—

Everything depends on childhood, Martin, and if you ever have children of your own, remember that, just as I, remembering my childhood, intend to make yours good to remember. When I was a boy of seven my parents died and I went to live with an uncle who kept a newspaper and stationery shop in Shawgate, and living in his house gave me, I think, the germ of all my later interest in printed things—perhaps even in politics too, because it so happened that at the time of my arrival there was an election in progress, and Uncle Joe, who was a Liberal (the only thing he had in common with my father), sent me out to distribute handbills. All I had to do was to walk about Browdley slipping them under doors and through letter boxes, yet I don't think the world was or ever could be more wonderful to me than during those few weeks. I kept hearing about some mysterious person called the Candidate, who was opposed in some mysterious way to another person who was called the Other Candidate, and it seemed to me that the great battle of Good and Evil was being fought in the streets of this town, and that I and my uncle were soldiers fighting it. I suppose it was then, before I really knew what things were all about, that I had the first hankering that made me later decide to go on fighting the same sort of battle when I grew up. And if that's a strange reason for a young man to enter politics, then perhaps it isn't the real reason, but just the flick of a button in the signal cabin that can send a train to any one of a hundred different places.

But of course all that was years ago—and in another age, because 1914 was really the end of an age. It was not only that things happened differently before then—they happened to people who *felt* them differently. Take chapel-going, for instance. If you had walked up Mill Street almost any Sunday forty years ago, you would have seen from the notice board outside that William Boswell was to preach there. That man was my father. It would be a cold, raw night, maybe, with mist peeling off the moors, but the folk who wanted to hear him were hard-wearing stuff; in twos and threes they mustered, till by six o'clock the little gaslit pitch-pine interior was almost full. Punctually on the hour old Jack Slater went to the pedal harmonium (the Methodists of the sect my father belonged to did not believe in pipe organs) and let his fingers wander over the keys according to a style of his own, beginning softly and working up to a great roar, his feet pounding as if he were bicycling uphill to save a life. By this time my father had emerged from the side vestry, Bible in hand, and climbed the steps to the pulpit, where he prayed standing (for the sect did not believe in kneeling or stooping), and announced the opening hymn in the boom-ingest voice I ever heard. He was a fine-looking man, as you can judge from the photograph in my study; his hands were big and thick-fingered; his hair, black and bushy, crowned a well-shaped head set firmly on broad shoulders. He never drank, smoked, played cards, went to Browdley's one theater (there were no cinemas in those days), or read a novel or a Sunday newspaper. A life that might have seemed, to an outsider, full of hardships relieved only by boredoms had some-how or other produced in him an air of somber majesty that I could never come to terms with, and I don't think my mother ever could either. We lived at Number 24, a four-roomed house identical with eleven on one side of it and thirty-two on the other. Parallel with Mill Street stood Jenny Street and Nathaniel Street, composed of houses exactly similar. From the pavement one entered by a single step through the usually unlatched front door; at the back, however, there was an exit through the kitchen into a small paved yard where coal was stored and clothes were hung to dry. I suppose there was no labor-saving device in general use in those days except the Singer sewing machine that, surmounted by a plant pot with or without a plant in it, stood behind the lace curtains in nearly every front window. And there was gaslight downstairs, but not upstairs; and sanitation had but re-cently progressed in Browdley from the stinking midden to the back-to-back water privy. There were no bathrooms, and baths were taken once a week by heating pans of water over the kitchen fire. I give you all these details because I hope by the time you grow up most of them will be a bit historic—at any rate I hope Mill Street won't be in existence for you to verify. Mind you, these houses were not slums (as they are today), but typical dwellings of respectable working folk such as my parents were. Respectability even imposed a toll of extra labor, for it was a sort of ritual to wash and scrub the street pavement from the front door to the curb, a task undone by the next passer-by or the next rain shower. When my mother was ill, as she often was during the last years of her life, this necessary tribute to tribal gods was made on her behalf by an obliging neighbor, though I doubt if my mother would have cared much if it hadn't been. She was a merry little woman with an independent mind uncoupled with any determination to stake out a claim for itself; this made her easy to get on with and rather hopeless to rely on. My father only saw her between six and ten in the evenings (the rest of the time he was either at work or asleep), and during the annual holiday which they took together, always at Blackpool, the strain of trying to seem familiar to a man whose life was so separate from hers made her almost glad when the week was over and she could return to the far more familiar routine of Mill Street. She loved my father well enough, but the emotion of being in love had probably not survived courtship, and by her thirties, with an already numerous family to look after, she had worn her life of household drudgery into an almost comfortable groove. Every morning in the bedroom overlooking the backs of the houses in Nathaniel Street, the alarm clock rang at five-fifteen; without a word my mother would get up, come downstairs in her nightdress, and poke up the kitchen fire that had been banked with small coal overnight. Then she would fill the kettle to make tea, and by the time this was ready my father would be down himself, washing at the kitchen sink and ready to leave as soon as the clock hand approached the half-hour. He was never exactly bad-tempered, but the fact that they were both sleepy made them reluctant to talk; there was, anyhow, nothing much to talk about. A few minutes after he had left the house the whole town resounded with the crescendo of the mill "buzzers," but by that time my mother was back in the warm bed, content to doze again while the clogged footsteps rang along the pavement outside. To her this pause between my father's departure for work and the beginning of her own was the pleasantest time of the day—and the only time she was really alone. By eight o'clock she was dressed and downstairs, glancing at the morning paper, making more tea and frying a rasher of bacon for herself. Then came attendance on us children, getting us off to school when we were old enough, and after that a routine of housework and the morning walk along Mill Street to the shop at the corner where nearly everything could be bought, from feeding bottles to fly papers. She would chat there to Mr. and Mrs. Molesworth while they served her; she liked a joke and an exchange of gossip, and often, if the jokes and the gossip were good enough, she would stay talking and laughing until other customers joined in, so that the shop became a sort of neighborhood club for housewives.

Then during afternoons, if the weather were fine, she would put the youngest of us (me, in fact) into a pram and wheel it round a few streets, sometimes as far as the canal bank or the Shawgate shops. Towards four she would be home again, in good time to prepare an evening meal. Then came the second pleasantest interval—the hour in the rocking chair with a cup of tea at her elbow before the children came home from school. While winter dusk crept across the sky, and until the passing of the lamplighter sent a green-yellow glow through the fanlight over the front door, my mother would "save the gas" by poking the fire to a blaze while she rocked and sang. She had a nice voice, small in volume but always true on the pitch, and though most of the tunes she knew were chapel hymns with rather grim words to them, she sang them somehow gaily and with a lilt, breaking off occasionally into a popular song of the moment, something half-remembered from the previous year's Blackpool holiday, or from summer performances of the Silver Prize Band in Browdley market place.

My earliest recollections, Martin, were of my mother rocking and singing like that. There was a brass rail that ran along the whole length of the mantelshelf, and as I first remember it this rail would shine in the firelight with the shadows darkening all around and my mother's face growing fainter and fainter as she swung backwards and forwards; till there was only the sound of her singing, the creak of the rocking chair, and the simmer of the kettle on the fire bar. . . . Then, all at once, I would wake up to see the room already gaslit, with my father standing, huge and unsmiling, in the doorway.

I feared my father and loved my mother and that's about the plain truth of it. On Sundays he locked up all story books, picture books, and even bricks that spelt out words; but while he was at chapel my mother used to unlock them with a key of her own and let me play till just before his return was expected; then she would whisk away the forbidden things with a knowing glance that finally became a sort of joke between us.

That is the home I was born in, Martin—not as happy as it might have been, but not as unhappy either. So I don't complain of it, but I do want to make *yours* happier. Which is why I intend soon to begin putting books in your way, because the more freely and vividly you see things while you are young, even if you can't fully understand them, the more actively they will possess you when you grow up—especially if, in adult life, you have hard battles to fight and bitter disappointments to face. New worlds, Martin, are for the young to explore; later one is glad of a new room, or even of a view from a new window. . . .

He put aside the fragment then, thinking he would add to it on many succeeding nights, but he never did; perhaps the rare mood never recurred.

.   .   .   .

As the postwar slump deepened and unemployment filled the street corners with lounging, workless men, George encountered new opposition to his Mill Street housing scheme. Many of the cotton mills were closing down completely; some of them went bankrupt as catastrophically as had Channing's a generation before, but without the criminal taint, though the short-lived boom had been pushed by speculators to limits that were almost criminal.

Among the mills that closed was the one still called Channing's, though long operated by another firm; now, when George walked down Mill Street, the mill loomed up, symbolically as well as actually, at the dead end of the street. Derelict, like Stoneclough five miles away, it stood for the dead end of what the Channings themselves had stood for. Still physically intact, with machines inside that could spin and weave, nobody would buy it or use it, because nobody wanted what it could do. Yet the illusion that it still had some real value was preserved; it was regularly taxed and insured; the Browdley police kept an eye on it, the fire department were ready to quench the blaze should any lightning or arsonist strike. But neither did, though lightning had once, when George was a boy, struck the Methodist chapel at the other end of the street.

The chapel also stood, a little less forlorn than the mill—derelict, one might say, only six days out of the seven. For Methodism in Browdley, like the cotton trade, was not what it had been. People could not afford to give so much to their chapels, nor were there so many Methodists. George, walking along the street where he was born and which he planned to rebuild for others to be born in, remembered those early days when both mill and chapel had flourished, and when his own father, sharing the week between them in that mystic proportion of six to one, and with his house halfway between, had served a life sentence longer though less stigmatized than that of his boss.

The reason George visited the Mill Street area so often was not a sentimental one. Indeed, it was concerned with drains rather than dreams; for the more graphically he could report to the Council how bad the houses were and what disease traps they had become, the sooner he hoped to get his scheme actually started.

He found a powerful ally in Dr. Swift, Browdley's medical officer, who had himself issued many warnings. After a long struggle

and against the bitter opposition of a few of the town's old-estab-
lished doctors, a system of free immunization against diphtheria had
been set up, enabling parents to have their children inoculated at a
municipal clinic. It was, however, impossible to make this compul-
sory, and the whole question became impregnated with political
and even religious prejudices that George deplored and perhaps at
the same time aggravated by his own constant argument that it
was not enough to immunize; the *causes* of epidemics should be
tackled, and the chief was bad housing. To which the opposition
retorted that George was using the health issue for his own political
ends, that Browdley was in no greater danger than other manufac-
turing towns, and that though the Mill Street area was somewhat
less salubrious than the rest, what could be done about it when local
tax rates were almost the highest in the country? And since the opposition, fighting on this tax issue, had won seats at recent Council
by-elections, George found his slum-clearance project losing rather
than gaining ground for the time being.

He often walked with Dr. Swift through the worst of the streets,
the medical officer supplying scientific ammunition for George's
continuing struggle on the Council. For George would not give in;
there was a point, even though at times it was hard to find, beyond
which he would not even waver or compromise. Indeed, his mere
mention of Mill Street had begun to send a smile or a sigh across
the Council Chamber, so well was the subject now recognized as the
bee in George's bonnet. But he did not mind. "Sooner or later I'll
wear 'em down," he assured Swift, to which the latter replied
grimly: "Better be sooner." For it had been a hot summer. Towards
the end of September over twenty diphtheria cases appeared in and
around Mill Street, mostly among young children, of whom five
quickly died.

In such an emergency Dr. Swift was given command almost without restrictions; everything remedial was promptly organized—the
quarantining of families, wholesale inoculations, closing of schools,
and so on. The Council had adjourned for its four weeks' annual
recess; many Councillors were still on holiday. But George, who had
the *Guardian* to look after and could not afford a holiday, was right
on the spot to say "I told you so" to any former opponents he might
meet. They were not so much his opponents now. They all agreed,

in principle, that something would have to be done about the Mill
Street area. And most agreed, in principle, with the *Guardian* editorial in which George wrote:—

We must learn our lesson from this tragic visitation. Though the
epidemic has now (according to the latest assurance of our eminent
and indefatigable Medical Officer, Dr. Swift) been checked, we can
never again feel secure until preventable disease has been
ABOLISHED AT ITS SOURCE. Let those citizens who live in the
more fortunate parts of Browdley and whose children have remained
unscathed, bear in mind the joint responsibility of us all for what we
allow to happen anywhere in our town, and let them do their share,
and *pay* their share, in making Browdley safe for our children's future.

The only adverse comment George got about this was from a
new Catholic priest, Father Harry Wendover, of St. Patrick's, who
questioned the phrase "what we allow to happen in our town."
Having been introduced to George at a meeting, he immediately
buttonholed him with the query: "Isn't that a bit arrogant, Mr.
Boswell? After all, even if you don't believe in the hand of God, you
might at least recognize that there are limits to what the hand of
Man can do."

George noted the newcomer's tall gaunt frame and deep-socketed
eyes, the strong chin and the cultured accent, and decided that here
was a man to be both respected and tackled. Rumor had already
informed him that Wendover was something of the proud cleric,
so George answered, giving as well as taking measure: "Aye, there
are limits, I daresay, but in Browdley we're still a few thousand
miles away from 'em. And as for the hand of God, what makes you
think I don't believe in it?"

Wendover smiled—a rather pleasant smile. "To be frank—just
gossip. That's all a priest has to go by when he comes to a new place
and wants to find out who's who."

"So they gossip about me, do they?" And immediately George
was thinking about Livia and what sort of gossip might still be cir-
culated about her.

"Oh, nothing malicious. In fact, you seem to be extremely popular. But they also say that you're not a God-fearing man like your
father, that you don't often go to church or chapel, and that you're
on good terms with atheists and agnostics."

It was all spoken with a twinkle that made it inoffensive and not quite serious, but George would not have been offended in any case. He was already too interested in what promised to be an argument.

"Aye," he answered. "I'm on good terms with anyone who'll help me make Browdley better. Romans, Church of England, Methodists, atheists, agnostics—they're all one to me if they'll do that."

"So religion has no place in your better Browdley?"

George appreciated a nicely laid trap, especially when he was in no danger of falling into it. He smiled as he had so often smiled across the Council Chamber or a meeting hall. "Nay—I'd rather ask you if *my* better Browdley has a place in *your* religion? Because if it hasn't you'll not do so well at St. Patrick's. I've got a lot of supporters there."

"Is that a threat, Mr. Boswell?"

"No—just a tip. I've no hell-fire in my armory. All I can tell folks is that diphtheria comes from bad drains, but of course if they're more interested in pearly gates that's their lookout."

Wendover's smile broadened. "If I were old-fashioned I'd probably say that God would punish you for blasphemy. But my conception of God isn't like that. I doubt that He'll find it necessary to strike down you or one of your family just to prove a point."

George grunted. He had an idea that Wendover was enjoying the encounter as much as he was, and already he recognized an agile mind. Agile minds were useful, and it might be that Wendover would take the progressive side in many of the town's controversial issues. George also realized that priests and parsons had to stand on some ground of their own, not merely on what they could share with every liberal-minded thinker, politician, or social worker. All this weighed against his impulse to continue the argument combatively, so he replied: "I assure you I didn't intend to be blasphemous, and I hope you're right about God. I don't think I know enough to agree or disagree with you. So I'm sticking to what I do know something about, and that's Man. Seems to me Man could give himself a pretty good time on earth if only he went about it the right way, but he just won't. You'd almost think he didn't *want* a good time, the way he carries on." But that looked like the beginning of another argument, so he shook hands with a final smile and left the priest wondering.

A few days later Wendover wondered afresh when news spread over the town that Councillor Boswell's baby had been stricken. But being honest he did not exploit the situation. Nor did he actually believe that the hand of God was in it. He just thought it an extraordinary coincidence, which it was, and wrote George a note that merely expressed sympathy and hoped the child would be well again soon. For he liked George.

.   .   .

During those dark days Livia and George hardly spoke, except when she asked him to do this or that; and he obeyed her then, blindly as a child himself.

They hardly spoke because there was simply nothing to say after the one sharp, inevitable, and rather dreadful argument.

When George came home late after a meeting and found Livia sitting up with Martin, who was ill and had a temperature, he was concerned, but not unduly so; and when he guessed that the thought of diphtheria was in her mind, he told her confidently not to worry, since the boy had been immunized. She just looked at him then and shook her head.

Over the small tossing body and whilst waiting for the doctor, they thrashed the matter out.

The fact was that when the free immunization scheme had gone into operation and he had told her to take Martin to the municipal clinic, she simply had not done so. And she had lied to him about it afterwards.

He kept pacing up and down the bedroom, trying to grasp the situation. "So you *didn't* do it? Oh, Livia, *why* didn't you? How *could* you not do what I asked about a thing like that? Did you forget and then tell me a lie to cover it? . . . Oh Livia . . . Livia. . . ."

She answered: "I didn't forget, George. I went to the clinic once and saw the crowd lined up outside. I didn't want to take Martin to a place like that."

His anger mounted. "Why not? For God's sake what was wrong about it?"

"I didn't like it. I didn't like the people there—I mean the other people with their children."

"*Snob!*" He shouted the word. "Weren't they well-dressed enough for you?"

"Most of them were as well-dressed as I could afford to be."

Yes, he knew that; he had let his anger tempt him into an absurdity as well as a side issue. "Then why—*why?*" he reiterated. "Why didn't you have it done?"

"I told you—I didn't like the place. Some of the children looked dirty, and they had bad colds—"

"And Martin might have caught one! Or a flea perhaps! So to save him from that you let him catch diphtheria—"

She interrupted in a dead-level voice: "I don't want to quarrel, George. But don't you remember I asked if it couldn't be done by a private doctor? And do you remember what you said?"

Yes, he remembered. There had been a wrangle, though a less bitter one, about that also. Couldn't she realize, he had asked her indignantly, that for months he had been making speeches all over the town in favor of free public immunization? What would it look like if, after all that, he took his own child to a private doctor? Couldn't she see what a fool and a hypocrite it would make him appear? So Martin *must* go to the clinic. "Livia, I wouldn't insist if it meant that the child would be getting anything second-best. But the free immunization's just as good—just the same, in fact— as anything a private doctor could give. The only difference is in where you take him to get it. Don't you see we have to set an example to the town in these things? If we don't use the new facilities ourselves, if we behave as if we thought them not good enough for our own children, how can we expect anyone else to trust them?"

Thus the argument when Martin was a year old. George had thought it ended in his own victory; now, six months later, he realized that the end was neither victory nor defeat, but just post-dated disaster.

He cried out, desperately: "I know all that, Livia. . . . And I don't want to quarrel, either—it's no good now—it's too late. But why . . . whatever you did . . . why didn't you do *something?* Why *didn't* you take him to a private doctor if you absolutely refused to do what I wanted? Oh, anything—*anything* rather than this. . . . Or why didn't you let *me* do it? . . . Why didn't you *tell* me, anyway? Why did you *lie* to me?"

He saw her hurt, stung face, and knew she was suffering so profoundly that his accusations made little difference. But she could sting back and make *him* suffer more, as when she answered with deadly irrelevance: "I did tell you one thing. I said we ought to leave Browdley."

"Oh no, that's not the point—"

"It is and always will be. If we hadn't stayed here, nothing like this would have happened."

Even that wasn't certain, he knew, but he saw the certainty in her eyes, and knew also that she would never believe otherwise, however much he went on arguing.

The arrival of the doctor interrupted them. His visit lasted an hour, and when it ended there was nothing more to argue about, only a dreadful possibility to face.

The local hospital was already overcrowded, so Martin lay in the spare room above the printing office. Livia shared it with him, while George slept on his study couch—so far, that is, as he could sleep at all. Becky, banished from upstairs, curled mournfully under the desk. George had not realized till then the depth of his affection for the child. He was like that with all his affections—they grew, and then lurked, and then sprang to give him pain. He was torn unutterably by remorse at having been so busy those past few months, so busy with the affairs of the town, too busy to look after the physical safety of his own household. He should have made sure that the immunization had taken place, instead of just mentioning the matter to Livia and taking it for granted that she had done it. It was *her* fault—and yet it was *his* fault too, for leaving everything of that sort to her. It was the streak of unreasonableness in her cropping up again, and this time tragically—he should have been prepared for it, in all vital matters he should have watched for it. He wished . . . he wished . . . and one of the things he did wish now, but dared not wish aloud, was that he *had* left Browdley. He almost dared not wish it in thought, lest there should pass some spark between his eyes and hers, some spark to set off a conflagration, or—even worse—to indicate a mood which she would take to be surrender. So it had come to *that*—that he thought of her as an enemy, or of his love for her as an enemy? Which—or both? He puzzled over it, far too modest to think his own emotions unique, but wondering if there were outsiders who would understand them better than he did—novelists, say, or psychoanalysts. Or that fellow Wendover, if ever he got to know him well enough? Though how could a priest . . . and yet, after all, it *was* a spiritual matter in some ways. Thus he argued with himself, and as the days passed and Martin did not improve, it occurred to him that the greatest single difference between Livia and himself was that she was too utterly fearless to be reasonable, while he was too reasonable to be utterly fearless. And at a certain level of experience there was simply no compromise, between them.

Just before dawn one morning he dozed off in the chair and dreamed of his own boyhood, a dream he had had recurrently before, though never with such clarity. It was about his Uncle Joe, whom he had gone to live with when he was seven years old, and of whom he had had more fear (on one occasion only) than ever before or since of anything or anyone. What had happened actually, though not always in the dream, was that uncle and nephew had met for the first time at the house in Mill Street, when no one else was there. This was about six months after his father had died, a week after the funeral of his mother, and a few hours after the door had closed on his elder brother Harry, his elder sister Jane, and the furniture removers.

George had been the youngest of a family of six, with a gap so wide between himself and the rest that at the time he was left parentless all the others were grown-up and some of them married. Their bickerings about who should take care of him (each one having a completely plausible alibi) had made them jump at an unexpected offer from their mother's brother, despite the fact that he and their father had quarreled years before over some point of behavior which (according to the latter) "just shows what a wicked man Joe is." Nobody ever told George more than that; all Harry would add was an especially sinister: "You'll find out soon enough, Georgie." And when the Mill Street household was broken up, Jane and Harry watched the last of the furniture stowed away in the van, then looked at George as if it were somehow disobliging of him to be alive. Finally Jane whispered: "We might as well go now, Harry —George'll be all right by himself till Uncle Joe comes—he said he'd be along as soon as he closed the shop."

Which made an excellent excuse to go about their respective affairs and leave a boy of seven alone in an empty house in which both his parents had recently died, there to await (with no lights and dusk approaching) the arrival of a man he had never seen before, and who, from mysterious hints and rumors he had heard, must surely be some kind of monster.

And about nine o'clock this legendary Uncle Joe, having paused longer than he intended at the Liberal Club, came striding along Mill Street to knock at Number 24. George could not, at that moment of panic, decide whether he were more frightened of the darkness or of his uncle; he could only crouch under the stairs until the knock was repeated. Then he decided that the unknown peril was worse and that he would not open the door at all. But in the meantime Uncle Joe had gone round to the back of the house and found a door there unlocked, so that he simply walked in, stumbling and making a great commotion in the dark while he struck matches and called for George.

George saw his face first of all in the light of the quick-spurting flame—not, perhaps, the most reassuring way for anyone bordering on hysteria to encounter a feared stranger. He saw a big reddish face, with bristling mustaches, tufts of hair sticking out of the nose and ears, and eyebrows which, owing to the shadow, seemed to reach across the entire forehead.

The result of all this was that by the time Uncle Joe, groping after a series of wild screams that jumped alarmingly from room to room, finally traced them to the corner of an upstairs cupboard, George had fainted and the old man had used up all his matches.

The only thing he could think of was to carry the boy downstairs in his arms and thence out of the house into the street. They had reached the corner before George came to, whereupon Uncle Joe, panting for breath, gladly set him down on the edge of the curb with a lamppost to lean against. Then, being a man of much kindness but little imagination, he could think of nothing further but to relight his pipe while the boy "got over it," whatever "it" was.

Presently George looked up from the curb, saw the big man bending over him, and, despite the now less terrifying eyebrows, would have raced away in renewed flight had there been any power left in his legs. But there seemed not to be, so he sat there helpless, resigned to the worst as he heard his captor fumbling around and muttering huskily: "Bugger it! No more matches—wasted 'em all looking for you, young shaver!"

Suddenly then, by a sort of miracle, the heartening message came through—that everything was *all right;* but only years afterwards was George able to reflect that in that same first kindly breath there had been the two things that had made his father call Uncle Joe a wicked man—namely, a "swear" and the smell of whisky.

All this was what *really* happened . . . but in the dream it did not always end like that; sometimes the fear of the stranger's footsteps in the empty house lasted till the crisis of waking.

And now, years later, while his son lay desperately ill in the room above, George dreamed of this fear again, and was wakened by the doctor's hand. "Sorry, George . . . but I think you'd best go up."

"Is it—is it—bad?"

"Pretty bad . . . this time."

George went upstairs, still with the agony of the dream pulsating in his veins; and then, from the bedroom doorway, he saw Livia's face. There was no fear in it as she glanced not to him, but to the doctor.

The doctor walked over to the bed, stooped for a moment, then looked up and slowly nodded.

.   .   .

One thing was now settled more definitely than ever; George would not leave Browdley, and if she should ever ask him again he would answer from a core of bitterness in his heart. But she did not even mention the matter. She seemed not to care where they lived any more, and if an absence of argument were the only test, then they were at peace during the days that followed. But George knew differently, and he knew that Livia knew also. It was no peace, but an armistice on terms, and one only tolerable so long as both parties fenced off large parts of their lives as individual territory.

They both grieved over Martin, and comforted each other up to the boundary line, but that was fixed, and beyond it lay inflexibility. When, for instance, she said a week or so later: "Tom Whaley telephoned while you were out to say that the Council reconvenes on the seventeenth—" George simply nodded, and went to his study.

She followed him, adding: "He wanted to know if you'd be there." She waited for him to reply, then said: "*I* don't mind you going, George. I don't mind being left alone in the evenings."

He answered: "Aye, I shall go."

"Perhaps you'd better let him know then—"

"Don't worry—I met him in the street after he telephoned you. I told him I'd be going."

And there was finality in that.

He went to the meeting and found there an atmosphere not only of warm personal sympathy, but of eagerness to accept him as a prophet; so that he scored, almost without opposition, the biggest personal triumph of his career. The housing scheme he had urged for years went through the first stage of its acceptance that very night; even his bitterest antagonists gave way, while to his friends he became manifestly the leader of a cause no longer lost. There was irony (unknown to any but himself) that at such a moment of easy victory he had never felt grimmer in spirit. When he reached home late that night Livia was in bed, and he would not disturb her, for the news he had did not seem enough excuse; she could read about it if she wished (and there was irony there too) in the pages of the next *Guardian*. But the excitements of the evening had made him sleepless, so he sat up in his study till daylight, reading and writing and thinking and working out in his mind the terms of the unspoken armistice.

One afternoon he found her with Fred, the messenger boy from the printing works, busily engaged in clearing up the yard behind the office that had always (as far back as anyone could remember) been a dumping ground for old papers, cardboard boxes, tin cans, and so on. It was such a small area, enclosed on two sides by buildings and on the remaining ones by high brick walls, that nobody had ever thought of any other use for it. But now, when she saw his curiosity, she asked if he would mind her turning it into a garden.

"Why, of course not," he answered, pleased that she should show such an interest. "But I doubt if anything'll grow there."

"We'll see," she said.

"I'll give you a hand with it if you like."

"No, there's no need. Fred will dig it over, and then I can do all the rest myself."

"What'll you plant?"

"I don't know."

"I'll get you some books about gardening if you like."

"Oh no, no . . . I don't want *books*."

And there was just the hint of a barb in that. It was as if she had chosen books as a symbol of *his* world, just as flowers were to be of *hers*. The books, too, were increasing all the time; some of them came as review copies addressed to the *Guardian* by publishers who did not realize how small and unimportant the paper was; many he bought, a few were sent him as chairman of this or that municipal committee. He had no collecting spirit, no special desire to make a show of what he had read. Yet as the books filled up the room, and new shelves had to be rigged till they covered most of the wall space, he could not help a little pride in them to match Livia's pride (and his own too) in the transformed dumping ground below. And his pride grew definite from the moment that Councillor Whaley, visiting him once while Livia was out, exclaimed: "George, I reckon this must be just about the best library in Browdley—in anyone's house, I mean. What does your wife think about it?"

"*Livia?* . . . Why . . . why do you ask that?"

"Only because she once worked in a library herself—I thought maybe books were in her line too."

"No," George answered. "She likes gardening better." And he took Tom to the window and pointed down to the rectangle of cleared ground. "She says she'll plant roses."

"Why, that'll be fine." And then as an afterthought: "Nobody'll see it, though—except you. Maybe that's the idea—to give you something to look at."

George smiled. "I don't know, Tom. But *my* idea is that it gives her an interest in life. She needs it—since losing the boy."

"Naturally. But I'll tell you what, George, if you don't mind plain speaking from an old bachelor." He whispered something in George's ear about Livia's youth and having more children. "Aye," George replied heavily, and changed the subject.

. . . . .

Martin's death seemed to bring him into immediate friendship with Father Wendover. Neither ever referred to the curious "coincidence" that both must often have recollected; nor did the priest talk much from the standpoint of his profession. He showed, however, considerable interest in George's family background, and once he said: "You'd have made a fine upstanding atheist, George, if only your father had lived a bit longer."

"Maybe," George answered, "but Uncle Joe didn't continue the training, and the result is I'm no more an atheist today than you are. . . . Not that he was *against* religion, mind you. He even sent me to Sunday School."

"Why?"

"To be frank, I think it was because he thought Sunday Schools were a good way of giving kids something to do when they were too dressed up to do anything else."

"An appalling idea."

"Oh, I don't know. He was all right." George mused for a moment. "It's odd we should be discussing him, because I dreamed about him the night Martin died. . . . Aye, he was all right. And he liked his Sundays too—in his own way. To my father they were days of gloom and mystery and foreboding, and that was the way he wanted 'em, but to my uncle they were nice comfortable days when you had a late breakfast and took a walk along the canal bank while dinner was cooking and then had a snooze in the afternoon and high tea at five o'clock—and that was the way *he* wanted 'em."

"Did he ever go to church?"

"Aye, when he felt like it. It's true he felt like it less and less as he grew older, but he still counted church as part of a proper Sunday program. He used to say he'd attend regularly if only Aunt Flo were a bit better on her feet, and he'd have liked to put more in the collection plate if only he hadn't lost so much in cotton investments, and he'd have been proud as punch if I'd had a voice to sing in the choir—but I hadn't. . . . Altogether what he'd have liked to do was so well-meaning you could hardly call him irreligious, while what he actually did was so little that he interfered with nobody— not even me."

Wendover, having watched George's face during all this with a growing conviction that its look of guilelessness was sincere, now slowly smiled. "Is that your portrait of a good man, George?"

"Well, he was good to me," George answered, simply.

Trade remained sluggish in the town, but the *Guardian,* due mainly to Livia's reorganization, began to show a small profit. George was then able to give her more money, but she seemed to care as little about it as about anything else over which he had any control. Yet she did not mope, brood, or look particularly unhappy. Nor did she nag, upbraid, or quarrel. It was merely that she seemed in some peculiar way to have withdrawn into a world of her own, where George was not invited nor could have followed her if he had been.

One evening early in 1921 he came home after a long day out of the town on municipal business, having left in the morning before she was awake. But now, hearing him enter, she came scampering down the stairs, and at the instant of recognition he gasped with the sensation of pain suddenly switched off inside him. Then, as always when he saw her afresh after even a few hours' absence, recognition dissolved into a curious feeling of never having seen her before, but of experiencing some primitive thrill that the few years of their marriage had neither enhanced nor made stale. Whatever that was to him, it had been from their first moment of meeting and would be till their last; it was something simple that only became complex when he sought to analyze it. Just now he was glad to hold her in a brief hug of welcome and feel that everything was miraculously all right, even if it wasn't, and that nothing needed explaining, even if it did.

He said he was sorry he was late, and she answered brightly: "Oh, that's all right—the dinner won't spoil. Lamb stew—can't you smell it?"

He sniffed hard and joyfully; lamb stew was one of his favorite dishes, and he would relish it all the more from thinking that perhaps she had prepared it to please him.

"Ah," he gasped.

"And we'll have it in the kitchen to save time," she said, evidently reaching an impromptu decision. "Annie—did you hear? We'll all eat in the kitchen, so hurry up."

That was like her; the knack of taking short cuts to get what she wanted—the quick plan, or change of plan, generally based on something so elemental that only a child could have avoided the mistake of reading into it more than was there. This eating in the kitchen, for instance, had nothing to do with any feeling on Livia's part that Annie was an equal (only George could, and did, sometimes think of such a thing); really, it was just that Livia was hungry and, as with all her desires, could not bear to be kept waiting. George was generally amused by this, and often quoted the occasion when, having attended a Council meeting at which he presided, she had left exclaiming: "Oh, George, I'll *never* go to one of those affairs again! They drive me silly—all that proposing and seconding and moving the nominations closed and appointing a subcommittee to report to the next meeting. . . . No wonder nothing ever gets done!" But something *does* get done, had been George's slightly hurt rejoinder—unspoken, however, because he knew she would then argue that what he called *something* was not much more than what she called next to nothing. . . .

But now, walking after her into the kitchen, his spirits rose, crowning the physical ease that came over him as he entered the warm small room and sat at the scrubbed table between the gas stove and the meat safe. A curious half-painful happiness clutched at him as he watched her across the table top; she was, he had to admit, as sheerly fascinating to him as ever, with those dark, almost violet-blue eyes that glowed rather than sparkled and gave her whole face a rapt, almost mystic expression; the hair so straw-pale that it could look white against mere gold, the mouth too big for the nose, but the nose so small and perfect that he had sometimes thought that if he were a sculptor he would model it and stick it on a model of someone else's face—yet he had never found that more matching face, and doubtless never would.

She was talking—most unusually for her—about events of the day, conditions in Europe, and how interesting it must be to visit foreign countries now that the basic comforts of peacetime travel had begun to return.

"Aye," he agreed. "I'll bet it's interesting. I've got a book about postwar Europe if you'd like to—"

"Oh, I don't mean *books,* George. It isn't here where you can understand things always—" and she touched her head—"it's more like *this*—" and he expected her to touch her heart, but instead she put up her small fist and shook it in his face, laughing meanwhile. "Oh George—you and your books and meetings and speeches. . . ."

He did not mind the mockery he was accustomed to, especially as she seemed so happy over it. She went on chattering till the meal was ended; then, as they left the kitchen for Annie to wash up, he said—and it was the truth: "Livia, that's the best lamb stew I ever tasted. How about a cup of tea with me in the study before I get down to some work?"

"You've got work to do tonight?"

"Aye—just a bit to finish up. The Education Committee meets tomorrow and I've got to hammer at them again for that new school."

She accompanied him to the study and presently Annie brought in tea. He was so happy, sitting there with her, in his own room with the books in it, and with her own garden below the window outside. And suddenly, as if to signalize the height of his content, the vagrant thought came to him that this was the moment, if a man were a smoker, to light up a pipe, or a cigar, or a cigarette. He laughed to himself at the notion, and then had to tell her what he had been laughing at.

"Well, why don't you?" she asked. "I've got some cigarettes."

"Nay . . . I was only joking, Livia."

"But George, if you *want* to—"

"I don't want to—it was just that now would be the time if I ever did want to."

And then he saw her face cloud over as if something in his words had sent her into a new mood. She went to the window, stared out over the dark garden for a moment, then turned round and said very quietly: "Now's the time for me too. George, I want to leave you."

"*What?*"

The happiness—so passing, so brief—drained away from mind and body, so that he felt older by years within seconds. "Livia . . . *what? What's that?*"

"I—I *must* leave you, George."

"But Livia—*why*—what on earth—" He was on his feet and crossing the room towards her.

"No, George—don't—don't. . . . Or you can if you like—I don't mind. It isn't that I've changed in how I feel toward you. And there's nobody else . . . but I'm not happy, George, since Martin died."

"Livia—my little Livia—neither am I—you know that—but after all—" And then he could only add: "I thought you *did* look happy tonight."

"That's because I'd made up my mind."

"To do what?"

"To leave you, George."

Then she went into further details. It seemed that years before (and he had never known this) she had been to some school in Geneva and had made friends with local people there; she had lately been in correspondence with them and they had asked her to visit them and stay as long as she liked. So she had accepted.

"But . . ." And even amidst his unhappiness the germ of optimism began to sprout. "But Livia—that's another matter altogether! You have friends in Geneva, so you want to spend a holiday with them! Well—why not, for heaven's sake?" And he began to laugh. "My little Livia—what a dramatic way of putting it—that you're going to *leave* me! Of course you are—for as long as you like —I daresay you *do* need a holiday—I'd come with you if I could spare the time—but as you know, I can't. I don't mind you going at all—or rather, I don't mind so much, because although I'll miss you I'll be happy knowing you're having such a good time."

"I may not have a good time, George."

"Of course you will, and when you've had enough of it you'll come back to smoky old Browdley like a new woman. I'll take care of things here while you're away—I'll look after Becky—"

"Oh no, I'll take Becky with me."

"You will? . . . All right, if you want. Anything you want. . . . You're run-down, Livia—a holiday's just what you need— I'm sure a doctor would say so. And don't worry about money— I'll go to the bank tomorrow and see if there's a bit extra I can find for you. . . ."

"Thank you, George, but I have enough. . . . And now I know you want to work."

"I did want to, but I don't know as I'll do much after this. When —when are you going to go?"

"Tomorrow. I have all the tickets and things and I'm pretty nearly packed."

"Oh Livia, *Livia*. . . ." And for a moment the battle was on again between despair and optimism, the latter winning by a hair-line in the end. "All right, Livia—all right."

"Good night, George. Please do your work. *Please.*" And she ran out of the room.

A little later, when he went up to bed, she was asleep. He smiled gently and with relief as he saw her thus, for he had already schooled and drilled his optimism, and that she could sleep so soon, as calmly as a child, was reassurance to all his hopes; while into his bones, as he watched her quiet breathing through slightly parted lips, there came an ache of pity for her—as if in sleep she told the plain wordless truth, that it was not in his power to make her happy enough. She was so small, so mysterious, and to him a part of something so incurable that he wondered, watching her in the light that came in from a street lamp, what would have happened had he been a shade less eloquent at that Council meeting three years earlier—if, for instance, the voting had been seventeen to fifteen *against* the motion instead of *for* it? Why then, so far as he could see, he would never have met Livia at all. And he would have taken that second examination according to plan and have obtained his university degree. And possibly also he would have won the by-election that would have sent him to Parliament as Member for Browdley. And also he would not have known such happiness, or such unhappiness either. . . .

"My little Livia," he whispered, stooping to touch her forehead with his lips. He knew she would not wake.

The next morning she left. He traveled also as far as Mulcaster, shepherding her and her luggage and her dog during that first stage of the journey, and fending off all sad thoughts by the resolute pre-tense that it was just a holiday. He was disappointed when a friend and fellow Councillor entered the same compartment at Browdley station; it was hard to concentrate upon a discussion of local political news, but then, later on, he thought it was probably easier than to have made conversation with Livia. She sat cozily, almost demurely, in a corner by the window, staring with quiet interest upon the familiar scenes. The hour-long journey, with stops at every station, built up in George a certain resignation, so that when the train reached the terminus he was well able to take command of the situation when Councillor Ridyard noticed the luggage. "Why, what's all this?" Ridyard exclaimed, reading the labels. "*Geneva?* Who's going to Geneva?"

"My wife," said George, as if it were the most natural thing in the world. "She's visiting friends there."

"Well, well! You don't say! Just for the moment I thought they'd appointed you to the League of Nations, and I was wondering how on earth we'd manage without you on the Housing Committee. . . ."

At which they all three laughed.

Just before George saw her off on the London train, Ridyard's joke put him in mind of something to say at a time when it is always hardest to think of anything to say to anybody. "Geneva must be pretty interesting these days, Livia. There's probably a place for the public at the League of Nations meetings—you might find some of them worth looking in at . . . but of course they do everything in French, don't they?"

"Do they?" she answered. "But I know French, anyhow."

"You do?"

"Yes."

"I never knew you did. You never told me."

"I never told you lots of things."

"Aye, that's about it. . . ."

And then the train began to move, and there was no more time for anything but the last shouted good-byes.

Two hours later he was back in Browdley, desperately unhappy, fighting again to believe that it was just a holiday. But after a little while to get used to it he established a fairly permanent victory over his misgivings; for she wrote several letters, quite normal ones, reporting what sort of time she was having, where she went, and whom she met. And he, in return, reported upon his own doings in Browdley—his continuing struggle to maneuver the housing scheme towards its first stage of accomplishment. When she had been away a couple of months she wrote that she had found a job with a tourist agency, conducting travel parties about Switzerland and Austria, and this, though it seemed to make her near return less likely, reinforced his belief that she was benefiting by the change. After all, it was quite natural not to stay too long as a guest in a friend's house, and if a temporary job offered itself, was it not sensible to take it? What really cheered him was the knowledge that those tourist-guide jobs *were* temporary—the season began about May and did not last beyond October. So that when October should come . . .

But before October came, Lord Winslow came, on that first of September, 1921, to lay the foundation stone of the first unit of the Mill Street Housing Scheme.

Part Four

———— ✦ ————

BETWEEN 1921 and 1938 much happened in the world; America had the biggest boom and then the biggest slump in history; England went on the gold standard and then off again; Germany rose from defeat to power and then from power to arrogance; flying became a commonplace and radio the fifth estate; people changed from being bored with the last war to being scared of the next— with one short interval of cynical, clinical absorption.

And those were the years during which, in Browdley, the Mill Street Housing Scheme was progressing unit by unit.

One afternoon in the first week of October, 1938, the Mayor of Browdley presided at official ceremonies to mark the scheme's completion. It had taken a long time, with many intervals of delay and inaction, but at last it was finished, and clusters of cheerful little red-brick semi-detached cottages covered the entire area of what had once been slums. George Boswell himself was also cheerful; in his early fifties he wore both his years and his mayoralty well; except for gray hair he had not changed much, it was remarked, since the day so long before when the foundation stone had been laid upon the first unit.

"Remember that day, George?" someone buttonholed him afterwards. "You had Lord Thingumbob here, and my wife slipped on the way home and busted her ankle—that's how it sticks in my mind."

This ancient mishap seemed to amuse the husband more than it did the Mayor, whose face momentarily clouded over as he answered: "Aye, I remember that day."

"And so you should, after the fight you've had. Seventeen years, George, and without a Council majority till lately, so that you couldn't vote 'em down, you just had to wear 'em out. . . . Well, it's all over now, and a big job well done."

"Aye, but there's plenty more to do."

The cloud then lifted, and the Mayor was seen to be enjoying the triumph he deserved. True, there was no noble lord on hand this time, but there was to have been a personage of equal if not superior importance, none other than a Cabinet Minister—and everyone knew that his absence was not George's fault, but Hitler's. George did not like Hitler—for other reasons than that; but now that the Pact of Munich had been signed he could not help seeing a certain symbolism in what had happened—the removal of the threat of war by a last-minute miracle so that the final ceremonies of the Mill Street Housing Scheme could take place as planned. And a further touch: the very same workmen who had erected the flags and platform had been taken right off the job of building an air-raid shelter under the Town Hall. George mentioned this in his speech, and again in a *Guardian* editorial that concluded:—

We people of Browdley—quiet folks who ask for nothing more than to do our work in peace and live out our lives in decency— we do not profess to understand the complicated geographic, ethno-graphic, and historical problem of the Sudetenland which has come so close to plunging a whole continent into the infinite disaster of war. We cannot be sure even now that the settlement just reached will be administered fairly to all parties, or whether, in certain phases of the negotiations, the threat of the sword did not prevail over the scales of justice. What we *do* know, by and large, is that at the eleventh hour a decision has been made that every honest citizen of every country will endorse in principle—because it is AGAINST WAR. Let every man of Browdley whose death sentence has thus been commuted, let every woman of Browdley who will not now face sorrow and bereave-ment, let every child of Browdley who will grow up to inherit a happier world—let them face anew THE TASKS OF PEACE AND RECONSTRUCTION.

After the ceremonies George walked home across the town and had tea alone in his study—the same study, though enlarged by a bay window built over the garden, as well as by inclusion of a book-lined alcove that had formerly been part of the lobby. For George's library was now more certainly than ever the largest private one in Browdley, the years having just about doubled its contents.

Everything else was much the same, including Annie, and the printing office, and Will Spivey. When George handed in his Munich editorial, the old fellow, a little crustier but otherwise unchanged by the years, read it through, grunted, and said at length: "Do you want this *as well as* the one about the new sewage scheme?"

"No," answered George. "Instead of."

"What'll I do with the sewage one then?"

"Keep it till next week."

But by the next morning George's slight misgiving about Munich had thriven, and he took the opportunity to cut out that final sentence. Instead he wrote:—

. . . For the rest, we must wait and see whether Hitler's word is to be trusted. If his desire for "peace in our time" is as sincere as our own, we should expect to see some corresponding reduction in German armaments, and until we have evidence of this we can only continue, however reluctantly, the process of bringing our own armaments up to a minimum safety level. THAT THE GOVERNMENT WILL DO THIS WE DO NOT DOUBT.

George's optimism had merely swerved in another direction.

.   .   .

Like most Englishmen, he was shocked rather than surprised when war came. Nineteen thirty-eight had been the year of hypnosis, the sleepwalk into tragedy, but the first half of 1939 brought a brand of disillusionment that made the actual outbreak of hostilities almost an anticlimax. After that there was so much to be done, and so little time for self-scrutiny, that George was spared the full chagrin of awakening; like all mayors of towns, he found his office had become practically a branch of the national government, with his own tasks and personal responsibilities greatly increased. He shouldered them with gusto from before dawn till often past midnight, while England slowly dissolved into a new era—slowly, it seemed, because it had been natural to expect change and catastrophe overnight. When no bombs fell on London, and when all continued to be quiet along the Western Front, a curious hangover of illusion recurred; it was a "phony" war, said some; perhaps it was not even a war at all. One morning at his editorial desk, aware of this unreality and not knowing how else to handle it, George indulged in a little spree of optimism. After all, he reflected, the good citizens of Browdley deserved a pick-me-up; they had done wonders in response to all his war-emergency appeals, had enlisted splendidly for air-raid protection and civilian defense, and were resolutely creating a strong Home Front while across the Channel hundreds of their sons were already facing the enemy, but so far, thank heaven, not being killed by him. It was astonishing, compared with the First World War, how few casualties there were along that Western Front. And thinking things out, George composed the following:—

We have now been at war for almost six months, and though it would be premature to offer ourselves any congratulations, nevertheless we may justifiably wonder whether the Germans are able to do so either. True, their tanks and mechanized armies have scored victories over the farm carts and cavalry of Poland, but at the cost of overrunning that country they have brought against them a factor which, with memories of a quarter of a century ago, must chill the blood of even the most ardent Nazi—namely, THE FULL FIGHTING STRENGTH OF ENGLAND AND FRANCE. For today that strength is assembled, not in a line of half-flooded trenches hastily improvised, but along the mightiest system of steel and concrete fortifications ever constructed by man—THE MAGINOT LINE. No wonder that the Nazi Juggernaut has satisfied itself with triumphs elsewhere. No wonder that (as some people are whispering, almost as if there were a mystery about it)—"nothing is happening" on the Western Front. If nothing is happening, then surely that is the measure of our victory, and of the enemy's defeat. For that is precisely what the Maginot Line was built for—in order THAT NOTHING SHOULD HAPPEN.

George thought this rather good, for it rationalized something that had begun to puzzle even himself slightly—that so-called phony war. But of course the Maginot Line was the clue. A high military officer had shown him some photographs of it—after which the whole business became no puzzle at all. A pity the general public couldn't clear their minds in the same way, but naturally the photographs were secret; and it was to substitute for them, in a sense, that George had felt impelled to write his editorial.

. . .

Perhaps as a result of this, he wrote fewer editorials after the war ceased to be phony. For one thing, he was overworked, and if he ever found himself with an hour to spare he preferred to drop in at St. Patrick's to see Father Wendover, who had long been his best friend. As George had somehow suspected from the first, Wendover was not only agile-minded but considerably sympathetic to George's work in the town. He had always held what were considered "advanced" ideas for a priest, with the result that he more often had to defend himself for being one than for having them; and that, he claimed, was as good for him as for his opponents.

Such controversies had flourished in peacetime, and George had often joined in them; during the war, however, and especially after the Norwegian fiasco and the French collapse, nothing seemed to matter but the bare facts of life and death, disaster and survival, enemy and friend. And George found Wendover congenial because, beneath the surface of the proud ecclesiastic, there lay a deep humility which, in a curious way, matched his own. Thus it was to Wendover that George took his thoughts during the difficult days of 1940, and there was one day, just after Dunkirk, when he brought over some notes of a speech he was due to make to a local patriotic organization. He wanted to know what Wendover thought about it.

And the latter, while he was listening, smiled slightly. Here was George Boswell, Mayor of Browdley—this decent, hard-working, well-meaning, quite talented fellow—a good citizen and a stout-hearted friend—a man whose powers of leadership were considerable and might have been greater had he not been so personally likable, and had he not liked to be so likable—here was George Boswell, with the Germans poised along the European coast line from Narvik to Bordeaux, thinking it really mattered what he said to a few hundred people gathered together in Browdley Co-operative Hall. But then, as an honest man, Wendover had to admit that a similar comment might have been made on his own sermons at such a time . . . for were George's speeches of any less *practical* importance? So he listened patiently and said, at the end: "Not bad, George—not bad at all. Cheerful, anyhow."

"You mean it's *too* cheerful?"

"Well, you always were an optimist, weren't you?" Then he smiled, but it was a rather grim, troubled smile. "You know, George, I don't want to discourage you, but things do look pretty bad. We've lost our army and all its equipment, and we've about one plane for every ten the Germans have, and the Channel's only a ditch nowadays. . . ."

George's eyes widened with a sort of bewilderment. "Aye, I've thought of all that myself. I've even wondered—sometimes—if they've got a chance."

"You mean to invade us?"

"Aye."

"They might have. Recognizing the fact shouldn't alter our resolve to fight to the last man. On the contrary, it's the basis of it."

George swallowed hard, then said, after a pause of gloomy thoughtfulness: "So it boils down to this—we might even *lose* the bloody war?"

"I think we'd be fools to assume that it's impossible. But of course I don't say we shall. I'm only speaking the thoughts that came into my mind while I was listening to you—perhaps because you *have* been wrong before when you've made such gallant prophecies."

George suddenly stuffed the notes of his speech into his pocket. "Then by God I'll be wrong again!" he almost shouted. "After all, as you say, I've got no reputation to lose. Aye, and I'll not do it by halves either! I'll tell folks that Hitler's on the verge of his first great defeat, and that whatever else the Germans succeed in, they'll never lick England!"

So George did this, and it was among his most quotable prophetic utterances. It was certainly the only one he had ever conquered a qualm about, and one of the very few that proved completely correct.

.   .   .

But as the summer months passed and the air assaults that had been expected a year before began now upon London and the large provincial cities, it became clear that this was not like the First World War, when every rostrum and pulpit had resounded to the call of a somewhat romantic patriotism. George could remember the mayor of that day orating in Browdley market square about the injustices of poor little Belgium, and thereafter luring recruits from the audience as a revivalist preacher extracts penitents. Thank goodness we don't have *that* to do, thought George more than once as he began his work on those fateful autumn days; and besides, it wasn't poor little Belgium any more, but poor little England—yet was there any Englishman who wouldn't somehow resent that phrase? Why, even poor little Browdley didn't seem to suit. Indeed, as George went about his wartime business in the town, visiting factories and homes and organizations, it seemed to him it had never been less "poor," in any sense of the word. And it wasn't so little either. One day, in company with other local mayors, he was taken up in an R.A.F. plane (his first flight), and when he stared down from three thousand feet upon the roofs of the town, he couldn't help exclaiming: "Why, it looks like a city!" To which an Air Force officer replied: "Let's hope it doesn't, or it'll be put on the blitz list." For Browdley had so far escaped, though bombs had fallen in the neighborhood at several places.

And there were other curious things about the war—for instance, that even with all the new food-rationing restrictions, many Browdley families were being better fed than in peacetime, because they now had full employment and money to spend. And the children in the schools, so the Medical Officer reported, were actually healthier than ever before in the history of the town.

It was nervous tension that weighed most heavily during that first terrible year of the real war—the loss of sleep through air-raid warnings even if the raiders did not come or merely passed over; the extra hours of work without holidays, the ten-hour shifts plus overtime of men and women desperately striving to repair the losses at Dunkirk; the irritations of tired folk waiting in long lines for buses to and from their factories; the continual wear and tear on older persons and those of weaker fiber. But on others the tensions, hardships, occasional dangers, and ever-present awareness of possible danger, seemed to have a toughening effect; many men who had worked all day found they were no worse off attending Home

Guard drills in the evenings or patrolling the streets as air-raid wardens than they would have been in the pubs and cinemas of their peacetime choice. And in this George discovered (to his surprise, for he had never taken deliberate exercise and had rarely given his physical condition a thought) that he belonged to the tougher breed. He was fortunate. There was even pleasure to him, after a hard day of mainly sedentary work, in transferring mind and body to physical tasks of air-raid defense, in the long walks up and down familiar pavements, in chats with passers-by, in hours afforded for private thinking, in the chance of comradeship with men he would otherwise have missed getting to know. Not that he ever romanticized about it; he was ready to admit that any fun he derived from what, in a sane world, would be a waste of time was due to the fact that so far there had been no actual raids; if there were, he did not expect to enjoy them any more than the next man. But for all that, there *were* good moments, supreme moments, and if there were bad ones ahead, he would take them too, as and when they came, sharing them with his fellow citizens as straightforwardly as he shared with them so many cups of hot, strong, sugary tea.

A few things gave him emotions in which pleasure, if it could be called that, came from an ironic appreciation of events. For instance, that the old Channing Mill in Mill Street had at last found a use; its unwanted machinery was junked for scrap metal, while its large ground floor, leveled off, served as a headquarters and mess room for the air-raid wardens.

And also that Richard Felsby's land, which the old man had decided too late to give the town for a municipal park, had been compulsorily requisitioned for the drills and maneuverings of the Home Guard.

But no use could be found for Stoneclough. It remained a derelict in even greater solitude now that there were no holidays to tempt Browdley folks on hikes and picnics.

.   .   .

George was an exceedingly busy man. Not only was his printing business getting all the work it could handle, but his position as

Mayor counted for more and more as the national and local governments of the country became closely integrated. For the first time in his life he had the feeling that he really represented the town, not merely his own party on the Town Council; and it was a satisfactory feeling, especially as his tasks were far too numerous to permit him to luxuriate in it. He was not a luxuriator, anyhow. And when he came home after a fourteen-hour spell of work, it was rarely with time left over to indulge a mood. He did not even read in his study most nights, but made himself a cup of tea and went immediately to bed and to sleep.

The ordeal of the great cities continued. Night after night the wail of sirens and thudding of gunfire wakened Browdley, and sometimes a wide glow on one of the horizons gave a clue as to which of the greater near-by cities were being attacked. One night there came an emergency call for help from Mulcaster, and George accompanied several truckloads of Browdley men in a top-speed drive to the stricken area. Till then all his fire fighting and similar work had been a rehearsal; but that night, from soon after midnight till long past dawn, he knew what the real thing was, and of course, like all real things, it was different. Crawling into smoking ruins while bombs were still falling in the neighborhood, giving first aid to the injured before a doctor could arrive, he directed his squad of co-workers under conditions which, despite all the training they had had, were in a dreadful and profound sense novel.

A youngish doctor asked him when the raid was over: "Been in this sort of thing before?"

George shook his head.

"I'd have thought you had, from the way you handled those stretchers."

"Oh, I've done *that* before."

"The last war?"

"Aye."

"How would you compare it—this sort of thing—and that?"

George answered irritably: "I wouldn't. And nor would you if you could."

The men returned to Browdley with scorched and blackened faces, minor injuries, and a grim weariness of soul which, after sleep, changed to bitterness, determination, cheerfulness, even ribaldry—so strange is the alchemy of experience on men of differing make-up.

On George, after that first irritable outburst (which he later regretted as being needlessly melodramatic and quite out of character), the principal effect was a decision to do something which, at any previous time, would have been an acknowledgment of defeat, but which now, the way he could look at it, seemed more like victory over himself. He gave up the *Guardian*. He did not even try to sell it; he abandoned it. For years it had never more than just paid its way, and sometimes not even that; but the real issue, in George's mind, was not financial at all. He suddenly realized that the paper had been costing too much in human effort, including his own, that could better be devoted elsewhere.

"It's one thing with another," he explained to Wendover. "Will Spivey's getting old—it's all he can do to manage the job printing—I'll have to keep *that* going, of course—it's my living. And then there've been newsprint difficulties, and you can't get paper boys any more, and I've just lost another man to the Army. . . . And besides all that, I haven't the time myself nowadays. If we should get a big raid on Browdley one of these nights, we'd all have our hands full. I know what I'm talking about, after what I saw in Mulcaster. Because I'd be responsible for things here, in a sort of way. There's a lot more work in being Mayor than there used to be."

"And I haven't heard any complaints about how you're doing it, George."

"I'll do it better, though, when the paper's off my hands."

"You're sure you won't regret not being an editor any more?"

"*Editor?*" George grinned. "What did I edit? Births, marriages, funerals, meetings, whist drives, church bazaars. The *Advertiser*'ll do that just as well—and one paper's enough in a town of this size. Most folks always did prefer the *Advertiser,* anyway."

"But you used to write your own stuff in the *Guardian* sometimes."

"Aye, and there you come to another reason why I'm giving it up. D'you remember when I came to talk to you about that speech I made just after Dunkirk?"

"You mean the one in which you prophesied that Hitler would

never lick us? Yes, I remember. And I'm beginning to think you were right."

"For once. But as you said, I'd been pretty wrong before. I'm glad you said that because it made me think about it, and I never realized how wrong I actually had been till the other day I got out the back files of the *Guardian* and reread some of my old editorials. By God, they were wrong. After Locarno, for instance, I wrote about France and Germany finally burying the hatchet, and after Munich I said that even though the settlement wasn't perfect, at any rate it might keep the peace of Europe for a generation . . . and only a few months ago I was blabbing that the Germans couldn't break through in the west because of the Maginot Line. . . . Mind you, I was always perfectly sincere at the time, but that only makes it worse. Seems to me, Harry, I'm just not cut out to deal with world affairs."

"You've been as right as a good many of the politicians."

"Aye, and that's no compliment. Maybe it was a good thing I never got to Westminster—I'd have been just another fool with a bigger platform to spout from. . . . And another thing occurred to me—I was thinking about it last night on warden's duty—and it's this—that the nearer I stay to Browdley the more use I am and the fewer mistakes I make. Look round the place—I have done *some* good things—not many, not enough—but they're here, such as they are, and I don't have to try to forget 'em same as I do the stuff I used to put in the paper. . . . Look at the Mill Street Housing Scheme, and the new Council School, and the Municipal Hospital, and the electric power station the Government took over. Aye, and the sewage farm, if you like—that's mine too—remember what a fight I had over it? Those things are *real*, Harry—they exist—they're something attempted, something done. They're what I've been right about, whereas Czechoslovakia's something I've been wrong about. So give me Browdley."

"You've got Browdley, George."

"Aye, and it's got me. Till the war's over, anyhow."

"And afterwards, perhaps."

"Don't be too sure. There's young chaps coming along as'll make me a back number someday, but they're in uniform now, most of 'em. . . . 'Vote for Boswell and Your Children's Future'—that

was my old election slogan. I hope nobody else remembers it. I'd
rather be remembered for the lavatories I put in the market square.
Because they're good lavatories, as lavatories go. Whereas the children's future that I talked so much about . . ."

Wendover smiled. "I get your point, George. But don't over-
simplify it. And don't throw all your books on world affairs in the
fire."

"Oh no, I won't do that. In fact when I've got the time I'll
study more of 'em. I want to find out why we've all been let in for
what we have. And I want to find out why folks ten times better
educated than me have made the same mistakes."

"Maybe because education hasn't much to do with it, George."
Wendover added: "And another thing—don't be too humble about
yourself."

George thought a moment, then came out with one of those dev-
astatingly sincere things that endeared him to his opponents even
oftener than to his friends. "Oh, don't you worry—I'm not as
humble as I sound. That's what Livia once said. . . ."

He did not often mention her now, and when he did the name
slipped out casually, by accident, giving him neither embarrassment
nor a pang. So much time can do.

But the remark gave Wendover the cue to ask: "By the way,
heard anything of her lately?"

"No, I suppose she's still out there."

And then, after a silence, the subject was changed.

                    .   .   .

Even in Browdley by now the affair was almost forgotten, and
George could assess with some impartiality the extent to which it
had damaged his career. Probably it had lost him his chance at the
general election of 1923, though his subsequent failure at two other
Parliamentary elections might well have happened in any case. Undoubtedly the divorce had alienated some of his early supporters,
especially when (due to the legal technique of such things in those
days) it had been made to seem that he himself was the guilty
party. Many of his friends knew this to be untrue, but a few did
not, and it was always a matter liable to be brought up by an
unscrupulous opponent, like the old accusation that he had put his

wife on the municipal payroll. But time had had its main effect, not so much in dulling memories, but in changing the moral viewpoints even of those who imagined theirs to be least changeable, so that the whole idea of divorce, which had been a shocking topic in the twenties, was now, in the forties, rather a stale one. George knew that a great many young people in the town neither knew nor would have been much interested in the details that had so scandalized their parents.

Those details included Livia's remarriage, at the earliest legal date, to the Honorable Jeffrey Winslow, who had given up a diplomatic career to take some job in Malaya. Except that Lord Winslow died in 1925 and left a large fortune, some of which must have gone to the younger son, George knew nothing more. The Winslow name did not get into the general news, and George did not read the kind of papers in which, if anywhere, it would still appear. But when Singapore fell, early in 1942, he could not suppress a recurrent preoccupation, hardly to be called anxiety; it made him ask the direct question if ever he met anyone likely to know the answer and unlikely to know of his own personal relationship. "I think they must have got away," he was told once, on fairly high authority. It satisfied him to believe that the fairly high authority had not said this merely because it was the easiest thing to say.

·   ·   ·

Those years, 1941 and 1942, contained long intervals of time during which it might almost have been said that nothing was happening in Browdley while so much was happening in the rest of the world. But that, of course, was an illusion; everything was happening, but in a continuous melting flow of social and economic change; the war, as it went on, had become more like an atmosphere to be breathed with every breath than a series of events to be separately experienced. Even air raids and the threat of them dropped to a minimum, while apathy, tiredness, and simple human wear-and-tear offered problems far harder to tackle. But there were cheerful days among the dark ones, days when the Mayor of Browdley looked round his little world and saw that it was—well, not good, but better than it might have been. And worse, naturally, than it should have been. Sometimes his almost incurable optimism remounted, reaching the same flash point at which it always exploded into indignation against those old Victorian mill masters with no thought in their minds but profit, and the jerry-builders who had aided and abetted them in nothing less than the creation of Browdley itself. Yet out of that shameless grab for fortunes now mostly lost had come a place where men could have stalwart dreams. George realized this when—a little doubtfully, for he thought it might be regarded as almost frivolous in wartime—he arranged for an exhibition of postwar rehousing plans in the Town Hall—architects' sketches (optimism on paper) of what could be done with Browdley if only the war were won and the tragedy of peacetime unemployment were not repeated. And by God, he thought, it *wouldn't* be repeated—not if he had anything to do with it; and at that he wandered off in mind into a stimulating postwar crusade.

* * *

One day, over two years later, he was visiting a large hospital near Mulcaster on official business; as chairman of a regional welfare association it fell to him to organize co-operation between the hospital authorities and various local citizen groups. He was good at this kind of organizing, and he was good because he was human; with a proper disregard of red tape he combined a flair for sidetracking well-meaning cranks and busybodies that was the admiration of all who saw it in operation. Indeed, by his fifty-ninth year, and by the sixth year of the Second World War, he had won for himself a local importance that had become almost as regional as many of the associations and committees on which he served. More and more frequently, within a radius that took in Mulcaster and other large cities, his name would be mentioned with a touch of legendary allusiveness; somebody or other somewhere, puzzled momentarily about something, would say to someone else: "I'll tell you what, let's see if we can get hold of old George. . . ." And if then the question came: "Who's he?"—the answer would be: "Just the Mayor of Browdley, but pretty good at this sort of thing"—the implication being that George's official position gave only a small hint of the kind of service he could render. And if a further question were asked: "Where's Browdley?"—the answer to that might

well be the devastating truth: "Oh, one of those awful little manu-
facturing towns—the kind that were nearly bankrupt before the
war and are now booming like blazes."

After a meeting of the hospital board George was taken over the
premises, and here too he was good; he knew how to say cheery
words to soldiers without either mawkishness or patronage. And if
any of the men were from Browdley or district he would make a
point of drawing them into neighborly gossip about local affairs. It
was noticeable then that his accent became somewhat more
"Browdley" than usual, as if *how* as well as *what* he spoke made
instinctive communion with those whose roots were his own.

On this occasion his tour of the wards was to be followed by
tea in the head surgeon's room; and on the way there, waiting with
his nurse escort for an elevator, he happened to glance at a list of
names attached to a notice board near by. One of them was
"Winslow." It gave him a slow and delayed shock that did not
affect the naturalness of his question; she answered that the list
was of patients occupying private rooms along an adjacent corridor—all of them serious cases and most of them war casualties. He
did not question her further, but a few moments later, meeting the
head surgeon and others of the hospital staff, he found himself
too preoccupied to join in general conversation; the name was
already echoing disconcertingly in his mind—Winslow . . .
Winslow. . . . Not such a common name, yet not so uncommon
either. Surely it would be too much of a coincidence—and yet
those coincidences *did* happen. At least it was worth inquiry.

So he asked, forgetting to care whether any of those present
knew anything of his own personal affairs: "I noticed a name on
my way here . . . a patient in one of the private rooms . . .
Winslow . . ."

"Winslow?"

"Aye, Winslow."

Someone said: "Oh yes . . . rather badly smashed up, poor
chap. You know him?"

"Er—no. . . . But I . . . I know *of* him—that is, if he belongs
to the same family. Is he—er—related to *Lord* Winslow?"

The head surgeon thought he might be. Somebody else said he
was. The head surgeon then said: "You can see him if you want.
He's not *too* bad."

"Oh no, no—I wasn't thinking of that."

But afterwards, while he was trying to talk about something else altogether, George wondered if he *had* been thinking of that. For the idea, once in his head, engaged those sympathies of his that were always eager for a quixotic gesture. Years before, he had come near to hating the man who had taken Livia from him—hating him *because* as well as *in spite of* the generosity with which he, George, had treated them both. But now there was no hate or near-hate left, but only a wry curiosity, plus the warmth George felt for any man broken by the war. Would it not be worth while to clinch this attitude by a few words of well-wishing? Could it possibly do any harm? Might it not, if it had any effect at all, do good?

When he was about to leave he said that perhaps he would visit that fellow Winslow after all.

"Certainly . . . Briggs here will take you over." The head surgeon singled out a young colleague who responded with respectful alacrity. "Don't stay too long, though."

"Oh no, only a few minutes. Not even that if you think it might—"

The surgeon smiled. "It won't. You're too modest, Boswell." But he added quietly to Briggs: "Better go in first, though, and see how he is."

As George accompanied the younger man across lawns and courtyards to the block in which Winslow's room was situated, they discussed the weather, the big raid on Mulcaster (history by now), the new robot-bomb raids on London, the successful landings in Normandy, and the difficulties of obtaining whisky and cigarettes that had lately become so acute that George had begun to feel almost ashamed of his own total exemption from such common hardships. But they provided a theme for conversation, and only when Briggs left him in the corridor did his thoughts recur to the nearer urgency, and then with a certain qualm. Was he doing a wise or a foolish thing, or merely an unnecessary one? While he was still wondering, Briggs emerged, his face youthfully flushed as he stammered: "I'm afraid, sir, he—I mean, if you could perhaps come round again some other time—"

"Why, of course. . . . Not convenient, is that it?"

"That's it." But the assent to such a vague explanation was so eager that George went on: "Is he asleep? Or isn't he feeling good?"

"No . . . he's no worse . . . and he's not asleep . . ."

"Then what?"

"Well, sir, to be frank, he—he said he—er—he'd rather not—er—"

"Didn't want to see me, eh? Well, that's all right. Don't bother about it."

"It's a mood they get into sometimes. They feel so low they just don't feel like having visitors at all."

George said he perfectly understood, and then, to cover an embarrassment that was more the young doctor's than his own, added: "I'm glad it isn't because he's worse."

"No . . . he's getting on as well as can be expected."

They walked away together, again discussing topics of general interest. At the hospital gate George said: "You did give him my name, I suppose?"

"Oh yes. I also said you were the Mayor of Browdley, but—but—"

"But it made no difference, eh? Well, why should it?"

George laughed, and then they both went on laughing as they shook hands.

.   .   .

But by the time he reached Browdley he could not see much of a joke in the situation, nor did he feel his usual zest for tackling the pile of clerical work on his desk. So he walked across the town to St. Patrick's clergy house. Wendover was in, and George, on impulse, told him all about his visit to the hospital and his discovery of Winslow there. This led to a longer talk about Livia than George had had for years with anyone, and also to a franker expression of Wendover's personal attitudes than George had yet encountered, despite his many years of close friendship with the priest.

"You see, George, I never felt it my duty to discuss your affairs—especially as you never told me much about them."

"Aye, I never felt like it—which is no reflection on you, of course. And I wouldn't say you've missed much. I'll bet you find it hard listening to stuff about other people's private lives."

"Even if I did, it would still be part of my job. Another part is to offer advice."

"And that's even harder, I should think."

"Well, you know, a priest has one advantage—so many things are decided for him by authority. Take divorce, for instance. The view of my Church is very simple—we think it's wrong, and therefore we're against it."

"Aye, I know. And that makes me guilty of compounding a felony because I made it as easy as I could for the two of them? Isn't that how you'd look at it—and at me?"

Wendover gazed at George very steadily for a moment before saying: "Do you really want my opinion of you?"

"Mightn't be a bad moment to get it out of you."

"All right. I have it ready. Nothing new, either—I've had it for years. I think you're much more like a Christian than many people who come to my Church."

"Quite a compliment."

"Less than you think."

It certainly failed to please George as most compliments did; indeed, for some reason it made him feel uncomfortable. He said, almost truculently, after a pause: "I'd do the same again if I had to. You can't hold a woman if she'd rather be with someone else. And anyway, twenty-three years is a long time to go on bearing a grudge. That's what puzzles me—why should *he* bear a grudge? . . . Well, maybe I can guess. I can remember a few things Livia once told him."

"About what?"

"About *me*."

"Do you mean *against* you?"

George nodded.

"Why should you think that possible?"

And then, for the first time, after an almost quarter-century interval, George disclosed to another human being the events of that memorable day, September the first, 1921—the day of the foundation-stone laying at which Lord Winslow had officiated, and after which the two had had their long conversation in George's study.

When he had finished Wendover made no reply at first, though he did not seem particularly surprised. And George, with his usual revulsion of feeling in favor of someone he had lately been criticizing, hastened to continue: "Mind you, don't get too bad an impression. If I've given you that, then—"

"No, George—and I don't rely on impressions. You've only told me that she lied, and that she may have been unfaithful while she was still legally your wife—"

"Aye, it sounds bad enough. But the funny thing is, she had her good points."

"It would be very funny indeed if she hadn't."

George caught the note in the other's voice. "I know—you probably think I don't blame her enough. But after all, she was *my* choice—and when she was only nineteen, don't forget. Might have been my own fault for not making *her* happy too. Maybe she's been really happy with this other chap. I've nothing against either of 'em. And if he's ill or crippled, if there were anything I could do— though I don't suppose there is . . . Well, I took the first step today and got snubbed for it, and that's about the whole story. So with all this off my chest, I'll now go home and try to work."

Wendover accompanied him to the street door. "Snubs are unimportant, George."

"Of course—and I've got a hide like an elephant for 'em. I'd call it my secret weapon, only it's no secret."

"It never was. Most of the saints had it."

George grinned. "Oh, get along with you. Don't you go calling me names!"

"All right—I won't. I can't teach you much, but perhaps there *is* one thing—a piece of advice that Christians need sometimes. While you're trying so hard to be fair to everybody, remember to include yourself. That's all."

"I suppose the truth is, I get a bigger kick out of being fair to the other fellow. So there's no credit in it."

"Was I offering you any?"

George's grin turned to a laugh. "Good night, Harry. Thanks for listening to me. That's the help I really needed, because there's nothing I can do if Winslow feels the way he does. Nothing at all. . . . Good night."

"Good night, George."

George walked slowly across the dark town. From St. Patrick's to Market Street was about a mile; it took him past the library and the Town Hall and the main shopping length of Shawgate. The night was moonless and cloudy—almost pitch-dark, therefore, in the blackout; but to George this made for no more than a little groping, and in the groping there was a sudden awareness of his whole life, shaped by and shaping those familiar streets and walls. It was as if, at the moment that things half-forgotten were coming back to trouble and confuse, the town rallied invisibly to his aid, assuring him that what he had done so far had not been in vain, and that what he had yet to do could be limitless within the same limits. That these were circumscribed, even narrow by some standards, was evident; but there was gain to match that loss—the gain of warm personal contacts, the "Howdo, Tom" and "Good night, Mr. Mayor" that he would not by now have exchanged for empire. And tonight, as he received and answered the greetings that his known footsteps drew from passers-by, he felt upon his heart the touch of benediction. These were his people, from whom he had sprung, and whom he would serve to the end, because he believed in them and in the destiny of their kind to make this world, if it can ever be, a happier place.

Comforted, he reached his house, entered the study, and turned over the papers on his desk, driving himself to concentration. He still felt disturbed by the day's curious incident, but somehow not as hurt as he had been or might have been. Presently he carried papers over to his armchair and settled himself in comfort. They were the minutes of the last Council meeting and required his approval. The dry official phraseology merely emphasized the part of his life that had gone on for so many years, and would continue to do so—whether or not, whether or not. Like the rhythm of train wheels that go uphill and down dale, through cities and across country . . . *whether or not*. But that again, the blessed rhythm and routine of work he knew so well, led deeper into springs of comfort already found along the dark pavements; and soon a measure of tranquillity was on him. He read every item of the minutes carefully, corrected a few, initialed others, then soon after midnight went to bed and slept dreamlessly till dawn, when the early morning buses wakened him as they started up in the garage just beyond the garden—Livia's garden, as he still thought of it. Then he got up, went back to his desk, and dug deeper into the pile of work there; and at eight, when Annie brought in the morning mail and some tea, he was still working.

Among the envelopes was one that bore the Mulcaster postmark. Like so many that reached him it was addressed merely to "The Mayor, Browdley," but the handwriting looked like a child's. Inside he found a note scribbled in pencil with the heading "Hospital," and so briefly worded that he hardly grasped what it was all about till he had read it over twice. Just—"I don't know what there is about mayors that got my goat this afternoon, but next time, if you want to see me, drop in." And signed with the initial "W."

The note chilled George with its contrast of childish script and adult irony. Presently he surmised that the look of childishness might have come from writing with the left hand—doubtless an effort, yet not too great for the extra words that hurt and were probably meant to.

Nevertheless, he caught the nine-five to Mulcaster.

. . .

At the hospital the nurse on duty told him he could see the patient "now" if he wanted. He asked, because of her peculiar emphasis on the word: "What made him change his mind?"

"Well, I think it was because of what Dr. Briggs and I both said." She blushed as she explained further: "We said you were awfully nice and that everybody liked you."

George's smile was a little ghastly, as if he had heard what might be his own epitaph. He answered: "Thanks for the testimonial. . . . All right, I'll see him. That's what I've come for. Does he have many visitors?"

"None, so far. He's only been here a fortnight."

All this as they walked along the corridor. She opened the door and George followed her. The room was cheerfully bleak, and contained bed, side table, two small chairs, and a table in front of the window surmounted by a large bowl of roses. The shape of a human being was recognizable on the bed, but the face was so swathed in bandages that nothing could be seen of it, while the legs, similarly swathed, were held in an up-slanting position by an assembly of

slings and frames. George was appalled, but the nurse began cheerfully: "Well . . . here's Mr. Boswell *again*."

George waited for her to go out, but she stayed, fussing around
with the pillow and drawing a chair to the bedside, so he said the
only possible thing, which was "Good morning."

From the bed came a curious muffled voice returning the greeting.

"You'll have to stoop a little to him, then you'll hear better. . . .
His words get all tied up with the bandages."

The voice grunted, and George placed his chair closer.

"There's only one rule," she added, finally moving to the door.
"You mustn't smoke."

"I don't smoke," George answered.

When the door had closed on her George heard what might have
been a sigh from the bed and then the question, abruptly: "Has
she gone?"

"Aye," said George.

"She's a good nurse, though."

"I can believe it." And then after a pause: "I got your note this
morning. It's a bit quick to have taken you at your word, but I
thought—"

"Oh, not at all. And don't be impressed by all these bandages
and contraptions. I'm not as much of a wreck as I look."

"I'm glad to hear you're getting on all right."

"Yes, they seem to be patching me up. Would you mind giving
me a tablet out of that bottle on the side table?"

George did so. He saw that the left hand was comparatively us-
able, though the skin was pink and shriveled.

"Thanks . . . they're only throat lozenges."

"I hope talking doesn't bother you. I won't stay long. I just
wanted to bring you my good wishes."

"Thanks . . . I can listen, anyway."

But George for once found himself without chatter. He said,
stammering somewhat: "There isn't much else I have to say—except that I'm sorry we meet for the first time under these somewhat
awkward circumstances. I used to know your father—slightly. I
met him—once—several years before his death—"

"*What?*" The exclamation was so sharp that it discounted the
enforced motionlessness of the body. And a rush of words continued:

"What do you mean? His *death!* Have you heard anything? Who told you that? Have they been trying to keep it from me?"

George realized there was a misunderstanding somewhere, though he could not yet tell what. For a moment the wild thought seized him that this Winslow might not be of the same Winslow family at all. He said: "I'm sorry if I'm making a mistake. I was referring to *Lord* Winslow—the one who used to be Secretary of Housing—"

A strange muffled sound came from the bed, uninterpretable except as one of relief, though the words that followed were still tense with excitement: "You certainly have got it all balled up, Mr. Mayor. . . . That was my *grand*father."

.   .   .

George described the rest of the interview to Wendover the same evening. "Aye, it was my mistake all right, but even when I realized it I didn't realize everything else immediately, because he kept on asking me about his father—did I *know* anything, had there been any news, and so on—and of course I could only repeat what I'd heard from the man in London—that they'd both got out of Singapore in time. But then he told me they hadn't been in Singapore at all, but in Hong Kong, where his father had a job.

"I didn't stay long after that. I could see I'd put him in a nervous mood, and I felt it was my fault, in a way, for not verifying things beforehand. And I was a bit excited myself, because it was hard to realize that he must be Livia's boy—and not more than twenty-two, if that. . . . Charles, he told me his name was. . . . I could have talked better to his father, if it had been him, but with the boy I felt tongue-tied . . . because as he went on talking it became clear to me that he hadn't the faintest idea who I was—or rather who I had been in his mother's life."

"You didn't tell him?"

"No, Harry, I didn't."

"He must have thought it odd that you should take all that trouble to visit him."

"Aye, and he said so, before I left. He got quite cordial—in a nervous sort of way. He tried to apologize for having refused to see me the day before—he blamed what he called the superstition that provincial mayors are pompous old bores—'I wonder why people think so,' he said, and although it was a backhanded compliment, I knew he was meaning it all right. So I answered: 'Probably because many of 'em are'—and we had a good laugh. Or rather, he couldn't laugh, but I knew it was the same as if he was laughing. . . . I promised to visit him again. He made a point of asking me to, if ever I was in that part of the world."

"Don't you intend to tell him?"

"Not just yet. I don't see that it can matter much—to *him*. Or if it did, it wouldn't help. You see he *needs* help. His nerves are all to pieces and he's pretty low-spirited about things in general—I gathered that. Maybe I can cheer him up . . . and if I can't—if he finds me a nuisance—then it'll be easier for him to tell me so if he thinks I'm only the Mayor of Browdley."

Wendover smiled. "You'd make a good Jesuit, George. You can find more reasons for doing what you want to do. . . ."

. . . .

George visited the Mulcaster hospital every week or so from then on. Not all the visits were on account of Winslow; some would have had to be made on official business in any case. But he found himself looking forward to them all, and not grudging the length of the journey, which meant less sleep, for it was in the nature of his own work that hardly any of it could be postponed, shortened, or abandoned. And gradually, as the youth continued to improve, there came to George the intense pleasure of noting definite improvements each time—the slow removal of bandages; the first time the cradles and slings were discarded; the first step from the bed to a wheel chair; and most of all, the lifting of the mind from despondency. All this took months, and the visits, though regular, could not last long. The Mayor of Browdley was curiously shy during the early ones—almost desperately afraid of intruding where he might not be really as welcome as it appeared—reluctant, it would seem, to believe that the invitations to come again were genuine. It was unlike George, who was so used to being liked, to have such diffidence; and yet there was in him all the uncertainty of a man in whom the touch of bravado masks only a deep humility and an awareness of personal inadequacy.

They talked of many things, from hospital gossip to world affairs, with no plan or aim in the talking; and this, perhaps, was as good a way to get to know each other as if either had deliberately tried. George was often tempted to lead the subject to Livia, but always forbore; he had an odd feeling of conscience about it—that his own concealment of identity could only be justified so long as he did not take such advantages. Sometimes, however, information slipped out without any probing. Charles liked to talk about the family home in Berkshire, the big centuries-old house that belonged now to his uncle, the inheritor of the title—"and thank heaven it does—my father never wanted it, and neither do I, though it's a lovely old place to visit." He spoke affectionately of both parents, but seemed to have spent comparatively little time with them since he was very young. "But that's the way it is when your people are overseas. They pack you off to school in England and you hardly see them for years at a stretch, and then when you do they're almost strangers. It was better for a while after 1934, when Dad gave up his job and they went to live in Ireland, near Galway. It was a sort of farm, and I used to stay there during the school holidays. Mother made a good farmer—she had a knack for anything to do with crops or animals. She could squeeze warbles on a cow, and that's a thing you can't do without being sick unless you really love farming."

George didn't inquire what squeezing warbles was.

"And yet she could be the great lady too—doing the society stuff if ever she felt like it. I've often thought she'd have made a damn fine actress. . . . And when she made up her mind about something, nothing on earth or under heaven would stop her. . . . My God, the wires she pulled to get out to Hong Kong after the war started."

"I thought you said he'd given up the job."

"He had, but he didn't much like farming, and after a year of it he went abroad again—for an oil company. Mother didn't like it, but she followed him, and I didn't see either of them again till 'thirty-nine, when they came home on six months' leave. They were still in London in September, and Father offered his services to the Government, but they told him he couldn't do better than go back to his job with the oil company. So he did—alone at first, because of the war and because Mother was mad with him for wanting to go back at all—but of course she soon followed as before. She always followed him everywhere, though I guess they neither of them expected to end up in a Jap prison camp."

"End up?"

"Well no, I didn't mean *that*. Oh God, I hope not."

"You don't really know what happened?"

"Not a thing—except that they *were* in Hong Kong when the Japs took over. That's definite. All the rest is rumor."

George caught the sudden tremor in his voice, and made haste to change the subject.

Once—and for the first time since the initial interview and misunderstanding—they mentioned the former Lord Winslow. "I don't really remember him," Charles said. "I think he disapproved of Dad's marriage, or something of the sort. But from all accounts he was a very distinguished piece of Stilton in his way."

George was not quite sure what this meant; besides, he was thinking of the phrase "something of the sort" and wondering how much, or little, it concealed. "A great authority on housing," he remarked safely.

"So are you, aren't you?"

George smiled. "I was one of six kids brought up in four rooms. Not a bad way to become a *practical* authority."

"I should think it was also a pretty good education for your father."

"Well, no—because he wasn't interested in earthly houses so much as in heavenly mansions." George chuckled.

"A good thing his son didn't take after him, then. I hear you've done rather well for that town of yours."

"Not so badly. I reckon Browdley's five per cent better than it might have been if I'd never been born."

"That's modest of you."

"Nay, I'd call it swelled head. Takes a lot for one man by himself to make five per cent of difference to anything."

"Same in flying. The idea of the lone hero soaring into the blue on a mission of his own is a bit outmoded."

"Aye, it's all teamwork nowadays." George added hastily: "Not that I'm much of an expert on military affairs."

"Is anybody? What about all the so-called experts who've been wrong? About the Maginot Line, for instance?"

George sighed. "I was wrong about that too, without being an expert."

"I suppose you were fooled by the last war—superiority of defense over attack, and so on?"

"To some extent. I couldn't help remembering the Somme."

"You were there?"

"Er . . . yes."

"What were you in—the poor bloody infantry?"

"No."

"Artillery? Sappers?"

"No . . . I . . . I wasn't in the armed forces at all."

"War correspondent? You're still in the newspaper business, aren't you?"

"I was—in a small way—until recently."

Charles laughed. "I *won't* be fobbed off with a mystery! What *were* you in the last war, for God's sake?"

George then answered the question that he had not been asked for a long time, and never went out of his way to encounter, but which, when it was put directly, he always answered with equal directness. "I was a conscientious objector," he said.

There was a little silence for a moment—not an awkward one, but a necessary measuring point in the progress of an intimacy. And this was the moment that made George sure he was liked and not merely tolerated by the youth whose less injured hand moved slowly across the arm of the wheel chair towards him.

"Conchy in the last war, eh?" The hand reached out. "Shake, then. Because that's what *I* might be in the next—if they have a next."

George took the wrinkled burned-red hand, though he thought it an ironic occasion to have first done so. Presently Charles went on: "What happened? You had a bad time?"

"Well," answered George, a little dazed at the extent to which they were talking as if they had known each other all their lives, "I was on the Somme, as I said, and *that* was a pretty bad time. My brother—one of my brothers—and I—were in the same Ambulance Unit. He was killed."

"Driving an ambulance?"

"No. We were both stretcher-bearers."

"Not exactly the safest job on earth."

"No."

"But you came through all right?"

"I was gassed—not very badly, but it led to pneumonia and a medical discharge. Probably saved my life in the long run."

Charles said, with a touch of pathos: "What did it feel like— after that? When you were out of hospital, I mean, but still not well enough to do things normally? How did you get used to things again?"

"I didn't, because the things I'd been used to before the war were things I didn't intend to get used to again—ever. . . . But of course in your case it's different."

"I don't know that it is, particularly. . . . But tell me about how you got started again. In business, wasn't it? A newspaper?"

"Aye, but it sounds too important when you put it that way. Just a bankrupt small-town weekly. Nobody's bargain, they practically threw it at me, but I thought it would help me in local politics."

"And it did?"

George nodded. "I was lucky. One of those handy by-elections cropped up, and there I was—the youngest Town Councillor Browdley had ever had."

"How old were you then?"

"Let me see . . . it was April 'seventeen when they let me out of hospital, and the election was in the September following. I'd be thirty-one."

"You didn't lose any time." Charles thought for a moment, then added: "Wasn't it against you to have been a conscientious objector?"

"Quite a bit. The other side used it for all they were worth, but Browdley's got a mind of its own in local matters—even in wartime." George chuckled. "I was for lowering the fares on municipal buses before eight in the morning. That got all the factory workers."

Charles smiled. "You weren't a pacifist in the election, then?"

"I was if anybody asked me, but I used most of my eloquence on the bus fares."

"The war must have been on your mind, though."

"Aye, it was—just as it still is."

After another pause Charles said thoughtfully: "So you think it's wrong to take human life under any circumstances?"

"I did then."

"You mean you don't think so any more?"

"That's about it. I'm not so sure of a lot of things as I was in those days. I don't hate war any less, but the problem doesn't look so simple for an individual to make up his mind about. Seems to me there are times when life's less important than a few other things, and those are the times when taking it—and giving it—are the only things we can do. It's the price we have to pay if we can't get what we want any cheaper."

"And what *is* it that we want?"

"I don't know what *you* want, but if I had a boy I'd want a better world for him than either your generation or mine has had."

"A world fit for heroes to live in, eh?"

"Nay, I'd rather call it a world fit for ordinary folks to be heroic in. . . . And I can't see it coming unless we win this war. I don't see it necessarily coming even if we *do* win it. . . . But there's a *chance* if we do."

"Quite a change in your attitude from last time."

"Aye—but that doesn't mean I regret what I did then. Seems to me I was right for a reason I couldn't have foreseen. Doesn't what's happening now prove it? What good did that first war do—all the misery and butchery I saw on the Somme? What was it for? To save freedom? There was less in the world afterwards. To crush Germany? Germany was strong again within a generation. To fix Europe once and for all? Europe got unfixed again worse than ever. . . ."

"I'll tell you one thing it did, Mr. Boswell—it gave some of you chaps who survived it twenty years of a damned good time. It gave you twenty years of movies and dog racing and charabanc outings and stock-market gambles and holidays on the Continent and comfortable living—twenty years of the kind of fun *we* may not have, even if we *do* survive."

George answered: "*I* didn't have twenty years of fun. I had twenty years of trying to improve a little town called Browdley— trying to put up a few schools and pull down a few slums—trying to make some headway against the greed and selfishness of those old Victorian shysters who ran the place for half a century like a slave barracks. . . ."

"And what does that prove? Merely that we all get saddled with old debts. You had the Victorian mess to deal with—I've got yours."

"Mine?"

"Who else's? You surely don't claim that you used those twenty years successfully? The last war mightn't have been so worthless unless you'd made it so. . . ." Charles added, smiling: "Not that I mean anything personal, of course. You risked your life, same as I have, and then you came home and did what seemed to you worth doing. But it *wasn't* worth doing—because the main thing wasn't right. And the main thing was the peace. Why weren't you a conscientious objector to *that?"*

George answered gravely: "Aye, you've a right to ask. I'm quite ready to take blame for plenty that I did—and plenty that I didn't do. I can see now, like a lot of folks, that I was living in a fool's paradise—if by any stretch of imagination you can call Browdley any sort of paradise. Maybe if I'd had a better education—"

"Depends on what you call a better education."

"I daresay I'd call yours one. What was it—Eton and Oxford?"

"No. Charterhouse and Cambridge . . . and also Berlin."

"What? You were educated in *Berlin?"*

"Not *in* Berlin—*over* Berlin." And then the boy laughed rather wildly. "Sorry. I've been waiting to work that off on somebody, but you were the first to give me a cue."

George smiled. "I see what you mean."

"You ought to. After all, you were at the University of the Somme yourself."

"Aye, but don't let's be overdramatic. War doesn't teach anybody much—except to hate it. If you hate it beyond a certain point you go out of your mind, so if you don't want to do that you have to forget it somehow or other, and I suppose that's mostly what I and millions of others did." George paused a moment before taking a further plunge in intimacy: "And that's what you'll do too, my lad, unless you're the exception that proves the rule. Maybe you are. But if you aren't . . . well, there's a maternity ward next door for you to think of. Aren't you afraid that someday all those kids will blame you as you're blaming me—not personally, but as a generation?"

"A damned hard question, and the answer is yes, I *am* afraid. I'm scared stiff . . . and I'm not hopeful. But what the hell can I do? Lads of my age, as you call them, have the war to win first, before we can bother with anything else. Give us a chance to do one thing at a time, for Christ's sake."

"Give *us* a chance, then, too—even if it's only a chance to help you. Some of us still have one foot out of the grave."

The door opened and the nurse entered. She had heard the raised voices and the laughter sound as she walked along the corridor, and now she was in time to catch George's last sentence. It must have seemed to her a strange conjunction, justifying the acerbity with which she approached the wheel chair, whipped out a thermometer, and said to George: "You mustn't make him laugh, Mr. Boswell —it would be very bad for the new skin. And you really have talked to him enough, I think . . . if you don't mind . . ."

It was true; it was the longest time George had yet stayed. "I understand," he said, smiling to both of them.

Charles then asked the nurse if she would fetch him some more of the lozenges.

She went out exclaiming: "My goodness, Lieutenant, have you used them up already?"

"Seems like it, Nurse." Then, when the door closed, he turned quietly to George. "Just a moment—before you go. I wanted to say this, but we got talking about so many other things . . . I've had the tip they mean to transfer me somewhere else—for facial surgery and what not. Probably before you come again . . . so if they do, and I send you my new address, would you—would you have the time—to—to write to me—occasionally?"

George laid his hand on the boy's shoulder. "Aye," he answered. "I will that." The long argument had given him such mental stimulation that now emotion came to him with an impact; after those four words he was speechless, stricken at the sudden thought of an end to the visits.

The nurse came hurrying back with a fresh bottle of lozenges, then spied one still half-full on the table beside the bed. "Well, I do declare—you didn't finish the others after all! He's so absent-minded, Mr. Boswell. . . . Aren't you, Lieutenant?"

George stammered his good-byes, and wondered as he left the hospital what was the matter with him to have used up so much time in talking politics. Of course it was the mere zest of a debate that had led him on, exhilarating him as it always did—recalling the remark once made by a teetotal friend that drink would have been wasted on George, since a good hard-hitting argument produced on him the same effects, even to the hangover the next day, when he wondered what he had said in the heat of the moment that might have given offense, or that he didn't exactly mean.

But now his emotions were of a different kind. Sadness grew in him all the way back to Browdley, coupled with and finally outweighed by a breathless satisfaction that the boy had asked him to write. Of course he would write.

* * *

Winslow was transferred during the following week to a hospital in the South of England, where specialists were reputed to work miracles with skin and cartilage; but it was not of this that he wrote in his first letter to George. He wrote:—

DEAR MR. BOSWELL—Just a line to let you know my new address. I expect to be here several months, as the work they do here takes time—and patience too, I expect, by all concerned. The men call it the beauty shop. But the main thing I have to tell you is about my mother. I've had news that she is among those to be repatriated after spending over two years in a Jap prison camp. The Foreign Office sent me word a few hours ago, and though they couldn't give me any information as to how she is, or about my father at all, it certainly is great news that she is actually out of enemy hands and on the first stage of her way home. They don't expect her to arrive for at least six or eight weeks, as the ship is slow and has to take a roundabout route. By that time I hope to be well enough myself to meet her— though the doctors here only smile when I say it. I'm a bit stubborn, though, when I set my mind on anything, which is a quality I inherit from her. Incidentally, I'd like you to meet her, because I'm sure she'll want to thank you personally for your great kindness to me while I was at Mulcaster. . . .

When George took this over to Wendover the latter read it through and turned on his friend a somewhat quizzical expression. "Well, George," he commented at length, "it settles one thing."

"Aye, I've got to tell·him."

Wendover nodded. "And quickly too. You don't want him writing to *her* about you."

"I don't see how he could."

"There might be some port of call where he could send air mail."

"That's so. Anyhow, I agree with you. Spill the beans and get it over. Might even have been better to tell him in the first place."

"One of the penalties of being too subtle, George. I could never quite make out what your aim was—or still is, for that matter."

"My *aim?*"

"Yes—in regard to the boy."

George answered: "I haven't got an aim—except that I'd like to help him because I like him. I never realized how much I like him till now that I can't see him. And I don't think it's because he's Livia's boy—it's because I like *him*. He's a fine young chap—and a brain too. . . . But I suppose it'll be an impossible situation when Livia gets back."

"It might be. You'll have to take that chance. But take it now— by telling him."

"Aye, I will. I'll write tonight."

George wrote a short letter containing the simple fact, and received in reply by return the following:—

DEAR MR. BOSWELL—What a hell of a surprise! I'll admit you could have knocked me down with a feather, as they say. I'm a bit puzzled why you didn't tell me earlier, but perhaps it doesn't matter. Of course I'd known that my mother was previously married, but I was never told any of the details. Frankly, the whole thing makes no difference to me, but of course it may to her when she gets here. I don't want to worry her, because from what I hear and can guess, she must have had a pretty bad time. . . .

George wrote back, and they both kept up the correspondence without ever referring to the personal matter again; nor did the youth even mention his mother, or the progress of her homeward journey across the world. George could not but feel that a barrier—

temporarily, at any rate—had come between them, and there returned to him his earlier shyness, diffidence, and reluctance to believe that Charles really wanted to continue the friendship. Then one day he read that the ship containing some hundreds of women and children repatriated from Japanese prison camps had put into an English harbor. It was his turn to write, but he put it off, thinking that even out of turn he could expect a letter from the boy about his mother—telling of her arrival, condition, and attitude. When such a letter did not come he eventually wrote briefly and rather meaninglessly about nothing in particular, but to that letter he received no answer, and when, after writing again, there was still no answer, he could reach only one conclusion.

"I'm not surprised," he told Wendover. "He probably thought it as good a way as any other to close an episode."

"That's a rather tragic interpretation, George."

"I don't think so. I wanted to help him, nothing more—and now Livia's back, perhaps he doesn't need help. Or at any rate, perhaps I'm no longer one who *can* help him."

"I hope it isn't going to worry you."

"No." George's answer was decisive. "Give me something to do and I'll worry over it. But when I can do *nothing* . . ."

But George did worry, nevertheless, if that was an adequate word for the quiet intrusion of thoughts about the boy into every momentarily unoccupied fragment of his time and mind. Those fragments, however, were few on account of increasing pressure of official work. There was, for instance, Browdley's annual budget which, as Chairman of the Finance Committee, he must prepare for annual presentation. More urgent still was a general tightening up of air-raid precautions and civilian defense, for which London had issued specific instructions, believing that northern England's long period of relative freedom from enemy air attacks might be coming to an end. There were also meetings and conferences on other matters— with the Medical Officer about a chicken-pox outbreak, with local union officials and plant-management committees, with regional groups in charge of War Loan drives, charitable funds, and so on. Least arduous of all—indeed, a kind of optional luxury in which George frankly indulged himself amidst all the urgent necessities— was an interview with an idealist town planner whose vision of a new Browdley included wide boulevards, American-style apartment houses, and glass-walled factories.

George almost forgot his personal affairs as he turned over the nicely water-colored drawings and marveled at large green blobs representing trees that could not possibly grow to such a size in less than twenty years. But there was an even more fundamental anachronism. "Do you realize," he said, a trifle impishly, "that your plan would mean pulling down practically the whole town?"

"That was rather the idea," came the quiet reply.

George laughed. "I see. And it might be a good one except that if you once did pull the place down I can't really imagine why anyone should want to rebuild it at all. It's really only here because it's here, so to say. A century ago they needed coal for the cotton mills, so they had to build the cotton mills near the coal—but now they don't need the coal so much, in normal times, or the cotton mills either. I doubt if they'd put up half of these towns if they had the chance to begin all over again."

"I know what you mean, sir. Growth and then decay. It happens with towns as with human beings."

"With countries, too, and empires."

"And down to the smallest villages. There's a place near here called Stoneclough—"

George started at the sound of the mispronounced word. "*Cluff* —they call it. You've been there?"

"Yes, I just happened along—by accident. Very interesting. Seems to be completely uninhabited, including the big house at the top of the hill."

"Aye—there's nobody at Stoneclough any more."

"I took some photographs—thought of working it up into an article—the Forsaken Village, or some such title. But I doubt if it would be of enough general interest till after the war."

"And maybe not then," George answered, moodily.

But he liked all such contacts with enthusiasts in their own special fields. As a contrast, it fell to him the same week to visit the Parliamentary Member for Browdley, none other than that same Wetherall (now Sir Samuel) who had defeated him in the 1919 by-election, again in the general election of 1923, and had represented the town in the House of Commons ever since. An old man now;

and like most former enemies, he had made his peace with George. The political truce since the war began had brought them even closer, so that George was genuinely sorry to hear that Wetherall was ill. They spent an afternoon together in the manufacturer's house just outside Browdley, talking over old times and old squabbles. Wetherall was still rich, still worried about taxes, still unaware that anything had happened to make the world vitally different since he was a boy. His solution for the problems of the postwar cotton trade was that all Indians should wear their shirts a few inches longer, and he couldn't understand how the Japs could possibly have taken Singapore after the place had cost the British taxpayer so much money to fortify. Capping it all, he persisted in believing that George had changed during the years into someone much more like himself; it gave him satisfaction to say (as if to justify his own liking for the Mayor)—"Ah, you're not such a firebrand as you used to be. You've seen a bit of reason these last few years."

George, reflecting what he *had* seen—the blitz raid on Mulcaster, for instance—hardly thought he would call it reason. But why argue with an old fellow who looked as if only his illusions could nourish him precariously for a few more years at most?

Wetherall went on: "Just as well I've kept you out of Parliament till you've grown sensible, George. You'll not do so bad when your time comes."

"Why . . . what . . . what makes you say that?"

"George, you old twister, don't pretend it never entered your mind before! Listen—and this is in confidence—I probably won't stand at the next election. God knows when that'll be—after the war or after I kick the bucket, whichever comes first. But I'm telling you this so you'll be ready."

George was suddenly aware of the peculiar truth that it *hadn't* been on his mind, not for quite a time, and that it revisited him now as an almost strange idea, with all kinds of new angles and aspects to be considered. He said, sincerely enough: "I'm sorry you're thinking of giving up, Sam. Over twenty years for the same constituency must be pretty near the record. . . ."

"Yes, and it's meant a lot of hard work, one way and another, but I don't grudge anything I've done for the town, any more than you do, George. After all, it's Browdley that made me what I am."

George thought that was very possible.

"So when they sent me to Parliament I made up my mind I'd do the best I could for them."

George thought that was very possible also, since during the entire period of his membership of the House, Wetherall had made only two speeches. One was about the local sewage scheme, which George had persuaded him to be for; the other was against the revision of the Anglican Prayer Book, which nothing could persuade him to be anything but against.

George said cheerfully: "Well, Sam—don't give up yet. And I wish you'd try to fix things with the Ministry about our Children's Home. We ought to get an extra grant for that, what with all the kids from the bombed areas we've taken in. . . ."

. . .

Sometimes the cheerfulness sagged a little and George saw the future in a hard bleak flash of momentary disillusionment; but even then he was prone to diagnose his mood as due to overwork, and therefore not to be taken too seriously. The cure was usually a good night's sleep or a chat with Wendover. The priest's help was all the more tonic because of the fixity of their disagreements, and also because (as George once laughingly confessed) he was far too modest to suppose that he could exercise any influence in reverse; but Wendover, with equal banter, wouldn't even concede that this was modesty. "It's your instinct for self-preservation, George. We authoritarians keep you going. How would you know your opinions were free unless you had ours to attack? . . . But I'll suggest this—that before the century ends, it may not be freedom that the world values, so much as order. Order out of chaos. A new world, George, with an old discipline."

"Aye, but suppose that road leads to Moscow, not to Rome— what would you chaps do then?"

"I should follow my Church, of course. But why assume that the two roads are ultimately so far apart? One thing I *do* know—that if the Church so decided, it would be very easy for a Catholic to change his mind about Communism, just as Moscow could doubtless make terms with Rome for as good a reason as Constantine ever had. . . . And what a tremendous bond that is in a chaotic world

—two major disciplined forces that know their own power to en-force a decision!"

"You've forgotten the Standard Oil Company. That makes three."

"Let's say, then, forces that can command not only obedience, but willing sacrifice."

"Which lets in Hitler. He could command all that at first. But in the end he was defeated by free men."

"Only when they themselves learned to organize, obey, and sac-rifice. And as soon as they forget that lesson there'll be other Hit-lers."

"Aye, and as soon as we forget we're free we'll have Hitlers in our own ranks."

"There's danger in whatever we do, George. . . . But don't misunderstand me . . . I'm not pleading a cause."

"Well, I *am*—and millions are fighting for it too! Today's my fu-ture—like theirs—and what happens by the end of the century doesn't give us much comfort—"

"Nor me either. It's merely that I'm content to let wiser men shape events that can't yet be properly foreseen. Whereas you have to settle the whole destiny of mankind here and now to satisfy an itching conscience. Quite a handicap!"

"I'd do better if I didn't think for myself, is that what you mean? Maybe I would—depends on who did the thinking for me. But I want to *choose* who . . . see? And that's democracy—even for a little fellow."

"You're not a little fellow, George. You're a very shrewd dictator who made up his mind years ago to have his own way in Browdley —and you *have* had it, against a big majority who've been either against your ideas or indifferent to them—and the methods by which you've succeeded have been slyness, smartness, blarney, im-portunity, intrigue, compromise, a certain amount of downright trickery, and a vast amount of personal charm! But you prefer to call it democracy!"

By the time they reached that kind of point in argument George was usually in a good humor and his normal cheerfulness renewed.

.   .   .

He never realized the majestic and in some ways rather terrifying alchemy of English life so much as when he attended official conferences in London. He had been attending them for years, until now they were something rather like routine, but he always remembered his first one—when, as a young man just elected to the Browdley Council, he had been sent as its delegate to a consultation with high officials of one of the Whitehall ministries. Because the government in power was of the opposite political party to his own he had expected to be frostily received and was full of carefully rehearsed truculence that evaporated at the first calm, polite, and curiously impersonal meeting with people whom he had thought of as his enemies. But it had left him baffled afterwards. "Talk about raising the standard of revolution!" he had reported, when he got back to Browdley. "It was hard enough to make anyone raise a couple of eyebrows!" Was it possible that London did not know what a potentially dangerous man he was? Or did not care? Or both knew and cared, yet was imbued with some classic spirit that would only return cool civility for warm antagonism? After he had attended half a dozen more such conferences, George's bafflement lessened, not because he had entirely solved the problem, but because he had come to terms with it; it was as peculiar, yet could seem as normal, as the normally peculiar smell of the London tubes.

By now, of course, he was not baffled at all. Whenever he visited the ministries on business he met important men who knew him, who called him George, who took him to lunch and kidded him good-humoredly about his being teetotal. The war years had only continued, with some intensification, the natural process of all the years; and when, as sometimes happened, George spent half a day at the House of Commons, he found himself surrounded by a platoon of ex-firebrands who held official positions. "Too bad you aren't here, George," he had often been told. "You'd have been at least an undersecretary by now."

"But then I wouldn't have been Mayor of Browdley," answered George, seeking to console himself from force of habit, yet no longer really needing to. He liked London; but to be a stranger to it, even a familiar stranger, kept him alive to that same majestic and rather terrifying alchemy of English life, as slow and sure and relentless almost as the grinding of the mills of God.

That it had helped to save England after Dunkirk and during the blitz autumn of 1940, George thought very probable. For then its virtue had shown like good bones under the flesh—especially its abiding combination of firmness and benignity, so that the same machine of government could jail a baronet for a rationing offense and organize the distribution to small children of Mickey Mouse gas masks. Nothing was too small, and no one too great, to be beyond the range of that cool-headed but never cold-hearted survey. And George, administering Browdley, had tried to generate something of that dual mood in microcosm.

And yet . . . whenever he went to London he felt the strength of Browdley in him, rebelling against certain things.

. . . . .

One morning, walking briskly along Whitehall after a meeting with officials, George ran into a man named Sprigge whom he had first met years before on the Terrace of the House of Commons. George was pleased to be remembered, and willingly accepted the other's invitation to have lunch at a near-by club. They talked about the war and politics; Sprigge said that since their previous meeting he had lived a good deal in China and the Malay States, getting out just in time after Pearl Harbor. It was natural then for George to ask, with an air of casualness, if he had ever come across the Winslows.

"You mean Jeff Winslow, brother of Lord Winslow?"

"Aye, that's him."

"Knew him well, my dear chap. Often dined at his house. Good parties he used to give—not so starchy as the really official ones, because, as he used to say, he wasn't really official. You see, he was attached to the Sultan of Somewhere-or-other, and that made a difference. The lady next to you at dinner might be an Italian spy or an Egyptian princess or a Javanese snake-charmer—used to be fun finding out. . . . Was he a friend of yours—Winslow?"

George answered: "Not—er—exactly, but I knew his father slightly—and I've also met his son."

"And as a result of that you're sort of interested in the middle-man, eh?"

"That's it," George agreed. And then, to steer the conversation very gently: "I remember his father expected so much of his career."

"Well, he was a brilliant fellow—no doubt about that." Sprigge paused, then added: "Wasted, though, the way things turned out."

"Wasted?"

"Perhaps that's too strong a word. But he'd have done well in the regular Diplomatic if he'd stayed in it . . . and also if . . . well, anyhow, perhaps it wasn't his fault that he didn't. Not *altogether* his fault."

George said nothing.

"Of course I'm only repeating things I've heard—but there was said to have been some scandal about his wife—an earlier divorce or something. And then other matters . . . later . . . well, one shouldn't gossip."

"Did you meet the boy?"

Sprigge shook his head. "He was at school in England. I suppose he's of age now to be in the fighting somewhere."

"Aye," said George thoughtfully. He would have liked Sprigge to go on chattering, but just then a fellow club member said "hello" in passing and Sprigge insisted on making an introduction—Henry Millbay, the name was, which to George seemed familiar though he could not exactly place it. Millbay shook hands, declined a drink, and regarded George with a certain friendly shrewdness while, to restart the conversation, Sprigge went on: "We were just talking about Jeff Winslow—the one who was in Malaya . . . Boswell knows the family. . . . Ever meet him out there, Millbay?"

Millbay shook his head, and the subject was dropped.

Half an hour later, after talk that would have been more agreeable had he not been thinking of other things all the time, George remembered an appointment and took his leave; but in the club lobby, as he was retrieving hat and coat, Millbay overtook him. "I'm a busy man too," he commented, with just the slightest derogatory implication that Sprigge was less so. "Wonder if we're going in the same direction?"

They found they were not; nevertheless Millbay kept George chatting for several minutes on the pavement outside. Presently he said: "I didn't want to talk much in front of Sprigge, who's the biggest male gossip in London, but he said you knew the Winslows— Jeff Winslow. . . ."

"I didn't actually know *him*," George answered.

Millbay's glance quickened. "Oh, you mean you knew *her?*"

George experienced again, and for the first time in years, that old sensation of a fist grasping his insides. "Aye, but a long while ago."

"Rather remarkable woman."

"Aye."

"She's just home from a Jap prison camp in Hong Kong. I saw her the other day." Something in George's face made Millbay add: "Part of my job, you know, to interview repatriates. The idea is to get information about the enemy. They all knew plenty, but it was mostly horrors. . . . Of course *her* story was particularly interesting to me because I'd known her and her husband before the war. . . . Remarkable woman."

"Aye."

"Even if I hadn't known that already I'd have thought so after interviewing some of the other women. They said she looked after English and American children in the prison camp. Seems to have been so bloody fearless that even the Japs let her have her own way as often as not. Anyhow, she got the kids extra food and medicines when nobody else could."

"What about her husband?"

"She didn't know. Nobody knows. After the first few months the Japs took to separating the men from the women and shipped the men to another camp—some said in Japan itself. Incidentally, she needn't have been interned in the first place—there was a chance for some of the women to get away, but she insisted on staying with Jeff. At the Foreign Office we're still pressing inquiries about him, but so far without luck, and it's hard to be optimistic."

George then asked, so softly that he had to repeat the question: "Do you know anything about the boy?"

"He was in the R.A.F. and got smashed in one of the Berlin raids. I think he's discharged now, and up at Cambridge. The mother's staying at the family place in the country." Millbay paused as if to give George time to realize where the conversation stood again, but George, though realizing it, said nothing. Presently Millbay smiled and added: "I've told you a lot—now you tell me something. What do you think of her?"

"Of . . . *her?*"

"Yes. Of Livia Winslow."

The utterance of the name made George stammer: "I—I thought she was what you called her—*remarkable.*"

"Did you know her at all well?"

"Aye, pretty well . . . but years ago, as I said."

"Then maybe you can answer one specific question: was she—er —when you knew her—politically—er—reliable?"

"Politically *reliable?* What's that?"

"Rather vague, I admit . . . but perhaps elastic enough to describe something a diplomat's wife should be. After all, Jeff had to handle fairly important matters—important, I mean, to British policy."

"And you're asking me if she always agreed with that policy? How on earth do I know? But I can tell you this much—*I* don't always agree with it, and if that's become a crime lately, by all means put me down on your black list."

George had reacted normally to a familiar stimulus, and Millbay reacted normally to that type of reaction, with which he was equally familiar. He smiled. "We're not as stupid as all that, Boswell, even at the Foreign Office. And our black list is largely a gray list—or should I use the phrase 'neutral tints'?" He paused a moment, then asked quietly: "Did you know her when she was in Ireland?"

"No." George caught the alertness of Millbay's glance and countered it with a more humorous alertness of his own. Suddenly he laughed. "Look here . . . what are you driving at? Are you a detective or something?"

Millbay also laughed. "I might be the 'something.' To tell you the truth, I'm just a government official who once wrote a few novels." George then knew where he had seen Millbay's name, and also why he had not clearly remembered it; he was not much of a novel reader. Millbay continued: "Perhaps that's why I'm handed all these wartime psychological problems. They're quite interesting, though, as a rule. . . . Take this woman we've been talking about —from all accounts she's top-notch for sheer physical and mental courage against appalling odds. Yet all that—and every novelist knows it—doesn't guarantee that she couldn't be a complete bitch in other ways. Did you, incidentally, ever discuss Hitler with her?"

"Good God, no—the time I knew her was years before Hitler was even heard of. You're not suspecting her of being a Nazi spy, are you?"

Millbay laughed again. "Stolen treaties tucked away in the corsage, eh? . . . Hardly. . . . So you don't think she'd have made a good spy?"

George answered: "From my judgment she'd make the worst spy in the world."

"What makes you say that?"

George answered: "Of course it's long ago that I knew her, but people don't change their whole nature. What I mean is—if they're . . . well, outspoken . . . not always too tactful . . ."

Millbay touched George's arm with a half-affectionate gesture. "Thank you for confirming my own private opinion. I never did believe there was anything really wrong with her in *that* way— especially on the basis of the incident that gave rise to most of the talk. . . . You heard about it, perhaps?"

"I don't think so. What was it?"

"Some big dinner party at Batavia, with a crowd of officials, attachés, Army people, and so on. I was told about it by several who were there. Before the war of course—1932 or 1933. Conversation turned on Hitler, and most of what was said was unflattering— especially from the viewpoint of the career diplomat. Suddenly Livia said—'Isn't it odd that people who profess to follow religion founded by a carpenter are so ready to sneer at someone for having once been a house painter?' Quite a sensation! Of course she was tabbed as pro-Hitler after that, but I really don't think she had to be. I think she could have meant exactly what she said. . . . Because it *is* odd, when you reckon it up. With all the perfectly sound reasons the democracies have for hating that man, they choose to sneer at him because he once followed a trade. How do house painters feel about it, I wonder? If I knew any, I'd ask 'em."

"I do know some, so I will ask 'em."

"And then tell me? Well, anyhow, you can imagine that sort of remark didn't do her husband any good professionally."

"Aye, I can see that."

They were still at the curbside, but a government car had driven up and the chauffeur was waiting. Millbay said hastily: "Sorry there hasn't been more time to talk. Always interesting to compare notes about people one knows. . . . Incidentally, if you're free tonight, why don't you dine with me? Then we'd have more time."

George was free and accepted, though not without a misgiving that grew and crystallized during the afternoon into a determination to pursue a certain course of action if Millbay should make it necessary. Before they were halfway through the meal, at a service flat in Smith Square, Millbay *had* made it necessary. They had discussed general topics at first, but then Millbay had continued: "You know, Boswell, I'm still a bit curious about Livia Winslow. She always rather fascinated me, in a sort of way, and to meet someone else who knew her . . . well, I suppose it's the novelist in me cropping up again, even though it's years since I last published anything. And I certainly don't intend to publish anything you tell me, so don't worry."

"Anything *I* tell you?"

"Yes—if you feel like it. I wish you would."

"About what?"

"About Livia . . . that is, of course, unless you'd rather not discuss her."

George then said what he had made up his mind to say if this situation should arise. He said: "I don't mind discussing her, but I'd better tell you something in advance. I was once married to her."

"*Good God!* You don't say?"

Till then George had felt slightly uncomfortable, but now, relaxed by his own candor, he could almost enjoy the other's unbounded astonishment. He grinned across the table. "I dunno why I felt I had to tell you, but now I have done, I hope you'll go ahead and give me any more news you have about her."

"So you're just as interested as I am?"

"Probably. That's rather natural, isn't it?"

"You haven't kept in touch with her at all?"

"No—not since . . ." He left the sentence unfinished.

"And that was—when?"

"September first, 1921."

"Well remembered, eh?"

George nodded.

Millbay gave him a slow, shrewd glance, then continued: "Jeffrey happens to be a friend of mine. . . . Would you like me to talk about his marriage?"

"Aye—if *you* feel like it."

"And you won't mind if I'm frank?"

"We'd both be wasting our time if you weren't, wouldn't we?"

"Glad you think so. And in exchange will you give me your own frank opinion . . . afterwards?"

George smiled. "Nay, I'll not promise that. Let's hear your story first."

.   .   .

I first met Jeffrey Winslow (Millbay said) in connection with the Kemalpan affair. I don't suppose you heard much about that. It didn't get publicized. Things like it are always apt to happen, and to happen with the same declension of eventfulness—that is to say, they begin excitingly—bloodshed in the jungle, perhaps—and end a year or so later with quiet voices pronouncing judgment across some departmental desk top in Whitehall. Mine was one of the quiet voices; I had all the papers relating to the affair before me, and I'd given several days to the most careful study of them. After all, you don't squash a man's career without good reason, especially if he belongs to a family like the Winslows. I was as tactful as I could be. I rather liked the look of the fellow from the outset; he was neither truculent nor obsequious, and heaven knows he could have been either. He just sat at the other side of the desk—a little nervous, as was natural; he answered questions briefly and clearly, and there was a pleasant ring in his voice that I would have taken for sincerity had not the circumstances of the moment put doubts in my mind.

Of course the Kemalpan affair needs some explanation—that is, if you don't already know about it. (George said he didn't.) Oh well, I can put it in a few sentences. Kemalpan is a technically independent Sultanate that the British Government has a treaty with; Jeffrey Winslow was adviser to the Sultan on matters connected with imperial relations—somewhat of a nebulous job, but semi-diplomatic, with tentacles reaching into commercial and military spheres. Decidedly no plum—but not badly paid, and easy enough, as a rule, if you didn't mind burying yourself in a place like Kemalpan. That, I should add, is the name of the capital city as well as of the state; the capital is inland, in the midst of jungle and rubber plantations; Winslow preferred to live with his wife at a settlement on the coast fifty miles away—healthier there, or so he reckoned. There's a telegraph line between the coast and the capital, and a sort of rough trail that you can drive over in a Ford—but no good roads, no railway, and in those days no airline. These details are important in view of what happened. Also I should add that a small colony of British and Dutch rubber planters lived on their estates near the inland capital, and were on good terms with the Sultan, whose subjects they employed. The Sultan didn't mind low wages for the tappers so long as he got a cut of the plantation profits —which he did, more or less, in the form of thoroughly legalized taxation. Quite a nice setup as long as it lasted, and it lasted throughout the twenties, when rubber rose to four shillings a pound; but later the fall to sixpence led to labor troubles, and by the mid-thirties these had reached danger point. All this is necessary to give the background to what happened in October '34, when an insurrection in the capital threatened to depose the Sultan in favor of some native "leader" whom the planters called a Communist—it's a conditioned reflex, you know. But it was true that the plantations couldn't pay higher wages without going bankrupt, and equally true that the mob was in a mood to overthrow things if the millennium didn't appear overnight. The Sultan, who was a sly old debauchee with no real interest in life but graft and women, rapidly slipped into panic; meanwhile the planters with their wives and families moved in from outlying districts to seek protection in the royal palace—protection being a few hundred of the Sultan's private army, poor in quality and doubtful in allegiance.

The crisis developed within a matter of hours, while the Winslows were at their home on the coast; Winslow wired the news to London, which was part of his job, and was told to await instructions. A day later those instructions were sent. He was told to assure the Sultan that the British Government would back him to the full in suppressing the revolt, and that therefore the capital must be held at all costs until such assistance was forthcoming. . . .

Now this was the point. Those instructions were *sent,* and we had evidence later that they reached the coast settlement where Winslow lived; but he swore he never got them. Thus he didn't give the Sultan any assurance of British help and the Sultan promptly gave in to the rebels. There followed a nasty little affray at the palace in which three white men and two white women were butchered. Well, that was the Kemalpan affair . . . nothing very remarkable, but thoroughly reprehensible from every official standpoint, and a year later we were still holding inquiries about it in Whitehall, still collecting more evidence that the instructions to Winslow had actually been transmitted and must have been received by him, though he still swore that they hadn't.

A further point cropped up: the telegraph line from the coast to the inland capital had been cut, so that if Winslow *had* received his orders he could only have properly obeyed them by making the fifty-mile trip in person over the rough trail; and this, with most of the intervening country in the hands of the rebels, might not have been so safe. In fact, it might have been decidedly unsafe—which was why he couldn't have relied on anyone else to do the job. So you see where all this is leading . . . and where it had already led on that foggy Friday in November '35, when I first talked to the fellow in my office. Was his denial of having received instructions just the only thing he could think of as an excuse for having been scared? If that were the true interpretation, it added up to something rather serious.

You know, it's a queer thing when you have to talk to a gentleman in the social sense who has somehow broken the code of a gentleman in the ethical sense. You can never quite come to grips with the situation. You fence and evade and know that he knows all the time what you're really thinking. I never, for instance, came anywhere near hinting to Winslow that he might be both a liar and a coward, yet he must have known that that was the inevitable implication behind all the questioning. And presently it all boiled down to that simple question: Had he or had he not received those instructions? He stuck to it that he hadn't, and he sounded convincing, but long experience has left me with the opinion that lies are, if anything, easier to tell convincingly than the truth. Besides, evidence that the instructions *had* reached him was almost watertight, so I had to accept it. But of course I did not say so. I said, quietly and politely: "Well, Winslow, we seem to have reached a deadlock. Maybe there'll be some further evidence . . . if so, perhaps you'll be good enough to come here again."

He answered then, with a certain austere dignity which I liked (whether he were a liar and a coward or not): "Of course I will, but it's nine months now since I was advised to come home on leave, and since then I've been kept waiting for the inquiry to finish. It's rather a strain, in some ways. Besides, I should very much like to go back to my job."

It was then my duty to tell him that there was little chance of his ever resuming that kind of job under government service. He took it very well. He said he was sorry—which I knew did not mean any kind of confession, but merely that the outcome was a blow to him. I said I was sorry too—and by that I did not mean that as a liar and a coward he deserved any special leniency, but merely that it grieved me, as a member of the so-called ruling class, to see another member acquitting himself out of style. You see what snobs we all are. . . . Anyhow, I shook hands with him and wished him well and didn't expect to see him again.

But I just couldn't get the fellow out of my mind. He'd interested me—not only because the departure from tradition is always more interesting than the tradition itself, of which one gets a little bored when one is, as I am, a somewhat cynical conformist. I should be believed, no doubt, if I said that after talking to Winslow I paced up and down my office floor wondering if, in his place, I should have behaved any better. Yet actually I didn't wonder at all, because I knew to the contrary. I have fought in wars, and there have been several occasions on which I risked my life, not because I was brave, nor because I hated the enemy, but because risking my life was the thing to do in those particular circumstances, and all my training had been to make me act both accordingly and automatically. That's one of the reasons why Winslow interested me— because his training had been, if anything, more traditional than mine. *Who's Who* and *Debrett* were sufficient authorities for that. He'd been to a good public school and to Oxford, had then passed into the Diplomatic and been an attaché at various European embassies. Quite brilliant at Oxford, by the way, and with his family connections he must have been exactly the type for whom one would

forecast a distinguished future. All of which added to the mystery—
for why, if one came to think of it, should such a fellow ever fetch
up at Kemalpan? That was decidedly *not* the thing to have done
. . . and since it was unlikely that anybody would take Kemalpan
from choice, what had forced him into it? Well, there were people
I knew who could throw out a few hints. Our friend Sprigge is the
expert there. Scandals, women, *mésalliances,* bad checks—he can
usually tell you. In Winslow's case it was a divorce—which in those
prim days didn't help anyone . . . and I needn't say more about
that to you.

I also discovered that Winslow had written a book of essays on
moral philosophy that had attracted some attention in its field, and
might have led to a useful subsidiary reputation had not his main
career gone off at such a tangent. I was interested enough to get
hold of the book. I found it a bit above my head, but I thought it
showed signs of a first-class mind, and first-class minds are such rare
things in our time and land that it becomes a crime, in my opinion,
to frustrate, sidetrack, or otherwise stultify them. And his, at least,
had been sidetracked at Kemalpan, for—apart from the career—
there had been no succeeding books.

During the following months a trickle of further evidence came
in, but none of it helpful to his case. A Chinese clerk reported that
he had personally delivered the coded cable message from the
telegraph station to Winslow's bungalow, where he had handed
it to a responsible servant; the servant said Winslow was out at the
time, so he had placed it on his desk along with other messages and
letters. . . . The case also began to look blacker from another
angle, for at the time the message was received it was known at the
coast settlement that the lives of white refugees in the Sultan's
palace were endangered, so that if Winslow had been concerned
with his own personal safety he must also have weighed it against
the safety of others. About twenty, to be precise—including women
and children. And to complete the indictment, it seemed reasonably
probable that if he had managed to get the message through to the
Sultan, the latter would have put up a defense instead of a surrender, and the five lives might have been saved. Altogether there
was very little excuse for Winslow, and when, just about the time
this later evidence came in, I got a letter from him in Ireland I was

in a rather unsympathetic mood for considering it, especially as the first few sentences showed me he was asking the impossible. Briefly, he wanted a job. Not, of course, the same job in Kemalpan, or even that kind of job in that kind of place; yet, he argued, could not a decade of experience in the East, plus the knowledge of several obscure languages and dialects, be put to some use somehow and somewhere? What he hinted at was a job in some government office, where he could continue in the public service, however humbly.

I wrote back and told him how little chance he had. And a week later Mrs. Winslow herself came to see me.

It was another interesting meeting. I had heard of this Mrs. Winslow once before, in connection with her oftquoted and misquoted remark about Hitler at the Batavia dinner party; I hadn't disliked her for that (because it seemed to me she had probably been misunderstood), but it had given me an impression that she was a dangerous partner for a man of affairs. And now, when I saw her across my desk, I was immediately struck by a certain controlled intention in her whole look and attitude. She faced me as if she knew what she wanted and meant to get her own way at all costs. After a mere good-morning she plunged right in—couldn't I possibly find her husband some desk job in Whitehall? Apparently my letter had been the final blow to his hopes, and she was afraid of a breakdown if he didn't find some work where he felt he could be useful. And though she herself preferred to live in Ireland, she would not say no to London if Jeffrey had to be there. She talked of living in London as a sort of sacrifice she would make for her husband if the Government in return would do its part.

I told her flatly it was impossible, and when she stressed the personal angle I delicately hinted that government posts were not handed out to prevent breakdowns. The Kemalpan incident, I said, was of a kind that they must both recognize had called at least a halt to Jeffrey's career. At that she began to protest and argue, but of course I wouldn't go over all the details with her. "Even assuming some tragic mistake, one can do nothing about it now. Men's careers have been ruined before by mistakes—it would be nothing new."

"You look at it very coldly," she said.

"I look at it very logically," I answered. "The whole incident, affair, or whatever you call it, is closed now and can't be reopened unless some totally new item of evidence should crop up. And that's so unlikely that we can almost say it won't happen."

She then said quietly: "It can happen. That's what I came here for—to tell you something. It was I who intercepted the cable. I decoded it, found out what it meant, then decided that Jeffrey shouldn't ever see it. Of course he doesn't know I did that, or that I'm admitting it now to you."

She waited for me to show surprise, and perhaps I did, but it was not surprise at what she said so much as surprise that she should expect me to believe it. Naturally I didn't. But it would have been equally unwise to dismiss the matter without further probing.

"What made you do such a thing?" I asked guardedly.

"I just had to," she answered. "The telegraph line was cut, so I knew he'd want to take the message himself, and as the country was in the hands of the rebels I didn't think he'd have much chance of getting through. And he might have got killed."

"He might," I agreed. "And five others did."

She said nothing.

"Probably as a result of the message not being delivered."

"I wouldn't say *probably*. *Possibly*."

"You knew the planters and their families were in danger when you intercepted the message?"

"Yes."

"And you deliberately let them take their chance in order to ensure your husband's personal safety?"

"Yes."

"Don't you think that rather indefensible?"

"I'm not defending it. I'm just saying it's what I did. My husband was dearer to me than a crowd of people I didn't know."

"How many people would you be willing to sacrifice for such a reason?"

She didn't answer.

I went on, with more sarcasm: "Or shall I put it this way—at what point would the lives of strangers, by sheer weight of numbers, tilt the balance against the life of the man you love?"

She answered: "Never."

"So you'd sacrifice millions, if one can conceive of such a situation?"

She nodded.

She really was at this point beginning to surprise me. It's rare that people, especially women, are willing to let a logical point be pressed home. I said, rather severely: "I'm glad to think you are probably unique in looking at things that way."

"Oh, but I'm not," she answered. "In wartime wouldn't you press a button, if you could, to destroy a million of the enemy rather than lose a single life on your own side? Then why is my attitude so extraordinary?"

What *was* extraordinary, of course, was her argument, and it was one that didn't seem to me profitable to continue. I was still disinclined to believe her confession, but I was clear in my mind as to the implications of the alternatives. Either she was lying to save her husband's reputation—in which case one could possibly like her for it; or she had actually told the truth—in which case she was ruthless, unprincipled, and wholly the kind of wife whom a man in a responsible position should not have.

But in any case nothing could be done. Even if her confession were accepted at its face value it would not help Jeffrey to get his job back. The most it could do would be to win him a measure of half-incredulous sympathy.

I explained all this to her, and it seemed to me that she picked up the cue, as it were, and from then on made a bid for the sympathy. Jeffrey, she repeated, was on the verge of a breakdown. All he asked was some job, however small and ill-paid, just to give him the feeling—perhaps even the illusion—that he had not been dishonorably discharged. It had even come to the point, she said, that their marriage might founder if he could not get such a job; he was finding it hard to settle down in Ireland, and the book he was trying to write was not going well. This was the first I had heard about another book and I asked her for details. She said it was a book about the Far East—one he had long projected—something rather scholarly and definitive. She had been urging him to use up his time that way ever since he came home, and surely conditions in Ireland were ideal for authorship—a quiet place in the country, nothing else to do, and ample money to live on. "Really," she added, "he's quite well off—there's no reason why he should worry about a career, or about writing books either, so far as that goes. The whole Kemalpan business wouldn't matter if only he didn't think it mattered."

"Perhaps, though, the relatives of the people who were killed there might still think it mattered."

"Oh, *them.* I wasn't thinking about *them.*"

And she wasn't. She was just thinking of herself and Jeffrey. That seemed to close the argument quite finally. I got up and made it clear that there was nothing more I could say or do.

During the next few weeks I found myself wondering even more compellingly about the Winslows. First, *he* had interested me, then she; but now my interest in each of them separately was more than redoubled in them both. What went on between such a pair? What sort of thing was their life together? If she had been lying on his behalf, it was possible that the appalling selfishness of her argument might not have been sincere. Or had she been telling the truth, as to both fact and attitude? To summarize it another way: if she were a liar, one liked her better and her husband less; but if she were not a liar, one disliked her intensely and felt sympathy for her husband. And I still could not properly make up my mind. I have rarely been so puzzled about anything. Then suddenly more evidence filtered through—I needn't go into details, but it was of a kind that weighed down one of the scales pretty conclusively. She *had* told the truth. She *had* intercepted the message. Which meant that Jeffrey himself was neither a liar nor a coward, but at worst a victim.

The revelation swung me into a mood in which I recollected our meeting and how much, from first appearance, I had liked him. I remembered his quietness, his austere dignity, the simple unassumingness which, I knew, concealed a mind whose quality had been demonstrated. So on impulse I wrote him a friendly letter, saying nothing much except that I hoped he was getting on all right and that if he ever visited London he might find time to have lunch with me. To my surprise he answered by return and took the invitation with far more seriousness than I should have thought. He would have been so glad, he said, to come to London and see me (I hadn't suggested that, by any means), but he was not very well and couldn't get away . . . would I, however, visit him in Ireland—stay a week or two—there was good shooting, fishing, climbing, if that sort of thing appealed to me? He would be very happy, and please make it soon, because the late summer (and it was then August) was perhaps the best time of the year at Carrigole.

It happened that I had not had a holiday that year, and though the idea of visiting the Winslows seemed quite fantastic at first, I soon found myself thinking of reasons why I might take Jeffrey at his word. After all, I liked him; it might even be that if he were feeling low-spirited I could help him by talk and companionship. But I will not disguise that my overmastering motive was sheer curiosity. I wanted to find out what sort of people they both were, in their own home and with their own domestic problems. And at least it could do no harm to call on them if I happened to be holiday-making thereabouts.

So I looked up Carrigole on the map and found it was a dozen miles from Galway—a small place, not very accessible, in a district of lakes and mountains. And that's why I asked you, Boswell, if you ever knew the Winslows in Ireland, because I should have liked your opinion of Carrigole.

It began to rain when I first came within sight of it. I had hired a car for the last stage of the trip and all the way I felt oddly excited about getting there. Actually I had never been in Ireland before, and crossing the country from Dublin it had occurred to me that even the trains were antique—and not contemptibly, as on so many outdated railways all over the world, but honorably, with dignity, like good sound Victorian mahogany furniture. And when, at Galway, my train reached its destination, there was again the contrast with other railheads I had seen; for here was no mere petering out into obscurity, but a grand finale in stone—the massive quayside station, far too large and almost quiet as a cathedral, shaking a granite fist into the sea.

But my first glimpse of Carrigole was equally memorable—or perhaps the mood I was in gave me extra percipience—a kind of mystic awareness I am naturally distrustful of, but can't deny exists, at certain rare times and places. I knew Ireland was supposed to be like that, and therefore I was perversely surprised to find it so. Through the rain-swept windows of the car I saw blue smoke drifting over the roofs of whitewashed cottages, and beyond them a mountain rising into clouds that totally covered the summit. I gathered, from the map on my knee, that this must be Slieve Baragh, not much higher than a hill, yet as I saw it then for the first time it seemed in another world of measurement. Presently the car slowed down for the village, and here the swollen clouds dipped lower, bringing no raindrops but emptying silently; Slieve Baragh was now hidden behind a curtain that suggested Himalayan heights —and yet, I remembered again, it was not much of a mountain— a mere two thousand feet. I couldn't help making other mental notes of the near and the practical—the uneven walls and mud-brown pavements, the butcher who called himself a "flesher" and the chemist's shop magnificently styled a "Medical Hall." I wound down the side window to catch the whiff of peat on the wet breeze as the car bumped over a bridge across a river—only a minor river, like the minor mountain, but turbulent now as it filled almost directly from the sky.

A mile or so past the village the Winslows' house stood behind a drenched garden, and Jeffrey was waiting at the gate in the rain. He looked pale and worn, and there was intense nervousness in the way he greeted me.

I ought to describe the house; it was substantially built, thick-walled and small-windowed, in a style conditioned by roaring Atlantic gales for half the year, and political troubles for half a century. These indeed had left the house with its most conspicuous attribute—a large, burnt-out wing, blackened and roofless, which provided a ready topic of conversation. "They tried to burn the whole place down in 'twenty-two," Jeffrey explained. "Livy got it cheap because it hadn't been lived in since then and needed so much repairing, but part of it's beyond repair—it would be too large for us, anyway. We have a couple of servants and the boy when he's home from school—that only makes five. . . ."

By then we were in the square hall, from which the main rooms of the house opened on all sides, and it was there that Livia met me. Perhaps because of the dark afternoon it seemed to me that she appeared from nowhere, a sudden distillation of shadows. I was not surprised when she greeted me as a stranger, allowing Jeffrey to make the unnecessary introduction. I played up accordingly and thought it equally unnecessary when, a few minutes later in the bedroom I had been shown to, she closed the door behind her and said with a sort of conspiratory quietness: "Jeffrey still doesn't know I came to see you in London."

I nodded and said I would have surmised that he didn't.

"And of course he doesn't know anything else either."

I knew what she meant, and I nodded to that also.

"I hope you won't ever repeat what I told you in confidence," she went on.

I said temporizingly and in the bland way which I have culti-vated as part of my official equipment: "My dear Mrs. Winslow, I wasn't aware that you were telling me anything in confidence, but as a matter of fact I don't usually gossip." I added, to change the subject: "It's so kind of you to have me here, and I hope it isn't too much trouble."

"Not at all," she answered, with cold politeness. "You're on your way to Limerick, aren't you?"

That was as broad a hint as I needed, and clear proof of what I had already guessed—that she didn't want me to stay, and that Jeffrey had invited me either without her knowledge or against her wishes. I had guessed this subconsciously enough to have wired my time of arrival too late for any cancellation of the invitation—and, as it happened, too late even for Jeffrey to meet me at Galway.

"Yes," I said. "I'm on my way to Limerick."

I had a bath, changed into drier tweeds, and went down to din-ner. I met the boy then, Charles I think his name was—a youth of thirteen, at Charterhouse—tall, good-looking, shy, likable. Intel-ligent, too, as I discovered after a few casual remarks. He was piling turf on the old-fashioned fire as I entered, for it was chilly enough to have one, and that set us talking of turf and electricity, old and new, the Shannon hydroelectric scheme and the ancient Irish tongue that nobody spoke except illiterate peasants and modern school-teachers. Livia then said: "We're all half-mad with our op-posites," which seemed to end rather than clinch any discussion. She had a curious way of saying things that were never quite clear, yet never so meaningless as to be easy to ignore. Jeffrey noticed my interest in the boy and soon found a chance to tell me, like any other proud father, that Charlie was keen on music and by no means a bad piano player. We went on chatting desultorily throughout the meal; then the boy made a polite excuse and left us three adults together. I somehow had an impression that he got on better with his father than with Livia, accepting the shy approach more readily than the frontal assault; and it has amused me since to reflect that Livia ranged against the polite taboos of the English public-school system would be a unique example of an irresistible force meeting an immovable body.

After he had gone there was a change of atmosphere that became almost baleful; it had been tense before, but now it was menacing, a curious hostility between Jeffrey and Livia that was due, I could not help feeling, to my own presence. A sort of invisible cat crouching on the table top to spring at any of our throats at an unknown signal—if the metaphor isn't too farfetched. In an attempt to ease the conversation into some harmless groove I said, unimportantly: "It's probably not a good day to sight-see, but I did at least get a good whiff of Ireland as I drove over."

Livia answered, as if she must dispute with me at all costs: "It *is* a good day to sight-see. Ireland's a sad country, so you see it best when it looks sad, but the sadness is alive—it comes out of the earth —it isn't like the dead sadness of London, especially the West End."

"Oh come now," I said facetiously. "The Café Royal at midnight hasn't got much dead sadness."

"Jeff and I love it here," she went on, defensively, as if I had ever denied it. "That is, he could if he wanted to," she added, as if Jeffrey had ever denied it.

"But what do you do all the time?" I asked, still facetiously.

"Livy looks after the farm," Jeffrey answered. "She likes that sort of work, though it's not very good land—far too stony, and the gales come in full of salt spray that sours the soil. . . . I'll take you round tomorrow."

"Mr. Millbay won't have time," Livia said pointedly. "He's got to leave for Limerick tomorrow." She added: "Jeffrey's busy too. He has to write his book."

"If he can," Jeffrey commented, with a note of ruefulness.

"He doesn't concentrate enough," she countered. They were both talking at each other, it seemed, with me as a needed yet somehow exacerbating audience.

The question of the book raised Jeffrey a notch higher in whatever emotion was being generated between them. "Livy," he said,
"appears to think that writing is just a simple matter of one page
after another."

"Well, isn't it?" Livia asked, appealing to me.

I tried to lower the tension by asking Jeffrey how far the book
had progressed.

Livia answered for him: "About a hundred pages, and it ought
to be easy for him to finish because it's all about Far Eastern affairs
that he's an expert on."

Jeffrey said, still in the same mood of self-scarifying irony: "Livia
thinks that with a record like mine people will be eager to accept
me as an authority."

I gathered that this had been argued between them before, since
Livia retorted: "What does his record have to do with what he
writes? . . . That's what I always ask him."

Jeffrey nodded. "Yes, that's what she always asks me, and I think
the answer is rather obvious. Wouldn't you say so, Millbay?"

I didn't want to get into such an argument, so I said nothing.

Livia went on, as if even my silence irritated her: "And what *of*
his record, anyway? Who bothers about it except a few people in
the Government?"

Jeffrey answered heavily: "I think Charlie would bother about
it if he knew—and perhaps he does know, or can guess."

"Charlie has no right to be ashamed of his father," Livia retorted, and then she added, astoundingly: "My father spent twelve
years in jail and *I* wasn't ashamed of *him*."

I hadn't known about that, and mentally made up my mind to
look into the matter when I got back to London. And of course I
afterwards found who her father had been. But in the meantime I
felt I had to be honest and side with Jeffrey about the book. He was
undoubtedly right, and his Far Eastern opus, however good, might
well fall under the curse of Kemalpan—the more so since, if it were
very good indeed, it might even attract publicity to what would
otherwise have been ignored or forgotten. I didn't bring up that
point, but my general support of Jeffrey's attitude led to what I had
feared—and that was the whole Kemalpan issue spouting up like a
volcano. Jeffrey muttered gloomily that he wondered if it were

worth while even to finish the book at all, what he really wanted was a job, something he could work at to prove himself more than a failure and an idler. A job, a job . . . to get away from the ever-lasting western gales and the stony soured soil and the clouds dripping over the mountain and nothing to do . . . nothing to do. . . .

I could feel the tension mounting now like a physical wave through the shadows, and again to ease it I said: "You know, Jeffrey, there *are* jobs, if you really want one. It wouldn't have to be in government service. Your Far Eastern experience would be a bargain for a good commercial firm, and it's true, as you know, that a man can serve his country in, say, British-American Tobacco quite as valuably as in an embassy."

I saw his eyes light up at that. "Do you think they'd even con-sider me?"

But then a strange and disconcerting thing happened. Livia got up from her chair and leaned across the table towards us with a gleam in her eyes that was of a very different kind. It gave her face a rather frightening radiance, emphasizing the curious profile of nose and forehead as she stared down at us like, I thought, the figure-head of a ship about to dive into a storm. "He's not going!" she screamed, in a wild angry whisper. "He must stay *here*. This is the place for him . . . *always*. . . ."

After that there was little I could say. The scene subsided, leav-ing us to stammer a few commonplaces about this and that; Livia seemed to realize she had said too much, or had somehow been caught off-guard.

We adjourned to the drawing room and sat up, the three of us, till it became clear that Jeffrey wanted to talk to me alone if there were any chance. Towards midnight I began yawning, to bring the thing to an issue, and Livia said it was time we all went to bed; whereupon Jeffrey announced that he and I would stay up and chat for a while. He said that with an air of challenge, and there was nothing much she could do about it except leave us together. Such a small victory, and yet, from his whole attitude, I gathered it was both a narrow and a crucial one.

When we were alone he asked me again about the possibility of a commercial job—had I meant what I said—did I really think there was a chance of it? Certainly, I answered, if that was what he really wanted, and I offered there and then to put in a good word for him. But the imminence of something practical and decisive seemed to reverse his mood and deflate his eagerness, so that I told him to think it over carefully; maybe he didn't want to go as much as he thought he did. He answered, far *too* carefully: "I'd go like a shot but for Livy."

Then he lapsed into a mumble of pitiful things about her—almost as if he had learned most of them by heart and were repeating them as much for his own benefit as for mine. She would be dead against his going abroad again; she had spent ten years in Malaya and that was understandably as much as she wanted; she loved Ireland and the farm; she worked so hard, was so good to him, they really got on all right together despite occasional bickerings . . . and so on.

And of course, knowing what I did, it antagonized me to the point of saying: "So you really mean you'll stay here for the rest of your life just to please her?"

He answered: "Perhaps I ought to stay here. After all, she's been very decent about the whole thing. The Kemalpan business, I mean. She's never reproached me about it."

That did the trick. Accustomed as I am to the severest verbal self-discipline I simply couldn't keep back my answer. "By God," I exclaimed, "she damn well oughtn't to, since she was the whole cause of it herself!"

Then I told him what I hadn't promised Livia not to tell him, though I should have broken that promise anyway.

Of course he was appalled. He wouldn't believe it at first, even when I said I had documents, depositions, and so on, that I could send or show him later. "Besides," I said, "she confessed to it even before there was proof." That appalled him also, and I had to tell him about her visit to my office. When he still seemed unable or unwilling to grasp the situation, I said: "You mean you don't think she's capable of it?"

He answered heavily: "She's capable of anything." And then he went on with a touch of anger: "Why did you tell me? Do you want me to think badly of her? After all, though what she did was quite dreadful, it only shows how much she loves me . . . in her way."

"Certainly, if you think so," I answered. "She shows she loves you by ruining your career—to say nothing of sacrificing the lives of five strangers. I didn't intend to say all this when I came here, and I admit I acted on impulse in doing so, but now I'm rather glad I did." I thought it was a good moment then to say good-night and tell him I'd be leaving in the morning early. "Perhaps there's somewhere in the village I can hire a car to take me on to Limerick. . . ." He said there was, and pulled himself together enough to telephone about it. Then he took me up to my room. At the door we shook hands and I repeated my offer to try to find him a commercial job if he wanted one. I also said that in any case I hoped he'd give me a ring if ever he were in London.

I slept badly and got up soon after dawn. The mists were over the mountain and a gale from the sea was already tearing them to shreds. I did not think Carrigole was a place I should like to stay in for long, much less to live in altogether. There was something elemental and primitive about it that would get on my nerves unless I could become elemental and primitive myself.

The car had already arrived and stood in the lane beyond the garden, but as I was crossing the latter from the house I saw Livia hurrying towards me from a side gate. She was dressed in a sort of waterproof smock, tied loosely at the waist; her head was almost hidden behind a low-brimmed sou'wester, and she wore also knee-high boots caked with mud. I don't know why I remember such things, except that I was aware of a curious half-hypnotized tension that made me stir my mind over details to keep it from somehow freezing at her approach.

I was prepared for a scene, but there was none. "So you're going now?" she greeted me.

I said I had thought it better to leave early, so as to reach Limerick by midday.

"Why yes, of course. Much better. I'm always up like this. There's so much to be done on a farm."

I said I was sure she was kept very busy.

"Of course Jeff's still asleep," she went on. "Nine's early enough for him to start writing, don't you think?" And then, with a bright smile: "What time would *you* begin writing if you were a writer?"

I answered, smiling back: "Any time I damn well felt like it— and I speak with authority because I *am* a writer."

She didn't seem to take offense—and yet I knew, from something in her eyes, that Jeffrey had told her I had told him everything, and that she hated me for it. And I had a feeling that to be hated by Livia Winslow was no mild experience.

She accompanied me to the car. "Jeff is really happy here," she said, as if I were again denying the fact. "And no wonder, is it?" And then she added, in a phrase I remember because I wasn't quite sure what it meant: "When I first saw this place I thought I had found where I was born in another world. . . ."

So I finished my Irish holiday and returned to London with such thoughts about the Winslows as you can imagine. Some months later Jeffrey rang me up at my office, the tone of his voice conveying a certain urgency, but also, I thought, a very welcome quality of decision. He sounded like a man who had finally yet in a sense firmly reached the end of his tether. We lunched at my club, and afterwards he asked if my offer to aid him in finding a job still held.

Not only it did, I told him, but it so happened that a few days before I had mentioned his name to a friend in one of the big oil companies, and the reaction had been distinctly favorable. "Only I didn't know whether you'd changed your mind, so I hardly cared to approach you about it."

"I'll take the job whatever it is," he said. "Where do I go and when can I start?"

"Look here," I answered, "I don't own the company. You'll have to fix all that yourself—but if you like I can telephone my friend this afternoon and let him know you're in town. I should imagine, from the way he talked, that it would be something fairly immediate, and he did also tell me where it was—Hong Kong. . . . How does that suit? You speak Cantonese?"

He said he did.

"They'll probably jump at you then."

He seemed so relieved that I told him how glad I was to see him in such a different mood from the last time we had talked.

"Yes," he said. "You can call it that if you like—a different mood."

I asked him what had happened to make the change, and then he told me something so extraordinary that if I hadn't known enough about Livia beforehand I should have disbelieved it, or him, or both of them, and even now I'm not a hundred per cent certain. It seemed that after my one-night visit they had had many arguments about his taking another job abroad, Livia becoming more and more obstinate in her insistence that he should stay at Carrigole. It was almost as if she had some obsession about the place—and perhaps, for that matter, she had. Most of her ideas were obsessions, anyhow, just as most of her affections were passions—she did nothing by halves. In such an atmosphere as had developed between them Jeffrey found it impossible to write his book and presently did not even wish to; what he craved was a job, and that too was for him an obsession. Their disagreements had culminated, he said, in an angry scene in which she accused him of pretending to want the job when what he really wanted was to leave her; this he denied emphatically, but in the very act of doing so caught himself wondering if it were half true. And then she staged an astonishing climax. She told him she would never leave him, that she loved him too much, that wherever he went she would follow, and that rather than lose him she would kill anyone who stood in the way of their life together. He took that for melodrama till she added, with a terrifying sort of casualness: "I did that once, you know."

He thought she meant the five victims at Kemalpan, and though he knew she could be held accountable for their deaths, he thought it was going too far to say that she had actually killed them. But then she always did go too far, and he always tried to drag her back by being severely and irritatingly logical; it was almost a routine. So he said: "Oh come now, don't put it that way. They might have lost their lives in any event."

"*They?*" she echoed. And then it turned out that she hadn't been thinking of Kemalpan at all.

"Then who?" he asked, puzzled but also wryly amused.

"Don't you remember Anne Westerholme?" she answered.

He told me that when she spoke that name he first had to make an effort to recollect it, but that when he did so he felt himself growing pale and cold with an emotion he would have called fear, except that he had known fear before, and this was nothing like it.

He also told me about Anne Westerholme, and the story took him back ten years or more, to the time when he was adviser to another Sultanate and lived with Livia at a place called Tanjong Palai. It was not such a good job as the one he obtained later, but the district was healthier and they had a pleasant bungalow in the hills, with the usual neighborhood society of tea and rubber planters. One of these, a friend of Jeffrey's, was bringing out a young governess from England to look after his three small boys, but as they developed scarlet fever while she was en route he had arranged with the Winslows that the girl should stay with them until the end of quarantine. So Anne Westerholme arrived one afternoon at the Winslows' bungalow, and the next morning she was dead. She had been bitten by a five-foot krait, the most venomous of Malayan snakes, and as it could be surmised that she had opened her bedroom window without fixing the screen there was no hitch in the presumption of accidental death. Thousands die from snakebite every year in that part of the world; it was tragic, but hardly remarkable.

But now, a decade later, Livia had more to say about this, and what she said was quite dreadful. She said that very early in the morning she had entered the girl's room and seen her asleep with the krait curled up at the foot of the bed. It would have been easy then to kill the snake (she had killed scores) but she simply did not do so. She went back to the kitchen, calmly gave the Chinese houseboy his daily orders, played some Mozart records on the phonograph, and waited for the call that summoned her, along with the servants, too late.

Jeffrey said that when she told him this, sitting over the turf fire at Carrigole late one night, he was so horrified that it did not occur to him at first that he had only her word for the story; but that later, when he did realize that, his feelings of horror hardly diminished. He made her go to bed, he said, and himself spent the night in his downstairs workroom, arranging the manuscript of the book he knew he would never finish—not at Carrigole, anyhow. And in the morning he took the train for Dublin en route for Holyhead and London.

We sat over coffee in the club smoke room discussing the matter throughout most of the afternoon.

"But do you really think she was speaking the truth?" I asked.

"I think she could have been," he answered, with no kind of reluctance. "But I also think she could have made up the story."

"But what motive could she possibly have had? A girl fresh from England—how could Livia have had any concern with whether she lived or died?"

"Jealousy," Jeffrey answered. "She saw in this girl some menace to her own life with me—or so she said when she made the confession."

"But that's equally absurd!" I persisted. "How long had you known the girl? A few hours, I suppose. . . . Had you had any chance to . . . but of course it's preposterous . . . and what sort of a girl was she? I suppose you hardly remember—even the name didn't stay in your mind—"

Jeffrey nodded thoughtfully. "Yes, I'd almost forgotten that, but I do remember *her*—she had reddish hair and a rather calm face."

"Not pretty, though?"

"No, but calm . . . *calm.*"

"And Livia was with you the whole of the time—"

"Oh yes. The three of us just talked during dinner, that's all."

"Well, it's still absurd," I repeated. "Even for Livia it's absurd. How could she possibly imagine there was anything for her to be jealous of?"

He nodded again, but then suddenly moved restlessly in the club armchair. "You know," he said at length, "I'll be perfectly frank with you, since you deserve that much for all you've done for me lately. . . . It's true of course that there was nothing between me and that girl. Yet . . . there almost might have been . . . eventually. I knew that, in a queer sort of way, while we were just chatting during dinner. Nothing special or exciting or significant or provocative—and yet—and I was aware of it—that girl's calmness came over to me . . . and Livy intercepted it, just as later on she intercepted the cable." He got up, clenching and unclenching his hands. "That's the really frightening thing about it," he exclaimed, when he had let me order a second brandy. "Livy *knew.* She *always* knew. She doesn't miss a thing. . . ."

. . .

The Mayor of Browdley sat for a long time in silence after Millbay had finished. He was—and he was aware of it—a little out of his depth. This world of rubber planters and Sultans and five-foot kraits was so foreign to him, or seemed so when he tried to get it into extempore focus; how different from that other world of cotton mills and council meetings? And yet, after all, it was the same world, governed by the same passions, the same greeds, the same basic gulf between those who take and those who give. True, there were no snakes in Browdley, but there was diphtheria that could kill (and had killed, hadn't it?) just as effectively; and there had once been a murder in a street not far from Mill Street, a particularly lurid murder that had made headlines in all the Sunday papers. From Browdley to Kemalpan and Tanjong Palai was only a matter of miles, but from Livia's mind to his own . . . how far was that?

Millbay interrupted his musings. "Well, Boswell, you stipulated for my story first. Now what about yours?"

George answered at length: "Aye . . . but I haven't one. Nothing to match what you've told me, anyhow. I can't say I'm glad to have heard it, but it's been good of you to give me so much time."

"No need to be grateful. I'd rather know how it all strikes you."

"That's just it," George answered. "It *does* strike me. It strikes me all of a heap."

"You mean you don't altogether believe it?"

"I don't disbelieve it, because I've been struck all of a heap before by some of the things Livia did."

"Oh, you have?"

"Aye. . . . When she left me I was a bit like that for years. But I got over it. . . ."

And that was all. Millbay, though disappointed, was tactful enough not to press him. "Seems to me," he said later, "that those who want to plan the future with everything neatly laid out in squares and rectangles are going to find the Livias of this world sticking out like a sore thumb."

"Maybe," replied George. "But maybe also if the world was planned a bit better there wouldn't be so many Livias."

"You evidently accept that as a desirable state."

"Nay," said George quickly. "I'll not say too much against her. We had some good times. And this jealousy you've talked about— I never noticed it particularly. . . ."

Millbay smiled. "May I be very personal?"

"Anything you want."

"It's perhaps such ancient history that you won't feel hurt if I suggest it . . . that perhaps she wasn't as jealous in your case because she didn't . . . love you . . . as much."

"Aye, that might have been it."

It was getting late and George took his leave soon after that. He thanked Millbay again, walked from Smith Square to his hotel in a street behind the Strand, and rather to his surprise slept well and did not dream. The next day was a Saturday and he was busy at a conference. The conference was about nothing more or less momentous than the co-ordination of local authorities in the grouping of road-transport services throughout the northern industrial areas; and George, again to his surprise, found it quite possible to intervene in the discussion and secure for Browdley favorable treatment in the proposed setup. The conference then adjourned till Monday, and with a day to spare George could not think of anything better to do than visit Cambridge. He had never been there before, and thought it would be a good opportunity to compare it with Oxford, which he had visited once, in a mood of envy and adoration, thirty years earlier. So he took the train at Liverpool Street and eventually arrived, after a journey in which wartime and Sunday discomforts were incredibly combined, at a railway station whose form and situation roused in him the most drastic instincts of the rebuilder. He then took a bus into the town, got off at the post office, had a late and rather bad lunch at a restaurant, and entered the nearest of the colleges.

Here at last he felt an authentic thrill that years had scarcely dimmed; for George still worshiped education and could still think nostalgically of never-tasted joys. To be young, to live in one of these old colleges, to have years for nothing but study, and then to emerge into the world's fray already armored with academic letters after one's name—this was the kind of past George would like to have had for himself, and the kind of future he would have wanted for his own boy, if his own boy had lived. The multiple disillusionments of the interwar years had not dulled this dream, because it had been a dream only—for George, in Browdley, had never heard about fully trained university men having to cadge jobs as vacuum-cleaner salesmen. So he could pass through the college archway and

stare across the quadrangle at sixteenth-century Gothic buildings
with the feeling that here, at any rate, was something almost perfect
in a far from perfect world.

Civilian sight-seers being rare in wartime, the college porter,
scenting a tip, came out of his office to ask George if he would like
to be shown over. George said yes, with some enthusiasm, and for
the next hour was piloted through various courts, and into a quiet
garden containing a famous mulberry tree; he was also shown the
rooms in which there had lived, during the most impressionable
years of their lives, such varied personages as John Milton and Jan
Smuts. George was entranced with all this, and by the time the
tour was completed had absorbed much assorted information about
the habits of undergraduates in pre-war days. It did not entirely
conform to what he had imagined, or even thought desirable. But
perhaps after the war things would be a little different in some re-
spects. He soon found that everything the porter was afraid of, he
himself most warmly hoped for; and presently he summed the man
up as an incurable snob, of a kind almost never met in Browdley.
However, all that did not matter in wartime, since the man, from
his own statements, was an air-raid warden and doubtless doing
his duty like everyone else. George gave him five shillings, which he
thought was enough; and the man took it as if he thought it just
about enough.

"By the way," George added, as an afterthought, "have you a list
of all the men in the University—not just this college only?"

He had, and George inspected it. It did not take him more than
a moment to find that Winslow was at St. Jude's. The porter then
told him where St. Jude's was and he walked there across the town.

• • •

He did not know whether he really intended to visit Winslow or
not, but as he was strolling towards the college entrance he saw a
man leaning on two sticks walk out towards the curb and there
hesitate, as if uncertain whether to risk crossing. George caught his
glance from a distance and immediately changed direction to help
him; whereupon the man turned away, evidently deciding not to
cross after all. But the whole maneuver puzzled George, so that he
approached nevertheless and asked if he could be of any service.

The man was a tall young fellow in a rather ill-fitting tweed jacket and gray-flannel trousers, with a hat turned down over his forehead in such a way that, with the further obstruction of dark glasses, the face was hardly to be seen.

Yet immediately—from some curious instinct rather than from any arguable recognition—George knew who it was. He had never seen him dressed before, or even standing up before, yet there was not a shadow of doubt as he exclaimed: "Why, Charles . . ." and took the other's hand.

The youth stared at him for a moment before forcing a smile. "I —I didn't expect you'd recognize me."

"Don't say you didn't want me to!"

"I won't say it if you'd rather not." The voice and the tone were ironic. "What are you doing in these parts, anyhow?"

George explained and added heartily: "No need to ask what *you're* doing."

"Isn't there? At present I'm going to have my hair cut by a barber who most obligingly does it for me privately every third Sunday afternoon. I can't face that sort of thing when there's the usual audience."

George nodded with understanding. "Then I mustn't keep you. But perhaps afterwards . . . How about having a meal with me?"

Charles declined with a brusqueness that softened into an only slightly irritated explanation that he hardly ever left the college after dusk. "For one thing there's the damned blackout." And then, either shyly or grudgingly (George could not be sure which): "I'm in Room D One in the First Court. Come up tonight after dinner if you like. About eight."

George had been intending to return to London by the seven-thirty train, but he canceled the arrangement quickly enough to accept without an appearance of hesitation. A later train, however inconvenient, would do all right. He said: "Thanks, I will. And now, since you *were* wanting to cross the street . . ."

He helped the boy as far as the opposite curb, then left him after a few conversational commonplaces. George's sense of timing was never, indeed, so infallible as when he found himself up against that rare phenomenon—someone who didn't seem particularly glad to see him.

He spent an hour or two in further sight-seeing, then made his way to St. Jude's after another bad meal. The night was cloudy, and the staircase leading to D One proved hard to find, even by inquiry. To George's astonishment, after he had knocked, the door was opened by a rather pretty girl in nurse's uniform who admitted him to a large pleasant room in which Charles, with one arm bared to the shoulder, had evidently been undergoing some sort of treatment which George's arrival had interrupted. George apologized for being early (though actually he was punctual), but Charles assured him the job was finished and introduced the girl, who joined in unimportant conversation while she packed her equipment. She seemed very charming, friendly, and efficient, and George, whose mind always flew to Browdley on the slightest provocation, wished he had her in the town's health department. He had also noticed the state of the arm, and Charles, aware of this, felt constrained to cover a certain embarrassment by making light of it. "Still have to be patched up, but I'm sure a lot of fellows would envy me the method." The girl laughed and made businesslike arrangements for her next visit. She demurred at first as George picked up her bag, but when he insisted she let him carry it down the stairs. Outside the door he said: "It isn't just that I'm being polite. I'd really like to know how that boy is, and I thought you'd be the one to give me the true facts."

She replied calmly as they walked across the court and through the gateway into the street: "He's not well at all—but that's a usual experience after the sort of crash he had. They seem to improve, and then they get worse again. It's partly because they expect to recover too soon and too completely—and it doesn't happen."

"But it will eventually—in his case?"

"He has a good chance. Physically he's doing fine. He fractured both ankles, and one of his hands and arms had bad burns—that's the one I'm working on—the muscle's damaged. And his face, too—that was burned, but they did a wonderful job with plastic surgery—I've seen a photograph of him as he used to be and it's really remarkable. Of course the shock is really the hardest thing to get over."

"But he *will?*"

"I hope so, though he's pretty bad at times. He has sudden nerve

storms—you can't imagine what they're like until you've seen him.
. . . But he should improve gradually."

"It all sounds serious enough," George said.

"It is—though I've seen many worse. And he has heaps of courage. You know he got a D.F.C.?"

"No? . . . When was that?"

She mentioned a time earlier than that of George's visits to the
Mulcaster hospital.

He said: "He never told me."

"I'm not surprised."

"But isn't he proud of it?"

She smiled. "He's just shy about those things, that's all. Do you
know him well?"

"Not very. But I—I like him a great deal."

"So do I."

They had reached the pavement where she said she would wait
for a bus. George would have liked to go on talking, but the bus
came up almost immediately. "And where are you off to now?" he
asked, curious as always about the lives and work of others.

"Back to the hospital here. They keep me busy."

"I'll bet they do," he answered admiringly. The bus moved away
and he walked back to the college room encouraged by a feeling of
community with all who worked with such quiet, cheerful skill—
the real aristocracy on earth, he reflected, if there ever were such a
thing.

Charles had put on his coat and was making sure the curtains
were drawn over the windows. George apologized again for having
arrived perhaps inopportunely.

"Not at all. . . . Sit down. You've had dinner, of course. How
about some coffee? I make it here, on my own."

George agreed and watched Charles as he busied himself with
the small but intricate task. It was as if he wanted to show how he
could do things—as if embarrassment, aware of itself, could find relief in a kind of exhibitionism. He made excellent coffee, anyhow,
and over several cups they fell to discussing the business that had
brought George to London, which George explained in as much detail as was interesting to himself until it occurred to him that Charles
might not be similarly enthralled. But the boy urged him to con-

tinue. "Go ahead. It's shop talk, but I always enjoy that from any-one who knows what he's talking about."

George acknowledged the compliment with a pleased "Aye," and then, to keep it modest, added: "So long as it's anything to do with Browdley. . . . Now tell me *your* gossip."

"Nothing to tell except a lot of dull stories about hospitals."

"They moved you about a lot?"

"Yes. Everybody who thought he could do anything had a go at me. Not that I'm complaining. They did rather well, I reckon. And the French johnny who fixed up my nose really improved on the original. I had to spend six weeks in his private nursing home in Leeds."

"Leeds? As near to Browdley as all that? Why didn't you let me know? I'd have visited you."

Charles looked embarrassed. "Well, you stopped writing, so I thought you'd got a bit bored with that sort of thing. I wouldn't blame you."

"*I* stopped writing?"

And then, of course, the matter was explored; it appeared that George's last two letters had never reached Charles; it was all as trivial as that. (They did arrive, eventually, after a series of fantas-tic reforwardings.) George exclaimed, laughing because his relief was so much greater than he could have believed possible: "And *I* thought it was *you* who didn't want to write!"

Just then the air-raid siren went off, effectively changing the sub-ject. "There's a shelter in the next court," Charles said, "if you'd like to go there."

"What do *you* generally do?"

"It's only happened two or three times before, but I've always stayed here. I don't think it's a very good shelter anyway."

George said staying where they were was all right with him, so they went on talking. Now that the contretemps of the letters had been cleared up, the mood came on them both for subsidiary con-fessions; Charles, for instance, admitted that when he had caught sight of George outside the college that afternoon he had deliber-ately looked the other way. "It was partly because I thought per-haps you really didn't want to see me—not now that you know I know who you are. There's also a bit of a phobia I have about my new face. It gives me the most conflicting impulses—for instance, in *your* case, because you never saw my old face, I didn't mind so much, yet because I also didn't think you'd recognize me I was glad to think you wouldn't realize I was avoiding you. . . . Or is all that too complicated?"

"Aye—and so are most human impulses, if you get down to analyzing 'em."

"I'm glad you think so. I've had a good deal of time to analyze myself lately—perhaps too much—and on the whole I prefer flying. . . . I suppose you know I'll never be able to do that again?"

George had all along thought so, but deemed it best to appear surprised. Charles went on: "The doctors simply hooted when I mentioned it. Asked me whether I wasn't satisfied with the way they'd fixed me up for a life of strictly civilian usefulness."

"And aren't you?"

"I guess I've got to be. I'm damned lucky compared with thousands. The fact is, though, I really *wanted* to fly again. . . . As long as I could be useful that way I was satisfied. But now that I have to wonder how I *can* be useful, I'm *not* satisfied."

"What's wrong with just being here?"

"Probably quite a lot. And that's what makes the big difference. There never was much wrong with the R.A.F., and even if there had been it was none of my business. My job was to fly."

"And now your job's to get ready for some other job that'll be just as useful in its way by then."

"I'd like to believe that. I'd like to think the things I'm being lectured about have the slightest connection with anything that matters. The Statute of Mortmain, for example—or the Amphictyonic Council."

"The Amphictyonic Council certainly has—because it was a sort of League of Nations, wasn't it?"

Charles gasped. "Good God! Now how the hell did you know that?"

"Because I once studied history for a university examination same as you're doing now."

"You *did?* You mean you . . ." The first gunfire could be heard in the far distance; it seemed to cause a break in the youth's astonishment, giving him the chance to reflect, perhaps, that it was not very polite to be so astonished. He stammered: "It's just that I didn't realize you were—well, what I mean is . . ."

George let him flounder with a certain grim joy. "Aye, I get what you mean," he said at length. "You thought education wasn't much in my line, I daresay. But you're wrong there. I had great ambitions when I was a lad, and to get a university degree was one of 'em. But it didn't come off—and perhaps it doesn't matter so much when I look back on it now. I've done other things."

"That's what my father used to say. His ambition was always to be an ambassador in one of the important capitals, but things didn't work out that way. In fact they worked out damned badly. . . . You know he's probably dead?"

George said gently: "Not *probably*. I don't think anyone knows enough to say that."

"I wish they did. I wish it was a certainty. I can't bear to think of him being—"

George caught the note of hysteria and checked it by putting out his cup for more coffee. "Come now . . . I know it could be bad, but maybe it's not as bad as that. . . . Isn't it possible to get word from him? Doesn't anybody have an idea where he is?"

The whole room began to shake as if a train were rumbling deeply underground. A flake of plaster fell from the ceiling with almost dainty nonchalance. Charles answered: "My mother thinks he's in Japan. I don't know what evidence she has—if any. She's— she's a little strange—in some ways. She's been writing to all kinds of people in the Government—making rather extraordinary suggestions for rescuing him. Quite extraordinary. I'm terribly sorry for her." His voice trembled.

The underground train noise began again. George took his refilled cup of coffee. "Thanks," he said. And then: "I'm sorry too, lad."

Charles lit a cigarette. "Air-raid warden in Browdley, aren't you?"

George nodded.

"Ever had a raid?"

"Not so far, thank goodness. But I know what they're like. I was at Mulcaster in one of the worst."

"I was in a few too."

"So I understand."

"Oh, I don't mean *those*. I mean as one of the underdogs. A few hours after my mother landed there was a bad one on the docks there. . . . She wasn't scared. I was, though." He smiled. "Not that I wouldn't rather be here than in a shelter. It's a bit of a bother for me to get down steps, and I hate strangers staring at my funny face."

"It's not funny to me."

"That's because you never saw it before. The really funny thing is that you should ever have seen it at all. . . . Just coincidence, wasn't it, that you noticed my name on the list at that hospital?"

"Aye—but when you come to think of it, there's a lot of coincidence in the world."

"That's so. . . . Boy meets Girl—always the perfect coincidence. My father meeting my mother. . . . *You* meeting my mother. Where was it? In Browdley?"

George nodded.

"My father met her first in Vienna."

"Aye."

"You knew that?"

George nodded. After a pause he asked: "By the way . . . did you . . . did you tell her you'd met me?"

"Yes."

"Did she mind?"

"She seemed a bit surprised, that's all." An explosion came, nearer than any before. Charles began to laugh.

George said: "Steady, lad."

"Oh, I'm all right. I was just laughing at something she said about you when I happened to mention you were Mayor of Browdley. She said you were like a lion when you talked at public meetings, and behind that you were rather like a friendly old dog that nobody need be afraid of, but behind everything else you had the secret strength of the dove."

"The *what?*"

Charles repeated the phrase, after which they both laughed together. "Well, it's the first time *I* ever heard of it," George said. "And I still don't know whether she meant that doves are strong or that I'm weak. . . . Maybe she didn't know herself when she said it."

"Maybe. My father once said she said things not because they meant anything but to find out if they *did* mean anything."

George made no comment.

"And sometimes her mind seems full of words waiting for other words to set them off like firecrackers." The distant underground rumbling died away and all was silence. "Sounds as if it might be over. . . . Where d'you think it was? Just tip and run on some little place—they do that, don't they?" With difficulty the boy got up and walked to the window. "George—do you mind if I call you George?—George, I *wish* I could be of some use—some *real* use— in this blasted country. . . . If only I could fly again—but that's out, and so far I can't seem to settle to what's in. I guess millions of us are going to feel like that after the war." He moved restlessly. "How about a stroll? I can, if I'm careful."

"Not till the All Clear sounds. Take it easy."

"All right, all right. I'll bet you make a good warden. When are you going back to that town of yours?"

"Tomorrow night, I hope."

"So soon?"

"I'll have finished my work in London and I've got plenty waiting for me at home."

"They can't do without you?"

"They could, but they mightn't want to."

"I'll bet you're a good mayor, too. I'll bet everything in that town runs like clockwork."

"Oh, not so bad. I'd match it against any other place in England for being efficiently managed, if that's what you mean." George smiled to himself as he thought of the matter, then saw the other's quizzical, slightly sardonic glance, and wondered if he were being baited. "Look here," he continued, in some embarrassment, "I'm showing off too much. . . . Aye, and I'd have been down that shelter too, but for showing off. Maybe that's what kept us both here like a couple of fools."

Charles shook his head, so George added: "Or maybe not in your case."

"No, George. Oh God, no. If you *must* have a reason, it's simply that I don't give a damn what happens. To me personally, that is. I'm scared, and yet I don't care. When you've seen a lot of your friends killed you can't think you've survived by any special virtue of your own. Then why the hell *have* you survived? And the next step in argument is why the hell should you go on surviving?"

George said quietly: "I don't like to hear you talk like that."

"It's better than having you think it was bravery—or even bravado. . . . Well, let's discuss something pleasanter. That town of yours, if you like."

"Provided it doesn't bore you."

"Not at all. I wouldn't even mind seeing the place sometime."

"Why don't you then—sometime?"

It was half an hour before the All Clear sounded, and George was just in time to catch his train.

* * *

Of course they began to correspond again, and within a few weeks it happened that George was called to London for another official conference. This time it did not spread over a week end, and he was far too conscientious to pretend it did; but by routing his return journey, with much extra discomfort, through Cambridge, he was able to spend a whole afternoon with Charles. He was delighted to note an improvement in the boy's physical condition; he could use his legs more easily, and since he had been recommended to do so for exercise, the two spent part of the time strolling slowly about the Backs, which at that time of the year were at their loveliest.

Less reassuring to George was Charles's state of mind, which still seemed listless and rather cynical, especially at the outset. He still questioned the value of anything he was doing at Cambridge, and George was too tactful to reply that even if it had no value at all, it was as good a way of passing a difficult time as any other. "But you like it here, don't you?" George asked. "Or would you rather be at home?"

"I haven't a home," Charles answered, so sharply that George did not probe the point. But then the boy smiled. "I'm sorry—you must think I'm very hard to please. Of course Cambridge is all right, and I've really nothing to complain of. Everybody's perfectly charming to me. The dons don't mind whether I work or not—the whole atmosphere is timeless. It's a bit frightening at first. And that air of detachment people have here. One of the St. Jude's dons—a little wizened fellow who's the greatest living authority on something or other—began talking to me quite casually the other day about the Channing case—took it for granted that I didn't mind everyone knowing that my grandfather served a long sentence in jail. And of course I don't mind—why should I? After all, my father didn't exactly distinguish himself either—ever heard of Kemalpan? Well, I won't go into that . . . and damn it all, I don't care— why *should* I care?"

"Aye, why should you?" George interrupted. "You haven't done so badly yourself—so far."

"So far and no further, though—that's what it looks like."

George looked straight into the boy's eyes. "You were talking about one of the dons here."

"Oh yes—the one who reminded me that my grandfather was a crook. But he must have studied the trial pretty closely from the way he talked. He said John Channing was quite a pioneer in his way, and that his scheme for reorganizing the cotton industry was very similar to the one sponsored by the Bank of England twenty years later. 'Unfortunate that your grandfather was tempted to borrow money by printing too many stock certificates. He should have become Governor of the Bank, then he could have printed the money.' " Charles imitated the high-pitched voice of the don. "So utterly detached—it made things rather easy between us afterwards. And then there's another fellow—a very famous scientist —who remarked pleasantly to a small crowd of us at a tea party— 'The Germans really do have the most God-awful luck—you almost feel sorry for them'—but nobody turned a hair or thought anything of it, because everyone knows he's working day and night on some poison gas to kill the whole German nation if they start that game themselves."

George answered: "You put your finger on a point, though, when you said 'a very famous scientist.' Anyone not so famous could get into trouble if he talked like that at the Marble Arch to a crowd."

"Oh, I don't know. He might be booted out of the Park by a few bus drivers. Probably nothing more. . . . Because the English, after all, are a race of eccentrics. They don't think it's odd that people should be odd. And they always bear in mind the possibility that the lunatic view might, after all, be right. That's what makes them tolerant of their enemies."

George nodded. "Which is rather wise, because often it's only from amongst your enemies that you can pick your friends."

"Has that been your experience, George?"

"Aye—as a minority member on a Town Council where I've had more of my own way, I reckon, than most of the chaps on the other side with all their voting majority. But it's taken time—and patience."

"But what happens to the battle, George, if you win over all your enemies to help you fight it?"

"Why, I'll tell you what happens—the battle's over, and that's what everybody's after, isn't it?"

"No, not exactly. What everybody wants is victory."

"And everybody can't get it. But you can make a lot of folks *think* they've got it. Remember Philip Snowden back in 1929—no, you'd be too young—anyhow, we all cheered like mad because he made France pay an extra million pounds of war debt! Think of it —one whole extra million pounds! The Fighting Yorkshireman! Wouldn't have been easy to forecast how we'd all feel about the Fighting Frenchman a bit later!"

"Does it prove we shouldn't have cheered?"

"Maybe not. Perhaps it proves that though it's hard to get the victory you want, it's even harder to want the victory you got ten years back."

"Which is the devil of a way to look at things in the middle of a war."

"Aye, I can see it might be."

Charles walked on for a little way, then said thoughtfully: "You know, George, you have a rather Machiavellian mind."

George laughed. "Twisty, you mean, eh? That's what my opponents say. But I'll give you one good tip in politics—keep straight from year to year, and you can twist as much as you find convenient from day to day. And as for the really big fellows—the great men of the world—if *they* keep straight from century to century, they can do *their* twisting on a yearly basis. Does that make any sense?"

Charles laughed. "What *doesn't* make sense to me is that you didn't try for Parliament. Or did you—ever?"

"Aye, a few times."

"And no luck? How was that?"

George answered after a pause: "Hard to say. Perhaps just what you said—no luck."

But the recollection was now without a pang, or at any rate the pang was smothered in much greater pleasure; for George had made a discovery—that he could talk to Charles as he had never been able to talk to anyone—even Wendover, with whom there had always been the prickly territory of dogma. But the boy, less schooled in dialectic than the priest, nevertheless had a clear, intricate mind—almost too intricate, almost ice-clear; and George argued with him joyfully every foot of the way from St. Jude's to Queen's and then back again, on that lovely May afternoon. All the time a curious happiness was growing in him—something he did not diagnose at first, but when he did, it came in the guise of a guess—that this must be what it felt like to have a grown-up son. During the last half-mile they increased pace, because Charles was in a hurry to get to his rooms. "That's what your arguments do, George—make me forget the time. . . . And I don't want to keep Julie waiting."

"Julie?"

"The . . . er . . . the nurse you met. Miss Petersham."

George didn't think it could matter much if she did wait for a few minutes, but he said merely: "And a very nice girl, too."

"You thought so?"

"Aye." George smiled and added: "We had quite a conversation on the way to her bus. She told me one thing you didn't let out."

To George's immense astonishment Charles flushed deeply and began to stammer: "You mean—about—our—engagement?"

George swallowed hard. "Well, no—as a matter of fact, it was your Distinguished Flying Cross."

"Oh, *that* . . ."

George could see that Charles regretted having given himself away. He held the youth's arm as they began to climb the staircase. He said: "I'm sorry if they were both things you didn't want me to know, but now I *do* know I'd like to offer my congratulations . . . and double ones."

"Thanks. . . . Of course there's no secret about a D.F.C. . . . The other thing *is* more or less—has to be—because—well, it depends on what sort of a recovery I make. I wouldn't have her tie herself to an old crock. Or even a young one."

He had left his room unlocked, and the girl was already there when they entered it. She greeted them both and immediately set about preparing the equipment for massage treatment.

Charles said abruptly: "He knows all about us, Julie."

She looked up, startled—to Charles, then to George, then to Charles again. "Did you tell him?"

"No . . . it sort of slipped out. But I don't really mind."

Then Charles laughed and George shook hands with the girl and said how pleased he was. "I was praising you to him even before I knew," he said. It was a happy moment. "And now I'd better leave if I'm going to catch my train. . . . I'll see you both again before long, I'm sure."

He shook hands again, but the girl followed him to the door. "My turn to see you to the bus this time."

"All right."

Crossing the court towards the college entrance she said: "I'm glad you know. Charles thinks such a lot of you."

"He *does?*"

Something in his voice made her laugh and ask: "Why, are you surprised?"

And George, who was so used to being liked yet could never somehow get over the surprise of having it happen to him again, replied truthfully: "In a way, I am, because it's hard for a lad of his age to get along with an old chap like me. Yet we do get along."

"I know. And you're not old."

"Older, then."

"You can be a great help to him anyhow."

"You too, lass. And far more than I can."

"Well . . . he needs all the help we can both give him."

"He's getting better, though?"

"Oh yes—physically. It's in other ways we can help him most."

"I understand. There's something he hasn't got—yet. It's a sort of reason to be alive. He doesn't know why he wasn't killed like so many others—he's said that to me more than once. Does he talk like that to you?"

"Sometimes," she answered.

They walked a little way in silence; then, as they reached the curb, she said: "Mr. Boswell, I'm going to be very frank and ask you something—as a friend of his . . ."

"Yes?"

"Will you . . . would you help him . . . *even against his mother?*"

A bus to the station came along. "The next one will do," George muttered. And then, as they stepped back from the commotion of passengers getting on and off, he went on muttering: "Help him—against his mother—eh? Why, what's wrong about his mother?"

She answered: "I only saw her once, when she came to visit him, and of course to her I was only a nurse. And I *was* only a nurse—*then*. But I could see that she wasn't good for Charles. She got on his nerves. She wants to *possess* him—her whole attitude was like that—and I don't think she's the right person, and even if she were, I don't think he's the sort of person who *ought* to be possessed—by anyone. He should be free." She continued after a pause: "Maybe you're wondering about my motives in all this. Well, so far as I'm concerned he *is* free. I love him, that's true, but I only agreed to the engagement because I thought it would help him—which it did, and still does. But when he's better he may feel differently. I shan't try to hold him. He's too young, anyhow, to decide about a wife. . . . I want him to be *free*. I don't want him to be possessed."

"And you think . . . his mother . . . ?"

"That's what *she* wants. I know it. I think he knows it too, but he can't easily resist, for the time being—that is, till he's recovered. She's so strong."

"Strong?"

"Yes, but there are two kinds of strong people. There's the kind that make you feel strong yourself, and there's the other kind that make you feel weak. . . . She's that kind. And he's so sorry for her —naturally, on account of what's happened. Everybody is—she's a tragic figure. . . . Which makes another reason. He's had enough tragedy."

George could sense the girl's emotion from the way she suddenly stopped at the word "tragedy" and laughed, as if that were the only thing left to do. She said, after the laugh: "Well, I've told you now. I don't know what you can do, but you're a friend of Charles and I took advantage of it. Don't do anything at all if you'd rather not. I really haven't any right to ask."

Another bus was approaching along King's Parade. George answered: "Nay, Julie, we've all a right to ask anything when it's a matter of helping somebody."

She smiled. "That's a nice way to look at it. . . . You'd better catch this bus or you'll be late."

He nodded. And then at the last minute: "I wonder . . . do you know who I am?"

She replied, in a rather puzzled voice: "Why yes—you're the Mayor of Browdley, isn't that it?"

"Aye," he answered, with a slow smile. "And I'll bet you'd never heard of Browdley till Charles told you. That's how important it makes me." He gripped her arm. "See you again soon, lass." And then from the bus platform: "I'll do what I can. I dunno how, but I will."

Inside the bus and all the way to Browdley, by various slow-train connections that took all evening and half the night, George still did not know how he would keep his promise, though his determination to do so surged into the familiar dimensions of a crusade.

·   ·   ·

George might have a Machiavellian mind, as Charles had said, or he might have made a Jesuit, as Wendover had once said; but there were times when he knew that nothing is more effective than the direct approach. So after pondering long on the problem of how to help Charles, he decided that the first step must be to meet Livia himself and judge what help was needed; and to meet Livia the simplest method seemed to write and ask for a meeting.

She returned a characteristic brief note that he could visit her any time he wanted while she was at Castle Winslow.

It was a week before George could arrange to be away from Browdley long enough to make the trip, and once again there was the complicated uncomfortable journey by a series of trains. He was not surprised when no one met him at Castle Winslow station, and as it was fine weather and there were no cabs he walked the three miles from the station to the lodge gates, wearing down by sheer physical fatigue a mounting excitement over the fact that at last, after over twenty years, he was about to see Livia again. It was curious how something had lingered to produce that excitement still. He remembered the months immediately after he had known definitely that she would not return to him—how she had been on his mind night and day, so that he had scarcely been able to work; he remembered how he would wonder whether to avoid the Stone-clough road with all its memories, or to exorcise them deliberately by the self-torture of walking there; and how for weeks he would try the one method and then, in despair, the other. But for years now there had been nothing particular to remember or to try to forget.

At the lodge an old man hoeing potatoes in a patch of garden pointed further along the road when George spoke the name *Mrs. Winslow.* "She's at the Dower House—that's about a mile. Turn left at the signpost and then it's the first place on the right behind the trees. There's a lot of kids there—you can't miss it."

George walked on, puzzled at the reference to "a lot of kids," and more so when he came near enough to hear their shrill cries and screams. At length he glimpsed a rather large rambling house, well set back from the road behind tall poplars. In the space between the road and the building children of all ages from three or four to ten or eleven were romping as in a school playground.

George walked in and the children took no notice of him, but a buxom middle-aged woman who looked like a farmer's wife changed her direction across the yard as he approached. He gave his name and repeated who it was he wanted to see.

"I don't know whether she will," answered the woman, doubtfully. "She won't see anybody as a rule. You're not from a newspaper, are you?"

George assured her he wasn't.

He waited till a moment later the woman beckoned him from a doorway. As she led him through the cool interior she explained the presence of the children. They had been bombed out of their homes in some of the big industrial cities, and this was one of the rehabilitation centers set up by the Government for the recovery of

special cases—"like shell shock," some of them, she said. George
knew all about it, for there was a similar center not far from Browdley, which he had visited. "And does Mrs. Winslow help in looking
after them?" he asked, eager for some clue to what he might expect.

"Yes, she helps. She's all right with the children."

Presently the woman opened a door leading to a kind of veranda
in which a few children were lying asleep or strangely awake in open
cots. That strangeness was another thing George had seen before
—the tense stare, the twitching muscles; these were the worst cases.
And beyond them, arranging pots of geraniums along a ledge, was
Livia. She wore a large shabby straw hat and a bright-colored dress.

At the instant of recognition he gasped with the sensation of
something suddenly switched off inside him, but it was not pain any
more; and as always when he had seen her afresh after an absence,
recognition dissolved into a curious feeling of never having seen
her before, but of experiencing some primitive thrill that time had
neither enhanced nor made stale; but it was no longer a thrill entirely of pleasure.

"Livia . . ." he said.

She looked up. "Hello, George." She gave him an odd sort of
smile. She had not changed much in appearance—at least, not as
much as he had expected. She went on: "I didn't think you'd be
coming today when you didn't get here earlier."

"I walked from the station."

"Oh, didn't Howard send the car? I asked him to."

"Howard?"

"My brother-in-law. He probably didn't do it deliberately. I
mean he did do it deliberately. I mean, he deliberately didn't send
the car. Just because I asked him. He doesn't like me. None of
them do—except these." As her eyes ranged over the cots something came into her face that made George reflect how beautiful
she still was, provided one had ever thought her beautiful at all.

"Well, it didn't matter. I enjoyed the walk."

"Come into the garden."

He followed her. She had been taking cuttings from geraniums,
planting them in pots for the veranda, and without a word of
apology or excuse she now resumed the task, and with such concen-

tration that George did not feel she was giving him more than a part of her attention. At any rate, there was to be no such dramatic or overdramatic encounter as he had half expected, and for this at least he was thankful.

He stammered: "I hope you're well, Livia—after—after all the —the trouble—you've had."

"Oh, I'm all right. Poor Jeff, though. He's in Japan, only nobody knows where. If only the Government would send me out I'd find him—surely it's possible by submarine? They could put me ashore on a dark night—like Casement in Ireland. Don't they do that sometimes? Do you know anyone at the Admiralty you could ask? I told Jeff I would. . . . People thought I was against his work—and so I was—because I could see all this coming. In Hong Kong, I mean. The place stank of what was coming. . . . And then he had to go back into it all like a fool. I'd never have left him no matter where he went, but they took him away. They took him away, George. I wish I was with him still, even in a prison camp. Where you are doesn't really matter. The earth is all the same." She began to pick up a handful of soil and sprinkle it into a pot. "I always liked planting things. Then you can let history slip through your fingers—like peasants do. That's why I want Charlie to give up Cambridge and live on a farm."

"To give up Cambridge?"

"Yes—what's the good of it? We argued about it but he didn't understand. Nobody ever does. They argue and argue but they don't *feel*. It's a little farm off the coast of Galway. I'd like him to settle down there and rest from thinking, arguing, books . . . all that . . . dead things that have caused all the upset. . . ."

George watched her with curious intensity. She went on: "You don't know what the world is all about, George. You never did. All your meetings and speeches—must have been thousands of them . . . what did they do? Or what did they stop?"

George did not reply. The heedless fever of her voice had not only been hard to keep pace with as a listener, but it had given him an inward tension that left him without power or will to reply. Presently she exclaimed: "Well? Don't say you agree with me—that would be too amazing!"

He still couldn't answer.

"Never mind," she smiled, after another pause. "Tell me about Browdley."

"Browdley's all right," he managed to say, in hardly more than a whisper.

"Not been bombed to bits yet?"

"Thank God, no."

"Annie still with you?"

"Aye."

"And Will Spivey?"

"Aye."

"And there's still the little garden I made?"

"It's still there." He added: "And Stoneclough too."

She suddenly began to cry, but without any sound. The tears fell into the soil as she went on filling up the pot. "Oh George, what a long time ago. I hope you've been happy."

"*You* have, haven't you?"

She nodded.

"I'm glad."

"Yes . . . it was a thing to try for, wasn't it? Love, I mean— not happiness." She stopped crying as abruptly as she had begun. "Poor Jeff . . . I wish I knew someone at the Admiralty—Howard knows them all but he won't help. He doesn't like me—Howard, I mean—Lord Winslow, that is. He thinks I ruined Jeff's career. And now he thinks I want to ruin Charlie's. Ruin . . . ruin . . . how can anyone make more than there is? I loved my father and then I loved my husband and now I love my son . . . anything wrong in all that? Or in these children . . . these have been ruined too, but not by love. I'll tell you what I do about them—are you interested?"

George murmured assent and she began to chatter with eager animation. "They're in need of almost everything when they come here—they have to be clothed, as a rule, as well as fed—I get some of the older ones to help in cooking and serving their own meals, also repairing their own clothes—that is, if they can—and of course we grow most of our own fruits and vegetables, so there's always plenty of work in the garden. But the worst cases can't do anything at all for a time—they just scream and cry and there's nothing helps but when I talk to them, and I do that. I talk nonsense mostly. When bad things are on their minds that's all they want to hear. Nothing serious. Not even politics." She smiled. "Charlie told me you were Mayor of Browdley now?"

George said that was so.

"You should have come here wearing your Mayor's chain. To make the children laugh. Always a good thing to make them laugh."

George smiled back. "Aye, I might have."

"You would, I know. You're very kind. It's just that you don't think of things, isn't it? Or rather you think of too many other things. . . ."

After that she continued to work on the geraniums for a long interval—so long that George began to wonder whether she had forgotten he was there.

But presently, with the air of a duchess at a reception, she turned to him brimming over with graciousness. "It was so nice of you to come. And you'll come again, won't you?"

"Do you—do you really *want* me to—Livia?"

"Of course. Any time. That is, before we go to Ireland. . . ."

"You're . . . going to take Charles . . . to Ireland?"

"Yes, for the vacation. And if I can I shall persuade him not to go back next term—he only likes Cambridge because he's got himself entangled with a girl there."

"*What?*"

"Of course he doesn't know I know, but it was plain as soon as I saw them together. Poor boy . . . rather pathetic to watch him pretending she was just a hospital nurse that came to give him massage treatment. Of course I don't blame *him*. In his state he'd be an easy victim."

"You mean . . . you . . . you think she's . . . *that* sort of a girl?"

"I don't care what sort she is, I'm going to put a stop to it."

"Why?"

"Because I have other plans for my own son. It's about time we got to know each other—what with all the separations of school, and then the war . . . and the peace isn't going to be much better, for most people. Or are you optimistic about it? You probably are

—you always were about most things. . . . I won't shake hands—mine are too dirty. But do come again—before we go. . . . Good-bye. . . ."

"Good-bye, Livia."

"And you will come again?"

"Aye." He walked to the door, then hesitated and said: "My advice would be to let that boy live his own life."

"And marry the first girl he meets? That *would* be optimism."

He wasn't sure whether she meant that such a marriage would be optimism, or whether it would be optimistic of him to suppose that she would ever let Charles do such a thing; and whichever she meant, he wasn't sure whether she were serious or merely ironic. Anyhow, he knew there was little use in continuing the argument, the more so as she had again resumed the potting of the plants. He said from the door, watching her: "I wish you were as good with grownups as you are with kids, Livia. You're doing a fine job with these. Their parents'll bless you for it."

"Their parents are dead, George. Dead—*dead*." Her eyes looked up, but her hands worked on. "Fancy you not knowing that."

George also felt he ought to have known it—though after all, why? But Livia had always been like that, possessed of some curious power to impose guilt, or at least embarrassment; and so he stood there in the doorway, staring at her till he knew there was nothing else to say. Then he walked off.

The woman who looked like a farmer's wife accosted him as he was leaving the house. "They telephoned from the Hall, sir," she said, with new respect in her voice. "His Lordship wished to apologize about the car—it had a puncture on the way to the station. But he's sent another car to take you back, and he also asked if you'd call and see him on the way."

"Where would I find him?"

"The chauffeur will take you, sir."

.   .   .

The Rolls-Royce swung into the last curve of the mile-long drive and pulled up outside the portico of Winslow Hall. It was an imposing structure, in Palladian style; and George's reflection at any normal time would have been concerned with its possible use as state or municipal property; but this was not a normal time, and to be frank, he did not give Winslow Hall a thought as he entered it. He was thinking of Livia.

Even the library, when he was shown in, did not stir in him more than a glance of casual admiration, though this was the kind of room he had all his life dreamed of—immense, monastic, and book-lined.

"Nice of you to drop in, Boswell," began Lord Winslow, getting up from an armchair.

The two men shook hands. The present Lord Winslow was a re-vised edition of the former one, but with all qualities a shade nearer the ordinary—thus a little plumper, rather less erudite, more of a dilettante, worldlier, colder beneath the surface.

George declined a drink, but began to take in his surroundings—the ornately carved mantelpiece, a smell of old leather bindings, the huge mullioned window through which a view of rolling park-land was superb.

"First time you've been in this part of the country perhaps?" And Winslow began to chatter about local beauty spots, while the butler brought sherry. "Good of you to take such an interest in Charles. He sends me glowing accounts of you."

"It's a pleasure to help the boy."

"That's how we all feel. . . ." And then a rather awkward pause. "Cigar?"

"No thanks—I don't smoke."

Lord Winslow got up and closed a door that had swung open after the butler had not properly closed it. Coming back across the room he said: "So you've seen Livia?"

"Aye, I've just come from seeing her."

"She's a little off her head, as I daresay you must have noticed."

George, despite his own liking for downright statements, was somewhat shocked by the coolness of the remark.

Winslow went on: "I suppose it's what she went through in Hong Kong."

"It might have been."

"Though to tell you the truth, she was rather—er—unpredicta-ble, even before that. . . . Of course it's a problem to know quite what to do. Especially in regard to Charles."

"Aye, that's what matters."

"I'm glad you think so. She's dead set on taking him to live with her in Ireland, but in my opinion that would be a mistake, even if it were feasible, which it probably isn't. I doubt if the Government would issue permits."

"Permits?"

"You see it's Southern Ireland. Neutral country. They wouldn't be quite sure what she was up to in a place like that. . . . I heard this in confidence from a chap in the Passport Office. They have everybody tabbed, you know."

"But I don't see—"

"Oh, nothing significant—nothing at all, I'm quite certain. She probably mixed with some of the wrong people somewhere—she's really rather eccentric in her choice of friends. Personally I don't think it ever meant a thing, though it certainly can't have helped Jeff . . . any more than it would help Charles." Suddenly Winslow rang the bell, and when the butler appeared turned to George with the remark: "I hope you'll stay to dinner." George was surprised by this on top of other surprises, and had hardly begun to stammer his regrets when Winslow interpreted them to the butler as an acceptance.

"It's kind of you," George said when the man had gone, "but I was thinking of my train. It leaves at six-fifteen."

"Oh, there's another one after that."

"Are you sure? Because I looked it up and—"

"Positive. . . . I'm so glad you'll stay. I'd like to talk things over with you. . . . I'm sure we both have the boy's best interests at heart."

So George found himself dining at Winslow Hall—just himself and Lord Winslow in the enormous paneled room that could have seated fifty with ease. The sunset slanted through the windows as they began the meal, but later, when the butler approached to draw the blackout curtains, Winslow left his seat and beckoned George to share with him a last look at the view. "You see how it is," he said quietly. "I have no children. All that—and this—may belong to Charles eventually." They went back to their places at the table. Winslow went on: "Oh yes, I know what you're going to say—one can't keep up these great estates any more—all this sort of thing's done for, outmoded, a feudal anachronism, and so on. That's the fashionable attitude, I'm aware. But fashionable things are usually wrong—or half wrong. All kinds of Englishmen are busy nowadays explaining to other countries how England has changed, is changing, and will change after the war. No doubt it goes down very well—especially with Americans. But between you and me England may not change as much as some people expect. And the kind of people who talk most about change don't seem to have changed much themselves—at least not to my somewhat jaundiced scrutiny."

"Aye," answered George. "You might be right about that. And there's certainly one thing about England that won't change—and hasn't changed."

"What's that?"

"Ninety-five per cent of us are working folks and have been for a thousand years."

A slight flush came into Winslow's face. He poured himself an extra brandy. "True, of course—as well as a useful demagogic statistic. . . . It only remains now for you to assure me that it's the rich what gets the pleasure, it's the poor what gets the—"

"Nay, I don't say that. There hasn't been much pleasure for your brother or your nephew these past few years—rich or not. And there isn't going to be much for them—or for any of us, maybe—in the years ahead. . . . That's why I'd like you to think twice about what you want Charles to do when he grows up." And George, now in a proper stride, became talkative for the first time since his arrival. "I'm very fond of the boy. He's taught me a bit since I knew him and maybe I've taught him a bit too. Don't saddle him with all this stuff. When I was a lad the rich had all of what were called advantages, but there's been a difference lately. It isn't that there's going to be a bloody revolution to take all this away, but are these things going to go on being such advantages? That's what folks are beginning to wonder, and once they start wondering, the bottom's out of the market. Take the Right School and the Right Accent, for instance. You've got the right ones, I've got the wrong ones, but suppose someday we all wake up and find the whole thing doesn't matter?"

"Of course. I'd be all for it. But what if some of your extremist fellows merely reverse the positions and call your accent right and mine wrong—what then?"

George gave a faint grin. "Aye, that would be a pity. But I daresay some of the chaps on your side are pretty good mimics. Our side always produced a few."

Winslow's flush deepened. "Maybe it will come to that. Lip-service to Demos could hardly be more literal."

George had to think that one out. Then he answered: "I don't know what you mean by Demos. I don't care for words like that. I don't like to hear people called 'the masses' or 'the proletariat' or even 'the average man.' Take my own town of Browdley. There's not an average man in the place—they're all individuals—different, separate, with their own personal problems same as we all have. And we don't know any Demos either. We've never seen the animal."

Winslow smiled coolly. "I think we're straying rather far from the point—if there ever was a point. . . . You obviously think there's no future in inheriting a title, a place like this, a seat in the House of Lords—and all the responsibilities as well as privileges it entails?"

George answered: "I never like to say what there's a future in. Sounds too much like a tip on the stock market. . . . It's *what's in the future* that matters more. I can't forecast that, nor can anybody. But I've often thought it's as if we're all in a train going somewhere. Some people don't like traveling, and just grumble about having to. And others think that trains go backwards or that you can push a train by leaning on a door handle. And quite a lot of folks seem to think that miracles can happen to a train. But it really doesn't matter what you think unless it's based on what you can see out of the window. The train's going to get you somewhere, wherever that is—and the one place it certainly won't be is the place you started from."

"Sounds very wise, Boswell. But whenever I hear a man enunciating a philosophy, I always ask him how has he handled his own life by its aid? Has he been a success or a failure? Has he been right when other men have been wrong? Has he made many mistakes? . . . Or is all that too personal?"

"Aye, it's personal, but I don't mind answering it. I've made plenty of mistakes, and I've often been wrong. And I've been a failure if you measure by what I once had ambitions about."

Winslow helped himself to more brandy. "Very honest of you to admit it . . . and if I might be personal again and suggest a reason —not perhaps the *only* reason, but *a* reason . . . might it not be the same one as in the case of my unfortunate brother?"

George was silent and Winslow went on, after waiting for some answer: "To put it bluntly . . . *Livia.*"

George pushed his chair back from the table. "I think we've discussed her enough," he said gruffly. "Perhaps I ought to be thinking of my train."

"Yes, of course." Winslow rang the bell again and told the butler: "Mr. Boswell will be catching the nine-forty. Will you telephone the stationmaster?"

"Very good, Your Lordship."

"Why do you have to worry the stationmaster about me?" George asked. "I can find a seat, or if I can't, it doesn't matter."

Winslow smiled. "My dear chap, if I didn't telephone you wouldn't even find a train. The nine-forty's fast from Bristol to London unless I have it stopped for you."

"You mean you can stop an express at that little local station just to pick up one passenger? And in wartime?"

"Certainly—but it isn't done by favor. It's a legal right, dating back to the time the railway was built a hundred years ago. My great-great-grandfather wouldn't sell land to the company except on that condition—in perpetuity. Damned thoughtful of him, I must say."

Soon afterwards Lord Winslow shook hands most cordially with George, and the latter was driven to Castle Winslow station in the Rolls-Royce. The station was normally closed at that time of night, but the stationmaster had opened it for the occasion and personally escorted him along the deserted platform.

"First-class, sir?"

"No, third," George answered grimly.

After that they conversed till the train came in. The stationmaster agreed that England was changing, but he also thought he never remembered farmers so prosperous or farmland selling at so high a price.

"How about taxes?" George asked. "I suppose the big estates are pretty hard hit?"

"Oh, they're all right if they did what Lord Winslow did. He made himself into a company years ago. He's a smart chap."

"Aye. . . . Knows how to keep up with the old and play around with the new, is that it?"

But the stationmaster was cautious. "He's smart," he repeated. "Travels third like yourself, as often as not . . . Because the firsts are just as crowded and he don't see why he should pay extra for nothing. You can't blame him, can you?"

George agreed that you could not.

But on the way to London the stopping of the express became a symbol—and a very handy one—of the kind of thing he found himself rather passionately against. And it was equally handy as a symbol of the kind of thing he felt Charles would be unlucky to inherit.

•   •   •

The university term was nearly over, and soon Charles would have to decide where to go for the vacation. His mother, he told George, wanted him to spend it with her in Ireland (she had been pulling wires, as only she knew how, to get the necessary permits); but Uncle Howard had asked him to Winslow Hall; and Julie, of course, though she would never suggest it, naturally hoped he would stay in Cambridge, like many other undergraduates in wartime. As for Charles himself, he didn't exactly know what he wanted to do. He was so damned sorry for his mother and anxious to give her a good time—especially after the nice letter she had written him about George's visit. So had Uncle Howard. In fact Charles showed George the two letters, and George, reading between the lines, deduced in both writers a desire to enlist him as an ally against the other. He did not, however, worry the boy with this interpretation, but kept it filed, as it were, in that department of his mind where the shrewder things took place.

Of course what Charles would really like best, he admitted, was to stay where he could see Julie, at least for part of the vacation. The only objection was that this, he felt sure, would either bring his mother to Cambridge forthwith (in which case he couldn't see

Julie at all), or else she would guess there was some girl in the case, and make a scene about it.

"What makes you think she'd do that?" George asked.

"Oh, just a few odd hints in letters and so on. And once in an air-raid shelter just after she landed. Some girl was a bit scared, and as I was too, we talked together till the raid was over. Mother of course couldn't understand it."

"That you talked—or that you were scared?"

"Both. . . . Anyhow, I can't stand scenes, and I know if she were to learn about Julie she'd make another one."

"But you can't keep it a secret indefinitely."

"I'll let her know when *I* know for certain I'm going to get all right. Because, as I told you, I wouldn't marry at all otherwise."

"You'll get all right."

"That's what everybody says, but of course saying so is part of the treatment. You can't really believe them—least of all doctors—in a matter like that."

"Well, what do *you* think? Don't *you* believe you're going to get all right?"

"Sometimes I do, sometimes not. So many things change my mind about it. Trivial—ridiculous things. . . . Sometimes I stop in front of a lamppost as if the future of the world depended on which side I walk round. Of course you may say it *does* depend on that. I mean, if you believe in predestination, every little thing must be charted out in advance, so that if it were possible for even a caterpillar to walk just once on the wrong side of a lamppost, then the whole cosmic blueprint goes to pot. On the other hand, you can say that my hesitation in front of the lamppost was itself predestined, so that—"

"That's enough," George interrupted. "You're much too clever for me. And if that's what you get from studying philosophy at a university—"

"No, George. That's what I got from piloting a bomber over Germany. You have to think of *something* then. Something fearful and logical, like predestination, or else mystic and mathematical, like the square root of minus one." The boy's eyes were streaked now with flashes of wildness. "Anyway, how did we get on to all this?"

"I was saying you're going to get better—and meaning it too. That is, if you tackle the future the right way."

"I know. And avoid scenes. Scenes don't help. And when I feel better enough to tell my mother about Julie there'll be a scene. And then I'll feel worse again. . . . Sort of a vicious circle, isn't it?"

George nodded. "All the same, though, I wouldn't wait too long."

"You mean, before I tell her?"

"Nay, don't bother your head about that. I mean, before you marry the girl."

A strained smile came over Charles's face. "Where's the hurry?" he asked, with sudden excitement. "What makes you give me that advice?"

George answered: "Because it seems to me there's another vicious circle knocking around. You say you won't marry till you know for certain you're going to get all right, but perhaps marriage is one of the things that would help to *make* you certain."

Charles laughed. "I see! Dr. Boswell's advice to those about to get married—*Do!* Advice based on his own experience of long, happy, and fruitful wedlock!" After a wilder outburst of hilarity, the laughter drained suddenly from the boy's face and a scared look took its place. He clutched frantically at George's arm. "Oh God, I'm sorry—I didn't mean that . . . I never thought . . . I forgot for the moment . . . George . . . Oh George, *please* forgive me. . . ." His voice and body began to shake convulsively.

It was the first time George had seen the kind of thing Julie had told him about, and it shocked him immeasurably. He put his arms round the boy and fought the enemy with a silent, secret strength of his own. There was not much to say. He kept saying: "Steady, lad . . . it's all right . . . all right. . . ."

"George, I didn't mean . . . I swear I didn't mean anything personal—"

"Aye, I know you didn't. And what if you did, for that matter? To blazes with everything except you getting well again. . . . Quiet down a bit more, lad, and then let's take a walk. . . ."

. . . .

All this took place during another of George's visits to Cambridge. He had been in London on business, as before—one of those fairly frequent conferences that had often been a nuisance in the past, but which now he looked forward to with an excitement entirely unshared by his colleagues. Nobody had at times been more severe than he in castigating the week-end hiatus in official circles, but now on a Saturday morning in some Whitehall government office he found himself almost gleeful over slow-moving procedure, actually hoping in his heart for an adjournment till Monday.

This had happened, once more, so he was enjoying the intervening day with a clear conscience. And another item of good fortune was that Charles could now walk short distances, with only one stick, and relish the exercise. Perhaps it was this that made him seem more boyish, even schoolboyish on occasions; and for the first time George ceased to be startled when he reflected that Charles was only in his twenty-third year.

But other startling ideas filled the gap, and one of them was unique because it came to George in—of all places—a public house.

Charles had mentioned this pub as being a rather pleasant place within easy walking distance in the country, and after an evening meal George let him lead the way there. The scene a few hours earlier seemed to have drawn them closer together, though in a way that neither could have expressed or would have wished to talk about; but George, at least, was aware of it and satisfied. It gave an edge to his enjoyment of the full moon over the fields, and the scents of crops and flowers that lay heavy on the warm air. Familiar as he was with the grimmer landscape of the north, he thought he had never known anything so richly serene as those rural outskirts of the university town—a quality enhanced, somehow, by the counterpoint of events overhead. For while they walked the hum and throbbing never ceased, sometimes increasing to a roar as planes in formation flew directly above. The R.A.F. was evidently out in force, heading for the Continent, and George guessed and was a little apprehensive of Charles's mood as he heard and was perhaps reminded.

For that reason George tried to keep the conversation on trivialities. During the walk they overtook several other pedestrians, which George commented must make a red-letter event in Charles's post-hospital experience, even though the slower movers were only old bent men plodding along at a mile an hour. Charles dryly rejoined that there was a good deal of rheumatism locally, which was a peculiar thing in an otherwise healthy district.

"Maybe not so peculiar," George countered, getting onto one of his favorite topics. "Give people decent houses, in town or country, and don't think that roses round the door make up for bad drains and damp walls."

Charles laughed. "Not bad, George. You might win a Parliamentary election yet. Castle Winslow would give you a chance, anyway. It's a family constituency—with the Winslow influence you'd probably romp home. Unfortunately the old boy who represents it now may hang on for another twenty years."

George laughed also, and in the same mood. "Pity. But in the meantime there might be a chance for *you*—in Browdley. Then I could demonstrate a bit of *my* influence."

They both went on with the joke till the passage of planes in even greater numbers changed the subject back to an earlier one. "I once tried to write a poem," Charles said, "about the contrast between those old chaps and the boys upstairs. I thought of it actually while I was flying back from Germany after a raid. You have to think of something then, when your nerves are all on edge. I can't remember more than one of the verses—I think it went—

> Each with a goal his own—
> Beginner's or Ender's luck—
> Four hundred miles to Cologne,
> Two to the Dog and Duck. . . .

It's less than two from where we are now, but some of those veterans wouldn't miss their nightly pint if it were twice that. . . . By the way, though, you don't drink?"

"No, but I'll swill lemonade while you have all the beer you want."

"All I can get, you mean. Don't be so bloody optimistic."

Presently they reached the pub and pushed into the already crowded bar, where Charles received a few cordial but quiet greetings from people whom he had presumably met there before. A few air crews from the near-by station were taking their drinks, and others were having a dart game, but perhaps half the crowd were civilians, mostly old farm laborers with tanned and wrinkled faces. The changing world met here with the less changing earth, tilled throughout the ages by men who had worked heedless amidst clashes of knights in armor, and were now just as heedless up to the very edge of runways and bomb craters. *Heedless?* But the word failed to express the rueful sagacity, the merry ignorance, that flourished nightly in the bar parlor of the Dog and Duck. Like all genuine English country pubs, it was always a cheerful but rarely a boisterous and never a Bacchanalian place—it was a microcosm of that England in which so many things are not done, including the act of wondering too truculently why they are not. George, even with his small personal knowledge of pubs, recognized at once the same spirit that usually obtained at Council meetings and Whitehall conferences, and thus he felt immediately at home. And in that heartwarming mood, while he leaned over his glass of lemonade and Charles over his tankard, George's startling idea came to him for the second time, but really startlingly now because, in a fantastic way, he half meant it. "Why *don't* you stand for Browdley at the next election?"

Charles looked puzzled. "You mean—for Parliament?"

"Aye. It's an idea."

"No, it's a joke, George, and not a very good one."

"Of course there won't be an election till after the war—so far as one can foresee. But there might be worse things that a chap like you could do when the time comes."

Charles smiled and drank deep. "And better things, I hope."

"Listen. . . . When I visited you in that hospital at Mulcaster you said something I hope you remember. You said you blamed my generation for not making a proper peace after the last war. And I asked you then if you weren't afraid that the kids now in their prams won't grow up to blame *your* generation for the same thing. . . . Well, lad, they will—unless you do something about it."

"Maybe—but not in politics."

"How else?"

"I don't know, George—don't ask me. I can't fly any more, or I might drop a few bombs somewhere. But I do know I couldn't face the political racket. Nobody would ever vote for me, anyway—I'm not the type that goes around kissing babies and promising every-thing to everybody. I'd say the wrong thing, and probably think it too—because, to be frank, I've never seen an election without feel-ing that the whole machinery of it is a bit ridiculous—"

"And it is. But it's the machinery we've got, and we'd better use it while we've got it."

"Oh certainly—but leave it to the right man. *You're* probably the right man for Browdley—you were born there, and you know the people. I wouldn't understand them—factory workers and min-ers—not because I'm a snob, but because I've never lived in that sort of a place."

"They'd understand you, that's the main thing. They'd under-stand you because they're doing a job same as you've done a job, and some of them are risking lives and health at it same as you've risked yours. You wouldn't be talking to them except as equals. Be-sides, it's probably years off yet—there's plenty of time."

"You really are a most persistent fellow, George. Anyone would think it was something I'd agreed to."

George laughed. "Aye, we'll not worry about it. Twenty-two's full young." And then he laughed again as he added: "Though William Pitt was Prime Minister at twenty-four. You won't beat *that*."

But a dark look came into Charles's face. "There's one final rea-son, George, even if there weren't any other. You've heard me spout my opinions, and you're taking it for granted I'd think it worth while to convert others to them. But I'm not sure that I would, even if I could. Don't think me cynical—it's merely that I'm not senti-mental. As I've found the world, so far, it's a pretty lousy place, especially when you get a glimpse of what goes on behind the scenes. Most people don't—and perhaps they're better off. That's why I wouldn't make a good vote-catcher. He has to be such a bloody optimist—like you. Even if he warns of doom he has to promise that if only you'll elect him he'll prevent it. Frankly, I don't kid myself to that extent and I don't think I'd find it easy to kid Tom, Dick, and Harry."

"Aye, things are bad enough, I'll admit that." George drank the rest of his lemonade in slow gulps. "But as for what goes on behind the scenes, that's just what gives me hope. Go behind the scenes of

everyday life and see the courage and decency most folks have—
see the raw material we've got to work on, if only those who have
the brains for the job can keep faith in it."

"I know what you're driving at, George. Just a simple little job
of rebuilding the world."

"Ah now, that *is* cynical. Of course it's not simple—was it simple to invent a plane? It's appallingly difficult and complicated—
and that's where chaps like you come in. It'll need all your brains
and education, but it'll also need something *I've* got—and that's a
bit of faith in Tom, Dick, and Harry." George then added softly,
administering the gentle shock with which he had wheedled so much
of his own way in his time: "Since you once said you'd like to, why
don't you come to Browdley when term ends and have a look at the
place?"

"You mean—*visit* Browdley?"

"Aye, why not? Or were you only joking when you said you'd
like to?"

"No, I wasn't joking—matter of fact I wouldn't *mind* coming,
only—" He hesitated and then added: "I hate disappointing so
many other people."

"But you can't please 'em all, no matter what you do. Why not
please yourself for a change? And of course you needn't stay longer
than you want. . . ."

.   .   .

George felt very happy as he sat in the London train that night.
Thinking back upon the long conversation at the Dog and Duck he
could not exactly remember when the idea of taking Charles to
Browdley had first occurred to him, but he knew that as soon as it
had, there had come to him the feeling of instant rightness. It was
like trying a new key in a strange lock and knowing, even before the
turn, that somehow it would work. And it had all happened, as so
many things happened in George's life, because he got talking and
couldn't stop. He hadn't, of course, been really serious about Charles
embarking on a political career. It was much too soon to be serious
about *any* kind of career for a youth who was still so far from mental and physical health. But that led straight to the point; for part
of the cure lay in *being* serious about something. And suddenly

George saw beyond the merely personal relationship between them; he saw the boy's problem as that of every boy returned from battle with body, mind, and spirit scarred by experience; and he knew that the problem must be tackled better than the last time, when millions who had faced the realities of war were too embittered, or too apathetic, or (like George himself) too easy-optimistic to face those of peace. But Charles was not optimistic enough; and that, for George, made the task of rehabilitation even more congenial. So if he could interest him in Browdley, why not? And if, in due course, interest should deepen into faith . . . faith in the things George had faith in . . . ?

George's heart was already warm to the prospect, but his head cautioned him against that same overoptimism while optimism gave him answer that the boy himself would check that. He's got a better mind than I have, George reflected humbly; *he'll* be good for *me*, too; he'll not stand any of my nonsense. . . . And then optimism soared ridiculously as George daydreamed them both as co-workers for Browdley—Mayor and Member—what a team! His eyes filled as he thought of it . . . highly unlikely, of course, but not quite impossible . . . and what more need a dream be?

Before taking the train he had mentioned to Julie his plan to have Charles at Browdley. He had had only a few moments with the girl because she was going on night duty; they had met by appointment in the market square where she had to change buses. She had told him then, since her arriving bus brought up the subject, that she lived in a suburb of the town and that her father was a schoolmaster there. George rode with her on another bus to the big hospital not far from the railway station, and perhaps because they found a seat on the top deck he was reminded of other bus rides, so many of them, years before, with Livia. And the reminder, of course, emphasized the difference of everything else, for no one in the world, he was sure, could be less like Livia than Julie was. . . .

She was delighted with his idea. "Oh, I'm so glad, Mr. Boswell. It'll be a real holiday for him."

"Not much of a holiday resort, Browdley, but I'll do my best to give him a good time."

"He'll be with you, that's the main thing, because I've noticed how good for him you are."

"You'll be better, though, one of these days."

"I hope so." And then she added: "By the way, I know who you are now. He told me."

"He did. That's fine. Now we none of us have any secrets from one another."

And suddenly again the same impulse he had had with Charles made him add: "Why don't you marry him soon?"

She seemed startled by a word rather than by the question. "Soon? . . . You mean—before he—before he gets better?"

"Aye, why not? Don't you want to?"

"I'd love to, but . . . in a way it would be taking an advantage. So many men in hospitals fall in love with their nurses—*think* they've fallen in love, anyhow. It often makes part of the cure, so the nurses don't mind. But a sensible nurse doesn't take it too seriously, even if she falls in love herself. That's why I don't consider our engagement as binding—not on Charles, anyway. When he gets better he may prefer someone else."

"And if he prefers someone else he may not get better. If I were you I'd take *that* seriously."

"You mean . . ."

"Aye, but think it over first. You're pretty right and reasonable about most things, I'd say."

That was all they had time for, but he was left with a comfortable reassurance that to be right and reasonable was not always to be prim and cold; and this, for him personally, was like a pat on the back from the Almighty.

So he enjoyed his thoughts during the journey back to Browdley.

A couple of weeks later, as he left a Council meeting, the Town Hall porter handed him a wire that read: HAVE JUST TAKEN YOUR ADVICE. HONEYMOON AT SCARBOROUGH. THEN MAY WE BOTH ACCEPT YOUR INVITATION TO THE MAYOR'S NEST? JULIE AND CHARLES.

George stood for a few seconds in the Town Hall lobby, holding the wire under the dim lamp; then his face broke suddenly into a wide slow smile that made Tom Roberts grin back with cheerful impudence. "Backed a winner, Mr. Mayor?" he quipped—the joke of that being the Mayor's well-known antipathy to betting of all kinds.

"Nay, Tom . . . *two* winners!" George answered, surprisingly, as he strode down the Town Hall steps into Shawgate.

.   .   .

On his way to Browdley station to meet them, he could not help reflecting what an extraordinary thing it really was that he should be welcoming Livia's son to his home.

He had spent the evening with Wendover, being far too excited to settle to any solitary work; and towards midnight, for a change and because of the bright moon, he chose the slightly longer route through the wasteland on the fringe of the town, where factories met fields and—less metaphorically—lovers met each other. And he thought of that evening, so many years before, yet so well remembered, when he had passed that way in the other direction, having taken old Lord Winslow to his train after the unforgettable interview. And now it was that man's grandson and a young wife whom he was meeting—as happily as if he himself were young again and happy about most things.

In fact he was momentarily so excited that when the train drew in and they had all exchanged the first greetings, he was glad that a heavy suitcase provided something immediate and practical to attend to—there being neither cabs nor luggage delivery till next morning. Meanwhile Charles was smiling and assuring George that he didn't in the least object to a walk on such a night, if it wasn't too far. "Not far at all," George answered, chiefly for something to say to the stationmaster as they passed the exit. "Except when I'm hurrying for the nine-five to Mulcaster—eh, Ted?"

They crossed the cobbled station yard and turned into the huddle of streets. A few other walkers passed or overtook them, even so late—men on their way to night-working factories, policemen, air wardens. George pointed out the stationer's shop in Shawgate that had formerly been his Uncle Joe's, and which still, after two changes of ownership, displayed the same mixture of leather-bound ledgers, morocco editions of the standard poets, Bibles, cookery books, and the works of Miss Florence Barclay. But as a concession to the day and age, and with that ironic innocence of which the English are so capable because they are unaware of it, a single modern edition occupied pride of place in the very center of the window—*Mein Kampf* in an unexpurgated translation. George did not point this out, because he saw in it nothing remarkable; but he did draw attention to the Mayor's office in the Town Hall with its rather florid stained-glass windows that an earlier generation had considered stylish. He kept up a running gossip, also, about Browdley people whom Charles and Julie would probably meet in due course. "The Vicar—he'll amuse you. He's writing a book about Roman numerals—has a theory about them—been busy on it for years—he's eighty-eight, I think. . . . There's a younger chap of seventy-odd—Catholic priest—Wendover, by name—my best friend —you'll like *him*. . . . That's the new municipal swimming bath— just finished before the war began. Like a fool I said I'd make the first dive when it was opened—used to be quite a swimmer when I was a lad—but I hadn't done any for years and I made a belly-flop that splashed all the other Councillors and their wives . . . it was the laugh of the place the day after. . . . Here's the real business center—the banks, Woolworth's, Lipton's. And down that street is where I managed to enter the world—the house isn't there any more, and that's another thing I managed."

Julie said: "You'd make a good guide, Mr. Boswell. Too bad there aren't any Cook's tours to places like this."

"Aye, it *is* too bad. Some of the London folks ought to come here once in a lifetime. They'd learn more than they would on the French Riviera—and about their own country at that. . . . And don't you go on calling me Mr. Boswell. Nobody here does."

Presently Charles remarked: "And you've never had a raid?"

"So far, not a solitary bomb. They say you shouldn't even whisper such a thing—but I'm not superstitious. All I sometimes wish is that I could clear everybody out of the town and organize my own raid. There's still a few thousand folks living in houses that oughtn't to exist, and it'll take me ten years to finish 'em off—the houses, I mean—even when peace comes."

George was silent again, and for a rather odd reason: at the very utterance of the phrase "when peace comes" he had been swept by a sudden illusion that peace *had* come, and that Browdley under the moonlit sky was the most peaceful spot, just then, on earth.

"Now you'll have to let *me* make *you* some coffee," he said, as they turned the corner from Shawgate into Market Street. "Because here we are—this is the old *Guardian* office—my printing works—this is where I live. You've seen most of the sights already—it's only a small town."

"And an honest one too," Charles commented, as George opened the front door by merely turning the handle. "You live alone?"

"There's Annie comes in every day to clean up a bit. She's an old woman now, but she'll be glad to see you because—" He was on the point of saying "because she knows who you are," but he changed it at the last moment to "because she's got three nephews in the R.A.F." Which was true.

While George was ushering them inside, somebody passed along the pavement and called out the usual welcome. " 'Owdo, George. Back again?"

"Howdo, John. Aye, I'm back."

It was the fourth or fifth exchange of similar greetings on their way from the station. Charles laughed and commented that George certainly seemed to be well known. George laughed also and said Aye, he wasn't exactly a stranger in those parts. The triteness of the remarks masked the tension they both felt as they entered the little house. George led the way along the hall and into his study, where he switched on a light after verifying that the curtains were drawn. Usually, on bringing anyone there for the first time, he watched for some sign of amazement at the shelves of books, but now he actually forgot to do so and was recalled from far different thoughts when Charles exclaimed: "Quite a library."

George then made his familiar boast that it was the best private collection in Browdley. But he added: "Not that I'd say the competition's been very keen." And then he heard himself launching into what now seemed just a ruefully amusing anecdote. "You know what your mother did once when I was away? Took off a lot of the paper covers and burned 'em. . . . Thought she was making the place tidy for me. . . . My, I lost my temper—and that's a thing I don't often do. . . . Well, how about some coffee? Come in the kitchen—it's easier. . . ."

. . .

They sat with the bare scrubbed table between them and had tea, after all, not coffee, because at the last moment George had felt shy of his coffee-making prowess compared with Charles's, and asked if tea wouldn't do as well. Charles and Julie said it would, so George made his own favorite brew, which he could not imagine anyone disliking, though for the connoisseur it would have been nauseatingly strong. He then put plenty of milk and sugar into his own large cup, stirred it round, and was reminded of innumerable times when, as a boy, he had carried a can of the same mixture to his father at Channing's Mill on cold winter mornings and had sneaked a sip or two on the way.

George talked about Browdley again—its industries, homes, and people. "You'll know what I mean tomorrow. The war seems to have solved our chief local problems—bad trade and unemployment—though it's only a fake solution, we'll have our troubles again later. But for the time being we're better off, in some ways, than we used to be—everybody's got money, the Council has a budget surplus, and as for jobs—why, we're even short of men to fill 'em."

"I suppose there's a good deal of female employment then?"

George began to laugh. "You mean, *do the women work?* Of course they do. . . . And I'm laughing same as when I read in some of those shiny-paper fashion magazines what a marvelous thing's happening in England because of the war—the women are actually not idling any more! But the women of Browdley never *have* idled. They've worked in their homes and in factories and in both together ever since the town began. Even when the men had nothing to do, the women had plenty. So don't you go praising 'em in your speeches for the novelty of getting their hands soiled!"

"You're still dreaming, George. I shan't make any speeches."

"Aye, I forgot. . . . I was just the same when I was your age— I could talk, but I couldn't make a speech. And even when I could I hated it at first. . . . But you're not such a fool as to do anything you hate."

"Who's speaking now, George—the lion, the dog, or the dove?"

The remark put them in a mood in which Julie told them to go back to the study and talk while she washed up in the kitchen; she insisted on this with such emphasis that George wondered if she were deliberately contriving a chance for him to talk to Charles alone. He was not sorry to have that chance, anyway. The boy entered the study first and was drawing the curtains aside before

George could press the switch. The sudden flood of moonlight criss-crossed the rows of books; it lay on his desk, on the litter of papers and Council reports; full of gleams and shadows, it caught the glass in front of photographs on the mantelpiece.

"Just wondered what sort of view you had, George."

"Not much, I'm afraid. That's the wall of the bus garage."

"But the *garden* . . . Come over here!"

George crossed the room, and as he approached the window, which was partly open, the scent of summer flowers came to him as he never remembered it before—geraniums, roses, carnations, stocks, mignonette.

"Aye, it's nice this time of the year. I'm not much of a gardener myself, but Annie likes it and does a bit now and again. . . . Liv-ia's garden, we still call it—used to be a piece of waste ground till she took it in hand."

At the word, uttered like a spell between them, Charles stirred uneasily. "Livia," he muttered. "My father used to call her Livy. . . . The lost books of Livy, he used to say, what wouldn't I give to look into them!" He breathed deeply into the scented air. "So she planted the garden and burned your book covers? Anything else?"

George did not speak.

Charles went on: "My father used to say she made you into a nerve of her own body and let you do the aching instead of her . . . unless you were ill or a child, and then she took all the aches to her-self and rocked you to sleep." He sat on the arm of a chair, fidget-ing nervously with his cigarette case. "But that wouldn't suit me. I'm not a child, and I don't expect always to be ill."

"You won't be. You'll get better."

"I want to work, too."

"You will."

"Mind if I smoke?"

"Watch the light if you're not going to pull the curtains."

"Good old warden. The moon's so bright you could turn on all the street lamps." He suddenly pointed to a photograph on the mantelpiece. *"That* her?"

"Aye."

"And the baby?"

"He died."

"She was young then."

"Aye. Nearly a quarter of a century ago."

"You make it sound a long time."

"It has been a long time."

"I feel so damned sorry for her, George. My uncle never liked her. Nobody seems to like her much, for that matter—not how she is now. And the chances are my father won't come back. She thinks he will, but to me it doesn't seem probable."

George exclaimed: "By God, though, if she thinks he will, he may. In fact he'd almost better!"

Charles stared for a moment, then slowly smiled. "Yes, I know. She gets her own way as a rule. That's why, when she learns about Julie and me—"

"You haven't told her yet?"

"Not yet. Do you think I should?"

George thought a moment, then said: "Aye, might as well get it over."

"I will then. I'll wire her tomorrow. Your advice has been pretty good so far."

"You mean you're happy?"

Charles nodded profoundly.

"That's good. I can see Julie is too. And don't feel you ought to be looking after your mother. It's she who feels she ought to be looking after you . . . but you're against that, and so am I."

"I know. And she doesn't really need me, she only needs me to need her."

"That's not a bad way of putting it."

"Because she's got a sort of secret strength to face things—and less fear than anyone I ever met—man or woman. I often used to think when I was sweating it out over Berlin—God, I wish I had guts of iron like hers. . . . It was crazy, sometimes, the things she'd do. We were at a restaurant in Munich once—it was just *after* Munich too—and a crowd of army officers sat down at the next table. They were pretty drunk and high-tempered, started abusing a waiter for something or other. Eventually one of them struck the man, and my mother, who was closer than I was, leaned over and bopped the officer over the head with a Chianti bottle. Suddenly—quietly—without a word—just like that." Charles swung his arm. "Pure slapstick comedy but for the time and place."

"What happened?"

"Blood and Chianti all over everything. A riot. Amidst which I managed to get her out by a back door. The restaurant owner was as keen to save his premises as I was to avoid an international incident."

George laughed. "It wasn't always so serious. Once she and I were arguing at dinner about something or other quite trivial when she picked up a piece of apple pie and threw it at me. And it happened that you could see in from the street and somebody *had* seen in—and also it was the middle of an election campaign. They called me Apple-Pie George after that for a time." George laughed louder at the recollection. "I used to think it harmed my chances—maybe it did. But I'm glad to know about the Nazi. I'd forgive her a lot for that."

"Didn't you forgive her anyway?"

"Aye, I always found it pretty easy."

"My father used to say it was easy to forgive her if she was wrong, but if she turned out to be right then you might as well never forgive yourself."

George said after a long pause: "I don't want to send you away, but if you're feeling sleepy . . . I've booked a room for you both at the Greyhound."

"The Greyhound?"

"Just along the street. More comfortable than here."

Charles crossed the room and George put his arm round the boy's shoulder as the two walked back to the kitchen. "Don't you worry, lad. If I can help her I shall. It won't all be your job. You can count on me for that."

"Seems to me I count on you for a lot of things, George."

.   .   .

George took them over to the Greyhound, said good-night, and began the short stroll back to his house. But he felt so wakeful he made a detour past the Town Hall, his mind being still full of thoughts, strange thoughts, such as that Charles had actually been under his roof, and that Browdley in moonlight was really a beautiful place. Not only the Town Hall, but the main office of the Browdley Building Society, Joe Hardman's fish shop, even Ridgeway's garage on whose doors, as a halcyon reminder, there could still be seen the painting of a very gay peacetime charabanc for hire . . . all so beautiful . . . which was absurd, of course; yet even as he admitted it, beauty and a little sadness remained in what he felt. He could not hope for sleep in such a mood; but he could work, there was always that. As he entered his house the hall was bright as bars of silver; he could even read the headline of the *Advertiser,* and a typical one, even after six years of war—"Shall Browdley Have Sunday Cinemas?" So *that* was how his old journalistic rival still looked at the world, he mused, with extra irony because the Sunday cinema question had been debated in Browdley ever since he had campaigned as a young man for his first Council election . . . and now they were at it again! . . . No wonder Lord Winslow could remark that England didn't change! But it did change, for all that, beneath the surface of dead issues regularly flogged to life. George slipped the paper into his pocket as he walked into the open study doorway.

Suddenly he knew he was not alone. Someone was standing in front of the window, staring out—as Charles had done earlier—into the garden. The figure turned, offered a profile against the moonlight, was unmistakable. . . .

"Livia!"

At the instant of recognition he felt his hands clench with shock for which he must brace mind and heart as well; and he did so, almost as instantly.

"Where is he? He's been here, George. I know that. I want to see him."

He answered in a level voice: "They're not here now, Livia."

"They? Who're *they?"*

He answered because it was the way he himself thought of them: "Charles and Julie."

He caught his breath, having spoken the phrase; he would have expected a scene, but for knowing that with Livia one could never expect the expected. All she did was to cross the room and sit on the arm of his armchair, while he drew the curtains and switched on the light. He saw then that she looked tired and rather pale, but not uncomposed. Because he wanted to give her time to grasp the situation, he did not speak, but went back to the curtains and pretended to be fixing them with especial care.

"Julie," she said at last, still quietly. "So that's her name. Charlie and Julie. How sweet! Where are they?"

"Why did you come here, Livia?" he countered. "What made you think it would help?"

"I don't want it to help. I mean to stop this nonsense. And I know they are here, now you've told me she's with him, because I went to Cambridge first and talked to his servant at the college. . . . I know, it's no use you denying it. Of course I know. And I know your part in it all. I *always* know."

"Aye, there's not much misses you—or ever did. But there's something extra to tell you this time." He added, in a kindly voice, with no note of triumph in it: "I told you, Livia, my advice would be to let the boy live his own life. That's what he's going to do, and I'll admit I'm all for it. So whatever you've come to stop you're too late."

"*I'm* too late?" She stared at him with glazed eyes. "Oh no, no. You're the one who's late. You have been all along. And he's where you put him because of that. You and your kind of people. You talk about letting him live his own life—why *didn't* you, then, when he had one to live—not just half a one? That's all he has now because of the mess you've made of everything. You said once my father's victims were all over the town—but yours are all over the world— people like you who went on making speeches . . . speeches . . . you were making them before he was born—just as you still are—"

"Livia, you surely haven't come here just for an argument—"

"I told you what I came here for. I want Charlie. I *want* him. What's left of him, that is, after your kind have said all their prayers and made all their speeches—"

"I don't know what you're driving at, Livia. If you mean that my generation's largely responsible for the war, then I'll agree with you. Charles and I once discussed the same point—"

"Oh, you did, did you? Just a nice friendly discussion. And he forgave you, I suppose. Man to man and all that. With his shattered nerves and smashed legs and burned eyes he forgave you—because he too may need to be forgiven someday."

"Aye, if he just sits back and lets things happen. I told him that. There was a children's ward next to where he was in the hospital, and I asked if he wasn't afraid that those kids when they grew up— or his own kids for that matter—"

Her eyes sharpened.

"*His?* He'll never have any. Maybe he can't. It's like that some- times. I hope so, because that would be the best way to end it. My father, me, him, full stop. . . ."

"Livia, that's a terrible thing to say."

"More terrible to mean."

"I hope you'll never let him know you do mean it."

"I shan't have to. It'll come to him when we're in Ireland."

"Ireland? I doubt he'll want to go there now so much."

"He doesn't know what he wants. He thinks he wants this girl, but that's absurd. I can make him want what he really wants."

"Livia . . . remember I said you were too late." George paused, then added: "They're married."

"What?"

"Three days ago in London. He was going to wire you about it tomorrow. Perhaps he ought to have done so before, but you can hardly blame him . . ."

George then saw something which, despite all Millbay had said, he had tried to believe did not exist. It was a look of implacability so vivid, so pure in a sense, that he recoiled from it less in revulsion than in elemental awareness of what it signified. For he was all against it, as a stream of yielding water is against the rock it will wear down in a million years or so. And suddenly, without bitter- ness, he saw Livia as a symbol of all that must so be worn down, no matter how hard or long the struggle, no matter how often the victories of greed and despair and intolerance seem to make non- sense of it.

With his own gentler implacability he stared at hers till the trans- figuration disappeared.

She said at length: "So . . . you think . . . you've done the trick?"

"It's no trick, Livia."

"Last-minute victory, then? Narrow majority? And a hearty vote of thanks to Mister Mayor . . . ?" But she was her masked self again, so that the stress on the prefix was only ironic. She went on: "Perhaps you still don't know what I'm driving at? You never did —and you're afraid Charlie might if he got the chance. You're afraid he might see things my way. So's Howard. He wants him to have lands and a title and riches—"

"Aye, I know, and I agree with you there. They'd be just a burden to him, and that's why—"

"That's why you'd rather give him *your* kind of burden. Speeches —promises—the same old never-again stuff. But you shan't, George —I can stop that, even now. And as for the little schemer he's been duped by, does she think *her* influence is going to count?"

"Nay, Livia, not hers. Nor mine, nor his uncle's, nor yours. Let him get on his feet, build up his own ideas, see things with his own eyes when he has the strength to see clearly—that's all I'm aiming for. He'll influence me as much as I will him—I'm not so sure of my own opinions that I'd try to ram them down somebody's throat. I'll take his—if he can convince me. Or we can keep our own. It doesn't matter. I know you look at things differently—"

"So does the man from Mars, maybe."

That stumped him; he blinked bewilderedly till she continued: "If he could see the world today he'd think it was in charge of raving lunatics and the asylums were for sane people who'd gone there for safety. So if anybody thinks I'm a little out of my mind— Howard does, I know—"

"Livia, *I* don't. But I do think—for the time being—you're not able to help the boy as he most needs helping. . . . Later, perhaps . . ."

"Too late—and already you talk of *later*. . . ." She suddenly got up and began walking towards the door. "I can see this is wasting more time. I'd better start on my way back. The five-ten, isn't it? I remember. Can I have a cup of tea first?"

"Why . . . of course. I'm only sorry you . . ." But then he stopped; he didn't know what he was only sorry about, except that she had come.

She said, from the hall as she crossed it to the kitchen: "No pressing invitation to stay a few days, then?"

"Nay, Livia, and you know why. I'm anxious that Charlie shouldn't have any shocks." He had called the boy Charlie because she had and it seemed almost something shared and sharable at last between them, something that warmed his voice as he added: "Give him a chance, Livia. Leave him alone a bit. God knows that's a hard thing to say, but I mean it."

She said after a pause: "Do you hate me, George?"

He shook his head. "I never did and I never could. I'm not much use at hating folks, to be frank. But I can fight 'em when I have to . . . and I'd have to now, if you made me."

"And you think you'd win?"

"I'm not so sure, but I'm not sure I'd lose, either. That's why I say give him a chance. Give us all a chance this time."

In the kitchen she prepared tea herself, not letting him do so, as if she were certain nothing had been changed (and practically nothing had). She began to cry a little while she moved about. George watched her unhappily, puzzled not so much by her behavior as by his own, for he found himself less moved by her tears than by her simple act of tightening a tap that had been leaking into the sink for days. Nobody could do things so deftly, quickly, tidily, uncontrovertibly. She had probably got her own way with Japs pretty much as she did with taps, George reflected whimsically; and then again he was touched by her next remark, clairvoyant in that old familiar blinding way of hers: "You think I'm acting, don't you, George? And you think that means I'm not sincere? . . . You don't understand that sometimes I mean things so much I *have* to act? . . . You don't understand that, because you *never* mean things so much. . . . Oh George, you don't know how terrible it is to be alive in this world!"

"Perhaps I do, Livia, perhaps I don't feel it the way you do, but I know it, and I also know this—there's not only terror—there's hope—and love—"

"But they're the most terrible of all—"

"Nay, nay, not how I see things."

"But do you see *anything?* Anything to match love and hate? I love my son and I hate that girl—I'd kill her if I got the chance. . . ."

"You would?"

"That shocks you, doesn't it?"

"Nay . . . it doesn't exactly do that. But it makes me think."

"And you think it's awful . . . yet all the other killing that's going on—killing without hate—oh, *that* you can take for granted. Duty. Honor. Jeffrey did too—and with better brains than yours. . . . What do you *see,* George? In the future, I mean? What chance is there? This humanity you do everything for—what do you see in it?"

George saw the grayness round the edges of the curtains; he looked at his watch, then crossed to the window and let in the summer dawn. Already it was staring the moon out of the sky. It seemed to him that the world, like Livia, was snarled with memories and desires, beauty and blackness and lies and truth and hope and despair; you might as well leave it alone unless you had a driving love for the thankless job of tackling it. But if you had that love, then you could go ahead. George saw the roofs across the street as they took form and substance, and knew that the love in his own heart was more than he could speak or even make a speech about— and least of all to Livia; but the thought of it, and the continual vision of it, had governed all he had ever done that seemed either weak or strong.

"Aye," he said as he turned back to her. "I've often wondered that myself, but it doesn't make any difference." He came over and touched her shoulder with a kindliness induced by his own thoughts rather than by any more personal emotion. "Drink up, Livia—we'll have to hurry if you want to catch the five-ten. And no more arguments, because we'll not change each other, I reckon, from now till doomsday. . . ."